HER DADDIES' SAVING GRACE

LAYLAH ROBERTS

LET'S KEEP IN TOUCH!

Don't miss a new release, sign up to my newsletter for sneak peeks, deleted scenes and giveaways: https://landing.mailerlite.com/web-forms/landing/p7l6g0

You can also join my Facebook readers group here: https://www.facebook.com/groups/386830425069911/

BOOKS BY LAYLAH ROBERTS

Doms of Decadence

Just for You, Sir

Forever Yours, Sir

For the Love of Sir

Sinfully Yours, Sir

Make me, Sir

A Taste of Sir

To Save Sir

Sir's Redemption

Reveal Me, Sir

Montana Daddies

Daddy Bear

Daddy's Little Darling

Daddy's Naughty Darling Novella

Daddy's Sweet Girl

Daddy's Lost Love

A Montana Daddies Christmas

Daring Daddy

Warrior Daddy

Daddy's Angel

Heal Me, Daddy

Daddy in Cowboy Boots

A Little Christmas Cheer

Sheriff Daddy

Her Daddies' Saving Grace

MC Daddies

Motorcycle Daddy

Hero Daddy

Protector Daddy

Untamed Daddy

Her Daddy's Jewel

Fierce Daddy (coming September 2021)

Harem of Daddies

Ruled by her Daddies

Claimed by her Daddies

Stolen by her Daddies (coming 2022)

Haven, Texas Series

Lila's Loves

Laken's Surrender

Saving Savannah

Molly's Man

Saxon's Soul

Mastered by Malone

How West was Won

Cole's Mistake

Jardin's Gamble

Romanced by the Malones

Twice the Malone

Men of Orion

Worlds Apart

Cavan Gang

Rectify

Redemption

Redemption Valley

Audra's Awakening

Old-Fashioned Series

An Old-Fashioned Man

Two Old-Fashioned Men

Her Old-Fashioned Husband

Her Old-Fashioned Boss

His Old-Fashioned Love

An Old-Fashioned Christmas

Bad Boys of Wildeside

Wilde

Sinclair

Luke

"Missy, would you like some tea? No? Well, tough. You're getting some. Now, don't give me that face. If you're invited to a tea party, then you should drink what you're offered, not turn up your nose like some fuss pot."

Juliet poured tea into one of her delicate cups. They'd been in Reuben's family for a long time, so she had to be very careful.

"Angelique, we're not having the cream cake yet. You have to eat a sandwich first. You're so naughty." She waggled her finger at the doll.

The ringing of her phone jolted her and she splashed hot tea across her hand.

She stared down at the red patch on her hand. She should probably put her hand under some cool water. But the pain felt almost cleansing. It cleared her mind and helped her think better.

You're a weirdo.

Wolf howls continued to fill the room. She set the teapot down carefully and ran to get her phone from where she'd set it on the small table by the couch. Reuben had bought her several cell phone holders to place throughout the house so there was less chance of her losing her phone.

Reuben tended to worry about those things. She loved the holders. The one in this room was a sloth and it always made her smile.

She picked up the phone and saw it was a video call.

"Hey, big brother," she greeted him cheerfully.

He didn't smile back but she didn't take offense. Reuben rarely smiled. He worked too hard. If he wasn't working, then he was fussing over her. It wasn't healthy. But she knew better than to try and tell him that.

Reuben didn't listen well. Plus, he thought it was his job to take care of her, not vice versa.

Stubborn man. She adored him, but sometimes she also wanted to shake him.

"Mini," he said on a sigh.

"You look tired. Aren't you sleeping?" His dark hair was up on end and there were bags under his eyes. She'd never seen him so rumpled and stressed.

"Are you in your playroom?" he asked instead of answering her.

She sighed. She knew that she was partly to blame for him not sharing any of his worries with her. She'd always be his baby sister. The person he had to protect and coddle. He tended to treat her like she was too young or delicate to burden with his concerns. It probably didn't help that she was a Little.

"Yeah. We're having a tea party."

"Missy and Angelique being naughty?"

"Like always," she replied. "Missy won't drink her tea, and Angelique wants to eat all the cream cake and none of the sandwiches."

She glanced down at her hand again. If he saw the injury, he'd freak. Especially as it was starting to blister. Not a good sign.

"And are *you* eating the sandwiches and cream cake?" he asked in a low voice.

Inwardly, she sighed. Being thousands of miles apart didn't stop him from fussing over her or bossing her around.

Then again, she'd never told him to stop. The only time she'd ever gone against him was when he'd wanted her to move to Boston to live with him. Wishingbone was her home. Her safe place. She couldn't leave. The anxiety attack she'd had at the idea of moving had been enough to convince him.

Of course, she'd had to give in to all his stipulations and rules, but he needed to feel like he was keeping her safe. And whatever he needed, she'd give him.

She'd give Reuben everything if she could.

"I'm fine."

"I am well aware that's not an answer, Mini," he replied, glaring at her through the phone.

"Are you sure you're all right?" She'd learned the art of deflection well.

"Actually, no."

Okay, that shocked her. He never admitted to any sort of weakness. At least, not to her.

"What is it? What's wrong? Are you ill? Is it cancer? Your heart? I'll get the first flight out there." Her heart raced with panic. Her fear of leaving Wishingbone was nothing against her fear of losing him. She couldn't live without him.

"Mini, I'm not ill."

How would she get to the airport? What did she need to take? She'd never booked an airline ticket before, but it couldn't be too hard, right?

"You never say you're not all right. It's the apocalypse. The zombies are coming." Zombies were terrifying. Maybe she should get a gun. Did bullets work on zombies?

Reuben narrowed his gaze at her. "Have you been watching zombie movies again?"

"What makes you ask that?" She made her eyes go wide.

Look innocent. Look sweet.

"Juliet Susanne," he said sternly. "What did I warn you about watching those movies?"

"That most rely on shock value to garner interest."

"Well, yes, but I was actually talking about the fact that the last time you watched one, you didn't sleep for three days."

Yeah, well. She hadn't slept for four days after the one she watched last week.

But she just couldn't stop watching them. It was a strange addiction.

"Sorry," she told him, knowing that was the quickest way to get out of a scolding.

He worked his jaw, his tension palpable through the phone.

"Reuben? What is it?" He was really starting to scare her.

"I've run into a bit of trouble here."

Did that mean he was coming home? Back to Wishing-bone? Excitement filled her. It had been ages since he'd come to visit. He'd kind of pissed off a few people in town, but Reuben was like blue cheese, you loved him or hated him. Most people just misunderstood him. He was simply, um, passionate.

"You're coming home?"

He ran a hand over his face. "I wish I could, Mini."

Mini was short for Mini-me because when she was a child, she'd always tried to imitate him.

"Oh." She tried not to look too disappointed.

"I'm not sure anyone would appreciate me coming to visit."

"Of course, they would."

Liar.

Last time he was here, he'd threatened no less than four

different people with lawsuits. He'd also bought the local hardware store and fired half the staff.

But everything he did was to protect her.

The manager of the hardware store was a complete dick. He'd been upset because she wouldn't go on a date with him and he'd spread awful rumors about her. Somehow, Reuben heard about it, and he'd taken care of that asshole.

"Mini, I've been working on a case that has brought some bad attention."

"From who?"

Her heart started to race. Shoot. She was going to give herself a heart attack at this rate. Bad attention? What did that mean?

"From one of the leading crime syndicates in the city."

"Oh God. Are they going to hurt you? You can't let them hurt you." Visions of him being tortured, waterboarded, his fingers chopped off filled her head. "I like your fingers!"

Nothing could happen to him.

"Of course, I won't allow that," he said arrogantly. That voice soothed her. It told her that he had everything under control. "I like my fingers too. Have you been watching mob movies?"

It was a sickness. She couldn't seem to stop. No matter how many nightmares these movies gave her, she just had to keep watching them.

"Juliet," he said sternly.

"I saw one a long time ago," she lied. A small lie wouldn't matter, right? "What happened? Why are they after you?"

"I failed to successfully defend one of their guys."

What? Reuben never failed . . . unless . . .

"What did he do?"

"Abused a child."

Ahh. That explained it. Reuben never defended anyone on charges of abuse.

"Why'd you take the case?"

"Because that wasn't actually one of the things he was charged with." His jaw worked. "But we had a meeting at his house, and there was this little boy . . ."

"Oh, I'm so sorry."

"I should have backed off then, but this asshole was adamant he wanted me. And I figured if he went away then that little boy was safe for a while."

This was a side of him she knew no one saw but her. Most people were terrified of him. For good reason. He had power. Money. Influence. He had information on a lot of important people. Reuben could move mountains. And he would. For her.

Which made her wonder why he was so worried.

"So, this criminal group is now angry? Don't you have something on them to make them back down?"

He sighed. "I've got stuff, but there's a lot of players to deal with, and it's going to take me longer than I anticipated to get things moving, and I need to make sure you're protected."

"You think they'll come for me?" She and Reuben had different last names for just this reason. While he'd paid for this house and everything in it, it had all been done through a trust he'd set up for her.

But plenty of people still knew that she was his sister.

"I'm not taking any risks, okay?" he said to her.

Panic filled her. "I don't like that you're in danger."

Nothing could happen to him. He was her anchor.

"Nothing is going to happen to me," he soothed, clearly seeing her panic.

"I . . . I . . ." She started to pace, excess energy coursing through her body. She was dressed in a long, black dress that completely hid her body. It swished around her bare feet.

"Mini, it will all be all right."

"What do you want me to do?" she asked. "Come to you?" Then she could watch over him, make sure he was all right. Yes, perhaps that was the best idea. She was definitely going to need a gun, though.

"I wish you could, but it will be safer for you to stay away from me. I've hired a security firm to guard you."

She shook her head. "No."

"Mini," he said in a firmer voice.

"No. No strangers." Her fingers started tingling, indicating a panic attack. When she had a panic attack, she tended to go into her own head, the panic eating her from the inside out.

"Juliet, there's no one in Wishingbone who can do this."

"Of course, there is. There's JSI."

"I've already asked them. Kent hasn't got anyone free for another month. He offered to let you come to the ranch, though. You'd be protected there."

Move out of her home. No . . . she couldn't.

"Mini, it's okay. Look at me. Look into my eyes." His voice was filled with command. She stared down at him. "Either you stay in your house, with strangers as guards, or move to the ranch. I'm sorry I can't offer anything else."

There was genuine sadness in his face. He knew how hard this was on her. And he had enough going on. She couldn't add to his worries.

She was being selfish.

"JSI is already monitoring my cameras." Reuben had arranged that. Even though Kent didn't like him much, he did like Juliet.

"They'll continue to do so," he told her. "But you need someone in the house with you."

Oh God. She didn't want that.

"Loki," she managed to get out, her lips growing numb.

"Loki is a nutcase."

She winced. She hated when Reuben talked about Loki like that.

"He's not. He has PTSD."

"And that PTSD causes him to behave erratically, and you know it." Reuben sighed. "I'm sorry. I didn't mean to be harsh. I know he's your friend. But he isn't reliable. And how fair would it be to put him in a possibly dangerous situation when he has PTSD?"

Oh, that wouldn't be fair at all. What was she thinking? What a terrible friend she was.

"You're right." The world around her was growing dark. She could barely focus on his words. "Do they really have to be in the house?"

"Mini, you know I wouldn't do this unless it was necessary."

Her free hand twisted in the long skirt of her dress.

"It's only for a short time. And I'll make sure that they know they're to bother you as little as possible. But I need your promise that you'll do what they say. That you'll let them in. Please, Mini?"

He was nearly begging. His desperation was clear. That, more than anything else, had her nodding.

She wouldn't be a burden to him. Well, no more than she already was.

"I'll be all right."

"I wouldn't allow you to be anything else."

One breath. Two.

"I'll get this sorted as quick as possible, all right?"

She nodded, unable to speak. Her hand gripped the phone so tight that her fingers hurt.

"Mini, I need you to talk. I need you to be okay. You know what happens if you're not."

He'd lose it. She knew he would. And when he lost it, well, any number of things could happen.

"If you can't do it, then I'm coming out there, grabbing you, and we'll head to the island."

Shit. Get it together, Juliet.

She loved the island. But she couldn't live there permanently.

People thought their relationship was odd. But it was a product of the way they'd grown up. They'd both developed ways to deal with what happened. And Reuben's way of coping was to guard her with a zealousness that would infuriate other women.

She wasn't other women, though. She needed him as much as he needed her.

"I'm fine," she told him. "I just want you to be safe."

Relief filled his face. "I will be. I can deal with these assholes easier if I'm not worrying over you."

"You always worry over me," she teased. "It's what's given you those gray hairs and crow's feet."

He barked out a laugh, running his hand through his dark hair, which didn't have a single gray strand. "You're the one thing in my life which doesn't give me gray hairs." A phone rang. He frowned. "I have to go. I don't like leaving you like this."

"I'm fine. You go deal with life. I've got a tea party to get to."

He studied her carefully. "I want you to have a nap today, okay? You look tired."

"I will." It was easier just to agree.

"Love you, Mini."

"Love you, Big Bad Wolf."

He rolled his eyes at her nickname for him. But when he ended the call, he was looking less stressed, which is what she wanted. Knowing a full-blown panic attack wasn't far away, she grabbed her weighted blanket from the chest under the window. Then she moved into the small space between the couch and the wall.

This was the only way to keep the panic attack from completely taking over. The weighted blanket was tucked around her. She buried her face into her knees and just tried to breathe.

Just breathe.

∾

DAMN REUBEN ANYWAY.

What kind of message was, 'go check on Juliet'?

That was it. Nothing else. What the fuck? Xavier had tried calling him, but the asshole hadn't answered.

He'd considered telling Reuben where to stick his order. He seemed to think Xavier lived to be at his command.

But now he was worried about Juliet. She was nothing like her brother. She was sweet, kind, and delicate.

He had the code to the gate, so he let himself in, driving up to the front of the castle-like house that Reuben had built for Juliet. This place was nearly a fortress. Cameras and alarms everywhere.

Getting out, he climbed the stairs and knocked.

Nothing.

He rang the doorbell.

Still nothing.

Reuben had said she was home. Xavier stepped back then walked around to check the garage. There sat the car she never drove, having lost her confidence after a few accidents. But her bike was still there.

He was kind of surprised that Reuben hadn't gotten her a driver. Riding her bike everywhere wasn't exactly safe. He hated when he saw her riding that bike. If only he had the right to insist she didn't ride it.

But you don't.

And his insistence would come with a red ass if she disobeyed. Something he was certain would terrify her.

Moving back to the front door, he rang the bell again.

He had the code for the house alarm too. Using it, he entered the house and reset the alarm.

"Twink? You in here?"

Nothing.

Fuck. What if she'd hurt herself? He moved through the house, going to the one place he knew she would be if she was scared or needed reassurance. He climbed the stairs up to the third floor. This entire floor was her private space. The second floor was for guests. Not that she ever had any other than her brother.

He knocked on the closed door to the playroom.

Nothing.

Opening the door, he stepped in. Yep, he was aware it was a complete invasion of privacy, but he'd come this far, and he was starting to get really worried. The playroom was enormous. Easily the size of four standard bedrooms put together. There was a door off it that led to her bedroom and bathroom.

He glanced around the airy space. There were storage drawers that were all painted in different colors. A huge mural had been painted on one wall of an underwater scene, complete with mermaids.

In the middle of the room was a round table that had been set up with a tea party. The dolls already in their places.

"Twink," he called out.

A small whimper came from next to the sofa. He glanced over, not seeing anything at first. Then he saw a pair of feet peeking out.

Aw. Fuck.

His heart broke as he moved closer and saw her crouched in there, her face hidden in her knees, a blanket around her.

"Juliet," he whispered. He sat in front of her but didn't reach for her. "Look at me."

Nothing.

"Baby, please. You're killing me."

Nothing. Fuck. What the hell had Reuben done to make her react like this?

He wasn't sure whether to touch her or not. To speak to her until she acknowledged him or just sit here.

If this was any other Little . . .

Yeah, he'd have already taken charge. But this was Juliet. His ex-best friend's little sister.

Getting out his phone, he sent a text to Reuben.

XAVIER: *What happened to her? What did you do?*

Asshole: *What's wrong? Fuck. I can't call right now. Just make sure she's all right.*

Xavier: *Tell me what's going on.*

NOTHING.

He sighed. "Twink?" Still nothing. Maybe he'd have to go with his gut then. He took a deep breath and hoped that this didn't wreck the bond they had.

"Juliet," he said sternly. "I want you to look at me."

Well. That worked. Not.

"I'm going to touch you now. If you don't want that, it's time to speak up."

Nothing.

Fuck it. Well, now he had to follow through, didn't he?

He wasn't sure who this would be harder on. Reaching over, giving her plenty of time to protest, he lifted her onto his lap.

Yeah, having her ass pressed against his dick? Definitely harder for him.

She was stiff as a board and he sighed. Shit.

He tugged at the blanket around her. It was black. What was with her love of black? If she was his . . .

Easy.

The blanket seemed to be weighted, which made sense as it should be good for her anxiety. Grabbing her right hand, he winced at how cold it was. It shouldn't be, if anything, it was overly warm in here. But her hand was freezing. He moved his fingers to her pulse.

Too fast.

"Twink, hold onto me. Hold my shirt." He knew that gave her comfort.

For a moment, he didn't think she would react. Then her hand twisted in the front of his shirt, holding on tight.

"Good girl," he murmured. "I'm going to stand now and sit on the sofa."

No reaction, but once he was on the sofa, she turned towards him, burying her face in his chest.

Okay, he hadn't expected that. He held his arms away from her, then realized how ridiculous he was being. She needed to be touched.

"Do you need my skin, baby?"

She nodded. He undid the first few buttons of his shirt and her cool cheek touched his chest.

Talk about torture.

Easy. Don't react.

"Hear my heartbeat?"

Another nod.

"Then you know you're not alone, right?"

Another nod.

But he wasn't putting up with that.

"I'm going to need you to use words, Twink."

Her breath hit his chest. Fuck. Think about something unsexy. Herpes. Warts. Reuben naked.

Yep. That did the job. Until Juliet shifted in his lap, wrapping herself around him like a baby monkey climbing to its mama.

"What's going on?" he asked her.

"Panic attack," she said quietly. Juliet only spoke to people she knew well and trusted. And if there were other people around, she'd only whisper.

"Okay, baby. Want to tell me why?" The need to demand that she tell him was on the tip of his tongue, pressing its way free.

Easy.

She shook her head and sniffled. So, he ran his hand up and down her back until she settled into him, her body growing heavier.

"You need a nap." He was pretty sure that she didn't get enough sleep, and he hated how pale she was. But getting her to come to him or another doctor for a check-up was impossible. Standing, he placed one hand under her ass, holding her to his chest.

Fuck, she was far too light.

This girl needed a keeper.

But not you, dickhead.

Her enormous bed took up one corner. It was only set about half a foot off the floor. It had a lacy black duvet cover on it. Around all four sides was a railing like you might find on a baby's cot. There was a small opening where she could climb in and out.

Leaning over the railing, he gently put her on her side on the mattress. Then he arranged the weighted blanket over her.

What now? He'd never put her down to nap before. What did she need? He searched through her drawers, coming across her panties.

Standing, he looked around as though searching for some sort of sign. A sucking noise had him turning back to the bed to find she was already asleep, a pacifier in her mouth which was attached to a soft-looking blanket. Okay, that must have been tucked under the pillow. Both of her hands were under the weighted blanket, so at least they'd be warm.

He quickly put her panties away because he really didn't want her to wake up and see him holding her panties like a creeper.

Grabbing a bottle of water out of the small fridge in the playroom, he walked back into the bedroom with it, setting it down next to the bed.

She looked so cute lying there. He wanted to just sit here and watch her.

But that was kind of creepy.

His phone buzzed and he drew it out. Christ.

Closing his eyes, he took a deep breath. If he didn't answer, it would make things worse. She'd keep calling and calling.

Moving out of the bedroom, he shut the door and walked over to the window before answering.

"Hello, mother."

"Xavier. It took you long enough to answer. I thought I was going to be sent to your voicemail. You know I don't like leaving messages."

Right. He knew. Because she told him often enough.

"My apologies."

"I'm calling because I want you to come visit."

Of course she did.

"I'm sorry, Mother. I'm very busy at work." He actually had a few days off, but he didn't intend to tell her that. He thought he might spend some time with Juliet, since she obviously wasn't doing well.

"I'm sure someone could take your shift for you. It isn't like much ever happens in that sleepy hospital. You should never have left your job at Massachusetts General. Think about how far ahead in your career you could be if you'd stayed."

He pinched the top of his nose.

"You know why I left."

"Pfft, ridiculous. That girl's death had nothing to do with you. And if you had to leave, why didn't you take the job your father offered you at New York-Presbyterian?"

Her death had nothing to do with him? It had everything to do with him. The guilt still ate away at him.

"Father worked at Wishingbone hospital for several years," he couldn't help but point out.

"He was the CEO, Xavier. Not a regular old doctor."

Right.

"And it was dreadful, living in that horrid little town. The only reason we didn't move sooner is because of your schooling. Despite it being such a strange place, the quality of the education was impressive."

High praise from Marigold Marson.

"Mother, I'm sorry but I really don't have time to come home." Not that he actually considered the apartment they owned in Manhattan to be home.

Home was here, in Wishingbone. With his friends.

"Xavier, I think you best come see me."

Her tone of voice had him freezing. She sounded almost distressed.

"What's wrong?"

"I've found a lump, Xavier."

"A lump? In your breast?"

"Xavier!" she said in a shocked voice.

He ran his hand over his face tiredly. "Mother, I'm a doctor."

"Yes, but you're also my son. There's no need to talk about breasts in front of me."

Lord, give him strength.

"What has your doctor said about the lump?" he asked urgently. "Have they done a biopsy?"

"I'm too scared to go," his mother whispered.

"Mother, you have to go."

"But they'll insist on examining me."

"Mother, please. Get father to take you. To examine you. He's a doctor."

"But he's not my doctor."

"Then please go to your doctor," he pleaded.

"Will you come home, Xavier? To take me? Please?"

He let out a deep breath. Then he glanced back at the doorway leading to the bedroom. He didn't want to leave Juliet.

But if his mother had cancer . . .

"Make the doctor's appointment for Monday. I'll get a flight out when I can." His phone started buzzing in his ear with another incoming call.

"Good. I knew you would come. I will see you then."

He blinked as she abruptly ended the call. But it was just as well since he saw he'd missed a call from the hospital.

After checking in to find one of his patients wasn't doing well, he checked on Juliet one last time.

He brushed his fingers down her cheek. He hated leaving her like this, but knew she would understand. He sent her a quick text to explain

Then before he could convince himself to linger longer, he left.

B rick checked his navigation system to see how far away they were. Fifteen minutes. Perfect. They'd been on the road for hours, setting out from Denver early. But they'd be right on time. He hated to be late for anything. His ex-wife had been the opposite. She'd been an hour late to their wedding. Perhaps he should have taken that as an omen.

"Earth to Brick, what's going on with you, man?" Sterling asked in concern.

"He daydreaming again?" Elias asked through the Bluetooth system. He was in the truck behind them.

Both men were his best friends. They'd been in the marines together. And when he'd called and told them the mess Linda had left him in, they'd dropped everything to come help him.

"He's got that line between his eyebrows which means he's thinking of—"

"Linda," Elias ended on a sigh. "Brick, man, you got to get her out of your head. You can't give her any more of your time."

His hands tightened around the steering wheel and his teeth

ground together. He knew that he had to stop thinking about Linda. And Mike. The bastard.

"I know," he said. "But it's hard to let it go when she cost me everything."

His house. His business. His credit rating. His reputation.

The only reason he'd managed to secure this job was because he was available on short notice. The client, Reuben Jones, needed someone to guard his sister for the indefinite future.

It likely wouldn't have been a job he'd have touched before he'd lost everything. The client was demanding. But his money was good. And since Brick was down to his last five hundred dollars, well, he was desperate. This job was his lifeline.

His friends were right, he had to get his mind back in the game.

"Sorry, you're right," he agreed, taking a right turn. "Have I thanked you guys again for helping me?"

The client wanted at least two bodyguards on site. One guarding his sister, the other patrolling the grounds and watching the cameras and alarms, even though there was an outside company monitoring the cameras and alarms.

Sterling scrolled through his phone. "Have you guys read the list of instructions and rules this guy has sent through for dealing with his sister?"

"He only sent them after I signed the contract, and then I was too busy packing everything up and getting ready," Brick said. "Why?"

"Did you know JSI put in her current security system?" Sterling commented. "Why didn't he go to them? They're monitoring her security anyway."

"Asked him about that," Brick admitted. And he'd been sweating bullets the entire time that Jones might turn around and go to JSI. "They didn't have anyone free, apparently. They're still monitoring the system, though. He said we can put in our system on top of theirs if we want. He also said something about Kent Jensen being a prick."

"Really?" Elias asked. "I've heard of Kent Jensen. Got a reputation as a fair man. Lots of the guys I was enlisted with talked about getting a job with him when they got out."

"I wouldn't put much stock in our client's opinions," Brick admitted as he turned into a quiet street. There didn't seem to be many houses out here. Just a lot of fucking trees. "I did a background check on him. He's got a reputation for being a shark. Ruthless and cunning."

"Yeah, but he's also loaded, I'm guessing," Elias said, looking around him. "As long as he pays the bills, do you really care?"

Once, he would have. But he couldn't pick and choose his jobs anymore.

"And demanding," Sterling said. "Listen to this stuff he sent through. No touching her without permission unless absolutely necessary. No going up to the third floor unless she's in danger. She doesn't talk."

"What?" Brick asked. "How the hell are we going to communicate with her?"

"Wasn't that something he should have told us first?" Elias asked.

Brick pulled into a driveway in front of a vast wrought-iron gate. A camera turned towards his truck. He knew there was likely another camera in a hidden position. The house wasn't visible from here. But just the gate held the promise of money.

"He should have," Brick agreed. Leaning back in the seat, he closed his eyes for a moment. He already had a headache.

"There's more," Sterling said as Elias pulled up behind them. "No changing her routine. We cannot talk to her with anything other than respect. When she gets nervous, she might grab hold of our clothing and we should allow her to do that. And if she goes still and cold, she could be having a panic attack. There's a number of a guy called Xavier to call in case of emergency."

"Wonder what's going on," Elias said. "She sounds—"

"Crazy," he barked.

"Brick," Sterling warned. "Just because Linda was a bitch doesn't mean all women are."

He closed his eyes and nodded. "Sorry. High-maintenance."

"Sounds to me like she has some problems," Elias said. "Bad anxiety."

All three of them were Dominants, and their protective instincts were strong.

"She works four days a week at the local library and that she uses a bicycle to get around," Sterling stated.

"That's out," Brick stated.

"Goes to a bar quiz night every Thursday," Sterling added.

"Also out."

"We're not supposed to disrupt her schedule unless necessary," Elias reminded him.

And he was being a jerk for the sake of it. Yeah, he knew that. But he would do whatever was necessary to keep this woman safe. This job could salvage his business. Losing it wasn't an option.

Winding down the window, he reached out to press the button on the communication system.

Elias got out of his truck and walked over to his open window. "This place is in the middle of nowhere."

Brick nodded. He didn't like all the trees surrounding the place. Too easy for someone to sneak close. But if there were any blind spots in JSI's security system, he knew he could plug them.

"Maybe if you tried smiling instead of scowling, she might be inclined to let us in." Elias raised an eyebrow, staring at Brick. "You do remember how to smile, don't you?"

"Fuck off," Brick snarled.

"Maybe she went out. Forgot we were coming," Elias said.

Humph. Probably out getting her nails done or shopping or whatever else rich people did. Like making a huge list of ridiculous instructions just to guard one woman. "Don't suppose there was a gate code on that list?"

"Nope," Sterling said. "But her number is here. And some information about her. Juliet Jackson. Age twenty-nine. Works at the Wishingbone Library four days a week for four hours a day."

He was kind of surprised she worked at all.

"Five foot three. Ninety-seven pounds."

Jesus. She was tiny. Didn't she eat?

"Allergic to shellfish. Carries an EpiPen."

He noted that all away as he pressed the buzzer again. Where the hell was she?

"How're we going to do this?" Elias asked. "Take shifts?"

"Jones wanted her to have one main guard," he replied. "Apparently, there's a guest suite in the pool house with two bedrooms. And then one of us can stay in the house."

When you were rich, you could afford to be quirky and different. Yes, he had a slight hang-up around money. Perhaps it was because he barely had two pennies to rub together. Or maybe because he had grown up watching his mother work three jobs to get food on the table.

Shit like that made you cynical.

"Quirks we can work with," Sterling said. "Just remember the money, man."

"Yeah, I know."

"You can't let her see that chip on your shoulder," Elias warned. "It's good money just to guard one woman."

And he needed it.

Frustrated, he put his finger on the buzzer again. Where was this woman?

"What's her phone number?" he asked. "I'll call her."

"Might be best to text her," Sterling suggested after rattling off the number.

He didn't care if he had to interrupt her manicure or whatever. Jones had told him that she knew they were coming. It was common courtesy to be here.

3

She had a headache. Her hand was throbbing from the burn. And she was really wishing that she hadn't freaked out like that around Xavier.

For as long as she could remember, she'd had a crush on the sexy doctor. He saw her as a sister, though.

She didn't blame him for not being attracted to her. She wasn't sexy. Or sane.

That seemed like something men might like. Someone who was sane. Right?

Kiesha was always saying that normal was overrated, but Juliet wasn't so sure. Besides, while Kiesha might be a bit crazy, she was also outgoing and fun, and she could actually talk to people.

That sort of thing helped, you know?

He'd rejected her once a long time ago when she was feeling surprisingly brave and kissed him. It still hurt all these years later. She wouldn't survive that rejection again.

Rubbing a hand over her face, she walked into the downstairs kitchen and opened the fridge. Grabbing the cranberry juice, she poured it into a glass. Her upstairs fridge was filled with iced coffee and water, but she had a craving for cranberry juice.

As she moved back towards the stairs, a buzzing noise frightened her.

She dropped the glass, which smashed on the ground, spilling juice everywhere. And she was standing in the middle of it, not wearing shoes.

"Crap. Crap. Crap."

Buzz!

Shoot. Whoever was at the gate was impatient.

"Keep your pants on, buddy," she snapped, feeling brave because she knew they couldn't see or hear her. Or even get onto the property without her letting them in.

She didn't want to let them in. She knew it had to be the security team that Reuben hired.

Buzz!

"Big girl panties, Juliet. It doesn't matter that you don't know them. Reuben sent them to protect you. They're doing a job. That's all. They don't have to like you. You don't have to like them."

She nervously tapped her fingers against her thigh, feeling her stomach churn. She wished Xavier had stayed. Not that she blamed him for leaving. After all, she'd fallen asleep on him. He'd had to put her to bed.

It was embarrassing that he'd had to take care of her like that.

Her phone dinged with a text message. Shoot.

She checked the text message.

UNKNOWN NUMBER: *Miss Jackson, this is Brick Sampson from Sampson Security. Your brother hired us. We are at the gate and would appreciate you letting us in.*

. . .

"THIS ISN'T GOING to work. His texts are so formal. What if he's like that in real life?"

She sent a text to Kiesha.

JULIET: *Can you trust people who txt in a formal tone?*

Kiesha: *Nope. Serial killer. 4 sure.*

YEP. That's what Juliet thought too.

Switching to her email, she went through what Reuben had sent her.

Brenton Sampson. Forty-two. Ex-Marine. Owned his own security company. Reuben had included a photo. He had a muscular build. Short, dark hair and tanned skin. He was also frowning. He looked kind of grouchy and hard.

Juliet rubbed at her temples. Her headache was still pounding. Her juice was all over the floor. There were shards of glass everywhere. And she was just standing here, doing nothing.

Her phone buzzed again with another text.

UNKNOWN NUMBER: *Miss Jackson? Are you home? Are you all right?*

YEAH, she was home. But whether she was all right, well . . . she guessed that depended on your definition. Closing her eyes, she took a deep breath. She couldn't stand here all day.

Stepping carefully around the mess, she moved to the panel up against the door. JSI had installed the system, and Kent had patiently shown her how to use it. She liked Kent. He was kind and he never rushed her.

She wished he or one of his guys could guard her. Then she wouldn't have to put up with this Brenton Sampson, who was not only impatient with a heavy buzzer finger, but had a scowly face and was obviously a serial killer.

Well, perhaps that last part was still up for contention. He could just be a lover of grammar. But the first two were definitely true.

Unfortunately, it seemed the man scowling up at the camera at the gate was almost certainly Brenton Sampson. Or his evil twin brother.

Her phone vibrated in her hand as wolf howls filled the room. Darn it.

She answered the call.

"Two calls in one day," she said cheerfully. "Are you sure you're not dying?"

There was silence on the other end. Drat.

"Let him in, Juliet."

"So, he's a tattletale too," she muttered.

"Mini," he sighed. She could feel the exhaustion in his voice and felt terrible. Here she was playing silly games and he was literally dealing with a threat to his life. If she could spank her own ass, she would.

She deserved a time-out at the very least. Or maybe writing some lines.

"I'm sorry, Reuben," she told him. "I know I'm more trouble than I'm worth."

"Excuse me?" he snapped coldly. He rarely used that tone with her. Only when she said something he really didn't like.

Oh. Like right now.

Good idea to anger him when he was already exhausted, worried, and in overprotective mode. She usually handled him better than this. It was just a sign of how stressed she was.

"What did you just say?"

"Nothing."

"Darn right. Because if you just said you're more trouble than you're worth, then I know I'm not talking to *my* sister. I know *my* sister must have been body-snatched. Because *my* sister would never say such a thing. Because *my* sister knows her worth, doesn't she? What's her worth?"

"I'm more important than anything and you'd give up everything you have for me."

The words filled her with a self-confidence she sorely lacked most of the time. When other people failed or left her, Reuben hadn't. He'd always had her back.

And you have to have his. Do this for him, so he doesn't worry about you on top of everything else.

Also, so he didn't kidnap her and take her to the island with him. Because he was also the most important person in her world, and if she killed him, then she'd be really upset with herself afterward.

"I'll let him in now. I'm sorry."

"It's okay, Mini. I know I'm asking for a lot. But I just need to know you're safe so I can do what I need to do to eliminate the threat. All right?"

"Yep. I can do that."

"I know you can. Because you're smart and brave."

"You're a good liar. Makes sense given your job," she teased him.

"Ha-ha, brat. You owe me some brownies for that."

"I might even leave out the walnuts this time."

Reuben hated walnuts but loved her chocolate brownies. So, when she was annoyed with him, she'd make him brownies with finely cut-up walnuts in it.

He laughed. A real laugh and she bounced on her toes, pleased with herself for relieving some of the stress in his voice.

"Listen, this guy comes with a lot of good references. He's had some financial difficulties, which was why he was available. I get the feeling he doesn't think much of me, so I doubt he would have taken the job unless he was desperate."

She frowned, not liking the sound of that. How dare this jerk think badly of her brother? Sure, Reuben could be a bit of a prick at times if you pissed him off. But the rest of the time, he was a teddy bear.

Yeah, okay, even she didn't believe the bullshit she was trying to spin.

"He looks scowly."

"Scowly, huh?"

"Kiesha thinks he's a serial killer."

"Kiesha thought the new pastor at her church was a serial killer."

"Yes, well, it turns out he was printing counterfeit money in his basement," she told him. "So Kiesha's instincts were right."

"It was play money and he was printing it off his computer."

"So he says. Kiesha says differently."

Reuben muttered something under his breath. She knew it would be nothing flattering about Kiesha, but it didn't matter. Reuben and Kiesha were oil and water, but they both loved her.

She hit the button to release the gate as he was muttering. Mr. Scowly gave the camera an even bigger scowl.

"He's going to give himself wrinkles," she muttered.

"What?" Reuben asked.

"Nothing, brother. I better go, I've let them in the gate."

"There are two guys with him?"

"Yep, looks like."

"Good. He's going to be your main point of contact. Kent said if one of his guys finishes a job sooner than expected that he'd send someone."

"Kent actually spoke to you?"

Reuben let out a huff of breath. "No. He's still sulking over something that happened ages ago. He needs to learn how to let go of a grudge. I spoke to Corbin. Who relayed the information to his majesty."

She rolled her eyes. She didn't know what the issue was between Reuben and Kent. But then, if she tried to keep track of every issue that someone in Wishingbone had with her brother, she'd never get anything else done in her life.

"They're here now."

"Okay, let Xavier do the talking. Wait. Why didn't he let them in? I sent him over to help ease you into this."

"You did?"

"What? Didn't he turn up? That bastard."

"No, he did. But I, ahh, doesn't matter. He left."

"You what?" Reuben asked suspiciously.

"Fell asleep." There was a knock at the front door. "Gotta go, they're here."

"I can't believe he left you! I'll kill him."

"Did you tell him that you'd hired a security team and that they were on their way?" she asked suspiciously. Because she was surprised that Xavier would have left her if that was the case.

"Well, no."

"Right, so you just ordered him to come over here instead of asking him or telling him any of the details."

Buzz!

What was with this guy? Was he trying to make her headache worse?

"Maybe," Reuben muttered. "Thought he would have stuck around for a bit longer."

"I've got to go. I got this."

She totally didn't. But she figured it wouldn't hurt to fake it.

"Love you, Mini."

"Love you too, BBW."

His sigh made her smile. Which faded as soon as she ended the call and faced the door.

Shit.

4

"Do you think she let us in just to leave us standing on her doorstep?" Elias said with amusement.

"Maybe you should let one of us do the talking," Sterling suggested.

"Probably a good idea," Elias agreed. "One look at you, and she'll likely run screaming."

He gave them both an exasperated look. "I can handle one woman. I've been doing this for a while."

Elias held his hands up. "Think I'll go start doing a recon of the area then."

"I'll see if I can find this pool house and unpack the stuff," Sterling added.

Wait. So, they were fucking leaving him? Assholes. He sighed. Great.

The door opened before he could call them back. Standing in the doorway was a tiny slip of a girl. She had her thick chestnut-colored hair in two braids. Her face was pale with smudges under her eyes.

She was dressed in a black dress that covered her from her

shoulders to her feet. Which he noticed were bare. And the nails were painted a pink so bright it almost hurt his eyes to look at them.

That was surprising. And kind of cute.

She's not cute, idiot.

It had been a long time since he'd been involved with a Little. Or even played at a club. Linda had been a sub, but not a Little. When they'd first started dating, they'd often go to the club to play. But after they were married, both of them had lost interest. Although, he'd come to learn that she'd simply found someone else to play with. His accountant.

He'd been fooled by his wife, his accountant, left with nothing.

Complete and utter failure.

But he wouldn't let this woman-girl see that. Sure, she might rouse his Daddy instincts, but that didn't mean anything. Maybe he was ready to move back into that scene.

His gut churned at the thought. Or maybe not.

Her fingers started tapping against the sides of her legs. A sign of agitation. And nervousness.

Because you're not talking, you ass.

Then his gaze caught on the red, blistered patch of skin on the top of her hand.

"How'd you get that?" he snapped, reaching for her hand. And why hadn't anyone taken care of it?

She snatched her hand out of his reach, stumbling back with a gasp. Her foot landed in something red on the floor. She let out a cry of pain.

Fuck, was that blood?

"Where are you bleeding?" he yelled.

Her eyes widened as she wobbled, about to fall. Acting on instinct, he grabbed her, pulling her towards him. She cried out, clasping her hands around his neck, and holding on tight. He swallowed heavily at the feel of her body against his.

Don't react. Don't react.

"You okay?" he asked.

She nodded, growing stiff. He saw the moment she realized that she was pressed against a strange man's body. He set her down before she could start to panic. Last thing he wanted was a hysterical, pint-sized woman on his hands.

Oh yeah? Because you're quite enjoying holding her in your hands at the moment.

"What did you slip on? Is that blood? Are you bleeding?" He looked her over but couldn't see any source for the red liquid lying on the floor.

Wait. Not blood.

Some other red liquid. Then he saw the shards of glass.

Bare feet.

Fuck.

"Did you stand on the glass?" he asked, remembering her sharp cry of pain.

She flinched, and he sucked in a deep breath. Fuck. He was messing this all up.

She's the client. Not someone he should be snarling at. His shortness with her came from worry. But she didn't know that.

Okay, he was also feeling short-tempered because he'd been made to wait at the gate, then on the doorstep for her, and Brick wasn't a guy who had much patience. Waiting around, doing nothing, it wasn't in his nature. He was a man of action.

But if he wasn't careful, he was going to lose this job before he'd had time to earn any money.

"There's sharp glass around and you have bare feet. That's juice?"

She looked from the liquid to him and gave a small nod. He wondered why she couldn't talk. Injured vocal cords? Something else? She wasn't what he'd expected. He'd thought she'd be perfectly composed. Maybe cool and haughty.

This is what Elias and Sterling were warning you about. Don't let your prejudices make you judge her before you even know her.

"Did you stand on some glass?"

Tears filled her eyes. Fuck. The urge to take her into his arms, to hug her and hold her was so strong that it nearly hurt trying to resist it.

Another nod.

He glanced over at her feet. One was hidden beneath her dress. Was she holding it up? Shit. How was he going to take care of her when she wouldn't let him touch her?

"I need to look at it." He tried to make his voice more soothing. But the wary look she shot him said that she wasn't buying it.

So, she was smart too. He wasn't much for soothing. Being calm and gentle didn't come easily to him. He was rough and emotionally unavailable, according to Linda.

But it was obvious that this girl needed him to ease his edges off, or she was going to bolt like a rabbit.

"I'm Brenton Sampson. Everyone calls me Brick, though."

She didn't react. It would help if she could talk. What had her brother said about communication?

"Do you have something you can use to talk to me?" he asked. He really wanted to check that burn, but he wasn't sure that she would let him touch her.

Yep, he'd really made a great first impression.

"I'm the security specialist that your brother hired to guard you."

She nodded slowly. Right. So, she knew who he was. But she still looked ready to run at the slightest hint that he meant her harm.

Easy. Just move slowly. Talk quietly.

"Would you let me look at your foot and your hand? They've got to be sore?"

She shook her head and he tried to work out which question

she was answering.

"You won't let me look at your foot and hand?"

She just eyed him. Not an outright no, but not a yes, either.

The need to pick her up and just take care of her was riding him hard.

You can't touch her without permission unless she's in danger.

A shrug was his only answer. Shit. This was going to be more difficult than anticipated. How did he communicate with her easily?

"A way of communicating with you would really help right now," he muttered.

She nodded then turned to limp away.

"Shit, don't walk around with a piece of glass in your foot."

Freezing, she shot him a look. He expected to see fear in her eyes, but instead, her gaze was filled with irritation. He ran his hand over his face. He needed to calm himself.

The job. You need this job.

Then he noticed blood on the floor. Actual blood this time. Fuck.

"You're bleeding. That's it. I'm touching you, so you need to deal." He didn't know how deep the cut was, it might not be a matter of life or death, but he was certain that her brother wouldn't appreciate him standing there while she was hurt and bleeding.

Fuck. His Daddy instincts were screaming at him. But as he reached for her, there was a noise behind him. Her eyes widened. He turned towards the threat, reaching for his gun.

"Whoa, it's just us." Elias held up his hands and Sterling shot him a look as they both walked through the door.

Shit. "Sorry, I didn't hear you coming." Suddenly, he felt someone press up against his back. Someone small, who was trembling.

"Juliet," he said in a low voice. Was that soothing? He

grimaced, fucked if he knew. The look Elias shot him was filled with surprise, so maybe he'd managed it. "Juliet, it's okay. These are my friends and work colleagues. This is Elias." He pointed at the dark-skinned, giant man who waved down at the woman peering around from behind him.

She twisted the back of his T-shirt in her hand and he remembered that being on the list of instructions. What had happened to this girl that she couldn't cope with meeting strangers? That she had to literally hold onto someone to ease her anxiety? Was that what she was doing? Holding onto him because he made her feel less anxious?

Something like satisfaction filled him.

Ease up, bud. You're like the lesser of three evils. She doesn't actually see you as her protector.

He might not have enjoyed being married to Linda, but he did like having someone to watch over, to protect.

"Hi Juliet," Elias said softly. Despite his large size, he was a big softie.

Brick expected Juliet's tension to ease, but she just tightened her hold on him. That was odd. Women usually much preferred Elias' gentle approach or Sterling's sense of humor. Not his grim personality.

"Hey, Juliet. Did the boss man here tell you some bad stories about us?" Sterling joked. "Promise none of it is true."

She still didn't react.

Elias looked to Brick, his eyebrows raised. "Anything we can do in here?"

Do?

"Did you guys spill something?" Sterling added. "There's glass on the floor, and is that cranberry juice?"

"Fuck. Her foot." He whirled around and nearly sent her flying. Grabbing her upper arms, he steadied her. "Are you all right? We need to check your foot."

Her eyes were too wide in her pale face.

"She hurt herself?" Elias asked.

"Yes, but I think more urgent is that you guys step back and give her some breathing space."

He'd seen several panic attacks before. Most people started to breathe in big gulps, as though they couldn't get enough air. But he had a feeling that Juliet's panic attacks were different. And that she was headed towards one right now.

Gently grasping hold of her uninjured hand, he placed it on his shirt. Something came over her face. Something that looked like relief.

That's right, baby. Let me anchor you.

Fuck. He was in trouble.

"Are you sure? Is there something we can do?" Elias asked. "Juliet, could I check your foot for you?"

She shook her head frantically.

"I got it," he said quietly. "I'm going to take Juliet and find a first-aid kit. Can you guys clean up this? Did you find the pool house?"

"Yeah, it's locked though," Sterling replied.

She pointed at the side table. There was a single drawer in it.

"Key's in there?" he asked.

She nodded.

Sterling moved to the drawer and opened it. She tensed, but that panicked look didn't enter her gaze again. Because she was holding onto him?

"Got it. We'll give you both a bit of space," Sterling said.

"I'll go find the broom and mop," Elias said in a falsely cheerful voice as he walked past them, careful to give her a wide berth.

Juliet watched him but didn't flinch. Her reactions were off. It wasn't like she was afraid of them exactly, just wary. But moments ago, he'd seen her panic. Almost felt it. Was she always this scared around people she didn't know? If so, how did she get on in everyday life? Hold down a job? Even just buy her groceries? Surely, she had to run into strangers. Or was it because they were big and male? Maybe because they were in her house?

He pushed those thoughts out of his mind. He'd ponder them later. She'd had a piece of glass in her foot for far too long.

"Juliet, I have to get that piece of glass out of your foot," he explained. "But I can't let you walk on it. Can I pick you up?"

She studied him for a long moment, then nodded.

"Good." He let out a sigh of relief. Reaching out, he lifted her up into his arms slowly. "You weigh nothing. Do you even eat?"

She stiffened, and he cursed himself for snapping like that. But when he glanced down at her, she was glaring up at him.

Okay, so the bunny had claws. Good to know.

"Not known for mincing my word, bunny," he told her.

She snapped her teeth at him, crossing her arms over her chest. Amusement filled him.

"More of a kitten, huh?"

She sniffed.

"Tigress."

Sighing, she looked sad all of a sudden, and he wanted the glaring, snappy Juliet back. She just shook her head.

"Right, point me in the direction of where the first-aid kit is."

She pointed down the hallway and they passed Elias in the corridor, carrying a mop, broom, and bucket.

He nodded at Brick, giving Juliet a concerned look but he didn't say anything. She tensed slightly but otherwise, she didn't show any sign of concern. Was it because she knew Brick would keep her safe? That was silly, right?

He'd known her fifteen minutes and spent most of that time snapping at her.

Yep. Ridiculous.

She pointed to a door and he stepped into a huge country-style kitchen. It was done in soft blues and creams with an enormous island. Reluctantly, he sat her down on the counter. Reaching over, she grabbed a whiteboard and pen that were on the counter.

First-aid kit is under the sink.

All right. He supposed at least now they could communicate. Although he wished he could hear her voice. Turning, he moved to the kitchen sink.

This was going to be a very strange assignment.

DON'T CHECK out his ass. Don't check out his ass.

Brick Sampson was too masculine to truly be thought of as handsome. Where Xavier's features were all perfectly proportioned, Brick's were all slightly off. His jaw a bit too firm. Nose a bit too wide. But it didn't matter because the man was raw power in a large package. But there was something radiating from Brick that just told you he was a force to be reckoned with.

He was gruff and impatient, there was nothing soft about him. She'd felt that when he'd held her pressed against him. Definitely all muscle. To her shock, her body had reacted to him. She had never shown sexual interest in any man except for Xavier. And he was a stranger.

She'd known Xavier for years. She'd first met him when he'd been in college and had come to Wishingbone to visit Reuben. Xavier was safe. Kind and caring. She trusted him.

She didn't trust Brick. She didn't know him. And from what she had observed of him, he was the opposite of Xavier. He wasn't a man who was used to being defied. She'd seen his frustration when he'd had to hold himself back with her. When he'd wanted to just storm in and take charge.

But he was here to do a job. Nothing more. Nothing less.

Still, she didn't have to trust him to check out one fine, fine ass.

He turned just as she had that thought. And she felt her

cheeks grow bright red. For the first time ever, she was glad that she wasn't able to talk. Because she had a feeling she might have just asked him if she could give his ass a squeeze.

Just a little one.

Thankfully, having to write things down rather than just blurting them out meant she had time to come to her senses.

Brick stood there for a moment, then he raised an eyebrow, and a hint of a self-satisfied smile filled his face.

Uh-oh.

She had a feeling that she hadn't hidden the fact that she'd been checking him out all that well

Look away. Act innocent.

How was she going to survive this?

He moved slowly and easily because he thought she was a bunny. Easily frightened.

And aren't you?

Although it was a wonder she hadn't had a full-blown panic attack just now. She'd managed to stop it before it had really hit her.

Because of him.

Placing the first-aid kit on the counter, he drew out a stool and sat on it, then using slow movements, he drew her foot up so he could examine it.

Her dress fell back to her calf, and she sucked in a breath.

Having her skin exposed made her feel raw. Vulnerable. But it was just her foot and calf. She could handle it.

"Walking around barefoot is a damn fool idea," he muttered.

She attempted to pull her foot away, scowling down at him. Plenty of people walked around barefoot. Who was this guy to keep snapping at her like he did? No one ever spoke to her this way.

He just kept hold of her foot.

"Especially with broken glass on the floor."

It wasn't like she'd done it on purpose.

She tried to pull her foot away again.

"Stay still," he ordered, giving her a firm look. "I know it hurts, but if you stay still, I can do it quicker."

She sighed but kept still.

"There, got it all, I think. But it would be better to wash your foot as well before we put on the antiseptic."

He picked her up and carried her over to the other counter where the sink was, setting her down and then gently washing her foot. A shiver ran through her, surprising her. Was she attracted to him?

What would it be like to have a fling? To have sex? Could she do that with a stranger?

She shuddered at the thought of him seeing her naked. Touching her.

"Easy," he said, breaking through the fear threatening to send her into another panic attack. "You're fine. All clean. Just need the antiseptic. Sorry if this hurts."

After the antiseptic, he put a bandage on, his movements brisk but gentle. Seemed like overkill to her.

"There, that ought to do it. But I don't want you walking on that foot for the rest of the day, understand?"

She raised her eyebrows at his bossy tone. Oh, he was definitely a man who was used to getting his own way.

Grabbing her whiteboard and pen, she wrote a message and showed it to him.

"Do I expect you to fly?" he repeated. "Are you sassing me?"

She tilted her head to one side. Was she? She'd never thought of herself as sassy.

She shrugged.

He eyed her for a moment, then let out a noise that was a cross between irritation and impatience. She hid a smile. It was fun poking the bear.

Best not poke too hard, Juliet. You don't know him. You don't know when he'll bite back.

Right. That somber reminder had her straightening. She knew that Reuben would have done an extensive background check on this man. Even with a short timeframe, he wouldn't hire someone who wasn't good at their job. However, there was a lot that could slip through a background check. It didn't mean he hadn't done bad things, only that he hadn't been caught.

And while her gut said she could trust him, she had nothing to base that on. She'd learned the hard way that her gut could be wrong. And that when she listened to it, she could end up hurt.

"Hey, you okay?" He reached for her chin and she flinched back.

He froze. She had to resist the urge to lean into him, to press against him and breathe him in.

"Would you prefer that Elias come and help you?" he asked in a voice that had grown cooler.

There was something in the way he held himself. Something that said he fully expected to be rejected. She wasn't sure who would ever reject this man.

Well, other than her. But she was an idiot. Flawed.

"I'll go get him to look at that burn." He took a step away and she shook her head, covering up the burn. He narrowed his gaze at her. "You need something on it. If the blister bursts, then it could easily get infected."

She shook her head again. He wasn't the boss of her. She wrote another message.

I'm fine. You probably need to settle in.

He crossed his arm over his chest. "It's not okay. It needs checking. And I'll settle in once you're okay."

I'm okay.

He sent her a skeptical look.

She went to slide off the bench, but he moved into her way. A small spark of panic started in her belly. Instead of trying to calm it, she let it grow. Because this was how she should react to him. No way was the desire to curl up in his lap like a contented kitten and purr actually real. Or sane.

But he didn't touch her. Or snap at her. Instead, he watched her carefully.

"For some reason, I don't think you're as scared of me as you're pretending to be."

She narrowed her gaze at him.

"Why don't you want me touching you? Is it just me? Or all men?"

None of your business. And I don't need a shrink.

She showed him the message.

"No, you need a bodyguard. Which is me. I'm in charge of you." He pointed a finger at her. If she'd been braver, she would have bitten it.

Nobody is in charge of me.

"I've been employed to keep you safe, and that means if there is any danger to you, then you're to do as I say. If you're hurt, then I'm in charge of taking care of you. If you need something, then I'm here to provide it."

That's not what bodyguard means.

"Does in my world, babe."

She wrinkled her nose at his arrogance. What he needed was a good, hard kick in the behind.

Fine. Then I'd like a double fudge sundae with whipped cream and sprinkles.

There. She sent him a triumphant look. He'd said if she needed something, he'd provide it.

"I'd say what you need is a medium-rare steak and an early night. Which I am happy to provide after I see to your hand and get you settled."

Arrogant ass.

5

Brick watched her eyes fill with temper.

He preferred her temper to her wariness. Something told him she had a good reason for being so guarded. He likely wasn't helping her feel more at ease around him. He was bossy and blunt, and he didn't know how to change.

One day he'd know all those nightmares he saw swirling in her eyes and he'd make every person that hurt her suffer. They'd rue the day they ever saw her.

Ease back.

You don't know her. You're here for a job. You have no right to her past.

And he shouldn't have any interest in her. She was the client. She was obviously damaged. There was far too much shit in his life going on right now for him to get into any sort of relationship. And he definitely couldn't fall for a client.

Perhaps it wasn't a good idea for him to be her main contact.

"Give me your hand," he said, injecting some Dom into his voice.

He waited impatiently for her to decide what to do. But before either of them could react or move, the door opened and Elias stepped in. "All clean, man."

Juliet let out a small squeal. Did that mean her vocal cords weren't damaged? She leaned into him, and he had to stop himself from preening like a damn peacock. Idiot.

There was definitely something weird here. He'd never felt such an instant draw towards someone.

"Sorry, didn't mean to startle you, Juliet," Elias said, holding his hands out at his sides. He held the mop in one hand and the broom in the other.

She made a noise of irritation, but he thought that was aimed at herself rather than Elias.

With a sigh, she picked up her whiteboard.

I'm not used to strangers in my house.

"I totally understand," Elias said with a smile.

A stab of jealousy hit him as he sensed her relaxing. Elias could soothe the prickliest personality and have them soon eating out of the palm of his hand.

"It's not easy for anyone having strangers in their home. But we'll do our best to be as unobtrusive as possible," Elias told her.

Will he?

He frowned as he saw she'd drawn an arrow pointing his way after those words.

Elias let out a bark of laughter. "Well, you've got Brick pegged right. And you've known him less than an hour."

Juliet smiled. Actually smiled. Her whole face lightened, and she looked so gorgeous that for a moment, his breath caught.

Fuck. He definitely needed to get away from her.

He crossed his arms over his chest. "I've got things I need to do. No time to stand around and chat. Elias, check her hand and don't let her walk on that foot."

Before he could change his mind, he left the room.

As soon as he left, he started cursing himself. Fuck.

Shaking his head and ignoring his gut, which was telling him to go back to her, he strode out of the house and headed towards where he figured Sterling would be, setting up additional cameras.

About twenty minutes later, Elias came into where he was sitting at the dining table. The pool house was as big as most people's actual houses. It had two bedrooms, both with attached bathrooms and a full kitchen. He could easily stay here while letting Elias stay with Juliet in the house.

"What was that?" Elias said.

Brick was aware of Sterling turning to watch them with interest.

"Why aren't you with the client?" he asked Elias.

"Because that's your job."

"Not anymore," he replied.

"What does that mean? Damn it, look at me," Elias snapped.

Sterling looked between them with wide eyes.

"I need you to take point with the client, Elias," he explained. "I should have done that from the beginning. She'll find it easier to be around you."

"I think you're wrong. She wasn't at ease with me at all after you left."

"What do you mean? Is she all right? Did you bandage up her hand?" he asked.

"Yeah, I bandaged up her hand, but she was nervous around me. Jittery."

"What's going on, Brick?" Sterling asked. "It was pretty obvious that she preferred you to the two of us when she grabbed onto you in the foyer."

"You gave her a fright and I was closest," he grumbled. "She'll be more comfortable with Elias."

"Fine," Elias sighed. "I'll go grab my stuff and get back in there, then. But I think you're wrong. I think she'd be more comfortable with you."

Brick didn't agree. He thought it was best that he kept some distance from her.

6

After limping into her playroom, Juliet set the electronic lock on the door.

Hurt flooded her, but she did her best to squash it. Ridiculous. Why should she feel hurt? He had other things to do. Besides, he unsettled her. He made her react to him in ways she didn't react to any man.

Well, except Xavier. But her reactions to Xavier were unwanted as well. Because he would never reciprocate them. And yet, she couldn't get him out of her mind. Right now, all she wanted was to talk to him, to tell him about what was going on so he could reassure her that everything was going to be all right.

Anxiety did a nasty dance in her tummy as she drew out her phone, rereading his text message.

XAVIER: *Sorry to leave you without saying goodbye but I've got to go see my parents. Call me when you can.*

· · ·

SHE CLICKED on his contact before she could talk herself out of it.

"Twink? You okay?" His voice soothed her even as it excited her. But she thought he sounded tired.

She sat on the sofa. "I'm all right. Are you? Why are you going to see your parents?"

Xavier wasn't that close to his parents. She'd never met them, but Reuben had told her a few things. They'd pushed all these expectations onto Xavier when he was younger. He'd always had to be the best at everything, and failure was never an option.

Xavier sighed. "My mother found a lump in her breast, and I'm worried she won't get it checked unless I'm there to help her."

"Oh no, I'm so sorry!" she told him.

"Thanks, Twink. I'm sorry I had to leave before you woke up. I got called into the hospital to check on a patient. Are you all right? Want to tell me why you had a panic attack and Reuben told me to go around and check on you?"

It always amazed her that with how much he had going on, he still took time to worry about her. She'd rang him with the intention of telling him what was going on, but she knew she couldn't now. Her problems were nothing against his mother being ill.

"I'm fine."

There was a beat of silence.

"Twink," he said in a low, warning voice that sent shivers through her body. If only Xavier saw her as anything other than a friend or little sister. "You know saying 'I'm fine' isn't acceptable. Tell me what's going on."

She sighed. "I'm really okay. There's stuff going on with Reuben, but when isn't there?"

"Well, that's true."

If he'd been here in person, he'd be able to tell she was lying. The last thing she wanted was to burden him with more stuff to worry about.

"When do you catch a flight out?"

"I'm heading to the airport early tomorrow morning. I just need to head home and pack then get some sleep."

"I'll let you get ready."

"Call me if you need me, understand?"

"Bye, Xavy. Be safe!"

"Bye, sweetheart."

After ending the call, she moved to the area in the back corner, she picked up Angelique and Missy. Curling up on the pile of cushions, she reached under one of the cushions for a pacifier. She had them hidden around this room and in her bedroom. The one in her bed was attached to her favorite blanket. It was something she'd had since she was a baby. It never left her bed because if she lost it, she'd be . . . devastated.

She wasn't sure how she was going to survive having them in the house. But maybe if she stayed up here, then she wouldn't have to have much to do with them.

That was the hope anyway.

Of course, she still had to leave the house. But that was a worry for another day. She didn't have to work until Monday, and today was Saturday. That gave her some time to get used to the idea, right?

She hugged Angelique and Missy tight.

Why couldn't she just be normal? Was that too much to ask?

BRICK SCOWLED DOWN at the steak on his plate as though it had mortally offended him. They were all seated at a table on the patio outside the pool house. All of them except her.

"This is a strange town," Sterling said. He'd gone out to shop for food for dinner.

"Strange how?" Elias asked as he dug into his large plate of food.

"Three different people propositioned me, and that was before I even got inside the grocery store."

Sterling could have graced the cover of any magazine and he was always getting hit on. So, he didn't see why it was such a great surprise.

Where was she?

"How long ago did you send that text?" he growled at Elias.

The other man just raised an eyebrow then purposefully took another bite of food and ate it slowly.

Asshole.

Then he picked up his phone. Brick tightened his hands around his knife and fork. He'd told Sterling to buy steak since he was worried about how pale she was.

"Ten minutes ago."

"What did you say to her?"

"I said that we were eating dinner and there was plenty if she wanted to join us."

"And what did she say?"

Elias sighed. "She said no thanks but to help ourselves to anything we needed."

"Why the hell did you let her go upstairs? She shouldn't be walking on that foot."

"I can't make her do anything. And unless there's a direct threat to her, I also can't order her to do anything."

Fuck that.

If he'd been the one watching her . . . but he wasn't. He'd given that job up. And now he was griping at Elias because he wasn't doing it the way he wanted him to.

He was absolutely being an asshole.

"What's so weird about women propositioning you?" Elias asked Sterling.

"They all had to be over eighty, and one of them was a man."

Elias grinned. "That is a new record for you."

Sterling shook his head. "And there's something else. There was this woman yelling at someone in a big red truck."

"How is that odd?" Brick asked, confused.

"She was wearing a T-shirt that said: Why be the bigger person, go slash their tires."

Elias's grin widened. "I already like her."

"I haven't got to the weird part yet. She was on roller skates, and she had a helmet on that had images of monsters on it and two googly eyes at the top. When I stepped out onto the road, she nearly ran me over then told me I was getting in the way of her righteous revenge and to go back to pretty boy school."

Sterling sounded miffed as Elias burst into laughter. Brick stood.

"Where are you going?" Elias asked.

"She could be hurt. She could have slipped over going up the stairs and cracked her head and be bleeding out. What if someone got to her?"

"Without setting off the alarms?" Sterling asked.

"She said she was going up to her room to rest, man," Elias added. "She's probably asleep."

"We should put cameras in her room," he said.

Both Elias and Sterling gaped at him.

"Bit far, don't you think?" Sterling said carefully.

"That would be a gross invasion of privacy," Elias agreed.

"We wouldn't watch it," he said impatiently. "Just check up on her when she isn't answering our texts. This house is so huge, we're already putting them at the entrances and exits, why not in her room?"

Even he knew he sounded like a crazy person.

"Fuck, I'm going to check on her." His glare warned them both not to say anything. Walking into the huge house, he stormed up the stairs. With each step, his worry grew. They could be sitting there eating dinner and she could be hurt.

Reaching the third floor, he was surprised to find just a small landing with one door off it.

He knocked on the door.

Nothing. Then again, it wasn't like she could call out.

"Juliet! Juliet, if you're in there, then please open the door."

Nothing. Fuck.

He reached for the door knob, but it wouldn't turn. Locked. He ground his teeth together. She couldn't lock them out when they were trying to protect her.

"Juliet!" He thumped on the door. "Open this door. Now."

Something slid out under the door. He blinked as his eyes took in the note.

No.

No? Seriously? That was it?

"Juliet, I'm not leaving until I have eyes on you. It's my job. Now open the door."

Another piece of paper slid under the door.

See previous note.

He ground his teeth together. The brat. If she were his . . . well, she wouldn't be on the other side of a locked door. That was for damn sure.

And defying him on a matter of health and safety would end up with her over his lap.

"Juliet, I'm not asking here. You're going to open this door and talk to me."

Fuck.

"I meant, let me see you," he added hastily. Good job, pointing out the fact that she couldn't talk. He still needed to find out why she couldn't speak.

"Juliet," he warned in his Dom voice.

Another note.

I'm fine. Go away.

"Your dinner is ready. I'll help you down the stairs. It's steak. It's good for you. It'll put hairs on your chest."

He rolled his eyes. Fuck, wasn't he on a roll? Hairs on her chest.

Another piece of paper.

Yay! Just what I always wanted. A hairy chest. Something else to make me a freak.

What. The. Fuck.

"Who said you were a freak? Did someone call you that?" he snarled. "Tell me who and I'll . . ."

He'd what? Chase down the bastard and teach them a lesson? Yep, that seemed totally not insane.

I'm tired.

He stared at the last note and sighed.

"If I bring the food up here, will you at least eat some of it? Please?" It went against his personality to practically beg her to do something. He was used to giving the orders and being obeyed.

No answer.

He sighed. "I'll bring it up. I just need to go over a couple of things before I go. I'll email you through some rules. We're setting up additional security. We'll do a big grocery shop tomorrow if you want anything. If you want to join us to eat at any time, you're welcome. Please make sure that if you get your bandages wet that you put on fresh ones. If you need anything, you have my number. You need anything, day or night, then text me. Good night, Juliet. Sleep tight."

7

"Where's your hat?"

The voice came from behind her, startling her so badly that she found herself slipping forward into the pool with a scream.

She landed with a splash, the cold water moving over her head. For a moment, she just floated there at the bottom of the pool.

Well, she had been thinking how nice a swim might be. She'd spent most of the morning in her playroom trying to gather up the courage to go downstairs, knowing she might run into one of them.

Mainly Brick.

Sexy, grouchy, Brick.

Somehow, the little sleep she'd got had been filled with dreams about him. And in most of them, he'd taken on the role of her Daddy. Which was ridiculous. Because the only kind of Daddy she'd ever want would be patient and kind and sweet.

Someone more like Xavier.

Not Oscar the grouch.

Something grabbed her around the waist as she lay there, floating, and she turned, trying to fight them off. Then she saw Brick's blurry face. He grabbed her, thrusting her up into the surface.

Darn. There went her swim.

Well, she didn't have her floaties anyway. Not that she needed her floaties or her blow-up lifesaver or her giant mermaid floatie. But really, what was the point of going swimming without those things?

Couldn't bring them out while she had Brick, Elias, and Sterling here. Which is why she'd been sitting forlornly, with her feet in the water, before Brick snuck up and scared her.

What a grumpy butt.

Speaking of Mr. Grumpy-Butt, he was currently losing his cool right now.

"What the hell were you doing by the water if you can't swim!" he yelled as he dragged her towards the stairs. "God damn it! Why do you have a pool if you can't swim? There shouldn't even be water in here. What were you thinking sitting on the side of the pool?"

She stared at him in shock as he kept raving at her. He started up the stairs with her in his arms. Why she wasn't panicking at being held by him, she wasn't sure. Maybe it was because one of them ought to stay calm.

Or maybe it's because you like him holding you.

Nope. It wasn't that. No way. No how.

But then he stopped and glared down at her. How could he be sexy even when he was insane?

It was hard to work out.

"Are you listening to me, Juliet?" he snapped.

She shook her head before she thought better of it. His gaze narrowed. He muttered something under his breath that she was certain wasn't at all flattering to her.

"Hey, what's going on? We heard yelling."

She looked over at Sterling who had spoken. Elias was behind him, studying them both with one eyebrow raised. They had strange looks on their faces that she couldn't figure out. She stiffened and attempted to get out of Brick's hold.

"Stay still," he commanded.

She glared up at him.

"I'm not putting you down until I know you're all right. Actually, maybe we should take you to the hospital. You could have swallowed water. Sterling, get her a towel. Elias, start the truck. We'll take her there now."

Now she started wriggling in earnest.

"I said hold still, little girl. If you were mine, you'd already be in . . ." his voice trailed off, a look of horror filling his face.

What? Was the idea of her being his so abhorrent to him?

Wait. Little girl? Did that mean . . . no, of course it didn't. He only said that because he probably saw her as young and immature.

Someone cleared their throat, and she glanced over to see that Sterling was holding out a towel. She shied away from him before she could stop herself. Even though all he did was hold the towel and give her a small smile.

Damn, he was pretty. Like movie star handsome.

"Give it to me," Brick snapped as he shuffled her weight around and grabbed the towel. He attempted to get the towel around her while holding her, which wasn't exactly working.

"Here, do you want me to . . ." Sterling attempted to help him, but a small panicky noise left her throat. Sterling stepped back with his hands up. "Maybe put Juliet down, and then she can do it herself."

"Juliet fell into the pool. She nearly drowned. We need to get her to the hospital." He half got the towel around her and started striding towards the truck.

No way. Not happening.

She wriggled around in his arms, trying to get down.

"Stay still," he bossed.

She growled up at him. He froze, his eyes widening.

"Um, Brick. She doesn't seem like her dunk in the pool has caused any issues. You sure she needs to go to the hospital?" Sterling asked.

"She nearly drowned!" Brick roared.

For goodness sake!

She slapped the palm of her hand against his forehead. He stilled, then he turned that dark gaze onto her. His eyes were actually dark blue, but they looked black. Like the devil.

"Did you just slap me?" he growled.

There was a bark of laughter from Sterling who was standing beside them.

"No, I'd say that she was trying to knock some sense into you."

She nodded. Sterling got her. Brick was just dense. He deserved that smack in the head and she wasn't going to feel bad about it. Nuh-uh. Not even with him glaring at her like he'd like to smack something of hers.

Something lower.

Her ass tingled just thinking about it.

"What's going on?" Elias hurried towards them. "I got the truck ready. I thought we were taking her to the hospital."

She scowled over at him, and he came to a sudden stop. "Or not."

"We're going," Brick insisted.

Smack!

Um, okay. She didn't actually mean to smack him in the head again. It just sort of happened.

"Did she . . . did she just . . ." Elias stumbled over his words.

"Try to smack some sense into him?" Sterling spoke through his laughter. "Yep, she sure did."

Elias burst into huge guffaws of laughter. "Holy shit. That's the funniest thing I've ever seen."

"Not funny," Brick snapped. "Hospital. Now."

She held up her hand.

"I swear, you smack me again and I'll . . ." his voice drifted off.

He'd what?

She raised an eyebrow as he obviously attempted to come up with something to threaten her with.

"Brick, she looks fine. Cold, but fine."

Brick's gaze swung back to her as Elias said that. Sterling had disappeared somewhere.

"She's going to catch pneumonia and die."

She huffed out a breath. She was not. It was hot as hell out here. Although she was a bit cold with her clothing all pressed against her body. And he was in the same state. Hm, now if she could just get a good look . . .

You're an idiot, Juliet.

Chill.

"She won't if you let her have a shower and get into warm clothes," Elias said reasonably.

"She nearly drowned. She needs the hospital."

"Why don't we ask her?" Sterling said, coming back with her whiteboard and pen in hand. Her hand shook as she wrote on it, which made Brick growl. Well, she thought that was why. Hard to tell with him.

He seemed to be awfully fond of growling. Especially at her.

Didn't drown. No hospital.

"You fell into the water. I had to rescue you," Brick said.

I can swim.

"Then why were you just lying there?" he snapped.

She shrugged.

Peaceful.

Elias cleared his throat. "I'm going to go turn off the truck."

"And I'll go get started on dinner. Juliet, you want to join us for dinner?" Sterling asked.

Eat dinner with them? No, she didn't want to do that. Right?

"She'll be coming for dinner," Mr. Grumpy-Butt said.

She was scowling up at him and didn't notice that they were on their own until he started to set her down on her feet. Needing to get away from him, she stepped back too quickly, tripping over her own feet. She would have gone flying if he didn't grab her, pressing her against his body.

A gasp escaped her, and it wasn't because they were both cold and wet. Nope. This was a reaction that sizzled deep inside her. She could feel his hard, muscular body. And she wanted to feel more. To strip him off and lick every inch . . .

Whoa, girl.

Brick stared down at her. There was something in his gaze. Something that looked like hunger. He licked his lips, his gaze caught on her lips.

Was he going to kiss her? He was, wasn't he? Her fingers tingled and her lips parted as she went up on tiptoes in preparation.

All of a sudden, Brick stepped away from her. He took several steps back then ran his fingers through his hair.

"Sorry for . . . for everything." He turned away, took another few steps while she gaped at him.

Then he turned back. Right, this was it. This was the part in the movie where the hero would run towards her, wrap his hands around her waist and spin her in the air before setting her gently down and kissing her.

Except real life wasn't a movie.

And truthfully, she'd rather be pressed up against a wall, with his hand wrapped in her hair while he ravaged her mouth.

Yeah, she kind of had a thing for the sort of romance books where the man was all possessive and dominant. Where he wanted the heroine so much that he was constantly bending her over pieces of furniture or ordering her to suck him off, or pulling her over his knee.

Not that she was ever going to get that. Because she had less than ten people who she could stand touching her, let alone trust to do any of that with. And of those ten people, there was only one she was attracted to.

And Xavier definitely wasn't the push her against the wall and fuck her until she screamed kind of guy. He was more of a roses, champagne, and sex under the covers guy. Which there was nothing wrong with. That was absolutely what she wanted.

Right?

Stupid Juliet. Just because something sounds sexy in a book doesn't mean it is in real life. She'd probably immediately freak out and then make a fool of herself.

She could totally see that happening.

"Get out of those wet clothes," he ordered.

Why don't you make me?

Sheesh. Where had all this sassiness come from? This wasn't her. Well, she was a bit sassy in Little space. But not in the rest of her life. She was sweet and compliant, mostly. Unless she didn't want to do something

Hm. Okay, maybe she was more disobedient than she'd thought.

"Have a shower. Or you'll get ill."

She rolled her eyes at him, but he'd already turned and started stomping away.

To Brick's surprise, she came to dinner. She stood shyly at the edge of the patio, watching them as they got dinner ready.

Well, Sterling was at the grill, and Elias was putting out some condiments while he set out the plates and cutlery.

Part of him had been hoping she wouldn't turn up. Even though he'd been the one who'd basically demanded she come.

There was something wrong with him. Really wrong with him. When he'd seen her floating on the bottom of the pool, he'd nearly had a heart attack. He'd felt sure she was drowning. And then when he'd picked her up, well . . .

He hadn't wanted to let her go.

He hadn't felt this attracted to someone since Linda. And Linda was the reason why he shouldn't trust himself. Because it turned out he was a bad fucking judge of character when it came to the women he was interested in. His dick didn't make good decisions.

And doing anything with Juliet wouldn't be a good decision.

He could kiss his reputation goodbye if Reuben Jones decided to blackball him.

So, no way was he going to go any further with this girl.

But that didn't mean that his dick wasn't still interested in her. When she'd been pressed against him, he'd been so close to kissing her. To ravaging that small mouth, picking her back up, and carrying her inside to strip her of her clothes.

But not because he was worried about her getting pneumonia.

Nope, he'd wanted to strip her for entirely different reasons.

Thank fuck he hadn't.

"Juliet, hi. Come on. Sit down," Elias said with a wide smile. "Not that you need an invitation since this is your place."

He watched her move forward warily. He was surprised she'd come.

"If you can swim, then why did you just float on the bottom?" he snapped.

Elias and Juliet turned to look at him. Her eyes were surprised. While Elias glared at him.

"Sorry about Brick, doll," Elias said. "He does have some manners. He just forgets to use them."

Brick scowled at his friend. What the fuck was he going on about? Then he noticed that Juliet looked like she was contemplating leaving.

"Sit down, Juliet," he said gruffly. He pulled out a seat for her, then looked pointedly at Elias, who rolled his eyes.

She moved slowly. Like a wounded animal who was worried that a gesture of kindness might turn into a trap. That made his heart ache. Who had hurt this woman? What he wouldn't give to know.

Easy, man.

He pushed her in. "Don't look so worried, Sterling's cooking isn't that bad." He took a seat next to her.

A plate filled with steak landed in the middle of the table. Her eyes widened as she took it in.

"Don't listen to him, I'm a fantastic cook."

"Finally!" Elias said, sitting across from Juliet at the round table. He reached out to grab a steak. Brick slapped his hand.

"Hey!"

"And you said that I don't have any manners. Ladies first." He picked up the plate and held it closer to Juliet. "Take one."

She shook her head. Then she picked up the whiteboard she'd carried over.

No thanks.

"You don't like steak?" he asked with a frown.

She shook her head.

"More for me," Elias said cheerfully as Brick set the plate down.

"Elias," Sterling said with a sigh. Then he turned to her. "Would you like me to make you something else? I have some chicken in the fridge. We should have asked you if you ate steak."

No problem. Bread and salad are fine.

"It's not fine," Brick countered. "You need protein. You're too pale. Sterling, get that chicken."

No!

She slapped the table with a frown as Sterling got up. He raised his eyebrows.

Please don't. I'll feel bad.

Brick grumbled under his breath. Obviously, she was so pale because she didn't eat enough meat. Salad and bread weren't a proper meal.

But he took note of Sterling's warning look and backed down. After she put a ridiculously small amount of food on her plate, he added more.

"If you're not eating meat, then you need to eat twice as much of everything else."

That's not a rule.

"Is now."

Elias and Sterling started arguing over the game they'd watched earlier that afternoon, and Brick leaned in to speak quietly to Juliet as she moved her food around on her plate rather than eat it.

"How's your foot?"

She gave him a thumbs-up. She hadn't been limping on it earlier, so he guessed it was all right.

"I want to check it after dinner."

She gave him an exasperated look, but he ignored her.

"And your hand."

A long sigh came from her this time. His lips twitched, and he had to avert his face so she didn't see. Wouldn't be a good idea to let the brat know she amused him.

After dinner, Elias and Sterling insisted on cleaning up. He turned his chair.

"Foot."

She glared at him.

"Please," he managed to get out.

She picked up the whiteboard. *That wasn't so hard, was it?*

Actually, he thought he might have pulled something. But then she raised her foot so he could look at it. He sucked in a breath as he realized she was walking around on bare feet. How had he missed that?

Because you were too worried she was about to bolt.

"Where are your shoes?" he snapped.

She tried to draw her foot back but he held onto her ankle. "Could have gotten infected."

But the bandage looked like it had been recently changed and when he drew it off, her foot was looking good.

"Looks fine. Hand." He held out his hand for hers.

She wasn't wearing a bandage, but the burn on her hand looked much better. She made a funny sound and he suddenly realized that he was stroking her hand with his thumb.

Holy. Fuck.

Abruptly, he let her go and then stood. His chair went crashing back.

"Everything okay?" Elias asked, rushing out.

Brick strode towards the door to the pool house, needing to get away from her.

"Yeah. Fine. Everything's fine. I've just got some paperwork to do. Good night."

Like a coward, he fled.

8

J uliet was still smarting over his hasty retreat the next morning as she got ready for work.

She sighed. She was being ridiculous. There had been several times yesterday when she'd picked up the phone to call Reuben and tell him that his bodyguards weren't going to work out.

But truth was, they weren't the problem. She was. And it wasn't fair for them to be out of a job because of her issues.

Abandonment issues. Check.

Nightmares. Check.

Anxiety. Check.

Panic attacks. Check.

She was just a bundle of fun. Honestly, it was a wonder anyone wanted to be around her. Even Missy and Angelique. Not that they had much choice.

Here were these gorgeous, normal men. In her house. Interrupting her routine. Messing with her mind. It was no wonder she was mixing up signals.

Just because she was attracted to Brick didn't mean he felt the same.

Standing in front of the mirror, she took in her appearance. A long black skirt. Black, loose shirt. Her brown hair was tied back in a single braid. No make-up. Pale skin. Sharp cheekbones. Shoot, was she losing weight? Reuben would have a fit if he thought she wasn't eating. Darn it.

She'd worry about that later. She had to get to work. Urgh, she hated work. Pretty much everyone who came to the library was a local, which made it easier. But they weren't all nice. And her boss was a total dick.

However, if she didn't have a job to go to, people who relied on her to turn up, she worried she'd never leave the house.

So, she got up four days a week to go to her job, which she didn't particularly like with a boss who sucked because that's what people did. Well, most people. It was something that was normal. And it also made Reuben feel better knowing she was getting out of the house. She would do anything to make Reuben stress less.

Including putting up with Darin the dick.

Nobody liked her boss, and she knew he would love to get rid of her. But he was also scared shitless of her brother.

Sometimes having a scarily powerful, autocratic, insanely overprotective brother came in handy.

Other times, like when he sent three strange men to live with her, not so much.

Picking up her phone, she texted Xavier.

JULIET: *How r U doing?*

Xavier: *Remembering why I don't visit my parents that often. Soon as I got off the plane, they were trying 2 convince me 2 come work at NY-Pres.*

.   .   .

HER STOMACH ROLLED IN PROTEST. He couldn't do that. She'd be devastated if he left. She didn't even want to think about it.

XAVIER: *Mother's appointment this morning, hope 2 be home by Wed. U okay?*

Juliet: *Yep. Hope everything goes ok.*

Xavier: *Me too, Twink.*

Juliet: *Miss U.*

Xavier: *Miss U more.*

MORE THAN HE PROBABLY REALIZED. She felt bad about not telling him the truth, but what was he going to do? He had enough going on without her problems.

Walking into the kitchen, she grabbed an iced coffee from the fridge. Her whiteboard and a marker were sitting on the kitchen counter. She probably needed to carry those around.

Or you could just talk to them. You know, be normal. That's the new quest, right? To be normal.

She drank the coffee slowly. She still felt half-dead.

What she needed was some of her special chocolate. The stuff that had enough caffeine in it to really kickstart her brain. She hid it up high in case Reuben surprised her with a visit. He claimed too much caffeine was bad for her.

Lies. All lies.

Setting down her drink, she climbed up onto the counter. Then she reached for the top cupboard, the one Reuben would never guess she'd use, and opened it.

"What the hell are you doing?"

Turning, she saw Brick striding into the room, a scowl set on his face. But then again, when didn't the man scowl?

"Get down."

She shook her head. She didn't have her chocolate yet. She reached back into the cupboard, searching around with her hand. Where was it?

Two big hands wrapped around her waist and pulled her down to the floor. Juliet glared up at him, hands on her hips.

Brick glared back. "Were you trying to break your neck?"

Yes. Yes, of course, that had been what she'd been doing.

He must have seen some of her sarcasm in her face because his eyes narrowed and he pointed at the counter. "No climbing onto things."

She grabbed her whiteboard.

How else can I reach up there?

"How about you ask me to get it?"

And what about when he wasn't here? Well, she guessed once he left, then his rules were no longer in effect.

There's a bag of chocolate up there. Can you please get it?

She added a sugary sweet smile to her request.

"Why is there chocolate up there?"

She just stared at him. Was he getting it or not? She wasn't in the mood for twenty questions.

Even he had to go onto tiptoes, but he grabbed the bag and she nearly clapped her hands in delight.

He read the front of the bag. "Two pieces of chocolate have the same amount of caffeine as one cup of coffee."

She attempted to snatch the bag from his hand, but he held it above her head.

Oh, he didn't just do that. The jerk.

He pointed at her iced mocha. "You can't have that drink and this chocolate."

Why not?

She held out her hand and tapped her foot.

You're not my doctor.

He scowled then handed over the bag. She grabbed a piece of chocolate and then offered him some.

He shook his head. His loss. This stuff was gold. She ate a piece then washed it down with her mocha.

"That's not your breakfast."

Was that a question or a statement?

He moved over to the fridge and drew out some eggs. "Sit. I'll make you an omelet."

She sighed. *No, thank you.*

He glanced at the whiteboard. "Wasn't a question."

She refrained from stomping her foot. It was hard. She never stomped her foot. She never lost her temper. She always did what others wanted.

Well, mostly.

She wasn't sure how often the sheriff had lectured her on riding her bike in winter. And Noah was always telling her off for coming to the bar in the dark on her own for quiz nights.

She watched him cracking eggs expertly. He could cook?

Somehow, he must have sensed the question. Or maybe he just wanted to fill the silence. That's why she and Kiesha worked well together. Kiesha never shut up, and Juliet barely spoke.

"Sterling is the best cook. I can make breakfast and that's about it." He opened the fridge again, frowning. "Sterling grabbed some groceries for us. Looks like he needs to get you some. There's nothing in here. Guess it's just a cheese omelet."

I don't want the omelet.

"You need something in your stomach other than that." He gave the coffee drink a disparaging stare.

Why?

"Because you're so tiny, a stiff wind would knock you over."

She couldn't actually argue with him since that had happened once. She'd flown into a building and got bruises all up her side.

Reuben had nearly had a cow. He'd bugged Xavier into checking on her every day for two weeks.

But she wasn't going to tell Brick any of that.

Would not.

Yes, she was completely aware her reply was childish. However, she didn't have a clever comeback. She might be smart, but communication obviously wasn't her forte.

He plated up the omelet and took it to the island. He stood there, arms crossed. She stared back then with a sigh, gave in, and climbed onto the stool.

"Eat," he said gruffly.

Knowing she'd feel rude if she didn't try it, she cut off a piece and slid it into her mouth. Then she washed it down with a mouthful of cold, sweet coffee. It wasn't that it tasted bad, Juliet just had a tough time eating in the mornings.

Well, a lot of the time.

He shifted around on his feet, clearing his throat a few times. He seemed nervous, but that couldn't be right.

"Look, I know this is hard," he said, surprising her. "Us invading your space. We'll try to keep out of the way as much as possible."

Shit. Why did that make her feel bad? She bit her lower lip. They seemed like nice enough guys.

It's okay. I know you just have a job to do.

Which was the only reason he was here.

"Your brother wanted one of us in the house, so Elias has moved into the second floor. But you don't need to hide in your room, he'll give you space."

She didn't want him to think she'd been hiding.

I wasn't hiding. I like spending time in my room.

He frowned. "Do you have another kitchen up there? What about getting fresh air? Vitamin D?"

I cracked a window and took a vitamin.

He gave her a skeptical look. She just stared back innocently.

"Eat." He pointed at the omelet. Drat, she thought she'd pulled his attention away from the fact that she wasn't actually eating. With a sigh, she took another small bite.

"Did you read all the instructions and rules I sent back to you? Any questions?"

No.

She had no questions because she hadn't read the rules. Angelique and Missy had been playing up, and she hadn't been in the mood for rules.

"How is your foot? Are you up to work today? Did you rebandage it? What about your hand?"

She gave him a frustrated look. Which question did he want her to answer first? With a huge sigh, she wrote on the whiteboard.

Fine. Yes. Yes. Fine.

He gave her a narrowed look. "Strange world where I'm the verbose one."

She flinched. She didn't think he meant it as a criticism. But it still hurt.

"Why don't you speak? Is it a medical condition?" he asked.

She thought about that then nodded. She guessed it was. Of a sort. Slipping off the stool at the island, she scraped the omelet off into the garbage disposal.

"Juliet, I didn't mean—"

"Right, are we ready to go," Elias' cheerful voice filled the room.

Thank the Lord. Grabbing another coffee, she turned and headed towards him, not looking at Brick.

And he didn't say anything.

Which said it all, really.

❧

He was a total creeper.

There was no other way to describe the fact that he was standing to the side of the window, staring out at where Juliet and Elias were headed towards Elias' truck.

She looked stiff and unsure.

It was a good idea letting Elias take her to work. He just kept putting his foot in his mouth and making things between them worse.

Yes. This was the best idea.

So why was he standing here like a creeper, watching her? Why had he spent most of the weekend worrying about her? Fuck. He had to concentrate on the job. Sterling was sleeping after being up on shift all night. He needed to get some shit done.

Not worry over their client.

Who was currently refusing to get in Elias' truck. For someone who couldn't communicate verbally, she sure did make what she wanted known. Even without her whiteboard. Which she hadn't taken with her. How did she get on in day-to-day life? Did she use sign language? Maybe he should learn some.

Urgh. Creeper.

He watched as she shook her head again and walked around Elias towards the garage. What the hell was she doing?

When she came out pushing a bike, he tensed.

Oh, hell no.

Not happening.

He had clearly stated in the rules he'd sent her that she wasn't going to be able to use her bike for transportation and would be driven everywhere by them, in one of their vehicles.

Hadn't she read the rules?

She shook her head while Elias spoke.

God damn it. She hadn't read the rules. And when he'd asked her just before if she had, she had blatantly lied to him.

Wait . . . she didn't though, did she? She simply didn't answer him.

Oh, the sneaky brat.

His temper sparked. If she wasn't prepared to follow the rules, then she wouldn't be going anywhere.

He stormed out of the house, heading their way. Elias saw him coming and shook his head. He ignored him, though, glaring down at the bratty girl. Who was again wearing black. Did she wear black all the time? It looked terrible on her.

"You didn't read the rules."

She gave him a wary look that he hated. He didn't want her scared of him. He stopped a few feet away so he wasn't looming over her. Much as he wanted to. He also wanted to put his foot up on the truck's tailgate, then draw her over his thigh and spank her ass.

He was damn proud of his self-restraint.

Instead of shaking her or pulling her over his knee, he put on a professional air.

"In the rules, it clearly states that you can no longer ride your bike until the danger has passed. If you need to go somewhere, one of us will drive you in one of our vehicles. Now, go put the bike away and get in the car."

There. That was said calmly. Behind him, he thought he heard Elias mutter the word idiot, but he had to have misheard that.

If he'd expected her to immediately do what she was told, well, turns out he was mistaken. This girl was full of surprises. She scowled up at him instead.

Then she shook her head.

"Yes."

Another shake. She pointed at the bike then went to climb onto it. His temper fired.

"No," he shot out at her, placing his hand on the handlebars.

Elias sighed.

Brick glared at him. What was his problem?

"If you want to leave, you're going in the truck. I'm sorry, but we can't keep you safe on your bike."

He'd thought her brother said she was shy and quiet and would give them no trouble.

Huh, seemed he didn't know his sister well at all. She was causing him no end of trouble. But instead of giving him attitude, her face grew blank. There was an air of sadness around her that he didn't understand. Disappointment filled her face, and he suddenly felt like a complete ass. He couldn't back down, it was safer for her to ride in the truck. But for some reason, he really wanted to.

He opened his mouth to say something else, something that might wipe away that blank look when she tugged the bike from his hold. Surprised, he let go. She wheeled it back into the garage then walked out, her gaze on her feet. Opening the door to the truck, she climbed in.

The urge to apologize, to soothe her, was riding him hard, but he pushed it down. She was the client. This was to keep her safe.

That was what was important. Right?

9

J uliet pushed the cart of books down the aisle, shelving the last few.

She'd been at work for hours and she was still obsessing over what happened earlier. Not being able to ride her bike wherever she needed to go felt like losing a limb. She knew people thought she was crazy for riding everywhere. But she loved riding her bike. It was one of the few times that she felt normal. Carefree.

And that had been taken away from her. As well as her privacy. Her ability to make her own decisions. Everything was getting on top of her, and it had been less than seventy-two hours since they arrived.

Please let Reuben get this sorted quickly.

Because she didn't know how much she could handle.

"Hey, it's lunchtime. You usually go out for lunch or something?" Elias asked with a hopeful smile.

She shook her head. Her lunch was the protein bar in her handbag. But she guessed that going halves on a protein bar wasn't going to fill the big guy up. He looked like he ate a lot of food.

Grabbing her phone from her pocket, she typed a message.

I have lunch with me. There's a diner down the next block if you want to go get something.

Elias huffed out a breath, grimacing briefly. "Not the way it works, doll. If you're here, so am I. My fault for not asking you about the food situation before we left."

No. Her fault for not telling him.

Let me get my bag and go to the bathroom, then we'll go.

Elias shot her a relieved grin. "If you insist."

She just shook her head at him and they walked into the break room. She grabbed her bag from her locker.

"Juliet, have you finished shelving those books yet?"

She glanced up with a sigh as Gladys walked in. Gladys was four years older than her and loved to pretend she was in charge. Juliet mostly ignored her. Like right now, when she didn't bother to look around as she searched through her bag to make sure she'd brought her wallet with her. Now that they were going to the diner, she was in the mood for a chocolate milkshake.

"I know you can hear me, you're not deaf. Just fucking rude."

"Hey!" Elias said in a sharp voice she'd never heard from him.

Juliet glanced over at him in surprise.

"Who are you?" Gladys asked. "What are you doing back here? Juliet, you're not supposed to bring customers back here."

"I'm not a customer," Elias said. "I'm Juliet's bodyguard. And I'm going to have to ask you to step away from Juliet."

"Or what?"

"Or I'll be forced to step in."

"I'll be telling Darin about this. You can't bring a bodyguard to work just because you're paranoid, Juliet. No one is after you. God, nobody even notices that you're here most of the time. You just blend into the background."

Juliet spun and Gladys took a step back with a gasp. She knew it wasn't nice to smile at the other woman's fear. But then, she didn't always claim to be nice. As she stepped forward, Gladys was forced to move back.

Elias moved with her, frowning at Gladys.

To her surprise, as she walked out of the library, she realized she'd worked up an appetite.

JULIET HUGGED Missy and lay on her bed, sucking her pacifier.

She'd changed into her Halloween onesie, since that was her favorite holiday. It had pictures of pumpkins with carved faces on them. She'd put on her ruffly panties. And she was rubbing her blankie under her nose as she sucked on the pacifier. She'd chosen Missy to cuddle since Angelique was in time-out.

Angelique could be such a bitch.

Sometimes she thought she'd be happier if she could permanently be in Little space. Of course, she'd still have to do things like order her food and clean and other adult stuff. She wasn't really good at remembering to do things like bathe or eat or drink water when she was in Little headspace either.

Gladys had been a bitch today. After getting back from lunch, Juliet hadn't been feeling great. She'd ended up giving her burger to Roger, the homeless guy in the park.

Once they'd gotten back to the library, she found that Gladys had left her a list of jobs that she knew Juliet would hate. Once, she'd tried to get close to her, but Elias had stepped between them.

Why had she let Gladys get to her?

She sucked harder on her pacifier.

Her phone buzzed with a text. Reuben checking in on her. Then another came through from Kiesha. Then Isa.

Okay, so she needed to remember that she had friends. She

wasn't on her own anymore. Gladys might be a bitch, but she couldn't truly hurt her.

She replied to everyone then brought up Xavier's contact. She shouldn't bother him. He was busy. But, she was upset and she wanted to hear his voice. Besides, if she told Reuben or Brick what a cow Gladys was being, they'd likely go all psycho on her. Xavier was more level-headed.

JULIET: *U have time 2 talk?*

Xavier: *Let me go somewhere private.*

HER PHONE soon buzzed with a video call. She hastily tugged out her pacifier, putting it down before answering.

Then he was there, smiling down the phone at her. His eyes narrowed in concern.

"What's wrong?"

"Nothing," she said cheerfully. "I hope I didn't interrupt anything."

"You can interrupt me anytime."

That was so sweet. She smiled at him.

"But you weren't interrupting anything. Just my mother lecturing me about my job, my life choices. All of that crap."

"Oh, Xavy, I'm so sorry. How did today go?"

"I took Mother to her appointment today. Now, we just have to wait on the biopsy result."

The poor guy looked exhausted. And he was asking her if she was okay?

"Is there anything I can do?" she asked.

"Distract me. Tell me about your day."

Hm. What could she tell him that would cheer him up?

"Roger's got a new sweatshirt. Kiesha got it for him."

"Oh Lord, what does it have on it?" he asked.

"Well, it's black then in neon written along the front it says: *Sarcasm and orgasm. Two things most people don't get.*"

Xavier huffed out a laugh. And she grinned, pleased she'd amused him.

"Kiesha is trouble."

"She's so much fun, though. I wish I was brave and funny like she is."

"You're perfect just the way you are," Xavier told her firmly.

She didn't reply. Because that just wasn't true.

"Juliet," he said in a low voice. "I want you to repeat this after me. I am perfect the way I am."

"Xavy," she sighed.

"Uh-uh. Don't Xavy me. Repeat it."

"I am perfect the way I am."

"With more conviction."

"I am perfect the way I am."

"Good girl, now what's going on? You look upset."

She bit her lip.

"Twink," he warned. "Stop chewing on your lip. Tell me."

"Just tired of my job, I guess. And Gladys. The bitch."

"Language," Xavier scolded. "What did she do?"

"Nothing much."

"Twink. Tell me."

"Just her usual stuff. Talking down to me. Leaving me all the jobs I hate. Being a regular old meanie-pants."

Whoops. She hadn't meant to say it like that.

Xavier frowned. "Have you told Darin?"

She snorted. "What use would that be? Her nose is brown from sucking up to him."

"Juliet!" He tried to sound horrified, but she saw his lips twitching.

"I should put salt in her coffee," she told him.

"Or glue on her chair," Xavier added.

"Ooh, good one, Xavy." Just talking to him was making her feel so much better.

Then Xavier scowled. "I'm not happy about the way she treats you. And Darin should do something about her. Soon as we hang up, I'm calling the weasel."

He was *such* a weasel. But she shook her head. "You can't."

"I can," he countered.

Okay, she hadn't expected this.

"It will make it worse. Trust me."

"I don't like it," he stated. "Quit that job. It's not making you happy and I hate when you're not happy."

So sweet.

"I hate when you're not happy too. I wish you were here."

"Me too, Twink. You look a bit pale. Is there anything else going on? Are you sleeping? Eating? Taking your medication? Bowel movements okay?"

"Xavier!" she cried. "You can't ask me that."

"What? If you're sleeping?" He gave her an innocent look.

"No, about . . . urgh, stop teasing me," she told him as he grinned. "You're so mean."

"What? Being regular is important."

"Xavier!"

He chuckled. "You going to put salt in my coffee, Twink?"

"Maybe," she threatened.

"Seriously, are you sure you're all right? I can come home if you need me."

He really was an amazing friend. She was lucky to have him, even if he could never feel the same way about her that she did about him.

"I'm fine, Xavy. Don't worry about me."

"I'll always worry about you. You're my best girl. Now, have you eaten dinner?"

"Not yet. I'm hungry."

"You need to eat. Be a good girl and I'll bring you back a present."

Ooh. "A present? What is it? I love presents!"

"You best behave yourself then, huh?" he replied.

"Eh, you'll bring me one anyway."

"Brat," he said affectionately. "I want you to eat dinner, maybe watch some TV but no zombies! Then get a good night's sleep. Okay? Doctor's orders."

Hm. What happened if she didn't obey? But she wasn't brave enough to ask that.

"All right, I'll do that. Miss you, Xavy."

"Miss you more."

"WHAT DO you mean there's some bitch at her work being mean to her?"

Brick glared at Elias as they stood outside the pool house. He was supposed to keep her safe.

Elias sent him an impatient look. "Just what I said. Bitter. Mean. I think she bullies Juliet."

He'd kill the bitch.

"Maybe she needs to stop working." It wasn't like she needed to. Her brother was rich.

Elias ran his hand over his face. "Maybe she likes it. I need to go make lunch for tomorrow. For both of us. Juliet doesn't eat enough to keep a mouse going."

"She didn't eat?" he asked sharply. "Why didn't you make her?"

"Because she's a client, not a child or your sub. You can't force her to do things."

Be much easier if he could.

"If you're so pissed off with my decisions, then maybe

tomorrow you should take her to work." Elias turned and stormed off.

Fuck. He was messing this up with everyone.

10

She shot a look at Brick as he walked her over to his truck. It was even higher than the one that Elias had taken her to work in yesterday.

This morning, she hadn't come down until five minutes before they were due to leave so she didn't run the risk of him trying to make her breakfast. He'd been waiting in the foyer, pacing back and forth.

The scowl he'd sent her almost had her freezing on the stairs. But then she'd forced herself to keep moving.

He'd simply grumbled something about women who took too long to get ready. She'd let that roll off her back. She didn't care what he thought.

They reached his truck and he opened the door. She shot him a look.

"What? You don't think I have manners?"

God, he was surly. Who peed in his Wheaties this morning? She grinned, wishing she had the courage to ask him.

"It's amusing to keep me waiting? There's a thing called common courtesy."

She froze. Had she been rude, not coming down until the last moment?

"Get in," he grumbled. "We're already late."

It was her job. Why was he so worried about being late? He wouldn't get fired.

She glared at him. He was such a jerk, and she didn't feel like getting in the truck with him in this mood. He let out a long sigh, filled with irritation.

"Come on. I hate being late. Although I guess when you're rich, you don't worry about losing your job."

Far as she could tell, he hated everything. Grabbing out the small whiteboard in her purse, she wrote a message.

Where's Elias? Why isn't he taking me to work?

He glared at her. "Why don't you just tell me what you want to say?"

She sucked in a breath. He knew. Was that why he was so surly this morning?

"Talked to your brother last night about your *medical condition*. You lied."

Her heart raced, making her feel ill.

"You can talk. You just don't want to."

That wasn't true. But she couldn't explain how she struggled to talk to anyone beyond her closest circle. "Get in."

Don't react. Don't show him how his words hurt.

If only he knew the truth.

She wrote another message. *You're a jerk.*

The muscle in his jaw was ticking. It was clear he was angry. Yeah, she'd lied to him.

But she'd had her reasons. He just thought she was some sort of rich bitch.

Fine. Maybe she wouldn't prove him wrong. Maybe she'd just be that rich bitch until he gave up and left.

You can't do that. Think of Reuben.

Crap.

But she really, really wanted to.

"No Elias. You're stuck with me. Problem, Duchess?" he asked.

She shot him a look then attempted to climb into his truck. But her long skirt got tangled in her feet and she went flying backward, falling into him. Thankfully, he had better balance than she did. He caught her, steadying them both.

A shiver of desire ran up her spine. What was wrong with her? She shouldn't be attracted to this grumpy jerk. Even though he'd been grouchy since she'd first met him, he hadn't been mean. Not until he'd found out she'd lied to him.

Tell him the truth then.

Yeah. Right. She never talked about what had happened.

"If you wanted to touch me, all you had to do was ask."

She jabbed her elbow back into his gut. It didn't do much. The guy was muscle everywhere. Damn, though, it felt good.

Until he grasped her around the waist and set her down, unceremoniously, on the passenger seat of the truck. Hard.

Ouch.

"Kid gloves are off now, Duchess," he told her in a cold voice as they drove out of the driveway. "Maybe your brother panders to your quirks because he thinks they're cute or whatever. But not me. You need to grow up. This shit is serious."

He thought she didn't know that? Seriously?

Raising her fist slowly, she pushed up her middle finger. *Take that, asshole.*

He turned his head, his mouth dropping open. "Are you serious right now? What—fuck!" He'd spun his gaze back to the road, just as a dark-haired woman wearing a bright orange jumpsuit roller-skated across the road.

Brick slammed on the brakes, swearing. His arm moved across her chest so she barely even moved despite the way the truck came to a sudden stop. She wanted to point out that she was wearing a seatbelt, but she was too busy trying to catch her breath after they'd nearly hit . . .

Kiesha!

A fear-filled noise escaped her mouth as she scrambled for the seatbelt.

"Juliet! Juliet!"

Gradually she became aware of Brick yelling. Finally, he grabbed her chin, turning her face towards his. "Are you all right?"

She nodded frantically. Of course, she was all right. She was in a truck with a safety belt around her. Kiesha had just skated past with nothing more to protect her than a helmet. She had to get out and check on her.

"Good. Stay here. I've got to check on that fool who raced out in front of us." Brick climbed out of the truck.

Stay there? Yeah, there was no way that was happening.

BRICK CLIMBED QUICKLY from the truck, looking around him carefully. If this was some sort of trap, he didn't want to fall for it. Best thing to do was lock Juliet in the truck and call Sterling. He turned, just in time to spot Juliet jumping from the truck and running towards the woman lying on the side of the road. He hadn't hit her, so he was guessing she'd just fallen. But the noises she was making indicated that she could be badly injured.

Still, she wasn't his priority.

The brat falling to her knees beside her was.

"Juliet!" he roared. "Get back in the truck. Now."

Juliet ignored him, helping the woman sit up. Her helmet, which had googly eyes at the top, was off to one side. She was wearing a bright orange outfit and skates that lit up when she moved.

"Hey! Don't you yell at Juliet."

Wait. Juliet knew this woman?

"Juliet, you know her?"

Juliet nodded. She patted down her friend frantically.

"Hey, Juliet, I'm fine," the woman said soothingly. "I'm fine. I've just got some bruises and skinned knees. I'm going to be all right. This idiot didn't hit me."

"I'm the idiot? You raced out onto the road in front of me." She was just lucky that he had good reflexes, or he might have hit her. "What the hell did you think you were doing?"

Juliet leaned into the other woman who put her arms around her, as though Juliet was the one who'd been hurt.

Or as though Juliet needed protection. From him.

His temper, which hadn't been doing very well, went up another level.

"I'm calling the cops and an ambulance," he stated.

"Fine. You do that!" the woman said with a sneer. "And you can explain to Ed why you nearly hit me."

"You skated out in front of me," he said with exasperation.

"Who the hell are you anyway?" she asked after he'd spoken to the dispatcher. She eyed him suspiciously then turned to Juliet. "Why were you in a vehicle with this asshole? Is he an Uber driver or something? Where'd he come from? Assholeland?"

What the fuck?

"Listen here, lady. You're the one in the wrong here, not me. Juliet, get back in the truck. I'll keep an eye on . . ."

"Kiesha," the other woman said reluctantly. "And Juliet isn't going anywhere with you. You're obviously unhinged. Trying to hit helpless women just skating along the road, minding their own business."

"You skated in front of me!" he yelled, making Juliet jump.

Kiesha actually pushed Juliet partially behind her. Was she seriously trying to protect Juliet? From him?

He stepped forward just as Juliet put her lips close to Kiesha's ear.

"What? Bodyguard?" Kiesha asked. "Are you serious?"

Juliet was speaking to her. Whispering something to her. She really could speak. There had been a part of him that hadn't quite believed it when her brother told him that there was no medical reason for her muteness.

Who the hell would choose not to speak? He didn't get it. But that didn't matter. Or at least that wasn't why he was angry. Sure, it was kind of odd and sometimes confusing as fuck not to be able to communicate with her easily. But it wasn't a big deal.

What pissed him off was the fact that she'd lied to him. When he'd asked her if she couldn't talk due to a medical reason, she'd nodded.

He couldn't stand liars.

His ex had been a liar. She'd lied about everything.

That was something he couldn't forgive.

Best he knew this about Juliet now, though. He was feeling more protective and invested in her than he should.

"So, you do speak," he said coldly.

Juliet stared up at him. But there was no remorse or anger. She just looked infinitely sad. A siren sounded in the distance as the woman wearing the skates sat up straighter, glaring at him.

"Hey, asshole. Don't you judge her. You don't know anything about her."

He studied the woman. "How badly injured are you?"

"None of your business." She turned to look at Juliet. "Why the hell have you got a bodyguard? This is because of Reuben, right? What did that asshat do now? Piss off the wrong people with his charming personality?"

Juliet leaned in again.

"Do not," he said sharply.

Juliet jolted as though he'd hit her. Fuck, he hadn't meant to scare her. He took a step forward, ready to apologize, but the other woman growled up at him.

Like, actually growled. As though she was a dog protecting her owner.

"Stay back, asshat," the woman said.

He glared down at her. "I'm not going to hurt her."

"Newsflash, you already did. I'd give you a one out of ten for job performance. You're in the negatives for personality."

The sheriff's vehicle pulled up and an ambulance soon parked behind it. A big man climbed out of the vehicle and scowled as he looked from him then over to the two girls.

"What the fuck happened here? Kiesha? Juliet? Are you all right? Who are you?" He turned to Brick, who'd stepped closer to Juliet. "Gonna ask you nicely to step away from the two women and over towards your truck. Keep your hands where I can see them."

Brick didn't move, but held his hands out to his side. "I'm not hurting them. I'm Brick Sampson. I'm Juliet's bodyguard. We were driving to her work when this woman roller-skated out in front of my truck. I slammed on the brakes. I didn't hit her but she looks to have fallen over."

"That what happened, Kiesha?"

Great, so the sheriff and Kiesha obviously knew each other well. And the sheriff seemed like he would take the dirty-mouthed woman's word over his. He guessed that was to be expected.

A car drifted slowly past them and the sheriff waved them on. There wasn't much traffic out this way.

"He appeared out of nowhere!" Kiesha said in her defense. "I was in a rush because I was running late, and he just turned the corner all of a sudden."

"All of a sudden?" Brick thundered. "It's a damn road. Of course, I was driving along it. And I wasn't even going that fast. You jumped out in front of me, lady. You're lucky we didn't crash. If Juliet had been hurt . . ."

"Juliet, you hurt?" the sheriff asked.

Juliet was pale and wide-eyed as she shook her head. The medic was with Kiesha by now, checking her over and taking off her skates.

"I'm fine, Ryan," the crazy lunatic said. "Just a bit bruised with some skinned knees."

"Take her to the hospital, Ryan," the sheriff barked. "I want her checked over."

"I didn't get hit, Ed. It's no different than any other time I've fallen over. Juliet, can you get my shoes out of my backpack?"

Juliet jumped to grab them. Brick's eyebrows rose as he saw her pull out two completely different shoes. She held them up and Kiesha nodded.

"I know they're different shoes. It's a new trend I'm starting, it's going to be big."

Why would that be big? But everyone just nodded at the strange woman's declaration.

Juliet hadn't been hurt, but she looked to be having a hard time processing everything. The need to take her into his arms and comfort her was almost overwhelming.

The medic put his arm around Kiesha's waist, leading her over to the back of his rig. The sheriff turned to him. "Going to need to see some identification and registration. Juliet, honey, come here."

Honey? Was he kidding him? Anger and jealousy raged inside him. Especially as Juliet walked over to the sheriff.

"You grab hold of my shirt if you need to, honey," the sheriff said in a soft voice. He was far gentler with her than he had been with the other woman, who was complaining loudly about the way the medic was bandaging her up.

Brick's jaw became so tight as she wrapped her hand up in the sheriff's shirt that he thought he might crack a tooth. He could definitely feel a headache pounding in his temples.

"Juliet, why don't we sit you down in my truck," the sheriff said in that easy voice of his, but his gaze was wary as he stared at Brick. "You're looking a bit pale."

Brick shook his head, his hands curling into fists to hold himself back from grabbing her and slinging her over his shoulder. "Can't let her do that. Juliet, come here."

The sheriff raised his eyebrows. "You're going to have to come back to the station to make a statement. Juliet can ride with me."

Brick narrowed his gaze as the sheriff dictated to him. "I'm her bodyguard. She's not leaving my sight." There was going to be trouble if the sheriff forced him to leave her.

"And why would Juliet need a bodyguard?" the sheriff drawled.

"Ow! Shit! Fuck! What is that stuff? Liquid fire?" the roller-skating devil woman yelled.

Juliet jumped and looked behind her, stepping away from the sheriff, although she kept her hand twisted in his shirt.

Jealousy bubbled in his gut. It was a hard pill to swallow. He didn't want to feel this way about her.

Liar. She's a liar.

"That's none of your business, sheriff."

"If one of my citizens is in trouble, then I need to know."

Juliet tugged on the sheriff's arm and he leaned down so she could speak quietly into his ear. Great, so she'd talk to him too? What the fuck?

The sheriff studied him as Juliet spoke then he nodded and patted her hand gently. So, he got to touch her too? Without her even flinching?

"All right. Juliet said that it happened like you said. Still need that license and registration and a quick statement. Kiesha, you'll be going home for the day."

"I'm going to work," Kiesha argued back.

"You're not."

"You need me."

Good God, don't tell him this woman was a deputy?

"We'll be fine without you for the day."

"No, you won't. I'm indispensable," Kiesha replied.

The sheriff started muttering something under his breath as Brick reached into his truck for his license and registration. When he walked over to hand them to the sheriff, he caught Juliet's worried gaze. She looked close to tears.

"Right, I'll run these, then we'll head to the station," Ed said. "Ryan, can you take Kiesha home?"

"Yep," the medic replied. Obviously, they all knew each other well.

"I'm taking Juliet home. She's pale and needs to rest," Brick said stiffly. "You can take our statements there."

"If Juliet's going home, I'm going with her," Kiesha stated.

Juliet shook her head. He wasn't sure what part she disagreed with. But he hoped it was with the roller-skating devil coming home with them.

Ed leaned down as she spoke to him again. Brick's ire rose until he was certain his blood pressure couldn't get much higher.

"Juliet wants to go to work. You sure, honey? I can call Darin and tell him what happened."

Juliet nodded her head.

"You're not going to work," Brick stated.

Ed's eyebrows rose and he could feel the attention of the other two people on him.

"Who are you to boss her around?" Kiesha stated. "She can do what she likes."

"I'm her bodyguard. I have the final say on what is safe." Brick turned to look down at Juliet. "You're pale and shaky. You need to go home and rest."

He expected immediate acquiesce from her. Especially when the sheriff nodded and glanced down at her. "He's right. You don't look so good. Maybe Ryan could check you over."

"I'll touch you as little as possible," Ryan told her gently.

Did they all pander to her quirks? Juliet shook her head at the medic, leaning into Ed slightly.

"Want us to call Xavier?" Ed asked. "He could meet you at your place."

Xavier. The guy who was written as a point of contact in their instructions from Juliet's brother. Brick's curiosity piqued at the mention of his name. He fully expected Juliet to agree.

But she shook her head again.

"You don't want Xavier to check on you?" Kiesha asked, walking over to them. Well, she was limping, but he wasn't sure if that was because she'd hurt her foot or the two different shoes on her feet.

Maybe Sterling was right. There was something odd about this town.

"Why? Did something happen? Was he a jerk? Want me to slash his tires? Because I have a knife that will do it." Kiesha's voice was fierce and his eyes widened. Was she for real or joking?

The sheriff rolled his eyes up towards the sky. "Lord, help me. Why me? Why?"

"Oh, stop being so dramatic," Kiesha told him. "You know you love me."

So, they were a couple? That explained some things. Although if his woman had been lying on the ground injured, then nothing would have stopped him from going to her as soon as he came on the scene.

Of course, that wouldn't be his woman, lying there injured, as he would never allow her to roller-skate along the road like that. If she needed to go anywhere, she'd go in the safest vehicle he could get for her. Preferably with him driving since he was a bit of a control freak.

"Like a sister," the sheriff said dryly. "You cannot go around slashing people's tires."

"Can if they're assholes." She looked over at Brick's tires. "Nice looking tires you have there, bodyguard boy. They look new."

Brick glared at the crazy woman. The sheriff suddenly stepped between them. He shot Brick a look.

"Do not look at her like that."

"If my tires are slashed, I'll know who is to blame," Brick warned. "And if you won't arrest her, then I'll go over your head."

To his surprise, Juliet slid out from behind the sheriff to glare at Brick. She pushed her finger against his chest. Then she pointed at the truck and stomped her foot.

Kiesha burst into giggles. "Ooh, someone got told off. And by someone half your size. You go, Juliet. Never seen you tell someone off before. Must mean you're making her real angry, bodyguard."

He glared over at the crazy woman.

"Juliet, we're going. Get in the truck. Sheriff, you want a statement, come to the house."

Instead of moving towards the truck. Juliet folded her arms over her chest and shook her head.

"Whoa, girl, I've never seen you like this before. I like it. You've got sass. Ed, did you know Juliet had sass?"

Ed just shook his head, staring down at Juliet thoughtfully then over to him.

"Juliet, do you not want to go home with him?"

Great. The last thing he needed was the sheriff trying to run interference.

"She's coming home with me. Her brother hired me to protect her."

Ed and Kiesha both flinched. What was that about?

"Ed, I've got to go."

Ed waved Ryan away. "I'll get Kiesha home. Reuben hired you?" The sheriff looked worried. "Juliet, are you all right? Are you in danger?"

Now he was taking him seriously?

Juliet shook her head then patted the sheriff's arm with a smile.

"I'm coming to stay with you," Kiesha told her abruptly. "Is this dude staying at your house? Why didn't you tell me? I would have come over right away."

Juliet turned to the woman and said something to her quietly that had the other woman looking even more worried. "There's two more of him? How have you not murdered them all?"

What the hell?

"Juliet, we're going. Now." He knew he sounded like an asshole. Both the sheriff and Kiesha scowled at him.

But the only one he stared at was Juliet. She shook her head at him again.

Disobedient brat. She knew the rules.

"Yes."

Another shake of her head.

"Yes."

Brat was testing his patience.

"Do you think his head is going to explode?" Kiesha mock-whispered to the sheriff.

"Think it just might. Don't think he's used to hearing the word no." Amusement filled the sheriff's voice.

"Juliet," he warned.

This type of disobedience couldn't be allowed. If he gave an order, he expected it to be obeyed.

Their audience watched on with rapt attention as Juliet took a step back from him and shook her head once more.

"Wow, I've never seen Juliet defy anyone. You must be someone real special," Kiesha told him, eyeing him. "Or just a class-A asshole. But Reuben is an asshole and she loves him."

Juliet shot her friend a look.

Kiesha raised her hands into the air. "Sorry. It's true, though.

I've known the guy for years. He's an asshole to everyone except you."

Juliet's gaze narrowed. She obviously wasn't happy with the other woman talking about her brother like that. He was just happy to have her ire away from him.

"He offered to help with Georgie after she came out of the hospital," the sheriff said.

"That's right," Kiesha said. "That was weird."

Who was Georgie? Actually, it didn't matter. He didn't care. He was done.

Just then, a red truck drove slowly past them. The windows were tinted so he couldn't see inside it. But something about it made Kiesha mad as hell. She held up her fist, shaking it at the truck.

"What do you think you're staring at?" she yelled as the sheriff tried to soothe her. She started moving after the truck. "You come back here, Jonny Jacks!"

The truck continued to move away.

"One of these days, I'll get my revenge. See how easy it will be to drive around on slashed tires."

"Lord. Help me now. Juliet, where do you want to make your statement?" the sheriff asked.

Juliet leaned up to whisper to the sheriff and Brick swore his vision went red.

"Good," the sheriff said to her. Then he looked at Brick. "She said you'll both come to the station later. Don't make me come looking for you." The sheriff turned the dark-skinned woman towards his truck. "Come on, Kiesha. I'll take you home."

"But I want to go with Juliet and watch her make the big guy sweat some more. I'm pretty sure that vein in his head is about to pop. I don't want to miss the popping vein," Kiesha whined.

"None of us do," the sheriff added. He got her into his truck then turned to Brick and Juliet. "Juliet, you sure you're okay with him?"

Juliet nodded, to his relief.

"You know where I am if you need me." The sheriff sent Brick a warning look. What was he warning him about? He was being paid to take care of her. He wasn't going to harm her.

"Juliet, we're going home," he said in a low voice.

And that, as far as he was concerned, was that.

11

B rick pulled up into the parking spot behind the library.
How the fuck had this happened? He'd fully intended to take her home. But then she'd pulled out the big guns.

When he'd told her they were heading back to her place and there was going to be no arguments, she'd pulled out her phone and brought up her brother's contact, turning the screen around so he could see it.

Brat.

Rich, spoiled brat.

But she'd gotten her way. However, he wasn't happy about it.

He turned to her as she undid her seatbelt. "We'll be having a talk about this when we get home."

She rolled her eyes at him. He regretted the words as soon as they were out of his mouth. Even he could hear how ridiculous he sounded.

"Don't even think about it," he warned as she moved her hand to the door handle of the truck. She looked tiny sitting in the huge bucket seat. "You need a booster."

She eyed him warily. As though he was losing it.

Maybe he was.

Maybe he was having some sort of episode or he was in the middle of a nightmare.

"Only a nightmare would explain this," he muttered.

A flash of pain entered her eyes, and he could have kicked himself. He went to apologize but she held up a finger, pointed at him then at the door imperiously.

"Sure thing, Duchess," he snarled. "I'll get right onto it."

He got out of the truck, slamming the door. Then he paused to take a deep breath.

You're being ridiculous.

You're the one who insisted she wait until you opened the door. Now you're mad at her for wanting you to open the door.

Yes, but it was the way she'd done it that had pissed him off. Or at least that's what he told himself. Because when she got all sassy and bossy, well, part of him thought it was cute as fuck.

Screwed. He was so screwed.

SHE DIDN'T KNOW what had put his panties in a twist this morning, but Mr. Grumpy-Butt had turned into Mr. Unreasonable-Grouchy-Surly-Butt-Pants.

A sigh escaped her as she stared down at the ass encased in those pants.

Damn, it was fine.

Focus, Juliet.

She was over an hour late to work. Her friend nearly got run over by her bodyguard. Although that was more Kiesha's fault than theirs. Still, it had shaken her when she'd seen Kiesha on the ground. She couldn't stand for anything else to happen to someone she loved.

Just the thought of it . . .

"Juliet? You okay?" Brick asked in his gruff voice.

What? Like he cared. He'd been like a bear with a sore paw all morning. And worse than usual. Usually, his blunt manner was tempered by an awkward sort of caring. But there was a coldness in his eyes that hadn't been there before.

Because he thinks you're a liar.

Well. She kind of was, she guessed. She'd agreed with him when he'd asked if she had a medical reason for not talking when there wasn't exactly one . . . it was more that she was fucked up.

But she couldn't tell him that. Because it was humiliating. Because it meant telling him about the past. Because she knew he'd turn away from her.

So instead of trying to communicate the whole fucked up mess inside her head, she shrugged.

His shoulders tightened and he turned away, his jaw tense. He didn't want to know. He was just here to do a job.

"Juliet?"

The irritated voice of her boss broke through her morose thoughts. She jumped with a gasp and felt Brick stiffen beside her.

"Who the hell is this?" Darin demanded, coming into the break room where she'd been stashing her handbag into her locker. She slipped her phone into her pocket. Technically, they weren't supposed to have their phones on them. But everyone did.

"I'm her bodyguard, Brick. And watch your language when you're talking to Juliet."

Darin's cheeks went a blotchy red at Brick's firm reprimand. She sighed. No doubt he thought he was helping. But he wasn't the one who had to work with Darin once she no longer had bodyguards. He could be a vindictive little creepazoid.

"I thought that other guy was her bodyguard."

"He is. She has more than one."

Darin's eyes narrowed to slits. He already looked like a weasel.

Now, he looked like a weasel sucking on a lemon. "Juliet, I'd like to see you in my office. Alone."

"Not happening," Brick said.

"Brick, was it?" Darin sneered. Today he was dressed in a waistcoat which just seemed to emphasize his pot belly. And the small amount of hair he had was slicked over his bald spot in an awful-looking combover. Whatever he used made the top of his head all greasy, so whenever he was under a fluorescent light, he almost glowed. "This is a private conversation. As Juliet's employer, I'm going to have to insist on speaking to her on her own."

Brick crossed his arms over his chest.

With a sigh, she grabbed her phone out.

There's a window. You can see in. He's a dick, but he won't hurt me.

"What did she say?" Darin demanded.

"If she wanted you to know, she'd tell you," Brick replied.

She wasn't sure if that was more of a jibe at her or at Darin. Although the way he glared at her boss, she was guessing it was aimed mostly at Darin. Still, she felt a mix of sadness and defeat mingling inside her. Maybe she should have gone home. Called in sick or something. She certainly felt nauseous. Rubbing her stomach, she followed Darin the dick, into his office.

Brick stood outside but kept an eye through the window.

"Charming, isn't he?" Darin sneered.

Feeling brave with a door between him and Brick, was he? She had to hide her grin. She was confident that Brick could take Darin with one hand tied behind his back. And Darin knew that too.

"Where is the other bodyguard? I didn't give approval for all these bodyguards coming in and out of the library, Juliet. Just how many do you need, anyway? What kind of trouble are you in?"

She just stared at him, waiting for him to get to the point.

"Because if it's something that could endanger my patrons, I'm going to have to ask you to take a leave of absence. I'm responsible for the safety of all the patrons and staff who work here. So, I'm sure you understand."

That sick feeling in her stomach grew.

It wasn't that she loved this job. She didn't. Gladys and Darin did their best to make it a crappy place to work. And while she mostly did shelving and research, there was still interaction with the public, which stressed her out.

But if she lost this job, she knew she wouldn't find another. Not without Reuben's help, and she wanted to rely on Reuben as little as possible. For both of their sakes.

Losing this job would unsettle her routine even more than it had been. She couldn't handle that.

Can't you?

Hadn't she been handling all the disruptions like a pro? But this was a temporary thing. On a day-to-day basis, she needed more stability or things started to unravel. She just didn't know what to do.

Usually, Darin wouldn't be brave enough to risk Reuben's wrath and do something like this. But this time, he actually had a good point. If she was truly in danger, then being here could endanger someone else. That obviously made him feel safer.

"Now, you were also late today, which normally I'd have to give you an official warning about. But if you're reasonable about staying away while there is some threat," the asshole made quote marks with his fingers as he said the word threat as though she was making it up, "then we'll call this the first day of indefinite leave, and there's no need to put anything official on your record."

Awesome. So now he was blackmailing her as well.

With a nod, she stood and walked numbly to the door.

"I knew you could be reasonable, Juliet. I hope you'll explain this to your brother." He blanched. "Please, when this is all over, let me know if you want your job back. But I'm sure you understand that we might have to hire someone else in the meantime."

Asshole. He was practically radiating with smugness. What she wouldn't give to pick up that cup of coffee and throw it right in his face.

But she didn't. Because she was a good girl. Juliet always did what was best for everyone else.

Well, mostly. She kind of liked sassing Brick for some reason. Maybe it was because he was so serious all the time. Although, now that he was actually angry with her, it wasn't going to be so fun.

As she walked out of the door, Brick stopped her by grabbing her arm. He drew back immediately when she flinched. "What did he say? What's wrong?"

She didn't feel like explaining it. So instead, she headed back to the breakroom.

Where Gladys sat with her best friend, Lorraine. Awesome. The two witches of Wishingbone.

Gladys looked up from her cup of coffee. Or hell's brew. Who really knew what she was drinking?

"Aww, Juliet, why are you looking so sad? Has something happened?" she asked with false sympathy.

Juliet clenched her hands into fists as she moved to her locker to remove her handbag. She knew just who had complained about Elias being around yesterday.

"You're leaving already?" Lorraine asked. "It's not even lunchtime."

"Juliet? It's rude to ignore people when they're talking to you," Gladys said snidely. "And aren't you going to introduce us to your man? My, you are hanging out with a lot of different men lately, aren't you?"

"We're her bodyguards," Brick said stiffly.

She grabbed her whiteboard from her purse and scribbled out a message.

I'm out of this hellhole. Have fun doing all the shelving yourselves, you dried-up old hags.

She grinned at the look of shock on Lorraine's face. Gladys had just taken a sip of coffee and she spewed it out as she read what she'd written.

Juliet slammed the whiteboard on the desk. She had plenty.

Take that mic drop, bitches.

With a smirk, she turned and strode out of the room.

"Juliet," Brick came up alongside her, putting an arm out to stop her from opening the back door. When she glanced up into his face, expecting to find a scowl of disapproval, she was shocked to find him grinning.

"I can't believe you wrote that."

It was a long time coming. They'd always been careful to wait until she was alone to say things to her. No doubt they didn't want to bring the wrath of Reuben down on their heads. Somehow they knew she wouldn't tell him. Maybe that had been a mistake.

But now, she no longer had to be around them.

She was free.

She felt about thirty pounds lighter. As though she could float.

"What happened? Why are we leaving?"

With a sigh, she pointed to his truck. He just shook his head. "Nope, we're not leaving until I know. Tell me what happened."

Getting out her phone, she sent out a quick text explaining her conversation with Darin. Well, she left out most of the crap he'd said.

"Fuck," Brick said after reading it. "Can't argue with his reasoning."

No. Exactly.

"Still a shitty thing to do. Want me to go scare him until he pisses himself?"

She grinned at the thought. Then she shook her head. She had to be a mature adult about this. Even though it sucked.

This was for the best.

That's what she told herself anyway.

12

The call took longer to come than she thought.

She was just serving cakes at her tea party. They had a special guest today. Mr. Prude had decided to come to tea.

"You have to be on your best behavior, Missy and Angelique," she told them as she settled Mr. Prude into his seat. He was called that because of the pinched look on his face. But when she'd seen him in the store, she'd known she had to have him.

After leaving the library, Brick had driven them to the station to give statements. Then he'd brought her straight home. She'd run up to her rooms, locking herself in and ignoring Brick's demands.

After settling Mr. Prude, she picked up her ringing phone. The sound of wolves howling filled the room.

"Hey, Big Bad Wolf," she said cheerfully, knowing that if she showed any hint of her true feelings, he'd lose his mind.

He peered up at her through the screen. "You've done your make-up."

"You like it?" It was a pre-emptive strike. The make-up hid the dark marks under her eyes, and hopefully, her pale skin. The puffiness of her eyes was harder to mask.

It was silly to cry over a job she hadn't liked. But it was more like a release. There was so much going on and it was getting harder and harder for her to deal. Her coping mechanisms were pretty poor on a good day. She'd had a series of bad days. She just didn't know how much more she could take.

But right now, she had to act like everything was fine.

"I did Missy and Angelique's too. Don't they look pretty?" They didn't. They looked like clowns. She looked like a clown. The only one who wasn't a clown was Mr. Prune.

"Mr. Prude is having tea with you?" Reuben asked.

"Uh-huh."

"Angelique done anything to get a spanking yet?"

"Not yet. Although I think she's close. Mr. Prude isn't too happy with her uppity attitude. And you know how he likes to spank her. Truthfully, I think he has the hots for her."

Reuben raised his eyebrows. "You could be right. Mini, we need to have a serious talk."

The lead in her stomach grew heavier.

"We really don't, Big Bad Wolf."

"We really do, Mini," he replied gently. But she heard the note of exhaustion in his voice, and she took a good look at him.

Shoot. He looked so tired. And drawn. "Are you eating, Reuben? Sleeping?"

"Are you?"

"I'm worried about you."

"Ditto, kid." She rolled her eyes at him. He was only four years older than her. But then, he'd never been a typical kid or teenager. She guessed growing up with the mother he had, he'd had to mature fast.

"I'm fine," she said brightly. "I'm having a tea party."

"Mini, what happened today?"

"Um, which part are we talking about?" she asked cautiously. She wasn't entirely sure who he'd been talking to. If it was Brick, then she was screwed. But she'd hoped that Brick wouldn't immediately go tattling to Reuben.

But who knew what Brick would do? Especially now he hated her.

"Why don't you just tell me all of it," Reuben said silkily.

"How about I don't, and you go back to worrying about the bad guy trying to hurt you and let me worry about what's going on here," she told him brightly.

He blinked at her, looking shocked.

"Juliet, do I need to come there?" His tone was completely serious. And she knew he meant it

Her eyes widened. "No!"

"Tell. Me."

"You have enough on your plate, Reuben. And nothing is wrong."

There was silence. Then he suddenly looked thoughtful. "How are the bodyguards working out?"

Reuben was exceptionally smart. He was very good at reading people, so she knew she had to tread carefully.

"Okay, I guess. Don't really like having strangers living with me. Have you fixed the problem yet?" she asked hopefully.

Well, she tried to sound hopeful. She wasn't sure why she felt this stab of sadness at the thought of Brick leaving. She didn't want him here.

"Not yet. I'm getting close, though. I wasn't sure you'd slip into Little space with strangers around."

Normally, she wouldn't. But she felt safe up here. No one could get in unless they had her pin code. And only Xavier and Reuben knew that.

Sometimes, there didn't seem to be much of a line between her adult and Little self. They were almost one. Which she wasn't sure was a good thing or not. It would be too easy to lose herself in Little space.

There are times when you have to adult, Juliet.

Those times just usually sucked.

"They give me lots of space." She was going to have to tell him something about what happened today to distract him.

"Do they? Not too much, I hope. They're supposed to be guarding you."

"They give me just the right amount of space," she added hastily.

"Hm. I spoke to Brick last night. He was concerned about the medical reason for you not being able to talk to them. Seemed shocked when I told him there was none. Did you lie to him, Mini?"

She shrugged. "Not exactly."

"Mini," he said softly.

"Reuben. I love you. But you have to stop worrying about me so much. I'm all right. You have enough going on."

"I'm never not going to worry about you."

"I know, just . . . I got this shit covered."

He studied her. She didn't have anything under control and he damn well knew it.

"Where's Xavier?"

She frowned at the question. "He had to go see his parents. His mom is sick."

"Really?" Reuban said thoughtfully. "I'll call him."

"Be nice," she warned, knowing they no longer got on well. It made her sad that they'd once been friends and had a falling out two years ago. Neither of them would tell her what it was over, either. But soon after, Xavier had moved back here to Wishingbone.

"Tell me about today. Please."

And because he said please, she spilled her guts. It actually felt good to get it out.

"Is Kiesha okay?" he asked sharply.

Despite what the entire population of Wishingbone thought, Reuben did care. It's just that he only cared because she did. There was a hierarchy in Reuben's brain when it came to other people.

There was her.

There was everyone she cared about.

Then there was the rest of the world.

She came first. And he forced himself to care about people that were important to her because he wanted her happy.

The rest of the world could rot. It wasn't healthy for him. For her either, probably. However, that sort of love was something she'd needed. Maybe she still did. Maybe she'd never have a relationship, not because she was a freak. But because nobody would love her the way he did.

Was that weird? Yep, it was weird. It was just that they'd both had very shitty upbringings that had brought them to this point.

"You need a girlfriend," she blurted out.

His eyebrows rose. "I do?"

"Yeah. You do. Do you even date? You never mention it. You've got to, though, right? You've probably got needs."

Dear Lord.

"I can't believe you just said that."

"Yeah, me neither. Think I might have thrown up in my mouth a little," she told him.

They both grimaced.

"Last thing I need right now is a woman in my life."

"A man then."

He glared at her. "Or a man. We're talking about you."

She sighed. It was always about her. "Why don't you ever tell me about what's happening in your life?"

"Mini, tell me everything that happened today."

Shoot. She winced. "You know about my job."

"I do. I'm going to do something very nasty to that dickhead boss of yours."

"Reuben, don't."

"How dare he fire you. He'll regret that."

"Reuben, you can't. And he didn't fire me."

"He's soon going to find himself demoted down to toilet scrubber and that might not be far enough."

"Reuben, I hated that job."

"What?"

"I hated it."

"You did? Why did you never say something? Did someone say something? Do something?"

"It's not that." Well, it was partially, but he didn't need any more targets. "It just wasn't something I was interested in."

"Then why did you stay at it?"

"It made you feel better."

He opened his mouth then closed it. "For me? You stayed for me?"

She shrugged. "You worry about me. All the time. When I do normal things like make friends or get a job, you worry less."

"Shit. Fuck." He ran his hand down his face.

"I'm sorry. I shouldn't bring this up now. It's just, I didn't want you to think I'm upset because I'm not. I'll find something else. There's probably a job at the diner."

He gaped at her.

"Not waitressing," she said hastily. "Maybe washing dishes."

"No. Nope. The next job you have will not be washing dishes."

"I don't mind." She knew he could be a snob.

"No. You're going to do something you want to do. You're not doing shit because you think it makes me feel better. Jesus fucking Christ."

She sniffled. "You're mad at me."

"Damn straight. Don't do stuff that makes you miserable for me. Damn. Damn. Juliet. I don't want you to sacrifice your happiness for me."

"Ditto," she told him.

"You are my happiness."

But he should want more, shouldn't he? He deserved more.

"I'm still destroying that asshole."

She sighed. She knew he wouldn't give that up.

"After I sort this mess out. You're really okay?"

"Really."

He gave her a skeptical look, but a phone started ringing in the background. "Fuck, I need to go. Listen to your bodyguards. All right? Promise me."

His phone stopped ringing then started again and he clenched his jaw.

"I promise, but please promise to be careful."

"Of course. Love you, Mini."

"Love you."

She ended the call then sent a text to Xavier.

JULIET: *Think I'd be any good at washing dishes?*

Xavier: *U should do something U want 2 do.*

Juliet: *Just got 2 figure out what that is.*

Xavier: *You'll figure it out. B patient. No rush. I believe in U.*

WOW. That was sweet. A knock came a few minutes after she ended the call with Xavier. She froze. The door was locked. She knew that.

"Juliet, it's me. Brick. We need to talk. Downstairs. Five minutes."

She rolled her eyes. She was pretty sure by talk he meant he wanted to lecture her.

"I'm still not in the mood to be lectured at," she told her companions. "Don't give me that look, Mr. Prude. I'm not in the wrong here. I'm not. I don't deserve a scolding." She gasped. "And I certainly don't deserve a spanking, Mr. Prude. So rude of you. Rude Mr. Prude. I like it."

Her phone buzzed.

KIESHA: *Spill girl. What's the deets with MrMcHottieAsshole.*

SHE ROLLED HER EYES. Then she texted back what she could tell her without spilling everything that was going on with Reuben.

There was a while before Kiesha texted back.

KIESHA: *Dude if he wasn't such a dick I'd tell u 2 bone him.*

NO WAY. Even if she did think he was attractive, he could also be a jerk. Nope. Not happening.

Never.

"WHAT'S GOT YOU SO UPSET?" Elias asked, walking into the living room in Juliet's house.

"Told her to be down in five minutes."

"Yeah? How long ago was that?"

"Fifteen minutes ago."

Elias grinned. Brick glared at the other man. "Why didn't you tell me her boss was a jerk?"

"Didn't meet him. That Gladys woman was more of a problem."

"Yeah. Met her too."

"You need to chill before you hurt something."

"She needs to learn to obey me when I give her an order."

Elias sighed. "What's your problem?"

"What do you mean?"

"You're an uptight prick, but you're not usually this bad. She's not going to jump when you say so."

She should.

He closed his eyes for a moment then moved his neck from side to side, trying to relieve the tension.

Even he could hear how much of a dick he was being.

"She lied to me." And it had been like a blow to the gut. Because he liked her.

Had liked her.

"About what?"

"When I asked if there was medical reason for why she couldn't talk, she nodded. There's not."

Elias leaned against the doorway. He seemed to think that through. "She's not a normal client."

No shit.

"Obviously there's something in her past that has caused her some trauma."

And he hated to think what that might have been.

"You do know that not all traumas are physical, right?" Elias asked.

"I was in the Marines, of course I know that," he snapped. Then it hit him.

Fuck.

He was a fucking idiot. Fuck. Fuck. Fuck.

With a pained groan, he sat on the sofa. "I wasn't angry about the not-talking. I was mad because she lied."

Elias sat across from him. "And that's a trigger for you. Always has been but especially after Linda."

Another moan escaped as he pressed his elbows to his thighs and buried his face in his hands. "Fuck. I'm a fucking idiot. The way I treated her today . . ."

"What's going on, Brick? I know these past few months have been hell. Having Linda leave you, losing the business, but while here you've been . . ."

"A complete asshole?" he guessed dryly.

"I wouldn't go that far. Although I don't know what you did today."

"Basically, treated her like I would someone who I thought had lied to me."

"Right. Awesome. So, should I start packing our stuff now? Because I'm guessing we're about to be fired."

Right now, he didn't care about the job. Which was insane since it should be all he cared about. But all that mattered was her. And the damage he'd done.

"If I've hurt her, I'll never forgive myself."

"Strange thing I noticed yesterday was the way everyone treated her," Elias mused. "Mostly, they went out of their way to avoid her or they treated her like she was made of the finest porcelain."

"Yeah, the sheriff did the same to her today."

He remembered how upset she'd been earlier. How her fear had called to him. How he'd wanted to erase all her worries. Christ. She wasn't his type. He'd always been attracted to women who were bolder, more confident. Juliet would always be shy and quiet.

Yet somehow, that seemed to be exactly what he wanted.

"Other clients have lied to you, Brick. Never seen you this worked up about it."

"Other clients weren't her."

"Yeah. And you feel things for her. That's why you were so butt-hurt over her lying."

He glared at Elias for the butt-hurt part, but he wasn't off the mark.

"Guess the question is: do you care about her enough to want to do something about it?"

"She's the client."

Elias grunted. "Small problem."

"Major problem. My reputation is already shot. I need this job."

"Then you apologize for being an ass. And let me take point."

His entire body rebelled at that. Not the apology part, he definitely owed her an apology. But he couldn't stand to let anyone else watch over her. Yesterday, he'd nearly worked himself into a heart attack from worry.

She was his.

He grimaced and rubbed his temples. "How pissed will you be if we don't get paid for this job?"

"Not as pissed as I'd be if you didn't grab hold of happiness when it was offered and run with it."

"You're a good friend."

"I'm pretty much your only friend. Sterling just tolerates you." He grinned at Brick.

"Wouldn't blame you guys for leaving me. I've been a dick to you too."

"Hormones."

"Fuck you, it wasn't hormones."

"So, now you've pulled your head out of your ass, what's the next move?"

He let out a breath. "Getting her to listen to me, to let me in."

"Don't envy you that job."

THERE WAS another knock on her door.

Huh. He'd lasted longer than she thought he would before coming back to yell at her.

Not that he yelled, but he didn't need to. A few cutting words in that cold voice were enough to slice her open.

"Juliet, I need to talk to you."

Awesome. Where were her headphones?

"Not like before. Not that sort of talk," he said hastily. "Crap, I wish I knew whether you were listening or not. I don't want to have to repeat this."

She frowned at that. Repeat what? She raised the headphones to her ears.

"I owe you an apology."

Okay. She was listening. This was starting to sound more promising.

"I was an asshole to you today. I have . . . issues that have nothing to do with you."

Why did that sting?

"And I shouldn't have taken them out on you. Thing is," he let out a pain-filled sigh, "eight months ago, I learned my wife had been having an affair for years."

Oh no. Her stomach dropped. Who the hell would be stupid enough to have an affair when they were married to Brick? How could they want someone else?

Like you want two people? You're attracted to him and Xavier.

Two completely different people. Maybe she was just the same as his ex.

Ouch. She winced at the thought. She'd never cheat, though. That just wasn't who she was. If she didn't want to be with someone, then she'd tell them. She wouldn't go behind their backs.

"Not only had she lied to me, and it's embarrassing that I never worked it out, but it was with my accountant. A man I trusted. They took everything I'd worked hard for."

They took everything?

"I was over-extended. And Linda had expensive tastes. By the end, all I was left with was debt. The business I worked so hard for was basically gone. Worst of all, I had to let all my employees go. They depended on me. I let them down."

And she knew how hard that would be for someone like him. He would take that responsibility seriously.

Boy, his ex-wife was a real piece of work. She clenched her tiny hands into fists.

"When your brother said that there was nothing medically wrong with you, I jumped to conclusions. I thought you'd lied to me."

She had. In the strictest sense.

"I overreacted. I had no right to talk to you like I did."

There was silence. He sighed. "I was so angry because I feel something for you. I know that's crazy. I've only known you for a few days. I have saved your life in that time, though."

Saved her life? Did he mean when he thought she was drowning?

"And fed you."

She shook her head, her lips twitching.

"That counts as a date, right? Two, if it's okay to have a date with your best friends along."

There was a thunk and she moved quietly over to the door. She touched the wood, wondering if he was sitting with his back to it. She turned and sat, leaning back against the door. Juliet understood why he'd gotten so upset. But it was difficult for her to get past it. Trust didn't come easily to her. And he'd eroded what little there had been between them.

"Don't know why you don't talk, Duchess," he said in a soft voice. For the first time, Duchess didn't come out derisively. It almost sounded affectionate. She sighed quietly and heard him move.

"So, you are listening," he murmured. "Okay, Duchess. Okay. It's all right if you're not ready to, uh, communicate with me. Listening is enough. Just know that I get that there's a reason for you not talking. Not sure I want to know what that is, if I'm honest. Not sure I can handle knowing you were hurt, even in the past."

Darn. That was kind of sweet. Sweeter than she'd expected from him.

"Just know, I'm not expecting anything. If you can be my friend, great. More than I deserve. If you wanted more. Well, fuck, I'd be the luckiest man on the planet."

More? Did he mean . . .

"But I don't want you scared to be around me. Rather have you mad. You're cute when you're mad."

She was?

"When you cross your arms over your chest, and your nose goes up in the air as you lay down the law, yeah, cute as fuck. Course, you do that when your health and safety are on the line, and you're gonna be in trouble."

Trouble? What sort of trouble?

"Damn, I need to shut up before you run from me."

She didn't feel like running away from him.

She looked down at herself. She was dressed in a pair of long striped socks. They were blue and white. She had on white rabbit slippers and this cute navy-blue skirt that barely went past her ass. Under the skirt, she wore a pair of ruffly panties. A simple white t-shirt finished off the outfit. What would he think if he saw her like this?

He'd only ever seen her in black. And completely covered. It was only in here that she felt safe enough to dress how she wanted.

She grabbed for the pacifier that was clipped to her shirt. She stuck it in her mouth, sucking on it to ease the panic. For some reason, it just wasn't doing the job it usually did, though.

"Anyway, you don't have to worry about any of that."

Why? Because he didn't think she could handle that? Handle him?

"I don't need that. I don't need anything. I just hope you can forgive me. We're having dinner in an hour if you want to join us."

She knew it was an olive branch. And she had a choice. Go down there and maybe gain a friend. Or something more? Was she ready for more? Could she be anything more? Especially with someone she barely knew.

But she was scared of ending up on her own, with just her dolls for company and Reuben occasionally calling her to let his kids talk to their crazy aunt.

Her breath came in sharper gasps and she pressed her eyes closed.

"I'm sorry, Duchess. I promise, you come downstairs, give me another chance, then I'll treat you the way you're supposed to be treated."

What way was that? With kid gloves like everyone else? As though she wasn't capable of doing anything on her own?

And whose fault is that? You're the one that acts like a lunatic. No wonder no one believes you can look after yourself.

She needed to change that.

But how? When she had no confidence in herself?

13

S hit. She wasn't coming.

Well, he had no one to blame but himself. He'd been a complete ass.

He sat in his chair, looking at the chops Sterling had grilled along with the baked potatoes, and didn't feel that hungry anymore.

Then Elias cleared his throat. Turning, he saw her. His heart caught. He wasn't sure exactly what it was about her. She wasn't the most beautiful woman in the world. Wasn't the most outgoing or funniest. She was quiet, introverted, and guarded.

And he wanted to take her into his arms and keep her safe. Wrap her up in cotton wool at the same time he wanted to fill her with self-confidence. So that the next time he invited her down for dinner with them, she'd just stroll right on up and plunk her ass down, instead of standing off to the side looking uncertain.

He frowned as he took in what she was wearing. He didn't like her clothes on a normal day. He knew that wasn't the acceptable way to think. It was her body, she got to decide what she wore. But Brick just hated that everything was black and shapeless. As though she used her clothing to hide. He really hated this outfit though, since she appeared to be wearing a man's hoodie.

Whose top was she wearing? And how could he get her out of it and into his clothing?

Hastily, he stood, sending his chair flying back and making her jump.

"Sorry," he said gruffly. Then he ran his hand over his face.

"Go to her," Sterling whispered.

Right. Go to her. Stop standing here like a freaking idiot. Quickly, he moved towards her. Her eyes went wide, and he slowed as he realized that he probably looked like a steam train, about to bowl her over. She was so tiny that he worried for a moment that he was too big, too rough for her.

Getting ahead of yourself, man.

Right. Dinner first. Then see how she feels. If she just wanted to be friends, well, he could deal.

"Hey, Duchess," he said quietly.

She barely managed a twitch of a smile.

"Hope you brought your appetite. Sterling cooked some lamb chops."

Her nose wrinkled. She held her whiteboard in one hand and wrote a message.

Red meat again, huh?

"Well, we are men." He winked at her. "Our tastes are simple."

Simple is one word to use.

"Is that so, brat? What other words would you use?"

Neanderthal. Caveman. Bossy. I could go on, but I'll run out of whiteboard.

He grinned, loving her sassy side.

"You two going to come have dinner before it gets cold or continue this weird flirting thing you have going on?" Sterling called out.

Juliet went bright red and took a step back. Turning, he glared at Sterling just in time to see Elias smack him around the head then say something quietly to him. Sterling sometimes didn't think before he spoke.

"Shit," Sterling muttered. "Sorry, Juliet. I didn't mean anything by that."

She nodded. But her free hand was curled into a fist.

"Come eat." He held out his hand to her, letting her make the decision whether to touch him. To his surprise and delight, she slid her cool hand into his. He turned it over, wanting to see if his suspicions were right. Yep, she had the indent of nails on her palm.

He ran his thumb over them soothingly, making her jump.

He had to be gentle. He couldn't order her not to do that again. Slow and steady.

"Come on, Duchess. We won't bite."

She raised her eyebrows at that. He wondered what she was thinking. Leading her forward, he hastily pulled out her chair, pushing her in. Right in. Until she was squashed against the table.

"She might want to breathe, man," Elias said dryly.

"Shit, sorry." He drew her chair back slightly.

She smiled at him nervously while his two best friends gaped at him like he was an alien. He might be possessed. He'd never been this nervous.

But he didn't want to mess this up.

Reaching for the platter of meat, he held it out to her, frowning when she refused it.

Again, he quelled the urge to just fill her plate.

Instead, he grabbed the potatoes. She took one and some salad, then smiled as Sterling started talking about his shopping trip today and how he'd had his ass pinched by some blue-haired woman with her hair in rollers. By the time he was finished, she was giggling.

Damn, he loved that. Loved the sound of her happiness.

"You've got it so bad," Elias whispered to him as they washed the dishes.

"Yeah. I do."

Elias' eyebrows rose. "Maybe you should be sleeping in the big house then."

"Not sure if she'd be comfortable with that." He looked out the double doors to the porch where she sat with Sterling. She seemed uncomfortable with just him. Her gaze met his and she started to relax.

"I think she'd be okay with it," Elias commented. "I'll go grab my stuff. Didn't unpack anyway. Why don't you ask her to watch a movie or something?"

He took a deep breath. He could try that, right? What was the worst that could happen? She'd reject him?

WHERE WAS THAT BIOPSY RESULT?

He'd been here for days, waiting. Maybe he should have gone into the appointment with his mother, but he hadn't wanted to embarrass her. He couldn't stay much longer. His missed Wishingbone, his friends, Juliet.

Sitting on the side of his bed, he knew he should get ready for dinner. His mother always insisted on formal dress and abhorred lateness. But he felt exhausted.

It wasn't just from being here with his parents and their relentless badgering about his job, although that was a big part of it. He worked long hours at the hospital, longer than any of his colleagues. An attempt to atone for past sins, but it was wearing on him.

He was lonely. And tired of it.

Grabbing his phone, he started flicking through the photos. And he realized most of them were of her. Juliet, smiling shyly into the camera. Juliet, at Wishingbone's annual fair holding a giant teddy bear he'd won for her.

Call her. She'll cheer you up.

Just as he was about to bring up her contact, his phone buzzed with an incoming call. He sighed as he saw who it was. It was getting harder and harder to hold onto his anger towards Reuben. He guessed it was easier to blame him for everything that happened two years ago than it was to actually deal with his guilt.

"Where are you?" Reuben asked as soon as he answered.

"Hello to you too, asshole."

"Xavier, I'm dealing with a lot at the moment, I don't have time for pleasantries. Juliet said your mother is ill?"

"She found a lump. I took her to the doctor on Monday."

"What did he say?"

Xavier frowned, wondering at the sudden interest in his mother's health. Reuben had never gotten along with his parents.

"He took a biopsy."

"Yeah? You talked to him?"

"Well, no."

"So you don't have any proof there is a lump?"

"No," Xavier answered. "What are you trying to say? That my mother is lying?"

"They want you to move jobs, right? Working at Wishingbone hospital isn't prestigious enough for a Marson. What better way to get you home than a possible cancer scare?"

"Reuben, that's ridiculous. This is my mother. Sure, my parents can be pushy, but she wouldn't fake being ill."

Reuben made a humming noise.

"I've got to go."

"Wait! Juliet needs you."

"What do you mean? What's going on?" he asked urgently. They'd texted often and spoke the other day, she hadn't mentioned anything.

"I just need you to get back to Wishingbone and check on her. Fuck, I've got to go. I know you care for her. So, just go check on her for me, all right?"

Before Xavier could reply, the call ended. He frowned down at his phone. What the hell?

A knock on his door had him half-turning.

"Xavier, please come down for dinner."

He closed his eyes with a sigh then quickly sent a text to Juliet.

XAVIER: *Everything ok?*

Juliet: *Of course, U?*

Xavier: *Fine. Gonna come home soon.*

Juliet: *Yay, miss U.*

Xavier: *Miss U more.*

HE RUBBED at his forehead then looked at flights back home. There was one leaving tomorrow at lunchtime. Hopefully, the biopsy would be back by then. He quickly got dressed. As he grew closer to the living room, he could hear laughter.

Walking in, he saw a tall, thin blonde woman sitting with his mother on the sofa. His father sat across from them.

Fuck.

"Oh, Xavier, there you are. You're late." His mother shot him a look. "I'd like to introduce you to Yvonne. She works with your father at the hospital. She's a pediatrician. Xavier loves children."

What the hell was happening?

Yvonne rose and smiled, looking him over. She held out her hand. "Such a pleasure to meet you, Xavier."

"You too," he said in a short voice.

His mother shot him a sharp look, but he didn't care. What the hell did she think she was doing?

He shook the other woman's hand. She was gorgeous, obviously smart, and he felt absolutely nothing for her.

All he could think about was Juliet's sweet smile.

"Your parents said you're considering moving here," Yvonne said as they all sat for before-dinner drinks.

"They're wrong," he said with a tight smile. "I'm happy where I am."

His mother let out a nervous laugh as Yvonne gave him a startled look.

"Xavier feels some loyalty to the town where he grew up. But his talent is wasted there."

"There are sick people in Wishingbone, Mother," he replied tightly.

"Wishingbone, what a funny name." Yvonne laughed, his parents joining her.

Xavier tapped his fingers against the arm of his chair, unamused.

When they went through for dinner, his mother pulled him aside. "You could make an effort, Yvonne is a lovely woman."

"I'm not interested in a relationship with a stranger, Mother," he said coldly. "Or in moving here."

She sniffed. "You can't stay in that awful town."

"I can and I want to. I'm leaving tomorrow afternoon and I'd like to speak to your Doctor about the biopsy results."

"The results aren't back yet."

He noticed she couldn't meet his gaze.

"They should be by tomorrow, or I'll call the lab myself."

"Don't do that," she said sharply.

"All right," he agreed. "But I'm leaving tomorrow and if they're not back by then, you'll have to send it to me."

"Xavier, you cannot just leave." She put her hand on his arm, her nails digging into his forearm.

"I have to go home, Mother. I have responsibilities."

She made a scoffing noise. "I cannot believe you're wasting Yvonne's time by not getting to know her."

"I'm not interested in Yvonne. I have someone else I care about."

He hadn't realized how much he cared about her until now. His head hadn't been in the right space. He still didn't fully believe he deserved to be happy, deserved her.

And he wasn't certain she could handle his need for control. Juliet was delicate and sweet. She wasn't going to want to be tied up and spanked. To have him torture her with pleasure without letting her come for hours. To get down on her knees and suck him off.

But if he had to suppress those needs in order to have her? Wasn't she worth that?

"Someone else? Who?"

No way was he telling his mother. He had to protect Juliet from her. From anyone who might harm her.

"I'm sorry you're ill, mother. And that you're not happy with me. But my life is my business."

Tension eased from her as Brick returned to the table. She set her phone down after texting Xavier.

It wasn't that Sterling wasn't a nice guy. He seemed fine. But she didn't know him well. Not like Brick or Elias. And he was so pretty that he was kind of intimidating.

Brick sat next to her.

"I'll just go check on how Elias is doing with the dishes," Sterling said hastily. "He forgets to rinse before he puts them in the dishwasher."

When Sterling left, Brick turned to her, looking unsure. In fact, he'd been kind of weird since she arrived.

She wished he'd say something. This was starting to feel really awkward and she had no idea what to do next. She'd never been on a date before. Well, this wasn't really a date. But . . . fuck. Did he want her to go?

"Hey, you okay?" He reached out and eased open her hand. "You're going to hurt yourself." He ran his thumb over the indents on her palm and she shivered.

Suddenly, he snatched his hand away. "Fuck. Sorry, didn't mean to touch you."

He didn't want to touch her?

"I know you don't like being touched."

Ohhh. That. She picked up her whiteboard.

I don't mind when you touch me.

"Really? You don't?"

She gave him a self-conscious look.

It's strangers I have trouble with.

"Oh. Right." He was still smiling, but there was less joy in his face.

Shoot. She was messing this up.

But I liked your touch from the first day I met you.

She knew she was blushing and dropped her gaze, suddenly worried about his reaction. There was a gentle touch on her chin, and he turned her face towards his.

"That true?"

She nodded.

"I like your touch too," he whispered. "You can touch me whenever you like."

That's good since I was going to touch you anyway.

"Oh, were you, Duchess?" A grin lit up his entire face. He leaned in toward her. "And just where would you like to touch me most?"

Her breath caught. Was she brave enough to tell him? She was tired of being a coward. To her shock, her finger moved up to his mouth.

His eyes widened and she heard him swallow. Heavily. "Yeah?"

She nodded.

"You want me to kiss you, Duchess?"

Well, she'd thought that was obvious, but she nodded. The more he made her wait, the more nervous she grew.

"You sure?"

Her bravery zapped out of her and she stood. But he reached up and lightly grabbed her wrist before she could run.

"Fuck. Sorry. I want to. I just want things clear between us."

She guessed she could understand that.

"Watch a movie with me."

A movie? Um, that wasn't what she expected. She pointed at him then at herself.

"You and me, yes." He cleared his throat, looking nervous. "Elias thought you might be okay with me taking his room in the main house."

She nodded.

"Good." He relaxed. "How about I grab my stuff? Won't take me long and I'll meet you in the living room. You choose the movie."

Huh, and here she'd thought he would want to choose. But she'd try to choose something they'd both like.

Twenty minutes later, she was sitting on the huge sectional in the living room. She'd made a bowl of popcorn and had a movie up on the screen ready to go. Her nerves had grown to the point she felt ill.

She wished he'd just kissed her. Now she was worrying about what would happen next. Maybe he'd changed his mind. Maybe she'd freak out. Who knew? It wasn't like she'd ever been kissed.

She'd grabbed a blanket for armor more than to keep her warm. She held it up over her until only her eyes peeked out.

When he came in, he paused, studying her. A tension came over her as she waited for him to say something. Slowly, he walked towards her. Instead of sitting on the sofa, he pulled the coffee table over and sat on it. His legs bracketed hers and he leaned forward until she got a hint of his aftershave.

Whatever it was, it was damn sexy and it made her insides stir. She'd only ever felt this way around Xavier.

Guilt filled her at the thought of Xavier. But she shouldn't feel that way. They weren't anything other than friends. That was the way he wanted it. She pushed Xavier from her mind. She shouldn't think about him while she was with Brick. It was wrong to want both men. It wasn't fair to Brick. It would hurt him. She would never want that.

She didn't know how Brick's ex had been stupid enough to let him go. But Juliet wasn't that dumb.

If he wanted her . . . if he could deal with her quirks . . . then she was going to do her best to open up to him.

He set down a hoodie he was carrying on the sofa beside her.

"Feeling nervous?"

She nodded.

"Me too."

Her eyes widened. He was nervous?

"I'm rarely nervous. Want to know why I am now?"

Um, yeah.

His gaze hit hers. And she sucked in a breath at the intensity she saw there.

"Because even though we've only known each other a few days, there's something pulling us together." He looked off into the distance. "Linda left me bitter. Angry. I don't want to be that person. And around you, I feel more at peace, happier than I have for a long time."

She lowered her blanket then reached out to touch his hand with hers.

"For you, I want to be a better person."

He was a good person. Didn't he know that?

"Know I'm not good enough for you. I jump to conclusions, let my temper get the best of me. But I'm gonna try to be better."

Drat, where was her stupid whiteboard?

"Even if it's only friendship you want."

Stupid whiteboard . . . where had it gone?

Maybe she should talk to him. If he was willing to work on himself, then she should do the same.

She opened her mouth. But all that came out was a pained groan.

His eyes flared. "That wasn't meant to scare you. We can be friends. Just friends."

But she didn't want to be friends. She wanted to be his. Irritated with herself, she smacked her hands against her thighs.

"What? Hell, no." He grabbed her hands, stilling them. "No."

That last 'no' was firm. And it made her pay attention. This was the Brick she knew. Not this more unsure side. She let out a breath, feeling more settled.

Was it a good thing he could settle her so quickly?

She drew her hand free, searching around for her whiteboard and finding it under the blanket.

"This is unprofessional of me. Your brother won't be pleased."

Oh no. Reuben would lose his mind. She grimaced.

"Yeah, he didn't strike me as the easy-going type."

Brick ran soothing circles with his thumb around the palm of her free hand.

"We don't need to talk about this now. I'd never expect more than you can give. You hold the reins."

Frustration filled her. She knew he meant well. She didn't want to immediately jump into something she wasn't prepared for. But at the same time, she kind of needed for him to lead. Because she had no clue what she was doing.

"Mind if I sit beside you? Or would you rather I sit down there?" He nodded to the other end of the couch.

See. This is what she was talking about. Before today, he wouldn't have hesitated to sit next to her. Or tell her what to do. Get bossy or grumpy.

And she liked that.

It sounded insane. But when he was grouchy and demanding, then he wasn't treating her as though she was breakable. The way most people did.

Would a relationship change how you act towards me?

"Well, yeah, I guess." He gave her a puzzled look.

Like you've been acting since you told me about your ex and apologized for being a jackass.

"I don't think the word I'd use is jackass," he grumbled. "And yeah, I'd treat you like you're precious. It's what you deserve."

I don't need to be treated like I'm defective.

He scowled at that. "Defective? Who the fuck said you were defective!"

Ahh, there he was. Relief filled her. And she found herself smiling.

"You think it's funny, calling yourself defective? Now, you listen to me, baby girl . . ." she saw the moment he realized who he was talking to and he reined himself in.

Frustration filled her. She started writing again.

You're treating me like I might break at a harsh word. I won't.

He eyed her skeptically.

I just want to go back to how things were before you thought I was a liar.

Something came over his face and he leaned back. Frustration bit at her. It was so hard to communicate.

"So, you don't want any sort of relationship other than a business one."

She thunked her forehead with the palm of her hand. Wait, no, she was hitting the wrong person. She reached out and smacked her hand against his forehead.

"Right, we need a serious conversation about you hitting me," he growled. Then he let out a huff of breath. "Fuck, this is harder than I thought."

What? Trying to suppress your bossiness?

He stared down at what she'd written.

I'm not as fragile as I look. I won't break if you growl at me. I just want you to be you.

Wipe. Write.

Because I like you.

He sucked in a breath. "Like like?"

She grinned.

"Fuck, you ever tell anyone I just said *like like* and I'll spank your ass."

Her face flushed and she was tempted to fan herself. Oh Lord. That was hot.

He was studying her closely.

"You really want to try a relationship?"

She hesitated then nodded shyly.

He placed his hands on the outside of her thighs. God, he was big. He made her feel so tiny. It probably should have scared her. But somehow, she knew he wouldn't harm her.

"And you want me to be myself? That's what I'm getting from this conversation."

She nodded.

"You like that side of me," he said arrogantly. "Because everyone else treats you like you're fragile, don't they?"

Shoot. He had noticed more than she'd thought.

She shrugged.

"Nope, you won't be allowed to use the fact you can't talk to me as a way of getting out of communicating," he told her sternly.

Uh-oh, what beast had she unleashed?

I guess so.

He gave her a knowing look. Then he seemed to think something over. "There're other things you don't know about me." He let out a breath. "You know that you were naughty today."

She froze. What was he talking about? And what did that have to do with anything?

"You didn't obey me when I told you to get back into the truck. As your bodyguard, I'm in charge of your safety. If I were a friend, I'd scold you."

She wrinkled her nose.

He tapped it. "Don't think I won't still do it."

But you were mean to me. I shouldn't get a scolding on top of that.

"You'll get more than that if you're mine."

She stilled, stared at him. Did he mean . . .

When he didn't say anything more, she let out an impatient noise.

"Think you've figured it out already, but I'm going to be clear. I'm a Dominant. And if you were mine, then I'd want to make rules for you. And punish you if you broke them."

Holy fuck. Her entire body felt like it was on fire. Thank God she was wearing a loose hoodie because her nipples felt like hard pebbles.

"Well, you haven't run screaming or slapped me," he said dryly, watching her intently. "Not sure if you're horrified, shocked, or a combination of both."

Not horrified.

"Okay, that's good. You know much about BDSM?"

Only what I've read.

He raised an eyebrow. "Might want to see those books."

Looking for pointers?

He grinned. "Never too old to learn something new."

I dunno, you are so very, very old.

"Brat. I am not." He gave her a mock-stern look. "Someone has their sassy pants on."

No way was she showing him any of her stories with hardcore Doms in them. No need to give him ideas.

"Tomorrow, you're going to show me your entire collection."

Her eyes widened.

He nodded. "Then you can choose your favorite. We'll read it together."

Oh fuck.

"Juliet? You okay?" Concern filled his face. "Too much? Too fast?"

She shook her head.

"Sure?"

She nodded.

"I can tone things down. We can go as slow as you want."

We might need to go slow. But I . . .

She chewed nervously on the end of the marker. Reaching out, he lifted her chin. "You what?"

I don't want you to tone anything down. I think I need your Dominant side as much as you need to let it out.

He studied her words for a long moment. "You ever been with a Dom?"

No.

"But you've thought about it? Thought you might be submissive?"

Her heart raced, skipped. Standing, she held out her hand to him. He raised his eyebrows.

I have something to show you.

He stood and slipped his hand into hers.

She could do this.

Or maybe she couldn't. Because she couldn't even make it out of the room, let alone up to the third floor. Her fingers started tingling and the urge to hide rushed through her.

"Hey, Duchess. Whoa, okay, breathe with me. You're safe. You're fine."

Suddenly she found herself pulled against his chest, and instead of feeling panicked or suffocated, a feeling of safety stole over her. This was right. She sucked in a deep breath, and he held her until she calmed, not trying to push her for anything.

It was exactly what she needed.

"Whatever it is you think you need to show me, you don't. Not yet, anyway. We go at your pace."

She stiffened at that.

He ran his hand up and down her back. "Or not?" He drew her back, studying her. "Shit, Duchess, I've no idea what you're thinking."

He grabbed her whiteboard and pen.

"Tell me what's going on. Now."

Yikes. He meant business.

"You don't get a pass on this, Juliet," he told her firmly.

She bit her lip in frustration.

Just because I have issues doesn't mean I'm not capable of making my own decisions.

He reared back as though she'd slapped him. "I didn't mean to imply you were stupid."

No, you didn't!

She was making a hash of this.

I can make my own decisions, but that doesn't mean I always want to be in charge.

"Right," he said slowly. "So, what you're saying is . . ."

I might need to go slow. But I don't want to always be in control.

He let out a sigh. "That, I can work with."

I feel safe with you.

His whole body softened. "Good."

I'm sorry I can't tell you everything.

"You will. There's something else we need to discuss if we're moving forward."

Uh-oh. What?

"I need to quit."

Quit? But then he wouldn't be here. He'd move away and she'd never see him.

"Whoa, easy. Hey, look at me," he said firmly, waiting for her gaze to meet his. "That's better. Deep, even breaths. You're all right."

He drew her back to the sofa, but this time, he sat beside her.

You're leaving?

"No, I'm not. I'm not going anywhere. But it wouldn't be right to be paid to guard you when we're in a relationship."

Oh.

Reuben will freak either way.

"Yeah?"

Yep. With Reuben, it's better to ask for forgiveness than permission.

Amusement filled his face. "Is that so?"

She nodded. And she knew he needed the money. So, win-win.

"Wouldn't feel right taking his money."

He has plenty.

"Not the point."

She decided to let that go for the moment. Her mind had enough to cope with.

"This is what we'll do. Go slow. But I'm in charge. We'll make rules. Talk about punishments. Work out a way for you to safe-word. But we'll do that tomorrow."

Relief filled her. She felt exhausted.

"Right now, let's just watch a movie and relax."

He drew her close. "Fair warning. I'm gonna want to touch you a lot. If it's too much, tell me."

She liked being touched by him.

"Oh, and Duchess?"

She looked up when he tilted her chin. "That whole asking for forgiveness rather than permission thing?"

She nodded.

"Try that with me, and you won't be sitting comfortably." He gave her a pointed look that made her squirm.

"And I haven't forgotten I owe you a spanking for being naughty today. That will come later."

What? Why?

"You disobeyed me."

He reached over and grabbed the hoodie he'd brought in with him.

"Off with this." He tugged on the sleeve of her hoodie. She gaped at him. Um, what? Had he lost his mind?

"You're mine. That means no wearing other men's clothes. This is getting burned."

She crossed her arms over her chest and glared at him. Not happening!

"Off. Now. This is non-negotiable. Call it my hard limit. No other men's clothing on you. Ever."

She grabbed her whiteboard and wrote frantically.

It's mine. I bought it.

He frowned. "Doesn't matter. Off."

He was being ridiculous. But when it came down to it, this seemed to be more important to him than this hoodie was to her.

But that was the only reason she gave in.

You're not burning it!

"Then get it off and out of my sight."

With a huff, she drew it off then threw it over the back of the sofa. She'd need to remember to grab it later. Then she pulled his hoodie over her head.

Oh Lord, help her.

It smelled like him. His scent surrounded her. Why had she fought putting this on? If he wanted to steal all her clothes and replace them with his, then he was welcome to. When the hoodie was on, he tugged her against him and put the blanket over them before placing the popcorn on her lap.

"Now, what are we watching?"

Dawn of the Dead?

Really? That wasn't what he'd been expecting. He'd thought maybe some rom-com or an action flick if he was lucky.

But zombies and gore? That surprised him. He hoped she didn't have nightmares. But when he'd suggested something else, she'd looked so sad that he'd let her have her way.

On the positive side, she'd kept grabbing him whenever she'd gotten scared. Which had made him puff up like a proud peacock.

Idiot.

On the negative side, he might not sleep well tonight.

When the movie was over, she pulled her legs up to her chest and buried her face in her knees.

"Duchess? You okay?"

She let out a cry when he touched her back, nearly falling off the sofa. He had to snatch her up and pulling her onto his lap. He held her shaking form in his arms, rocking her back and forth.

"No more zombie movies," he dictated.

He peered out the windows, wishing he'd pulled the drapes. Fuck. He was meant to be the big, bad bodyguard. He wasn't supposed to be scared of something that was fiction.

But zombies *were* terrifying.

Juliet pulled back to give him a sad look.

"Wait. You like them?"

She nodded.

Christ. He ran his hand over his face. "Will you even sleep tonight?"

She rocked her hand from side to side, meaning it was debatable.

He tapped her nose reprovingly. She already looked like she didn't get enough sleep. "If you get scared tonight, I want you to come find me."

She bit her lip nervously.

"Promise," he said firmly. "Or you're not leaving my sight. I don't want you having nightmares or being too scared to go to sleep."

What had he been doing, letting her watch that? She'd gotten to him with her big eyes.

"Besides, it's not like I'm going to be sleeping much tonight."

She grinned.

"Are you laughing at me? Because I'm now terrified a zombie is going to eat me?"

She giggled. There he went, puffing up like a peacock again.

"So mean, making me watch a zombie movie."

Her mouth opened and he thought she might speak. Then she frowned, looking frustrated.

"Easy," he told her. "I can wait as long as you need to. Even if it takes forever."

She relaxed in his arms and he knew he'd guessed the reason for her frustration. Made him feel even more like an asshole for the way he'd treated her earlier. It was obvious that not speaking wasn't a choice.

He just wished he knew why she couldn't talk to him. She'd spoken to the sheriff and her friend.

It had to be about trust. He just had to hope once she trusted him fully, she'd speak to him.

Until then, he'd be patient.

Leaning in, he kissed the tip of her nose, then her forehead, then both cheeks.

She tilted her head as though wanting his lips on hers. But he drew back.

She let out a small noise of protest and he had to hold back his smile.

"You're beautiful, you know."

She shook her head immediately. He'd expected that reaction. Most women didn't seem to see their worth. Juliet's beauty didn't hit you over the head. It was quiet. It snuck up on you. Then pow! It smacked you over the head when you weren't even looking.

"So beautiful. I could hold you all night. But you need sleep."

She shook her head.

"Yes. Sleep."

Standing, he drew her up next to him. He tried to discreetly adjust himself, but she stared down at him with wide eyes.

"Gonna need a cold shower tonight."

A smile crossed her lips.

That cold shower?

Totally worth it.

14

Juliet stumbled into the kitchen, moving towards the fridge.

"Good morning, Duchess."

Urgh. Was it?

Ahh. Mocha coffee. Sweet elixir of the Gods. She grabbed a can, letting out a cry as it was plucked from her hands.

No! What cruelty was this? She chased after the can, nearly crashing into the jerk holding it.

She held out her hands in the universal sign for gimme.

Or in her case, 'gimme my coffee before I kill you, you rat bastard'.

Brick raised an eyebrow with a laugh. "Oh, like that, is it? You haven't been this anti-social in the mornings before."

That's because she usually caffeinated before she came downstairs. But she'd run out of coffee drinks upstairs.

She huffed out a breath, staring at the coffee.

He read the back of the can. "This is filled with sugar."

Who was he? The coffee police?

"You can have it back—"

Damn right she could. Or he was toast. TOAST.

Her hand balled up into a fist. She knew how to hit. Reuben had taught her how to make a proper fist. If Brick thought she wouldn't dick punch him then he didn't know her well.

"Okay, Duchess. Not liking the way you're looking at my dick. I'm going to hand this over to you."

She pretty much snatched it out of his hand then opened it, gulping it down. By the time it was gone, she was feeling halfway decent.

Only now, she had a frowning man staring at her disapprovingly.

What was his problem?

"Are you addicted to these?"

Well, if by addicted he meant she needed at least five a day to survive and often substituted them for meals then . . .

"I'm going to take that as a yes. How many do you drink a day?"

Why was he asking her to do math? She hated math. She held up the fingers on one hand then shrugged.

He sighed. "As long as they're not replacing meals."

She smiled brightly. He gave her a skeptical look. Okay, so he wasn't buying her bullshit. Yeah, she wouldn't buy it either. She caught a glimpse of herself in the mirror on the opposite wall. She looked deranged.

Not good.

"Breakfast time."

She looked longingly at the fridge. She could really use another caffeine boost. She pulled herself up onto a stool. That's when it hit her. He wasn't wearing a shirt.

Holy. Shit.

He wasn't wearing a shirt. How had she not noticed that? Was she blind? Dead?

The man was seriously built. Muscles galore. And as he turned, she saw he had a tattoo high up on his back.

Strength over fear.

She wondered when he'd gotten that. And if she could lick it?

Lick it? Jeez, Juliet. You can't just lick him to lay claim. What are you? Six?

Well, sometimes. But she could also go younger.

She knew she had to tell him about her Little. But not yet.

He slid a plate of something in front of her. Sheesh. Could he fit any more food on here? There was bacon, scrambled eggs, poached eggs, hash browns, grilled mushrooms, sausages, and toast.

He couldn't seriously expect her to eat all of this.

Another plate was put down next to her and he sat. "Eat."

She didn't know where to start. She was overwhelmed. He didn't seem to have that problem as he dug in.

Then he paused and brushed his hand over hers. "Eat, Duchess."

Elias and Sterling walked in. Sterling looked more tired than she did, although he perked up when he saw all the food.

"Yes! Brick's breakfasts are the bomb! No pancakes?" Elias pouted, making her smile. It looked silly to see the huge man pouting.

"Not today. Protein and carbs. Pancakes are too much sugar."

Elias rolled his eyes and grumbled under his breath. She didn't blame him, pancakes were the bomb. The others sat and gave her the distraction needed so that Brick wasn't all focused on her.

Or so she'd thought. Probably should have known better.

"You don't have to eat it all, Duchess," he whispered in her ear, making her shiver. "But you need to eat some."

The 'or else' was left off the threat. But she heard it anyway. She gathered up some scrambled egg on her fork.

"So, what are you kids up to today?" Sterling asked. "Got any idea what to do with your days now you're no longer working, Juliet?"

Elias slapped him around the head.

"Hey! What?" He rubbed his head.

"Not cool pointing out that she doesn't have a job."

"I need to have a word with your boss," Brick said. "He should hold your job open."

She looked around for her whiteboard. Damn, where was it?

"Here." Sterling grabbed one from the top drawer of the kitchen cupboard. She stared at the brand-new whiteboard in surprise. His cheeks grew red. "Ah, hope you don't mind, but I put a few throughout the house and pool house. In case we needed them."

"Aw, look at you being all sweet," Elias teased.

Sterling slapped him around the back of the head this time. It looked like they were about to erupt into a tumble when Brick cleared his throat.

"Don't worry about them, Duchess. They still think they're fifteen rather than nearly forty."

I didn't like that job anyway.

Brick raised his eyebrows. "Why did you work there, then? It's not like you need the money."

Elias groaned. "I give up on the two of you. Idiots."

How could she explain this to people who had probably never had a day of doubt about themselves in their lives? Who had likely never lain in bed without the energy or will to get out?

Sometimes doing something you hate is better than doing nothing at all.

"Now you have an opportunity to do something you want to do," Elias said quickly with a smile. But what was the point of another job? What could she even do? Nothing.

She was useless.

Excuse me. I'm full. Thanks for breakfast.

Climbing off the stool, she headed out of the room.

. . .

Fuck.

What had just happened? He watched her walk out, shoulders slumped. It was clear she was sad.

He raced after her, found her halfway up the second set of stairs.

"Juliet! Wait!"

She gasped and missed the next step, flying backward. He braced himself, catching her.

"Fuck, baby. Fuck. Are you all right?" He carried her to the landing, setting her down so he could run his hands over her. Once again, she was wearing a black dress that covered her from neck to toes.

When he finished patting her down, he noticed how red she was. "You're flushed. Are you hot? You should put on something lighter."

She shook her head, stepping back away from him.

"How did you trip? Is there something wrong with that step?"

Another shake. But he noticed she wasn't looking at him. Her gaze was on her feet.

"I'm sorry if I said something to hurt you."

Her head rose and she stared at him.

"Linda always said I had no tact. I was always saying the wrong thing, putting my foot in my mouth."

She grabbed her phone out and typed something then showed it to him.

It's not anything you said. I hated that job, but it gave me a push to leave the house. If I don't have a reason to get up and leave, then I'm worried I'll stay in this house forever.

He read her words twice, thinking over what to say.

Just say it. Trying to be tactful will give you an ulcer.

She had a cheeky grin on her face.

"Brat." He let out a breath. "I had these ideas of what you'd be like, and you're nothing like what I thought."

You thought I'd be sane and normal? Not looney-tunes?

He frowned. "Putting yourself down isn't allowed." Taking hold of her hand, he led her to the stairs. Sitting, he patted the stair next to him. She placed her hand on his shoulder to steady herself as she sat, and at her touch, a thrill of heat raced through him.

He held out his hand and she slid hers into it.

"I like touching you."

She typed one-handed. *Same. You make me feel safe.*

"Good, baby. Because you're always safe with me." Leaning over, he kissed the top of her head, breathing her in. "You're in the unique position of having time to find a job you really want to do. If you're worried you'll become a recluse, then we'll come up with different reasons for you to get out and about."

She gave him a shy smile then leaned her head against his arm. He just sat there for a moment. "I don't like you putting your-self down."

She tensed.

"Do it again and you'll go over my knee, understand?"

I've never been spanked.

"Hm, that explains things."

She leaned back to smack his arm playfully, rolling her eyes.

"No hitting, little girl."

I'm not little.

She was kidding him, right? She was tiny.

"So, you haven't changed your mind? About being with me? We don't have to rush into, um, bedroom stuff."

She grinned at him and he let out an exasperated breath. "Yeah, I realize I sound like an eighty-year-old spinster."

A small giggle escaped her.

"Hey, are you laughing at me, brat?" He started tickling her, and her giggles turned into gales of laughter. Then he drew her onto his lap. As her giggles died away, he wrapped his hand around the back of her neck, then kissed her.

She was stiff for a start and he worried he'd made a mistake. But then she melted beneath him. But still, he kept the kiss light. Not wanting to push her too hard. When he drew back, she looked dazed, flushed.

Perfect. "I like kissing you."

She smiled. *Like kissing you too. I want to be with you.*

"Thank fuck." He kissed the tip of her nose then drew back. "Right. Then we need to go over the rules."

That smile dimmed slightly and worry filled her face.

"You already have safety rules. Those still stand. When it comes to your safety, you're to obey our orders immediately. Next rule, you have to spend at least an hour a day snuggled up on my knee."

She gave him a shocked look then her lips curled up in a smile.

"Breaking that one comes with severe consequences," he warned. "At least ten minutes of tickling."

Who was he? Where was the big bad Dom?

But he had gotten her to loosen up in his arms.

She was already softening his harsh corners. But he wanted to be softer for her.

"If I say the wrong thing, hurt you, then you don't shut me out. You tell me. Got me? Communication is important."

You'll do the same?

"Yep, it's not always my strong point, but I'll try. You feel sick, unsure, scared, I want to know."

Biting her lip, she nodded.

"I don't expect to know all your secrets right away, but I can't abide lies. That's a trigger for me. You'll tell me when you're ready. That will do for the moment. There might be more later. Any hard limits?"

No name-calling. Or humiliation.

"That won't ever happen."

No blood or scars.

Fuck. He wouldn't want to make her bleed anyway. He wasn't a sadist or that hard core.

"But spanking with my hand is fine? Maybe later with a paddle or the belt, that okay?"

She nodded shyly. *Yes.*

"We need to figure out a way you can safeword. Maybe a squeaky toy during punishment."

She nodded, looking shy.

"How about this? We'll go for a swim then I'll read one of your books to you. Tonight is your quiz night, right? You still want to go?"

Excitement filled her face and he was glad he hadn't told her she couldn't go. It had been tempting. She'd be safer here, but he didn't want to take away everything from her.

Yes.

"Meet you downstairs in fifteen. Don't go into the water without me."

15

Brick took one look at Juliet and shook his head. "Nope."

She paused at the bottom of the stairs and gave him a confused look. Then she glanced down at herself.

"Go change your shoes."

Exasperation filled her face. She took another step down.

Lord, she was trouble.

But the very best kind.

He moved closer and clasped her around the waist to whisper in her ear. "We're gonna be late if I have to take the time to spank your ass. Either way, you're changing your shoes. Now, it's your choice if you sit comfortably or not tonight."

A tiny sound of irritation escaped her. It was weird, but he treasured each noise he managed to extract from her like they were expensive jewels.

Pulling back, she got out her phone to type him a message. *What's wrong with them?*

"They're too high. You'll trip in them and break your neck."

Did she just . . . yep, she rolled her eyes at him.

"Three."

She frowned.

Three what?

"I'm counting down. If I get to one and you haven't started up those stairs, you're in trouble."

Her mouth opened in shock. He had to bite back a grin. Damn, he enjoyed playing with her. Although he wasn't playing about the shoes. She wasn't going out in them.

"Two."

With a huff, she turned.

"And take the shoes off before you attempt to climb the stairs."

Another huff. But she did as she was told. Satisfaction filled him. He had this under control. She absolutely knew who the boss was.

As she came back down the stairs, he realized that his assumptions were just that.

Because there she was, clutching at the banister as she took each step carefully, wearing black stilettos that had to be at least eight inches high.

She couldn't even walk on them. With each step, she wobbled. Damn fool woman was about to fall and break her neck.

And she'd done the exact opposite of what he'd just told her to. Storming forward, he plucked her off the steps before she could even get to the bottom. Then he swung her over his shoulder.

She let out a squeal that had Elias and Sterling racing into the foyer.

"What's going on?" Elias asked as he started back up the stairs.

"Someone needs new shoes," he called back, smacking his hand on her ass as she tried to wiggle away from him. "And an attitude adjustment."

She let out an outraged gasp that was drowned by the bark of laughter from below. She stiffened.

"They're not laughing at you," he reassured her gently. "Both of them are Doms too. And they're laughing at me."

Probably because they'd never seen him act like this. He'd always kept his head when playing. Control was important to him. But this brat had him tied in knots and the thing was . . . he didn't ever want to be set free.

As he moved up the stairs, he smacked her ass in between scolding her.

"Going to break your damn neck." *Smack! Smack!*

"No high heels." *Smack! Smack!*

"Got half a mind to go through all your shoes." *Smack! Smack!*

They'd reached the landing on the third floor, and he set her down gently. He knew she wouldn't appreciate him barreling through into her private rooms. Although he was curious. What did her bedroom look like? Was it all done in black?

She gaped at him as he crouched in front of her. "Hands on my shoulders." Without argument, which was likely due to her shock, she put her hands on his shoulders and lifted each of her feet. He pulled her high heels off and kept hold of them as he stood.

"Now, go put on some sensible shoes, because we're not leaving until I approve of them."

Beautiful hazel eyes studied him then she stomped her foot and turned to the door.

"Unless you want me to choose?"

She shook her head and held out her hand for the high heels.

"Oh no, you're not getting these back. Not until you convince me you can walk in normal shoes without falling over."

With a pout and a flounce, she turned to her door and he headed downstairs.

Brat.

CRAP. It was fifteen minutes until the quiz began. If she was late, then Kiesha would never let her hear the end of it. She shifted around anxiously on the front passenger seat. Elias and Sterling had taken the back seat. Brick reached over and placed his hand on her thigh, stilling her nervous movements.

"Easy," he told her in that low voice of his. She should be pissed off at him. He'd not only made her change her shoes. Twice. But he'd spanked her ass. Okay, she had gotten a bit bratty. But he was high-handed.

Grumpy-Butt.

Even though she'd stopped shifting around like a toddler needing the toilet, or a woman who'd had her butt smacked, Brick kept his hand on her thigh. It was hot and heavy. And it felt like a brand.

As though he was claiming her.

That made her insides rejoice, heat filling her.

She was in such trouble.

She still couldn't believe he'd thrown her over his shoulder and smacked her ass while carrying her up the stairs.

Damn caveman.

It was kind of sexy though, too.

Lord, Juliet. What have you gotten yourself messed up in?

When he pulled up outside the Wishing Well, Brick squeezed her leg while the other two got out. "Remember the rules?"

He'd gone over the rules this afternoon. Several times. She'd had to promise to a whole lot of ridiculous demands. Their table would be at the back of the room with a wall behind them. She wouldn't move more than two feet away from him at all times. If he wasn't there, she had to stick by Elias or Sterling.

If she needed to go to the toilet, one of them was to go with her.

No leaving on her own.

Then he'd handed her an alarm button that, if pressed, would emit a loud screeching noise, and a necklace with a GPS chip.

If she hadn't wanted to come tonight so badly, she might have argued with him. But she had given in. Not graciously, but hey, what did he really expect?

She gave him a salute.

"Juliet," he warned. "This isn't the same as wearing high shoes or getting into the swimming pool on your own. I get that I'm over-protective. Always been that way of people I care about, of which there aren't many. Maybe because I'm stifling."

She slapped his thigh and pointed her finger at him warningly. She caught his grin.

"But this is your safety. You fail to obey me, and I won't hesitate to haul your ass out of there. And I guarantee, you won't be back there until I know the risk to you is eliminated."

He grasped hold of her chin, it was firm without being threatening. "Understand me? Your safety comes first. Above everything else."

Butterflies moved through her tummy, growing bigger and bigger until she could barely breathe. But in a good way.

A really good way.

She nodded. Then like a good girl, she waited until he came around and lifted her down.

"Still think you need a booster."

That was the sort of thing a Daddy might say, right?

Suddenly, she felt exhausted from all of the secrets she held. Why couldn't life be simple? Then again, simple would be boring, right?

When they reached the door to the bar, it opened and someone half-stumbled out singing a bawdy Irish song.

Irish Mick.

He wasn't actually Irish, but he had red hair and when he got drunk, he sang this really vulgar song with a bad Irish accent.

Brick clamped his hands over her ears just as he got to the good part. Like she hadn't heard it a thousand times before.

"This place seems like fun." Elias rubbed his hands together. She didn't know where Sterling had gone, maybe he had to pee.

"Juliet! Ye better get in there, darlin', it's about to start." Irish Mick wobbled away.

"That was the worst Irish accent I've ever heard," Elias stated as he moved ahead to open the door.

When the door opened again, the noise hit her. Nerves jangled, the way they did every week. She both loved and loathed quiz night. She enjoyed being with her friends and the quiz itself. But being surrounded by all those people made her really anxious.

Moving towards Brick, she twisted her hand in his shirt under his jacket. He paused and glanced down at her. "You want to go home?"

She shook her head.

He didn't move so she gave him a nudge. She could handle this. She just got really anxious in these situations.

He moved her hand off his shirt and she let out a distressed noise.

"Easy, Duchess. Just hold on to the other side in case I have to go for my gun."

Right, she remembered that instruction now.

Brick moved forward and she slid up so close to him that she was bumping into him as he walked. She was probably putting wrinkles in his shirt.

Elias stepped in behind her and she had to remind herself that she knew him. That she was comfortable with him. It was only because of the situation that she felt so on edge. She glanced around.

"There's Sterling." Elias pointed to a table near the back, but she couldn't see anyone over this crush. Had Sterling come in to find her friends?

"He's talking to a tiny blonde wearing a sparkly dress and cowboy boots," Elias explained, seeing her issue.

Isa. She nodded.

Brick started moving and she walked behind him. People got out of his way immediately. He had that effect on people. She shivered, a weird feeling coming over her. Almost like being watched. She shook that off, though. Most of the bar probably had their eyes on her right now.

Weirdo Juliet with the two hunky men.

This would fuel the gossip mill for a while. She kept her gaze down, though. She knew from experience that looking around would just overwhelm her. Too much noise, too many colors and scents.

Sensory overload. So, she kept her gaze down and trusted Brick to get her safely to where she needed to go.

"Juliet! About time! We thought we were actually going to have to do some of the work tonight."

She looked up as Kiesha came barreling towards her. The other woman stopped and bared her teeth at Brick. "You."

Brick stared down at her. "You."

Kiesha pointed over at Sterling who was smiling at something Isa said while Cleo poured them all drinks from a huge pitcher. She wondered what was in it. Maybe she'd have a drink tonight. She didn't usually drink because it didn't mix well with her anxiety medication. But had she even taken that medication today? She couldn't remember, she wasn't great at remembering that sort of thing.

"I get that you sent him in to butter us up. But while Isa might be charmed, I'm not. And I'm watching you." Kiesha used two fingers to point at her eyes then at Brick. She did the same to Elias. "You too, cutie-pie. I don't trust any of you. You hurt my girl and I will come after you. See how you like driving on slashed tires."

Juliet tried to pull away to talk to Kiesha, but Brick held her back, glaring down at Kiesha. "You won't go anywhere near our tires."

"Oh yeah, why's that?"

"Because we drove Juliet here and you won't want your friend waiting in the cold while we get our other vehicle."

His answer took all the fight out of Kiesha. "Jeez, it's no fun fighting if you're gonna be all logical and shit."

Juliet had to hide a smile.

"Just watch yourself," Kiesha told him. "Juliet has all of us at her back and we ain't afraid to get dirty, if you know what I mean."

"Who's getting dirty?" Cleo asked with a frown. Cleo was tall, gorgeous, and very serious. She was in a relationship with the owner of The Wishing Well, Noah.

"We are, if they hurt Juliet."

"Who hurt Juliet?" Isa interjected. "Who are we hurting? Let me at'em."

Isa was tiny and tough. Also, her housemate was a crazy dude who knew how to kill a person and hide the body so nobody would ever find them. Nobody messed with Isa.

Speaking of Loki, she spotted him across the room sitting with his friends.

"Your team is going down tonight," he yelled out across the bar when he saw her looking. "Loki's Warriors are gonna win."

"Loki's Warriors," his friends all chanted.

"Not a chance, boys," Kiesha called back. "You should just give up now. Maybe go home and get in your jammies and ring your mommies because that will be less humiliating than the ass-whipping you're about to get."

"Oh good, I didn't miss the trash talk."

Juliet looked over as Georgie approached with Ed walking slightly behind her. He frowned at Brick, taking in Elias and Sterling.

"Georgie!" Kiesha cried, wrapping the other woman in her arms. "It's been so long!"

"I just saw you three hours ago," Georgie pointed out dryly.

"Yeah, a whole three hours. You've delivered her now, Ed, bye-bye." Kiesha shooed the sheriff. "It's about to kick off."

"Wait, weren't we going to kick off with whoever hurt Juliet?" Isa asked.

"Who hurt Juliet?" Ed rumbled.

"What's this about Juliet being hurt?" Noah asked as he approached with a pitcher of water. "Someone hurt you, sweetheart?"

Brick stiffened and she slid her hand into his without thinking. She should have known better. Eagle-eyed Kiesha spotted the movement straight away. She sucked in a breath.

"Oh, you've got some explaining to do." She reached for Juliet.

Brick frowned down at her, stepping between them.

"Listen here, bodyguard boy—"

Thankfully, before Kiesha could finish the threat, Red spoke into the microphone. He ran the quizzes each Thursday night.

"Five minutes until we start, ladies and gents, so grab your tables and get ready."

"Loki's Warriors are ready for war," Loki roared.

Noah turned to him, hands on his hips. "Fun, Loki. This is a quiz for fun."

"There's no fun in love and war."

"That doesn't even make any sense." Noah shook his head, turning to Isa. "Isa, he's your problem tonight."

"Loki's harmless, Noah," Isa said with exasperation.

"He doesn't look harmless." Brick frowned.

Ed, who was close enough to hear him, glanced over. "Don't worry, Loki would cut off his hand before he hurt anyone."

"But he is fond of kidnapping women he considers spoils of war," Georgie added.

"What?" Brick snapped, drawing Juliet close to his side.

The sheriff watched them. "You're awfully hands-on, even for a bodyguard. Something we need to know?"

"Nothing that has anything to do with the law."

Ed raised his eyebrows. "Yeah? And what about as Juliet's friend?"

"If she wants you to know, then she'll tell you," Brick replied.

Ed studied her and she smiled at him, sending him a wink. His eyebrows rose. "All right, then. Take it Reuben doesn't know?"

The whole bar seemed to quieten at her brother's name coming from Ed's lips, but she knew that couldn't actually be the case.

She shook her head.

"Thank Christ for that."

Brick gave him a curious look and Ed kissed Georgie. "I'm going to sit at the next table."

"Good. No men allowed," Cleo said loudly. She smacked Noah on the ass as he turned away. He spun and gave her a look that had her smiling.

Then he glanced at Juliet. "Sure, you're okay?"

She nodded as she slid into the chair that Brick pulled back for her. Always a gentleman.

Noah glanced at Brick with narrowed eyes. "Juliet has a lot of friends here."

She sucked in a breath, wondering how Brick would react to the threat in Noah's voice. Noah was generally pretty easy-going, but he had another side to him that was rarely roused unless Cleo was threatened.

And apparently, when he thought there might be some sort of threat to her. Which she hadn't realized.

"I can see that. I'm glad she has all of you. But she has me now too. And I'm not going anywhere."

"I like him," Isa said loudly.

"I don't." Kiesha glared at him.

"I'm on the fence. He has to prove himself," Cleo said with a sniff. Cleo wasn't fond of most people. Her being on the fence was as good as he could have hoped for.

"I'm a bit on the fence myself," Elias added with a grin as Brick glared at him.

"I'm with Cleo," Noah said. "Needs to prove himself worthy."

"Maybe we should strip him and send him out into the woods with a packet of matches and see if he survives," Kiesha said with a toothy grin.

Ed groaned. "I told you to stop watching *Naked and Afraid*."

"What do you say, Brick? You want to be out in the woods? Naked and afraid?" Kiesha asked as she pulled a sucker from her pocket and pulled off the wrapper.

"No."

That was all Brick said and Juliet had to hide another grin.

Brick leaned over her. "You need anything, you get my attention. I'm going to be standing by the wall behind you. Elias is over there. Sterling on the other side of you." They formed almost a triangle around her.

Sheesh, she wasn't stupid. Of course, she remembered. They'd only spoken about it again before coming into the bar. She'd been here hundreds of times without incident.

As he settled against the wall behind her, Kiesha leaned over. "Is he just the bodyguard? Or is there something more going on?"

The others leaned in.

Shit. She was going to need something to give her some courage.

She slid close to her friend to whisper. "Pour me a drink and I'll tell you."

Kiesha's eyes widened. "Holy. Shit."

"What?" Isa asked.

"What is it?" Cleo demanded.

"Are you okay, Juliet?" Georgie sat next to her, looking concerned.

"Juliet wants a drink," Kiesha stated.

Cleo and Isa just stared at her.

"So?" Georgie appeared confused.

"Juliet never drinks. Not once. Not ever," Kiesha explained.

She blushed. She shouldn't have asked.

"No reason why she can't have one, is there?" Georgie asked.

Well, other than her medication. But one drink wouldn't hurt, right?

Georgie poured her a glass. "Here you are. Go slow, though. If you're not used to it, these concoctions of Noah's can go straight to your head."

JULIET WAS DRUNK.

Not just a bit drunk, but she was headed to completely intoxicated drunk.

Maybe he should have stopped her. He'd considered it. But she'd only had one and a half glasses.

His girl was a lightweight.

And yes, somehow, despite spending half her time giggling over nothing, she'd managed to slaughter everyone else at quiz night. Her team didn't seem to do much but sit around and chat. While Juliet got every question right.

Damn, she was brilliant. That was sexy as fuck.

Elias stared over at him, wriggling his eyebrows as though to ask whether Brick was seeing the same thing he was.

Brick shrugged.

"And the winners are, Beersal Suspects!"

Kiesha and Isa jumped to their feet, high-fiving. Cleo

continued to file her nails although she smiled. The sheriff's woman was congratulating Juliet.

"Loki's Warriors are defeated," the big man across the room cried out. "The defeat is crushing."

"Told you, Loki," Kiesha said, shaking her head. "Face it. You're never going to beat us."

"I can do it. All I need to do is turn one of your own." He spun towards Juliet.

Brick stepped forward, moving closer to Juliet. Not happening.

Loki climbed onto his table, then he dropped to one knee. "Marry me, Juliet. Run away with me. We'll hide in the mountains where Reuben will never find us."

The room hushed.

And his possessive instincts went into overdrive. Before he could stop himself, it barreled out of him.

"She's taken," he boomed into the silence.

Now the whole room was gaping at him as she turned to stare up at him in shock. Okay, maybe he shouldn't have said that in front of half the town . . . but no, screw it.

"Oh fuck, if Reuben didn't know before, he will now," Kiesha said.

"I'm just glad I didn't spend any time getting to know you," Cleo added, not bothering to look up from her nails, "since you're a dead man."

16

Had he really just done that? Declared that she was his to all of Wishingbone? Okay, not the entire population. But about a lot of the town was here tonight.

Reuben was going to explode.

"Sorry I did that." He crouched next to her. "Juliet?"

He was sorry? Because he didn't mean it? Or because Reuben was going to murder him?

"Did you just say you were sorry you claimed her?" Kiesha scowled at him. "Why? Because you didn't mean it?"

"No," Brick snapped back. But he didn't explain himself further. "We should have this conversation in private."

"I don't think so," Kiesha said.

The other women all nodded and he noticed that the sheriff had moved closer with a frown.

Brick sighed and looked around. "I would rather get out of here, Duchess."

"Duchess?" Cleo asked. "Why Duchess?"

"None of your business."

Juliet frowned at him. These were her friends.

He grimaced. "Sorry. I don't have the best social filter."

"You want us to trust you with Juliet, then maybe you should start talking to us," Isa pointed out.

"She isn't going with you until we know she's going to be okay," Kiesha added.

"I would never harm her." Brick gave them all an insulted look. Of course, he wouldn't.

"Not physically," Cleo said pointedly.

"Why did you claim her if you didn't mean it?" Kiesha demanded. "We're not going to let you play around with her feelings."

"I didn't say I didn't mean it," he told them. "Just that I was sorry for blurting it out like that. We're meant to be going slow."

She smiled at him. Or she thought she did. It was hard to tell when her face felt kind of numb. She pressed her fingers to her lips. They were definitely curled up. Oh good.

"Also, Juliet is capable of making her own decisions."

They all gave him surprised looks while she sat up straight. She was capable, wasn't she? And she would just have to tell Reuben that this was her choice. She was an adult. And he could just butt out. Okay, she wouldn't say it like that.

She whispered to Kiesha, "Tell him I won't let Reuben kill him."

"She said that she won't let Reuben kill you," Kiesha repeated.

He eyed her. "Nobody is killing me. I'm guessing she doesn't drink much?"

"No, never," Kiesha told him. "But it isn't because she's drunk that she's worried about Reuben killing you."

"Yeah, you should be worried too," Cleo told him dryly.

No, he shouldn't. Because she would protect him.

Irritation filled his face. "I don't know why you all have this strange fear of him. He's just a man."

Everyone stared at him.

"You've never met him in person, have you?" Cleo asked.

"No. I've talked to him, though. I'm sure he's a reasonable man."

The whole table, including her, gaped at him. She lightly patted his cheek. Good thing he was so damn sexy. She moved her fingers to his lips, trying to get them to turn up in a smile.

"Duchess, we need to get you home. You're sloshed."

"So, you really are claiming her and risking Reuben's wrath?" Cleo asked.

"If he's that upset, I'll quit."

No. He couldn't quit. She didn't want him to walk away. She sniffled.

"Hey, I'm not going anywhere, Duchess." He took her hands gently away from his face. "I'm not leaving you."

"Wow, that's so romantic," Isa said on a sigh. She watched them with a dreamy expression on her face, her chin on the palm of her hand, elbow on the table. "Kiesha said you were a dick, but I think it's just an act. You're marshmallow on the inside, aren't you?"

Kiesha snorted. "He's not marshmallow."

"I'm not marshmallow," he stated at the same time. "Jesus."

She had to giggle at the indignant look on his face. That was cute. Because he totally was marshmallow under the gruff exterior.

Big old marshmallow.

Hm. That made her want s'mores. Yum-yum.

"Juliet, you with me?" He cupped her face between his hands.

Of course, she was, where else would she be?

"You know that it won't matter to Reuben if you quit or not," Kiesha told him. "Not with you playing hide the sausage with his little sister."

"Juliet is an adult. He'll respect her decision."

Her friends all just stared at him sadly. Yeah, he was delusional if he thought that. In his defense, he didn't know Reuben like the rest of them did.

"If I'm not working for him, I don't see what his objection to me being with Juliet would be."

Isa sighed. "If only you hadn't declared it to the whole room. We could have kept this a secret, but someone is going to tell him."

That was true. Darn it.

"I still think you're all exaggerating."

"When we were sophomores, we had this awful calculus teacher," Cleo told him. "He was really mean. He told Juliet that she was dumb. The next week, these photos of him started to circulate. Pictures of him in compromising positions with the old lady of the president of a biker gang a few towns over. The gang rode into town and he was never seen again."

"And you're saying Reuben did that?" Brick asked skeptically.

"I'm saying he'll do that and worse for his sister."

Juliet studied him closely. Would that horrify him? Would he run? Most men wouldn't want to risk being with her. Of course, most men wouldn't get past the fact that she couldn't talk to them.

Hm. She wondered if the alcohol would help her talk. Worked for Raj on *The Big Bang Theory*. She opened her mouth and tried to form words. Nothing happened.

"Duchess? You okay?"

"I think she's trying to talk," Kiesha said.

"Or she's having a fit," Cleo added.

"Or about to puke," Isa supplied.

"Okay, that's it. Come on." Brick stood and held out his hand to her. As she stood, the whole world spun and she giggled. Brick leaned into her and she attempted to hold him up. Whoa, he was heavy.

"Duchess? What are you doing?"

"I think she's trying to pick you up," Kiesha said with a giggle. "Juliet, wanna dance?"

"I don't know if that's a good idea," Georgie said.

"No, it's not," Ed added. He crossed his arms over his chest. "Think you best get her home."

Who? Her? Aw. That wasn't fair. It wasn't her bedtime. Did she have a bedtime? Who cared? She was a big girl!

"What is she doing now?" Cleo asked.

"Dancing?" Isa said skeptically. "I think."

"Come on, Duchess." Brick tugged her close and she spun out of his hold with a laugh, trying to move to the dance floor.

"Nope. You're not going anywhere without me."

Oh yay! He was going to dance with her. She hadn't thought he'd be the dancing type. She grabbed his hands and started moving them back and forth.

Was someone watching her? She tried to look around, but all the faces were starting to blur together.

Hm. That felt weird.

"Duchess," a low voice warned.

Ooh, that sent a shiver up her spine.

"We're going home now."

She shook her head. Whoops. More spinning. Bright lights. Fun!

Then she suddenly felt herself flying. Ooh, she could fly? She'd never tried to fly. Maybe she could be like Superman. She should totally try that. All she needed was a cape. Did she have a cape at home?

She put her arms out in front of her. She was totally going to fly!

"Juliet? Juliet, look at me."

She tried to look at Ed, but he was kind of upside down. He leaned into her. "You okay going home with Brick, or you want to come with me and Georgie?"

She loved Georgie. And Ed. But she wanted Brick.

"I'm gonna fly, Ed," she whispered to him as he bent down close to her mouth.

"No, sweetheart. You're not."

"Uh-huh."

"Think you better go home with me."

"No. Brick. Want Brick."

"You sure? You're drunk, you're not exactly making good decisions."

"Brick," she whispered. "Mine."

"Okay, sweetheart." Then he disappeared. She thought he might have said something about flying. That reminded her. She was going to fly.

Whee!

Then something rocked her. Oh. That didn't feel good. That felt like she might throw up.

"Careful you don't end up with puke down your back," someone said. Who was that? Who was going to throw up? Why would they do it down someone else's back?

Why did she want to throw up? Where was she? Why was the ground moving under her? Was she flying?

"Better than her trying to fly her way out of here."

That was Brick. Who was flying? Her? That sounded like so much fun. If she wasn't feeling so sick.

Wait. What was that? There was a mighty fine ass right in front of her face. Well, she couldn't let that go to waste, right? If someone was going to put their mighty fine ass in front of her, then she was going to squeeze it.

She grabbed it hard.

"Holy shit!"

She was jostled.

"What happened?"

"She just squeezed my ass."

Someone started laughing and she smiled. She must have

done a good job. She started hitting it. One-two. One-one-two-two. This was fun.

"Juliet, stop smacking my ass."

But it was such a cute ass. But maybe she should go back to squeezing it. That was just as much fun. Squeeze. Slap.

"Thank fuck," Brick muttered, then she was flying again. Whee! She came to a stop facing him. He still had a hold on her, so her feet dangled in the air. She wrapped her legs around his waist.

Did he want to dance?

"Duchess, I have to put you down in your seat."

Seat? What seat? She stared behind her at Brick's truck. Aww, she didn't want to go home yet.

"Juliet," he said in a warning voice.

She liked it when he called her Duchess. Reaching up, she attempted to get his lips to say the word.

"Maybe you best hop into the back with her," someone suggested. "I don't think you'll like it if she starts doing that to one of us."

Brick just grunted.

When he tried to move her away from him, she let out a protest.

"It's okay, Duchess," he soothed. "I'm just putting you in your seat." He sat her down and pulled the belt over her.

Urgh, the seat belt was cutting right into her neck. She had already unclipped the belt by the time he got in the other side.

"Keep your belt on, Juliet," he warned.

Duchess. She was Duchess. She frowned at him as he reached over to do the belt up again.

She reached down to undo it.

"Undo that belt and you're going to bed with a hot bottom," he whispered into her ear.

She leaned into him. Did he promise? Peering up at him, she

realized how much she trusted this man. It was insane. She never trusted people. It took her a long time to let people close. What was it about him?

"What is it? Do I have something on my face?"

She shook her head as he wiped a hand over his face.

He was perfect. Perfectly perfect.

Huh, say perfect often enough in your head and it started to sound weird.

Oh. They were moving. Fresh air. She needed fresh air.

She hit the window button, lowering the window, then she stuck her head out into the cool air. That was good stuff.

"What are you doing? Get in here."

Brick tugged at her, but she ignored him, opening her mouth and sticking her tongue out. She'd always wondered why dogs liked doing that. Now she got it. Maybe she could lean out of the window and pretend she was flying. She got up onto her knees and attempted to lean out.

"Sit on your butt. Right now."

He was such a worrywart. He needed to stress less. Poor guy would give himself an ulcer. Or diarrhea.

"Juliet," he warned, before grabbing her and pulling her back in. The window rose.

What was he doing? She glared at him. He pointed a finger at her.

Plop. Into her mouth it went. Hm. He tasted pretty good. She worked her tongue around his finger.

"Juliet, let me go."

She munched on him lightly and heard him take in a breath. Oh. Was she hurting him?

But when she focused on his face, he didn't seem to be in pain. Well, not exactly. His breathing was coming in fast pants.

Then he leaned in and whispered in her ear. "Fuck, you have no idea what you're doing to me, do you?"

No. What was she doing? She swirled her tongue around his finger. To her surprise, he gave her another finger, pressing them into her mouth then out. A small groan erupted from him. Sterling turned from the front seat.

"Everything okay? How'd you get her to settle . . . okay, forget I interrupted."

"She's quiet, isn't she?" Brick grumbled.

"Yeah, man. Like you're not enjoying the hell out of that. It's all to keep her quiet. Yep, I'd believe that if you weren't steaming up the truck."

"Shut up, Sterling," Brick gritted out.

She jumped at the snap in his voice and stopped what she was doing. Was she annoying him? Hurting him? She never wanted to hurt Brick.

"Shh, baby," he crooned. "You just go back to what you were doing. I'm good. You're good."

Was he sure?

"Suck on my fingers. That's it. That's my good girl," he whispered in her ear.

The truck came to a stop, and she found herself sliding along the backseat of his truck, his fingers still in her mouth. Huh, when had he undone their seatbelts? Had she been wearing one? She hoped so. It was dangerous to drive without a seatbelt.

"Need help?" Elias asked.

"I got it," Brick told him as he pulled her up against his chest. She wrapped her arms and legs around him, trapping his arm between them as she continued to suck on his fingers.

"Yeah, we can see that. Ouch, Elias, stop hitting me!"

"Leave them alone," Elias replied. "We'll secure the place. You take care of Juliet."

"On it."

Where were they going? Hey, this was her house. Cool. They were going up the stairs? And he was carrying her.

Whoa. He was strong.

She continued to suck and lightly chew on his fingers. A feeling of contentment ran through her. Sure, it could be the booze. But she was pretty sure it was Brick.

He'd claimed her. In front of everyone.

People in Wishingbone took that seriously. She hoped he did too.

Suddenly, they came to a stop. She looked around. This wasn't her room. They were outside one of the spare bedrooms. Was this the one he was sleeping in?

But she wanted to go to her room.

"Duchess, you listening to me? Look at me."

Uh-oh. She got the feeling he might have been trying to talk to her for a while. She drew her mouth away from his fingers to smile up at him.

"Jeez, you're a lightweight, baby."

She wondered why she'd never taken up drinking before. This was fun. Then again, it might not be fun without Brick watching over her.

"Hey, listen to me. You want to stay with me in my room?"

She shook her head. That would be a no, rubber-ducky.

"You want to go to your room?"

Ten-four, rubber-ducky.

"Okay, easy, you keep nodding like that, and your head is going to fall right off the end of your neck."

She giggled. That was just silly.

"I don't want to leave you on your own, though."

Sleep-over! She'd never had one of those.

"Your brother said we weren't to go into your rooms unless you were in danger. You sure you're okay with me in there?"

Why wouldn't she be? Silly. She pointed towards the stairs then tightened her thighs around him.

"Are you trying to ride me like a horse?"

Ooh, now that was an idea. She wondered if she had something that would work as a bridle?

"I don't like the look on your face. Fuck, I hope this isn't a bad idea. Just in the morning, try to remember that you insisted on staying up here."

They reached her door and she leaned over to put the code into the keypad.

"Juliet, are you sure?" he asked, turning her face to his. "I can get someone else here to stay with you if you don't want me. What I can't do is leave you on your own."

She wiggled in his arms and he set her down, holding onto her hips. He was always so careful with her. Yet, at the same time, he was the first person in so long to treat her as though she wasn't some delicate mess.

She was sure that was how Xavier saw her. This mess he had to keep cleaning up.

Don't think about him. That's not fair to Brick.

Guilt filled her and she turned towards her door, pushing it open.

Something niggled in the back of her mind. Some reason she hadn't wanted Brick in here.

But that wouldn't come to her. Because she'd just remembered that she wanted to try flying. She was certain she had a cape in here somewhere. Stumbling forward, she sat on her beanbag with a plop and tugged off her shoes. Then she crawled over to her costumes space. Reuben had bought her this large mirror that had lights around it. It looked like it had come out of some old-school Hollywood dressing room.

Hell, maybe it had.

There was a make-up table in front of it with play make-up. Next to it was a spacious wardrobe filled with play outfits. She found a superhero cape after about a minute of looking and attempted to tie it around her neck.

"Duchess?" Brick asked in a low, quiet voice.

Oh. How had she forgotten he was there? Whoopsie! She spun around then held the cape out to him. She shook it when he didn't immediately take it.

"You want me to put the cape on you?" he asked her.

She nodded.

"Juliet, you sure you want me in here with you?"

Why did he keep asking that? And why wasn't he putting the cape on her already? She pointed at the cape then at her neck.

"All right. Why do you want the cape on?" he asked as he tied it. As soon as it was on, she put her arms out and started to run around the room. "You want to fly?"

There was something in his voice that she couldn't work out. She gave him a thumbs-up.

"You know you can't actually fly, right? You're just pretending."

Hm, but was she? Or could she fly, but she simply hadn't accessed the part of her mind that would let her do that?

She raced to the double doors that led to the patio and unlatched them.

"No."

Suddenly, Brick was there, reaching across her to lock the doors.

She glared up at him.

Crossing his arms over his chest, he gave her a firm look. "No."

She stomped her foot.

"Still no."

What a party-pooper. Maybe it was a bad idea to have him here. He was cute, though. In a really masculine, sexy way.

And the way he filled out a pair of jeans? Hallelujah. She wondered if he'd let her squeeze his butt again.

"Why do you look like you want to eat me?" he murmured. "Duchess, it's time for bed."

What? No way.

She pointed at the door.

"No, you're not going out there."

She narrowed her gaze. He wasn't the boss of her.

"I don't like the look on your face. Let me make that clear. Touch that door and you're in trouble, baby girl. I'll smack your bottom until you completely forget about flying and put you to bed on your tummy."

They stared at each other before she looked away. Drat him.

"Come on. Show me where your bed is."

But she didn't want to go to bed. She let out a pitiful sigh and gave him her best sad look.

"If you're a good girl and get ready for bed, I'll read you a story."

She thought about that. On the one hand, she really wanted to try her new-found flying skills. They were going to be epic. But on the other hand, Brick did have this really sexy voice. And when he read to her, she got chills all through her body.

Okay, she supposed she could go flying tomorrow. That skill wasn't going anywhere. She slid her hand into his and she led him into the bedroom.

He stilled and took in her bed as she moved to her bookcase to choose a book. Ah, there was another favorite book of hers. It was by CJ Bennett, about a Little with three daddies. Juliet wasn't sure she could handle one Daddy, and this girl had three riding her butt. And smacking it. A lot.

Turning, she found him running his hand along the top rail of her bed. She gave him a curious look.

"Haven't seen a bed like this. Looks comfy and safe."

She handed him the book.

"Right. I thought you might want a fairy tale or something. But this makes more sense."

She didn't know what he was talking about. She needed to get changed. She grabbed her pajamas and headed towards the attached bathroom.

"Do you need help, Duchess?" he asked.

Help? Why would she need help? She stumbled into the doorway with a giggle. He came over and steadied her.

"I think I should help you."

There was some reason why that was a bad idea, but what was it? She hummed a tune as he helped her pull the dress over her head. She noticed he kept his gaze averted as he handed her a pajama top. She was just wearing a camisole with a built-in bra, since her boobies were like two fried eggs. Nothing much to see. She slid on the satin, long-sleeved pajama top over her camisole. But didn't do up the buttons. Then he held out her pants for her to step into.

"Hold onto my shoulders."

She grasped hold then put her feet in, grabbing the bottoms to pull them up.

Oops, she had to pee. She moved towards the toilet.

"I'll wait in the bedroom."

She peed, washed her hands and brushed her teeth, then clumsily made her way back into the bedroom. Brick was waiting there with some painkillers and water, which he insisted she take.

Then he led her over to her bed. Crawling into it, she climbed under the covers and grabbed her pacifier with her favorite blankie attached.

But when she put it into her mouth, it just didn't have the right feel. Something started to build in her tummy. A nervousness that she couldn't pin down. Something was wrong.

She shuddered out a breath.

"What's wrong, Duchess?" Brick sat next to her bed on a bean bag he'd dragged over. He looked kind of funny, like he was about to topple out of it at any moment. She guessed they didn't make mountain man-sized beanbags. Or maybe they did, she just didn't own one.

She let out a frustrated noise because she had no clue what was wrong. But she was starting to feel anxious, and if she didn't do something about it, then it was going to turn into a panic attack.

Brick slid his arm through the rungs towards her.

He didn't resist as she grabbed his hand and sucked his fingers into her mouth. That was better.

And as she suckled on his fingers, he read to her in his deep, gravelly voice.

Sleep came surprisingly easy.

XAVIER MOVED around the grocery store in a tired haze.

After two delays with his flights, he'd gotten home late last night. His parents had tried all sorts of things to get him to stay. He was starting to think Reuben was right. That his mother faked an illness to get him to come see them. And then they'd hatched some plot to lure him there by dangling poor Yvonne in front of him.

Now, he was headed out to check on Juliet. It had been too late to go there last night, but he wanted to bring her something. Flowers. She liked flowers.

"Xavier? You okay?" He looked over to find Ed staring at him in concern. "I said your name and you didn't reply."

Shit. "Yeah. Sorry. Hi."

"Been at the hospital?"

"No, I went to see my parents for a few nights and got back late last night."

"Hi, Xavier," Georgie said with a smile as she walked towards them. "I haven't seen you for a few days."

"I've been out of town."

She turned to Ed. "Sorry that took so long, I got stopped by three different people who wanted to know who the guy with Juliet in the Wishing Well was last night. People around here sure do love gossip."

"Small town living," Ed replied. "Most people here live for gossip. And a guy laying claim to one of our own is big news. Even bigger news when it's the town's sweetest, quietest, gentlest resident."

Xavier felt like his world narrowed around him. Like everything else turned blurry. His heart raced, palms grew sweaty.

"What happened?"

Ed gave him a curious look. "You didn't hear already?"

"Hear what?"

"Guess if you got home late, you wouldn't have," Ed said.

"Heard what?" he asked between clenched teeth. If someone didn't start talking, he was going to lose it.

Ed crossed his arms over his chest and Georgie sent her fiancée a strange look. Yeah, he was drawing this out. And Xavier had a fair idea why.

"You snooze, you lose," Ed told him.

Georgie's sharp gaze turned to him as she caught on to what he was saying.

"Are you saying that Juliet has a . . . has a . . ."

"Boyfriend?" Ed supplied helpfully.

"I don't know if I'd call him her boyfriend," Georgie said doubtfully.

Hope filled him. So, it wasn't like that?

"He's not the type of guy you could label a boyfriend," she added. "More like a man. He's Juliet's man."

"Hm," Ed said. "I agree. Juliet's man."

He could feel his blood pressure spike. There was a ringing in his ears. "Juliet's man?"

"That's what he claimed to be," Ed said. "Well, no, that's not quite right. He told the whole bar that she was taken when Loki proposed to her."

"Loki proposed to her?" How long had he been gone for? What was even happening right now?

"He only wanted her to join Loki's Warriors for the quiz," Georgie explained, obviously taking pity on him.

Right. That explained that part. But who the fuck was this guy claiming his Juliet in the damn Wishing Well? He'd seen her a week ago. How could she have met someone? Juliet, who couldn't speak to people she didn't know and trust well. She still wouldn't talk to Georgie, and she considered her a close friend.

"Who is it?" he asked in a strangled voice.

Ed gave him a puzzled look. "You don't know?"

"Know. What." Seriously, he was going to deck Ed if he didn't tell him what the fuck he knew.

"He's a bodyguard, someone Reuben hired to protect her," Ed told him.

Fuck. Fuck. Fuck.

Why the hell hadn't Reuben told him? Why hadn't Juliet? He was going to spank her ass so hard she wouldn't sit for a week.

Fuck. No, he wouldn't. This was Juliet. Besides, it wasn't like he had the right to do that.

"Reuben hired a bodyguard because he's paranoid or . . ."

"He thinks there's some sort of threat," Ed added. "There are three bodyguards. I don't think this is some paranoid delusion of Reuben's."

It was all starting to make sense. Reuben calling him because he was worried about Juliet. Her anxiety attack. Shit. Shit.

Okay, so there was some threat, something Reuben thought was credible enough to hire bodyguards for Juliet. But that didn't explain why this bodyguard guy was claiming Juliet as his. Was it so Loki would back off?

"Maybe he was just trying to protect her from Loki."

"Protect her by claiming that she was taken?" Ed mused. "I suppose it could be possible, if it wasn't for what he said afterward to her. The way he held her hand or picked her up, or she squeezed his butt."

His Juliet wouldn't do things like that. This had to be some weird joke.

"Although she was a bit tipsy," Georgie added. "I hope she's okay this morning."

"Wait. She was drinking?" She shouldn't be drinking on her medication. What was she thinking?

She needed him. He'd fucked up. He'd failed at his job to take care of her.

"Where are you going?" Ed called out as he turned and walked out of the door.

"I've just remembered I have somewhere I have to be."

17

Dying.

She was dying.

This was the end. An end to a short life. Her head throbbed, her mouth was dry, and her stomach was rolling. Why did people drink? Really? How was this fun? This wasn't fun. Sure, it had seemed like a good idea last night . . .

What exactly had happened last night? Had she been playing the drums at some stage? She remembered hitting something. And squeezing something firm and high.

Oh no. Had she squeezed someone's ass? And why did she think she could fly? She couldn't fly. That was ridiculous.

Please don't tell me I tried to fly last night.

With a groan, she rolled her over and opened her eyes. She tensed.

Oh no.

No. No. No.

This couldn't be happening. This was some sort of dream. Because there was no way that Brick Sampson was lying on a beanbag next to her bed, sleeping.

Because that would mean he was in her bedroom. And she was lying in her cot-bed. With her pacifier and blankie lying next to her. That he'd had to walk through her playroom to get into her bedroom.

And that definitely hadn't happened. She'd remember if something like that happened.

So, this was all just a bad, bad dream.

Sitting up, her head throbbed and her stomach rolled.

Sick. She was going to be sick.

Juliet quickly scrambled for the opening of her bed and managed to get to her feet, stumbling into her attached bathroom to land heavily by the toilet. She heaved, her body shaking violently. She abhorred throwing up. She sobbed, tears clouding her vision as her stomach revolted.

A warm hand landed on her lower back, making her jump.

"Easy, Duchess." His voice both warmed and horrified her. The last thing she wanted was for him to see her like this.

He'd seen her bedroom, her bed. Lord knows what she'd done while she was drunk. How irresponsible was it of her to drink? This was her punishment. Being violently ill in front of the sexiest man alive. Then having him turn away from her after discovering one of her biggest secrets.

"It's all right. Let it all out. You'll feel better afterward." He had her hair pulled back from her face.

Gross. Gross.

When the heaves stopped, he eased her onto her bottom and leaned her against the wall. She curled up into herself as she heard the toilet flush.

"Let's get you cleaned up. Look at me."

No way. She had to smell like booze and puke. She disgusted herself. And she couldn't bear to see that look on his face. He just needed to go.

"Duchess. Look at me," he repeated firmly.

This time, she managed to ignore the order. A sigh escaped him. This was it. Now, he would leave. And she could crawl into her bed and die.

There was the sound of running water. What was he doing? Taking a bath?

"Right, Duchess, here's the thing," he said in a no-nonsense voice. "I don't know what's going on in your head, but I know you're feeling miserable. Been there, done that more times than I care to admit."

What? He'd humiliated himself in front of someone that he was attracted to?

"Guessing you're also mad at me. I know I shouldn't have done it, but I can't say I'm sorry about it."

What was he talking about? He wasn't sorry about spending the night with her in a beanbag?

"Telling people you're mine, it felt right. We can still go slow. But I want people to know you're mine, and I'm sorry if you don't want—"

She raised her hand and tried to cover his mouth. But his muttered curse had her lifting her head sharply.

Her head protested the movement. Not a good idea.

Chagrin filled her as she saw the way he cradled his eye. Shoot.

You're such a clumsy idiot.

She reached out to touch him then thought better of it. Best not to keep hurting him.

"So, I'm guessing you're really not happy about me saying you're mine."

She shook her head. That wasn't it.

"You're not upset about me claiming you?"

She shook her head again.

He lowered his hand then stood and reached over for a wash-cloth that sat on one of the shelves. It was a pale blue color with a mermaid on it. He ran it under the water. She guessed he was going to put it over his eye. But then he crouched in front of her and grabbed hold of her chin. She tried to pull her head back, but he gave her a firm look.

"Stay still, baby girl."

He started to gently wash her face. And oh, it was bliss. She didn't realize how crusty and gross she'd felt until her face was clean. Then he moved away to turn off the bath. She noticed that he'd poured some of her colored bubble bath into it, turning the water and bubbles all green.

"Stay there."

She opened her mouth then closed it. Useless. She dug her nails into the palms of her hands in punishment. She hated that she was this way. That she couldn't even talk to the sexiest man alive.

Well, one of them. An image of Xavier floated through her mind. She pushed it aside.

"There is nothing in that fridge but water and an iced coffee."

There was a coffee drink left? It must have been tucked into the back of the fridge. She looked at what he held in his hand, disappointment filling her as she realized it was water.

He crouched in front of her again, frowning as he stared down at her. What was wrong? He took her hands in his, drawing her nails away from the palms of her hands.

"No."

She crossed her arms over her chest. He was awfully damn fond of that word. Especially when it came to her. He opened the water then lifted it to her mouth. She reached for it, but he shook his head at her. Puzzled she sucked some down then drew back.

"More," he demanded.

He'd gone from talkative to one-word sentences. She couldn't keep up. What had she done last night? She had these vague recollections of flying and playing the drums, but none of that made sense.

"Are you worried I'm going to push you for more than you're ready for?" he asked abruptly.

What? No. Even though she hadn't expected him to blurt that out, she wasn't upset. At least not for the reasons he thought.

She shook her head.

"Are you worried about your brother finding out? I know everyone seemed to think he'd be upset. But you don't need to concern yourself about that. I'll be the one to deal with him. If I quit, then he'll have no objections."

Oh, he'd have plenty to object about. And she knew she'd have to be the one to stand between them. It was the only way to protect Brick.

"I don't want you stressing about anything. I'll take care of everything."

As nice as it would be to hand over everything to him, that wasn't the way life worked.

With a sigh, she rubbed at her temples.

Brick grabbed some painkillers from the cabinet then handed her two pills before giving her another drink of water. Leaning her head back against the wall, she closed her eyes.

"You're upset because I breached your privacy, aren't you?"

Her eyes shot open. His jaw was clenched. "I told you that you'd be upset in the morning. But I couldn't leave you alone. You have to understand, I wouldn't have come into your rooms unless I was worried about your safety. Do you hate me?"

Hate him? Was he serious?

"I know you must feel like I broke your trust. Both last night when I claimed you in front of everyone and this morning, when you found me here in your bedroom. But I swear, Juliet, I didn't mean to—"

This time, she used her lips to shut him up. She shoved herself forward and pressed her mouth to his. He froze in shock. Then she realized that she'd just puked her guts out with that mouth and drew back just as quickly, putting her hand over her mouth.

Crap. Well, if it wasn't bad enough that he'd seen her drunk, discovered she had a playroom and a crib for a bed, oh, and she'd probably sucked on her pacifier. Although a memory tugged at her, where she sucked on his fingers. But that had to be wrong. Because even she wouldn't do something that embarrassing.

"Okay, so does that mean you're not so upset with me that you want me to leave?"

She shook her head, growing increasingly frustrated with herself.

"Hey, easy. Shh. It's okay," he soothed her, and she suddenly realized she was making weird noises. She stopped immediately and he stood. "I'm going to find your whiteboard."

She grabbed his hand. It was boiling up inside her. The need to set it free was overwhelming. She tugged at him.

"I'll only be a second, Duchess. But I don't think we can continue this conversation without some help. I need to know what's on your mind."

She knew exactly what was on her mind. She tugged at him again, even though she knew she wasn't strong enough to keep him there if he actually wanted to move.

Crouching, he cupped her chin. "What is it? What's wrong?"

She grabbed his hand and drew it down. Turning it over, she used her finger to write out a word.

M.I.N.E.

He sucked in a breath. "Mine? You're asking if you're mine? You mean last night's declaration wasn't enough to reassure you? Juliet, you're mine. If you still want me, that is."

There was still doubt in his gaze and she hated that. She was also making a hash of this. That bubble in her stomach was about to explode. Sweat broke out on her skin. He watched her worriedly. "Are you going to be sick again?"

Was she strong enough to survive him if she opened up and he rejected her?

No.

Could she live with herself if she let him go without trying?

Shaking her head, she got onto her knees just as an alarm on his phone blasted.

"Fuck." He jumped to his feet and raced into the bedroom to grab his phone. "What? Who? Yes, she's up here. How did he get in? All right."

She stood on shaky legs and moved towards the doorway.

"There's someone coming down the drive. They had the code to the gate, but we don't know that it's a friend. Elias will meet him at the door, I'm going to back him up. You're to stay in here. Until I get you. Understand me? Do. Not. Move."

The look on his face was furious intent and she nodded shakily. She hadn't thought about what might happen if Reuben wasn't just being overprotective. That Brick would actually be in danger if someone came for her.

Suddenly, it became harder to breathe.

"Juliet. Stay. Here."

Then he was gone, and she found herself sinking to her butt in the middle of her bathroom.

Breathe.

You don't have time to lose it.

Someone was here. Someone who could hurt her.

But they'd had the gate code. Who would be able to get through? Reuben. But he'd let them know. Kiesha. But she didn't drive.

Xavier.

That thought got her up on her feet and she stumbled towards the window, gaping down at the car she saw pull up.

Oh no.

She had to tell Brick. But he'd told her to stay here. She froze, indecision tormenting her. Juliet didn't want to do something stupid. But she was certain that was Xavier. And he wouldn't hurt her.

But what if Xavier got hurt? She couldn't let that happen. He was one of her best friends.

Shoot. Shoot. Shoot.

She moved to the door and opened it, hurrying out to the top of the stairs. Lightly, she raced down to the second-floor landing so she could peek over the edge and see the front door.

"Who the fuck are you? Are you the guy who thinks she's his?"

"I don't know who you are, but you need to calm down and keep your hands where I can see them," Elias urged.

Where was Brick? She leaned over the railing. She caught sight of Elias' broad back blocking the door.

"Get out of my way!" Xavier demanded. "I'm not letting you keep me from her. Juliet! Juliet, get down here now!"

Her feet were moving before she even thought about what she was doing.

"Juliet isn't coming down here," Elias warned. "And you're not getting near her. Now, tell me your name or I'm calling the cops."

"Call the fucking cops. Then you can explain to Ed why the fuck you're keeping her prisoner."

"Juliet isn't a prisoner," Brick said.

Oh shit. She sat and peered through the rungs of the stairs as Brick stepped up and Elias took a step back.

"Juliet!"

Xavier stepped forward. Brick pushed him back. She winced, feeling bad for Xavier. He was no slouch, but Brick was a wall. There was no getting through him.

"Let me fucking see her. Now!"

She jumped in shock. Xavier rarely swore. Rarely lost his temper. What was going on?

"Want me to call the cops, Brick?" Elias asked.

"Not yet."

"Juliet! Get down here!" Xavier called.

"You're getting nowhere near her. Not until I know who you are, what you want, and definitely not until you calm the fuck down," Brick told him in a low, dark voice she'd never heard from him before.

"I'm her close friend. And you don't get to come between us. Get Juliet, tell her Xavier is here." Xavier was growing quieter. She didn't think that was a good thing.

And then he shoved Brick.

Oh no. No, no, no.

She'd waited too long before intervening. Sitting here, feeling sorry for herself, and mourning what might have been. She would never have Xavier like she had once dreamed of, but she still loved him.

And she couldn't let Brick hurt him. She also couldn't let him attack Brick.

Because Brick was hers.

So, she found herself flying down the stairs, uncaring that she was still in her pajamas and hadn't yet brushed her teeth and that her hair was likely a rat's nest.

This couldn't happen.

When she got to the foyer, Xavier and Brick were toe to toe. This wasn't going to end well. She ran closer.

"Juliet, no!" Elias yelled out, moving towards her. Brick spun, startled, and Xavier started past him. Brick turned back and blocked him. Xavier saw the opportunity to land a punch which Brick dodged.

She had to stop them. Then she spotted the fresh vase of

flowers on the hallway table. Picking it up, she threw the water and flowers at them.

Both of them froze then turned to gape at her.

"What the hell?" Brick snapped. "Juliet!"

"Don't speak to her like that," Xavier growled at him. Then he turned to look at her, his gaze running over her.

She was heaving for breath, hardly daring to believe she'd just done that.

"Twink? You okay?" Xavier's voice immediately softened. Again, he tried to step past Brick, but the other man was suddenly between them. All she could see was his back.

"Last chance to leave before we call the cops," Brick warned.

"You can't keep her from me."

She stepped forward and put her hand on Brick's shoulder. He didn't look at her. She bit her lip, feeling worried.

"Juliet, go upstairs. Now," Brick demanded.

Oh, she wished she could do that. She really did. But she couldn't let him call the police on Xavier. She glanced over at Elias and shook her head.

"No cops?" Elias asked. "He really is a friend?"

She nodded.

"We're closer than friends," Xavier demanded.

They were? What did he mean? Well, she guessed maybe he meant he was more like her caretaker. Sadness filled her at the thought.

"Really?" Elias drawled. "Then where have you been this last week?"

"I've been away. I didn't know there was trouble, or I would have been here."

"So Juliet didn't tell you?" Elias asked.

"No," Xavier said shortly.

Was it her imagination or did Brick's shoulders ease?

"I only just heard that there was trouble and came over," Xavier said stiffly.

"You seem awfully upset," Elias said in a strange voice.

"Of course I am. Juliet means a lot to me. Twink, come here."

She tried to get around Brick, but he moved, blocking her again.

"Thank you for taking care of Juliet," Xavier told Brick. "But your services are no longer needed. I'll be taking care of her now."

"You need to go away and calm down," Brick told him firmly. "You're not getting near her in this state."

"Get out of my way," Xavier demanded.

Oh Lord. She just knew this was going to end in disaster.

18

Xavier felt crazed.

His heart was racing, adrenaline surged inside him. All he wanted to do was take down this smug asshole. To wipe that smirk off his face. Unfortunately, the bastard was built like a brick shit house.

He understood why Reuben had hired him. With his burly stature and craggy face, he'd be enough to scare off most people.

But Xavier wasn't most people. He'd watched over Juliet for the last two years. And now this damn bodyguard thought he got to claim her?

Nobody was stealing her from him. As soon as he got rid of this asshole, he'd tell her about his feelings.

"You can go pack your stuff. I'll make sure Reuben pays out what he owes you."

"You can't fire us when you didn't hire us," said the first man, who stood off to the side, watching them both.

"If Juliet needs bodyguards, I'll hire them."

"If?" the first guy asked. "You don't think there's a real threat?"

"Reuben is overprotective. He probably overreacted."

"You have no idea what's going on," the bruiser standing between him and Juliet said. "You'd put her in danger because you think you know best."

Fuck. He wanted to re-break this asshole's nose.

Because Xavier didn't know what was going on. Damn Reuben. Why did he never explain shit?

"Juliet, upstairs," the bruiser commanded.

Xavier stiffened. "Don't speak to her like that." Juliet needed gentleness, kindness. "Juliet, come here." He tried to peer around the bruiser to see her.

"For fuck's sake, will the two of you stop it." Elias glared at them. "Can't you see what you're both doing to her?"

The bruiser half-turned, letting him get a good look at Juliet. Her hair was a mess. She wore long, silky pajamas that covered her body, but her face was pale and there were dark marks under her eyes.

"Twink, aren't you feeling well?" he asked with concern, stepping towards her.

The bruiser moved between them again.

Xavier shot him a disgusted look. "I'm not going to hurt her. I'd never do anything to hurt her. I care about her." He turned to Juliet. "Baby, have you been sleeping? Eating?"

Her eyes widened as she stared from him to the big guy between them.

"Are you here as her friend or for some other reason?" the bruiser asked.

"What business is it of yours?"

"It's my business because Juliet is mine."

Anger flooded him. This asshole didn't get to come in and steal what was his. But he managed to keep himself under control. Just.

"You've known her less than a week. How do I know you haven't taken advantage of her? Does Reuben know about this? Because it seems highly unprofessional."

. . .

JULIET DIDN'T UNDERSTAND what was going on.

Her pulse was racing. The room around her spun. She knew she had to take a breath or she was going to pass out.

"I think the two of you should cool off," Elias told them. "Neither of you are thinking about Juliet right now. Have you even looked at her properly?"

Suddenly, everyone's attention was on her. Xavier seemed more upset than she would have thought. And he really couldn't fire Brick.

She hated the thought of upsetting Xavier. But she didn't want Brick to be upset either. The way Xavier was acting was out of character.

"Twink, look at me. I need you to breathe." Xavier stepped forward, and this time, Brick let him.

"Georgina said you were drinking last night. You know alcohol isn't good for you. I need to check you over, make sure you're all right. You're safe. I'm here. I'm going to take care of you."

She looked from Xavier to Brick.

"Why don't you head upstairs," Elias said to her. "I'll take care of things down here."

Xavier frowned at Elias. "Juliet, come here." Xavier crooked a finger at her. She wanted to go to him.

But she didn't want to upset Brick. Didn't want him to think there was something going on with Xavier. She was with Brick now. It was making her ill, not knowing what to do.

Turning, she ran.

That was what she did best, right? She ran from her problems.

BRICK WATCHED Juliet race up the stairs.

Why hadn't she told Brick about this Xavier guy? Was she like

Linda? Was she after the best offer? Xavier drove an expensive car and dressed like he had money. He could likely give her a life that Brick couldn't. Plus, he knew her well. He already had a considerable head start.

Hell, she couldn't even talk to Brick. What the fuck was he thinking?

Six days wasn't enough to build a relationship.

So, you're just going to give up?

Xavier moved towards the stairs, obviously intent on following her.

Are you just going to stand here and let him or are you going to do something?

"That's not happening," Elias said, stepping into Xavier's path.

"Get out of the fucking way." The other man's hands were clenched into fists. It was obvious he was in good shape. But there was no fucking way he could take either of them. And the two of them together? He was toast.

Elias shook his head, crossing his arms over his chest.

"She needs me."

"No, I'd say you're actually the last thing she needs." Elias aimed a furious look at Xavier, which made Brick feel a bit smug. Until his best friend aimed that look at him.

"She shouldn't be on her own right now. Her health is fragile. I'm her doctor as well as her friend."

Elias raised an eyebrow. "If I think she needs medical attention, I'll be sure to call you. In the meantime, my job is to protect her. Go calm down. Think about what the fuck you just did. Because neither of you put her first. What just happened was all about the two of you and what you want. If you'd once thought of her, then this might have ended up differently."

The doctor looked from Elias to him. His face was filled with cold fury that made Brick straighten. But he turned and stomped out the door.

Elias waited until he'd driven off to turn to Brick. "Brick, fuck, I know what you're thinking. That she and the doc have something going on. But you're not thinking clearly. Linda fucked you over, but not all women are like her. Juliet certainly isn't. That girl doesn't have a deceitful bone in her body. She's so sweet that she worked a job she hates to make other people feel better. When she doesn't eat all her lunch, she boxes it up to give to that homeless guy in the park. Oh, and she slipped fifty dollars into the box when she thought I wasn't looking."

Brick shot Elias a look. "He's got feelings for her."

"Seemed that way," Elias said.

"She might have feelings for him," he suggested.

"Maybe she does," Elias agreed, surprising him. "But I didn't take you for a coward."

"What the fuck?" He was no coward.

"What the fuck just happened?" Sterling asked, rushing in.

"You should be watching the monitors," Brick told him.

"I made sure he was gone, and an alarm will sound on my phone if someone tries to get onto the property," Sterling countered. "What's happening?"

"I'm trying to talk some sense into Brick," Elias answered, turning back to him. "Are you going to walk away? Let this guy, who hasn't been around all week, just have her? Are you going to let him come in here and take what's yours?"

"She's not mine." Except he remembered what she'd written against his hand with her finger. Had she meant it? That she was his? Or would she turn away from him?

"No?" Sterling asked. "Thought you declared her as yours in front of the whole bar last night."

"That guy is probably a better fit. He lives here. He's a fucking doctor. They know each other." He had nothing more than a bankrupt business and five hundred bucks in the bank.

"What if Juliet said she wanted you? That she chose you? Would you just walk away?" Sterling asked.

"And what if she says she wants him?" he countered.

"What if she wanted you both?" Elias asked.

They both stared at him.

Elias shrugged. "Didn't you share a girl with a friend of yours back when you first entered the Marines?"

"That was a long time ago," Brick said. "We were young."

"But you know it's possible. A girl with two guys. A guy with two girls. Sometimes more. There's a whole section of romance dedicated to reverse harems."

"Who are you?" Sterling asked, looking angrier than the conversation warranted. "You want a harem of women? That would never fucking work."

"A reverse harem is the opposite, dickhead. And who says it wouldn't work?"

The two of them glared at each other. Brick had often wondered if they had feelings for each other. Not that it was any of his business what they did.

Like they ever stay out of your shit?

"I wouldn't share my woman," Sterling declared.

Elias shrugged. "I don't see why it would be a bad thing, especially if it was what she wanted. Think about it. Life's so fucking busy, right? What if you had someone else that could help take care of your girl? Be there when you couldn't? What if you weren't good at something, like communication, but the other guy was? Way the economy is going, wouldn't surprise me if more people ended up in relationships like this."

"So, it should be a financial decision? That's bullshit," Sterling spat out.

"No. It should be what is best for them and who are we to judge? If your woman needs it, then would you really deny her?" Elias asked.

"All she should want is me." Sterling turned and stormed away.

"Somehow, I feel like this stopped being about me," Brick commented.

Elias sighed, running his hand over his face. "Just don't let her go because you think she's better off without you. If she's worth it, you'll fight for her. If you don't think she's worth it, then best to walk away before she gets hurt further. Because that girl doesn't have any shields, Brick. So, if you don't want her, walk away. But if you do, then march up those stairs and tell her."

"I did tell her."

"Then don't fucking ruin it."

Brick made it as far as the second-floor landing before he sat on the stairs. He leaned his head in his hands. What the fuck was he doing? Did he really want to do this all over again? Hadn't Linda turned him off relationships? Then he went and fell for this complicated, confusing, beautiful girl who needed him.

And Brick liked to be needed.

Had she lied to him? He shook his head. He doubted it. She hadn't mentioned Xavier before, though. But when would she have had a chance?

Had he pushed her too far too fast? Likely. He'd jumped in feet first. Claiming her like he was a caveman.

Did she have feelings for Xavier? That was the question. Maybe there had been nothing between them before, but that didn't mean she wasn't interested in Xavier. It would make more sense for her to be with him.

But then he remembered her curling into him. Sucking on his fingers. Her shy smiles. Those admiring glances.

Did he fucking deserve her? Likely not.

Did he want her? Fuck, yes.

Don't be a fucking coward.

Maybe she'd choose Xavier. But she wouldn't pick him because Brick hadn't fought for her. Decision made, he let out a breath.

Fuck. Fine. He was going to talk to her. Lay his cards out. And if she rejected him, then at least he'd tried.

What if she wants both of you?

Sheesh, Elias had really gotten in his head.

Climbing to her door, he knocked loudly. No answer. Crap.

"Juliet, it's me. Open up."

Nothing.

"I just want to talk." Still nothing. He should wait. That would be the right thing to do. The proper thing.

Good thing he never cared much about that. He'd seen the pin number she'd used last night, and he quickly inputted it, telling himself that he had to check she was okay.

He strode through the playroom, taking it in during the daylight. There was a tea party set up at a gorgeous antique table, along with what looked to be a complete play kitchen, with everything you could imagine.

The costume area was behind the kitchen. He frowned as he remembered her trying to fly last night. What was she thinking? She could have hurt herself. Damn woman needed a keeper.

Which is what you want to be, don't you? You want to be her Dom. Her Daddy. Her man.

Fuck, yes. He wanted it in a way that he hadn't wanted anything for a long, long time.

There was a massive mural on one side of the room. It was an under the sea scene with mermaids and treasure and fish.

He moved into the bedroom, not seeing her. Where was she? He walked into the bathroom. Fuck. Panic started to fill him.

Heading back into the playroom, he looked around. She was tiny. Maybe she was hiding. A muffled sound reached him and he froze. There it went again.

By the couch. Swiftly, he headed that way, coming to a stop as he found her. She was curled into a tight ball, wedged between the couch and the wall. A tremor wracked her body, and he kicked himself for taking so long to come to her.

Oh, his poor baby.

"It's all right, Duchess," he murmured soothingly. "You're all right."

Her hands were clenched into fists, and he knew she was pressing her nails into the palms of her hands.

"Duchess, look at me."

Nothing. She didn't even move, didn't flinch.

Well, you could stop looming over her.

He sat down abruptly then stared at her, wondering what the hell he could do to ease her anxiety.

"I'm a dumbass, Duchess."

Nothing. Okay then.

"How about a story?" He nearly rolled his eyes at himself. But he'd started this now. "About a guy. A guy who makes mistakes all the time. Who is blunt and grouchy and sometimes a bit mean. He thinks the worst of people. He wasn't always that way. But life kicked him often enough that he'd come to expect it to keep on kicking him."

Still nothing.

"And then one day, when this idiot was feeling at his lowest. When he didn't think life could get that much fucking worse, this gorgeous, sweet, confusing woman came into it, shaking it up. And she taught him that not everyone was out to kick him when he was down. That there was still good in the world. When she smiles, he wants to smile. When she's mad, he wants to make her happy. When she's hurt, he wants to destroy whatever made her cry. This guy knows he doesn't deserve her, but he wants her anyway. Even though he's a dumbass."

She shifted then her eyes peeked out at him. He let out a sigh. Thank God.

"There you are, Duchess. Give me your hands." Because he couldn't stand the idea that she was hurting herself.

She stared at him like she didn't know what he was saying.

"Duchess. Hands."

He held his hands out, watching her intently as she reached out towards him. Her hands shook and his insides clenched. He was such a selfish prick, thinking only of himself. Assuming the worst of her.

"That's it. Hands in mine."

She put her hands into his and he frowned as he noticed how cold they were. And that there were red marks along her palms. He fucking hated that.

"You're freezing. We need to warm you up. I'm going to run you another bath, okay? But first, let's get you out of here."

He let her hands go, then stood and reached for her. Thankfully, she held her arms up. He breathed out a sigh of relief. As soon as he lifted her close, she wrapped her limbs around him. Her legs went around his waist, her arms around his neck, and she shook in his arms, burying her face in his neck.

"Hey, little monkey. You're all right. You're all right," he soothed. She held onto him like she thought he might disappear.

He closed his eyes, chagrined. While she was stronger than most people might realize, she was also delicate in so many ways.

And he needed to remember that.

He rubbed his hand up and down her back, hugging her tight. "It's okay. You're all right. Did we scare you?"

Fuck. Why hadn't he thought of that? He'd been furious with her for disobeying him.

He still was.

She was in trouble for that. He'd need to reinforce that her safety came first, and she had to obey him when he gave her orders in those situations. This wasn't the first time she'd disobeyed him like that.

It would make his life easier if she obeyed him in all situations, but somehow, he thought he wasn't going to get his way in that.

She didn't reply. He huffed out a breath, wishing he knew what was going on in her head.

"Let's get you a blanket to warm you up with." He carried her into the bedroom and managed to get a blanket off the back of an enormous rocking chair. It looked big enough for two people to sit in it.

Deciding the bath could wait for a moment, he sat on the chair and attempted to pull her around onto his lap.

But she held on tighter.

"Come on, baby girl. I just want to move you so I can wrap this around you."

She shook her head again.

All right then. He settled back as well as he could and started to rock them. He didn't say anything, figuring they could both use a bit of time. Gradually, she began to relax in his arms.

"I'm sorry if we scared you. I didn't know who he was for a start. I thought he was a threat."

She nodded her head.

"You feeling okay? You need anything?"

She ran her finger over his chest. N.O.

Okay.

"I'm going to get your whiteboard. We can't have this talk without it."

She let out a noise of protest.

"Duchess," he warned. "We need to talk. I know you're upset. I know you were frightened. But we have to talk about who Xavier is to you. And me. About what I am to you."

NERVOUSNESS FLOODED HER.

Along with shame. Fear. A whole raft of emotions.

She'd been so sure that Brick was going to shut her out. That he'd go back to being the cold man who was just doing a job. And she wouldn't see those minuscule smiles, wouldn't get those heated looks or the small acts of kindness that he hid from most people.

But she'd seen that her secret stash of chocolate downstairs had been refilled. And that the pool had been cleaned of leaves when it wasn't the gardener's day to work. When she'd gone into the garage the other day to check on something, she'd noticed that her bike was shining and that the tires were pumped up.

She knew it was him. He never spoke about it, never tried to lay claim to what he'd done. Never looked for a thanks.

His ex was a fool for letting a man like this go. A man who took care of her in ways she didn't know she needed.

She didn't want to lose him. It would hurt. Badly.

And what about Xavier?

What sort of person wanted two men at the same time? What the hell did that make her?

"Duchess, I'm not good at talking about my feelings and shit. It's gonna be even harder if I'm doing all the talking. So, let's get your whiteboard, all right?"

She shook her head. She either trusted him or she didn't. And if she didn't, then they couldn't do this, because she had to trust someone to open up, to be vulnerable.

But God, it was hard.

"Juliet, I know this is difficult. It's fucking near impossible for me to sit here and wonder if you're gonna tell me to get lost. That you don't want me. But you have to tell me. Because hiding isn't an option right now? Got me?"

It welled inside her. She knew that she had to let it free.

"I know I acted like a dick downstairs. I . . . fuck . . . you know about Linda, what she did. For a moment, I was wondering if you had this thing going on with Xavier and I was just someone you were stringing along. But only for a moment. I've got fucking trust issues and I know I have to work on them. Just give me time."

She opened her mouth. It was coming.

"I know I don't fucking deserve you. You'd be better off with him. He's got a good job. Obviously makes good money. Knows you. Lives here. Fuck, there's no reason you should choose me. I get it."

Shoot. What made him so talkative all of a sudden?

She tried again.

"But give me a chance and I'll treat you like a fucking queen. Maybe I can't give you material stuff now, but I'll get there. I'll take care of you, protect you, I'll work every day to make sure you never regret being with me."

He was killing her. Killing her.

"Brick," she whispered in that broken, tiny voice of hers. The one that had made her feel so much shame and embarrassment. The reason she never spoke to someone she didn't fully trust.

He froze. He stared down at her, eyes wide, the pain in his eyes so clear that she wanted to hold him tight and tell him everything would be all right.

"I want you." She hoped it was enough. Because the lump in her throat wouldn't let anything else pass. The pain in her heart didn't lessen, but she knew it was the right thing to say. How could she feel so happy and so devastated at the same time?

Then he cupped her face, pulling her back so he could stare down at her fiercely. "You want me?"

She nodded, tears streaming down her face.

"Thank fuck. Because I don't think I could let you go." He sucked in a breath. "I wondered what you would say if you ever spoke. Fucking glad those are the first words you've ever said to me. Best words I've ever heard." Relief filled his face, that quickly turned to concern. He wiped at her tears. "Baby, don't cry. Why does that make you sad?"

She shook her head. There was no way to explain it.

"Tell me what's wrong. I'll fix it."

He didn't understand. Nothing was wrong. Well, there was plenty wrong. But that wasn't why she was crying. She'd managed to speak to him. It was cathartic. He'd seen parts of her that she usually hid from people. The only ones who knew about her Little side were Kiesha, Xavier, and Reuben.

"Stop crying," he pleaded. "I hate seeing you upset."

She let out a deep breath. Fuck. For a long moment, she closed her eyes and tried to pull the pieces of herself back together. He took her face between his hands and kissed her forehead. And all of those fractured pieces started to reform. They might not be perfect, might not be what they once were.

But they could be stronger.

When he drew back, his forehead rested on hers. "Are you crying over him?"

She opened her mouth. Closed it. How did she explain how she felt about Xavier? How could she explain when she didn't know what was going on inside her head? She cared about him, she'd fantasized about him for so long, but that was all he was. A fantasy. She wanted someone real.

"I have to know if you'd rather be with him. Because if you would—"

She slammed her hand over his mouth, frowning at him fiercely. "No."

He let out a deep breath. "Thank God, because I'm not letting you go. Ever."

His fierce statement eased some of the worry inside her.

She smiled at him.

"Told myself if you said you wanted him that I'd walk away. But that's bullshit. I won't walk away. I want you. I promise, I'll do what I have to do to make myself worthy of you."

What was he talking about?

"I'm not worthy of you."

Brick scowled, looking ferocious. Her warrior. Her protector.

"What bullshit is that?"

Her blunt man.

"Not normal."

He stared down at her. "Normal?"

She nodded.

"Who the fuck said anything about you having to be normal?"

"The world?"

"Fuck the world. Is the world here with us? Are you going to let other people dictate the way you live your life?"

Obviously, he'd never had the world turn on him.

However, the world didn't turn on her. Just some very nasty people. And it was her fault. She'd given them that power. She'd let them get in her head, hurt her.

"Do you think I'm normal? I've got so much fucking baggage I could fill a plane. Screw normal."

He said that, but he didn't know the extent of her issues.

"I've never . . ." She closed her eyes, thinking of Xavier.

"You've never what, Duchess?" he asked gently.

"Been with a man."

Tensing, she waited for his reaction. The ridicule. Or the smug acceptance.

"Open your eyes."

She shook her head.

"New rule. No hiding from me."

She scowled. That sucked. Also, she didn't think he could just keep adding rules.

"Open. Your. Eyes." A firmer tone this time had her eyes opening. Staring into his gaze, she saw acceptance, gentleness, and a hint of hunger. There was also an air of satisfaction.

"You think I care that you haven't had sex?"

She pressed her nails into her thighs.

"No." He moved her hands from her thighs. "Another rule. No using your fingernails as weapons against yourself. Actually, no hurting yourself at all. Understand me?" He cupped her chin firmly.

She nodded.

"So, you and Xavier have never been a thing?" he asked carefully.

She shook her head.

"Just the way he was talking about you, it sounded like maybe he cared about you as more than a friend."

"Xavier was Reuben's best friend. They had a falling out two years ago, just before Xavier moved back here." She sucked in a breath. Why was it so hard for her to talk about anything emotional or real? When she was in Little space, she could chat away, but when she was adulting . . . yeah, it was hard as fuck.

She cleared her throat. It was hard to speak so much when she wasn't used to it.

"I'll get you a drink." Standing, he set her down on the chair.

"Coffee," she demanded.

"Water," he replied with a firm look. He tapped her wrinkled nose then moved into the playroom. After he returned, he picked her back up, resettling her on his lap. Then he unscrewed the water and held it to her mouth. She settled in against him, feeling exhausted. After a few sips, she knew she couldn't put this off any longer.

"Xavier has always watched out for me." She paused, thinking about this next part. "Always seen me as a little sister. Nothing else."

"Maybe he used to," Brick said.

She shook her head, feeling embarrassed. "No, that's all I am to him. When I was eighteen, I tried to kiss him. He let me down gently." She bit her lip. "He's one of my best friends."

"You feel like you're betraying him by being with me?"

Sort of. She shouldn't feel that way. Distress flooded her. She didn't want to hurt anyone's feelings. Maybe she couldn't do this.

"I just don't want him to be upset with me."

"Duchess, look at me," he said firmly. "I'm sorry for the way I behaved down there. I've got things to work on. You want to call him, ask him to come back, then you do that. He's your friend."

"You're really okay with that?"

"I am. As long as you're honest with me. Remember, being lied to is a trigger for me."

"I get it. I'm a lot of trouble," she whispered to him.

He wrapped his hand in her hair and tugged her face back. The pain should have scared her, the aggressiveness. But it was tempered. She knew he wasn't using his full strength, not even close. And something about the movement just did it for her. Arousal spiked through her blood and she was nearly squirming in need. His glare was almost enough to send her crashing into an orgasm. And wouldn't that be embarrassing?

"You kidding me?" he growled. "Too much trouble? I don't want to hear bullshit like that from your mouth, understand me?"

She attempted to nod, but he had her pinned down tight. She licked her lips.

"Words."

"Yes," she replied. Her voice was so quiet she wondered if he could hear her, but satisfaction filled his face.

"You're not trouble. Got me?"

"What about . . ." She pointed at her bed.

He quirked an eyebrow. "You think I shouldn't want you because of your bed?"

He knew that wasn't exactly what she meant. She gave him a look.

"You know I'm a Dom."

She nodded.

"Before Linda, I used to go to a BDSM club a lot. You know my favorite room in that club?"

"The torture room?"

"No." He shot her a quelling look. "Not the torture room. Although, do you have a basement in this monstrosity?"

She shook her head, wide-eyed. Nope. That wasn't happening.

"Hm. Maybe I can convert a bedroom. I have a feeling you're going to earn a lot of punishments."

She would not!

"You've got more than one punishment owing for the way you keep disobeying me."

What?

"It was the Littles room," he said, not explaining about these punishments further. "You're a Little, aren't you, Juliet?"

Was he . . . did he . . .?

"Juliet?"

She nodded slowly.

"Now that you've trusted me enough to speak to me, I'd really love if you could keep using words. But is it painful to talk? Has your voice always been like that?"

She winced. Trust Brick to come out and ask. In fact, she was surprised it had taken him so long.

"Not saying it's bad or anything, Duchess," he quickly reassured her. "Just want to know if it hurts you."

Did it hurt her? Not exactly.

"My voice suffered trauma when I was a kid," she told him. "Then I stopped speaking for a long time. It's never been the same."

"That's why you don't talk in front of most people?" he asked thoughtfully. "But you'll talk or whisper to people you trust?"

There were two different issues there. She winced. "When I was in school, I went through some stuff. It left me with a lot of issues around trust."

He froze. "Fuck, baby."

She shrugged. "Easier not to talk. I know I sound weird. So I only speak to people I know won't . . ."

"Hurt you?" he growled.

Yeah. Exactly. She nodded.

"Fucking hell."

"When I'm in Little space, it's easier," she admitted.

"Thank you for telling me," he said, surprising her. "No secrets between us. I'm yours. You are mine. No more hiding."

He wanted to know everything? Her breathing started growing rapidly.

"Easy," he told her. "I don't need everything all at once. You feel safer in Little space?"

She nodded. She also felt safe around him.

"Sometimes, I think life would be easier if I spent all my time in Little space."

"That's why you went to your job even though you hated it," he guessed. "You were worried you'd never leave?"

"Yeah."

"So, you've never had a Daddy?"

"I told you I haven't been in a relationship," she whispered.

"You don't need to have a relationship to have a Daddy or Mommy or Caregiver. Not a sexual relationship. They can be someone who looks out for you, gives you rules and consequences, gives you the care you need without anything else."

Oh. She hadn't quite realized that.

"I've never had a Daddy."

"Would you like one? Only, one that comes with a relationship too, obviously."

She sucked in a breath. It was her wish come true. A stern but loving Daddy. But what could she give him in return?

"What would I give you?"

He raised his eyebrows at that. "Your submission. Your care.

Your attention. You give me you."

Her breathing quickened. "There're things about me, my past . . . it's not pretty."

"Like I said, I've got enough baggage to fill a passenger plane. Your past doesn't scare me. Does mine scare you?"

She shook her head. How could it? When it had led him to her. Sure, there would be bumps. He had issues, just like she did. But if he was here and hers . . . that was all that mattered. All she'd dreamed of.

Although that wasn't entirely true. But that other dream was a fantasy that never had a chance of coming true.

"Juliet, would you like me to be your Daddy as well as your man?"

"Yes." Her excitement was tinged with a hint of sadness, but she squashed the negative emotion.

"Good."

He cupped her face with his hands. He was going to kiss her!

Fuck!

"Wait!" she managed to get out.

He froze. "What is it?"

"Well, it's just, this is my second kiss—"

"Your second kiss? Then your first kiss was . . ."

"With you. But I—"

Brick looked shocked. "I wish you'd told me. I would have tried to make it more memorable."

"Hey, I thought it was plenty memorable."

"Your second kiss will be a proper one then. I have to redeem myself."

Proper one? What did he mean?

He leaned in.

"Wait!"

He froze. "What is it?"

"Can I brush my teeth first? I have puke breath!"

19

He ran her another bath while she brushed her teeth.

"I ruined it, didn't I?"

Her voice was raspy, husky. It didn't sound like it should come from such a slight body.

It was sexy as fuck.

Seriously, that voice was going to kill him. How was he meant to keep his fucking hard-on under control when she sounded like that? He was just grateful that she'd chosen him. Wanted him.

But there was still this niggle inside him, telling him something wasn't right. That he was missing something.

"Ruined what?" he asked.

"The kiss. I shouldn't have said anything. But then I would have had puke breath. And you might not want to kiss me again because you might think I always have bad breath."

"For a girl that barely talks, you sure can word vomit," he teased.

She blushed, dropping her gaze. "Sorry."

"Enough," he said firmly. "You didn't ruin anything. I should have remembered that you likely feel like crap, and you've been through a lot today. This can wait."

"But I don't want to wait."

He studied her. He wanted this kiss to be memorable. And fuck, he hadn't even brushed his teeth.

"Got a spare toothbrush?"

She nodded and fished through her drawers for a toothbrush still in its wrapper. It was pink, but he didn't give a crap. He turned off the bath taps. This time, the bubble bath was purple. It kind of hurt your eyes to look at it, but she had so much of this stuff, he figured she must like it.

Taking the toothbrush, he put some toothpaste on it. Then he handed it to her.

Her eyes widened then a look of chagrin filled her face. She covered her mouth. "OhmygodIstillhavestinkybreath!"

Shit. He gently pulled her hand away from her mouth. "No, Duchess. I wasn't giving it to you to brush your teeth."

"Then . . . I don't understand."

"Want to brush my teeth?"

Her mouth opened then shut then opened again. That was damn cute. Then she giggled.

"I get to brush your teeth?" Her strangely broken voice took on a different note and he knew her Little was close to the surface.

"Yeah. You want to brush Daddy's teeth?"

Her breath caught and she studied him for a long moment.

Take it slow, idiot.

Had he pushed her too fast? Damn it.

Then she grinned. "Have you not been doing a good job of brushing your teeth?" She wiggled a finger at him. "The dentist won't be happy. No candy for you."

"No candy? That's harsh."

She sighed. "Sorry, it's not me that makes the rules."

"No, Daddy makes the rules, baby girl. Now, brush my teeth."

"Okay, open wide."

"Open wide, what?" he asked, deciding to press her a bit since she still hadn't said the word he most wanted to hear. He lifted her so she was sitting on the cabinet as she was a bit short to reach his mouth easily.

"Um, open wide, please." She banged her feet against the cabinets and he winced at the noise, stilling her legs with one hand.

"Nice manners, but that's not what I want either."

"Oh." Her cheeks went red. "You're sure?"

"More sure than I've been of anything before."

"Open wide, Daddy," she said so quietly that he had to strain to hear her. That was all right. This was a start.

He opened his mouth. This was kind of odd. But it had definitely made her relax.

"Gosh, Daddy. These are really dirty," she told him as she started to brush his teeth with way more enthusiasm than he ever did. At one stage, he thought the toothbrush was about to go down his throat.

"Definitely no more candy. You don't want holes, do you, Daddy?" she said sternly. Then she pulled the brush out. "Spit. Rinse. Okay. Repeat."

By the time she was finished, he was pretty sure she'd scraped half the enamel off his teeth.

"All shiny, Daddy."

"Thank you, Duchess," he said dryly. He moved between her legs then put his hands onto the counter on either side of her, trapping her in. He studied her, waiting to see if she showed any sign of panic. But pleasure filled her face. Yeah, his girl definitely liked when he got all dominant on her.

"Time for that kiss."

He didn't give her too much time to think. Grabbing the back of her head with his hand, he held her still while he pressed his lips to hers. He kissed her softly, drinking her in. Goddamn. Need flowed through him, making him groan as his hard cock pressed against his pants.

Don't scare her off.

Drawing back, he ran a finger over her lips. As he'd hoped, they parted, and he dipped his finger in. She sucked on it with a quiet murmur.

"Keep your mouth open," he commanded as he slid his finger free, then he pressed his mouth against hers again, his tongue slipping into her mouth. For a moment, she was still, almost frozen. Then he ran his hand up the outside of her thigh, his other hand holding her head, and she sighed into his mouth.

Then her tongue started playing with his.

Oh, fuck yes.

He could have stood there all day, kissing her. Could have happily dropped to his knees, pushed down her pajama pants, and eaten her out until she screamed.

But slow. She wasn't ready for more.

Drawing back, he had to hold her to keep her from chasing his mouth.

"Duchess, stop now."

"Want more."

Damn, that was like an aphrodisiac, he could feel it in his dick. Shit. He was going to have to do something about his hard-on from hell. He needed a shower and a change of clothes anyway. But he didn't really want to leave her alone.

Bath. Clean. Food. Then he'd take a shower and take care of his dick.

"I know. But I can't guarantee I'll stop. And a kiss is all you get at the moment. Until I'm sure you're ready for more."

SHE WAS ready for more now, damn him. What was he talking about?

A frown filled her face as she glared at him.

"Don't give me that face, baby girl," he warned.

She crossed her arms over her chest with a huff. She wanted more kisses. Maybe she could sneakily kiss him.

Secret mission: Kiss Brick.

Brick eyed her warily. "Time for a bath."

"No bath."

"Yes, you need a bath."

"No bath." If she threw herself at him, he'd have to catch her, right? Then if her lips just happened to land on his . . . well, he'd have to kiss her.

It was a flawless plan, really.

"You're a brat. Since you're obviously feeling well enough to sass me, we'll be having a chat about you obeying me. Especially when it comes to safety."

"No chat."

"Well, you're right. It won't be much of a chat. More like a lecture, followed by someone getting a red ass."

"Your ass."

"No, not my ass. What's got into you-oomph . . . Argh!"

Oh shit. She froze.

Her secret mission to kiss him had somehow gone horribly, horribly wrong.

Blood hadn't been part of the mission! Somehow, instead of him catching her, and 'accidentally' kissing him, she'd managed to slam her forehead into his nose.

Which was now bleeding everywhere.

Oh no. Oh no.

Why couldn't she do anything right? Even though he was bleeding a lot, he'd still managed to grab hold of her with one arm so she didn't slip onto the ground.

"Fuck. Crap."

She stood frozen as he grabbed one of her mermaid towels and pressed it to his nose. Then as he turned, she did the only thing she could.

She ran.

CHRIST. That hurt.

And it was bleeding like a motherfucker.

Damn it. He pressed the towel to his nose to stop the bleeding. But it just kept going. He turned to check on Juliet.

Where the hell had she gone?

Shit. No doubt she was feeling bad about hitting his nose. But it hadn't been her fault. She'd been trying to jump off the counter, which he'd have to speak to her about since she could have hurt herself. Grabbing a fresh towel, he moved back into the bedroom.

"Duchess? Where are you?"

Alarm filled him. But she couldn't have gone far. Clearly, she wouldn't have left her rooms again just wearing pajamas.

He wasn't taking very good care of her. He should have at least gotten her clean and dressed before kissing her like his life depended on it.

"Duchess? Where are you?"

He moved out into the playroom, checking the sofa. Not there. Crap. He walked back into the bedroom. Where would a scared Little hide?

Well, there was one obvious place and he called himself an idiot for not thinking of it straight away. Crouching down, he stared right into the face of his girl, crouched under the bed.

"Hey, Duchess. What you doing under there?"

She flinched then whimpered. He frowned. She shouldn't be this upset.

"Duchess, it was just an accident."

She shook her head. What did that mean? That she didn't want to come out?

Or that it wasn't an accident?

Had she hurt him on purpose? But that didn't make any sense. Why would she do that?

He reached for her, but she backed away from him. Tears welled, spilling down her cheeks.

"Christ, don't cry. Please."

A sniffle. A sob.

Enough.

He wasn't putting up with this bullshit. He wasn't going to sit here while she suffered alone.

"Juliet. Out of there. Now." He used his Dom voice. The one that garnered instant obedience from any sub close by.

So, no one was more shocked when she defied him.

Damn. Talk about a blow to the ego. Maybe he was out of practice.

Or perhaps she was scared he would hurt her? Surely, she knew he wouldn't. The girl that never spoke to anyone she didn't know for years and trust implicitly, had spoken to him.

That was huge. He wasn't underestimating how huge.

So why was she under the bed?

Fuck.

"Okay, Duchess. We'll do it your way," he said in a soft voice, then he lay down and rolled under the bed. He heard her gasp. He'd expected to find dust and stray hair ties and bits of rubbish under here.

But it was spotless.

He rolled to his side. The cot-bed was far enough off the ground to give him some room, although his shoulders brushed against the slats of the bed when he was on his side. She was pressed up against the wall, watching him with wide eyes.

"This would make a good fort. You like playing in forts?"

She shook her head slowly.

"What?" he gasped theatrically. "You've never built a fort?"

Her thumb moved up into her mouth as she shook her head again. Great. They were back to her being silent.

He could deal. Just stay patient, calm.

An idea occurred to him about how he could ease her anxiety. He reached out slowly to tug her thumb out of her mouth. Then he ran his fingers over her lips.

His nose felt stuffed and he couldn't breathe through it. So, a long sigh left his mouth as she took two of his fingers into her mouth and suckled.

"That's a good girl. Take what you need from me."

To his relief, she moved a bit closer. Then she chewed lightly on his fingers. His dick hardened and he closed his eyes.

Think unsexy thoughts. Think unsexy thoughts.

They lay there for long moments until he felt the tension ease from her body. Thank fuck.

"Ready to come out from under the bed?" he asked quietly.

She jolted then shook her head, nearly losing his fingers. She let out a whimper and he made soothing noises, pressing his fingers into her mouth again.

"It's all right. You're all right. I'm here. I'm not going anywhere."

Eventually, she was the one that moved. He lay there, motionless, waiting on her, like she was an injured animal he was going to coax closer. Then she pressed herself against him.

Please don't feel the hard-on I'm sporting.

Letting his fingers slide free of her mouth, she buried her face into his neck and breathed him in.

That's it. Take what you need.

Slowly, so he didn't scare her, he put his arm around her. Putting his hand on the back of her neck, he held her against him.

"I'm so sorry," she whispered.

"What for?" he asked.

"Making you bleed. I hurt you." She had her hand wrapped in his shirt and he felt like a fucking King. He knew that was insane. Here she was, scared because she'd hurt him, and he felt this surge of arrogant satisfaction because she was curled up around him, clinging to him like a life preserver.

"Did you do it on purpose?"

"No," she gasped. "Of course not."

"Then why do you feel so guilty? It was an accident."

"I hurt you."

"And you apologized. That was all that was needed. So why did you hide?"

"I . . . I . . . felt so stupid. Can't do anything right. Couldn't even kiss you without hitting you. Idiot."

A growl rumbled out of him. Jesus. What was that? He sounded like a fucking animal. He half-expected her to crawl away from him in fear, but she was still clinging tightly to him.

"You're in trouble now, baby girl."

Okay, that time, she did stiffen up.

"But not for making me bleed or hurting me," he added hastily. "It was an accident. You hurt me. You apologized. It's forgotten."

"Really?"

"Really," he said firmly. "You know what's not easily forgiven?"

"What?"

"Talking about yourself like that. It's unacceptable and I won't put up with it."

"Sorry," she said hastily.

He moved his hand to her ass, tapping it softly. "Unfortunately, saying sorry doesn't wipe that clean. That's ten."

Maybe he was making a mistake. After all, she'd just been hiding under the bed and barely responding to him. He could send her running again.

But he had a feeling he wouldn't.

He thought she probably needed his rules and consequences. That they'd give her a feeling of security that she was desperate for.

"Ten what?"

"You know exactly what I'm talking about." He'd read her books to her. She might not have had a relationship with a Daddy before, but the Little in the book he'd started reading to her had been spanked plenty.

"You wouldn't," she breathed out.

"Oh, I would, baby girl. And that isn't the worst punishment you're owed."

"You're going to punish me for hurting you." She said it like it was a foregone conclusion. Did she think he was a damn monster?

"Never. It was an accident. Understand?"

She nodded.

"Nope. Words."

"Yes, Sir."

Fuck. His balls were going to be blue by the time he got to take care of this hard-on.

"Soon as you're over this hangover, you're going to be punished for disobeying me and coming downstairs. I specifically told you to stay up here, Juliet."

She trembled.

"Don't care if it was Santa Claus," he told her firmly. "You were told to stay upstairs. Then, when we were downstairs, I heard Elias tell you to stay away from us, and what did you do?"

"Threw water and flowers over you."

"One of us could have accidentally hit you when we were fighting. Do you know what that would have done to me?"

"I'm sorry. I didn't want you to harm him."

"That's not your concern. Your only job is to obey me. Understand?"

"I'm not sure I'm going to be very good at that job," she said forlornly.

Ridiculously, despite the seriousness of the conversation, he felt like smiling.

"Maybe you'll get better once you realize the consequences. I also owe you a punishment for not obeying me when Kiesha skated out in front of the truck."

"You can't! We weren't, um, anything then."

"Was still your bodyguard," he growled.

"You spank all your clients?"

"Course not. But none have been naughty like you."

She gasped, clearly offended. "I'm not naughty."

"You absolutely are."

She huffed out a breath.

"Ten for just talking badly about yourself. Fifteen for the other day. Twenty-five for today."

"What? Are you trying to kill me?" she groaned. "I won't sit."

"Kind of the point. Since you're new to this, I'll split it up. Fifty over two nights."

She moaned dramatically.

"Come on, it'll wait until you feel better. I need to get off the floor. Too old for this shit."

She giggled as he moaned and groaned his way out from under the bed.

"How about a bath, then we'll build a fort, and you can play in it while I make some lunch?" he asked her.

"Sounds perfect, Daddy."

20

"**D**uchess, time for lunch."

"No," she called back from the depths of her fort. This thing was awesome! They'd managed to find some large blankets which he'd put over the table and a few chairs. He'd grumbled about it not being big enough, but Juliet loved it.

And she wasn't leaving it.

"Excuse me?"

She trembled. In desire, not fear. Because his voice was deliciously deep and dominant.

Just what she liked.

She'd managed to spend the last hour playing in her fort. It had helped her keep her mind off everything that had happened earlier that morning with Xavier.

They'd had a bit of a stand-off when she'd wanted to bring some iced coffees in with her. Finally, Brick had relented and let her take one as long as she drank some water as well.

Which . . . oh barnacles. She picked up the water bottle, shaking it. Nearly full. Hm. Angelique looked like she needed some water. Naughty girl was getting dehydrated.

She grabbed her doll and attempted to give her a drink of water. It ran down the sides of the doll's face and she tutted at her.

"Naughty Angelique, drink your water."

A flap of the blanket was pulled back and she quickly put the water bottle behind her as Brick poked his head into the fort.

"Now, I must be hallucinating, because I could have sworn that when I called you for lunch that you told me no. But I know that my girl wouldn't have told me no. Would she?"

"Certainly not, Daddy," she said with mock-surprise. "Although it could have been Angelique. She is very naughty."

"Is she just? Well, she must be if she says no to her Daddy."

"Definitely. I should put her into time-out."

"Hm, do you think she'll learn anything in time-out?"

"What would you suggest then, Daddy?"

"Maybe what she needs is a smack on her bottom."

"Daddy! That's just mean!" She hugged Angelique tight.

"Come on, my naughty girls. Time for lunch."

"I don't think Angelique is hungry, though."

"Well, Angelique can stay in here then, and think about her behavior."

"But she might not like being in here alone."

"Pass her to me. She can sit in time-out out here while Juliet eats her lunch."

A huge sigh passed her lips, but she handed Angelique out.

"Baby girl?"

"Yeah, Daddy?" she asked as she crawled out into the room. Urgh. Too much light. She liked her dark cave better.

"Why is your dolly wet?"

Warning. Warning.

"Maybe she peed her pants?"

"Hm. Except it's her face that's wet. Where is your water bottle?"

"I don't know, Daddy. It must have gotten lost."

Please don't look in the fort. Please don't look in the fort.

She should have known her luck wouldn't be that good. He crouched down, then searched through the fort. When he came out, he held a nearly full bottle of water. "What did Daddy say about drinking your water?"

"Um, my memory is a bit faulty, Daddy."

"Oh, I think your memory is just fine," Brick replied sternly. "Daddy told you that you were to drink all of this water, didn't he?"

"But Daddy, it was a lot of water and I only have a little belly."

"That you do. But I bet if this bottle were filled with that iced coffee crap you drink, then you wouldn't have any bother."

He might be right about that. But she wasn't going to agree with him.

"What was the rule?"

"If I drank the coffee, I had to drink all the water."

"And did you?"

"No, Daddy." She thought that was obvious.

"What do you think we should do about that?"

"Get a smaller water bottle?"

"No. Although I think we should get you a special water bottle. I'll order one online."

"I have lots of bottles, Daddy." She led him to a cupboard and opened it.

Brick's eyes widened as he took in the mermaid-themed drink bottles, baby bottles, plates, cups, and cutlery. He drew out one of the larger bottles. "This might work. Can I write on it?"

She nodded curiously.

"Got a marker pen that won't rub off?"

"Um, I think so." She skipped over to her desk. Because why walk if you could skip? She found him a permanent marker, and he drew lines on the bottle then wrote numbers going up in twos beside each line. Then he did the same on the other side.

"This shows you how much water you should drink by ten a.m.

up until eight p.m. We need to refill the bottle at two p.m. Understand?"

She wrinkled her nose. "What's up with your obsession with water, Daddy?"

"It's good for you." He tapped her nose playfully. "Come and eat lunch, then we'll deal with your naughty behavior."

"I wasn't naughty."

"You were trying to make your doll drink your water."

"She looked thirsty," she defended.

He gave her a look. Then he took her hand and led her to the table, where he'd set a plate of sandwiches.

They were cut into triangles and the crusts were trimmed off. There was also a bowl of chopped strawberries and grapes.

He pulled back a chair. "Here you go, Duchess." He did an elaborate bow which had her giggling. She sat and he pushed her in, then he went back to the cupboard and grabbed a mermaid plate and sippy cup. He put some sandwiches on her mermaid plate. Then he poured some water into her sippy cup. She sighed but took a few sips of water in between a couple bites of sandwich. By the time he'd eaten two huge sandwiches, she'd managed one small triangle.

"Eat more," he insisted.

"I don't want anymore, Daddy. If I eat too much at once, my tummy gets sore. I don't think it's a big deal."

"It is when you're already so small a stiff breeze would blow you over."

A flush of embarrassment filled her. Did he not find her attractive like this? Maybe he wanted someone with curves?

"Come here." He pushed his chair back and lifted her onto his lap. Then he tilted up her face. "It's only because I worry about your health. Your happiness, health, and safety are my number one priorities. We need to make sure you eat well because you'll need all your energy once I get you naked and under me."

"Daddy!" she protested, growing red.

Then he reached over and picked up a strawberry, feeding it to her. "Good girl," he praised as she ate it. He fed her a few more plus some grapes before she shook her head. She didn't want to feel too uncomfortable.

Kissing the top of her head, he set her on her feet. "Tummy sore?"

"No, it's okay."

"Good." Standing, he took her hand and steered her towards the only corner in the room that didn't have stuff in it.

"Nose into the corner, bottom poking out."

Corner time? No way. She wouldn't survive.

"Can't you just spank me, Daddy?" she whined.

He raised his eyebrows. "Oh, you're getting a spanking. But corner time comes first."

She was wearing her favorite mermaid onesie, which had a drop seat. When he had her positioned in the corner, he lowered the drop seat then started to draw down her panties.

"Daddy!" She stiffened.

He quickly tugged her panties back up. "Too much? Fuck. Sorry, Duchess, I—"

"No, no, it's all right. I just . . . I wasn't expecting it, I guess."

"No, it's my fault. I need to go at your pace. Sometimes I don't always think. Is it okay for me to bare your bottom during punishments?"

She let out a deep breath.

Be brave.

Picking her up, he carried her to the sofa and sat with her on his lap. "Baby girl?"

"Nobody has ever seen me naked."

"Are you worried about what I'll think of your body? Because I can tell you right now, you could have a third hairy nipple and I'd think you were the most beautiful person I've ever seen."

"Ew, that's kind of gross."

He cupped her face with his hand then laid a soft kiss on her lips. "The point is that nothing you can tell me or show me will change how I feel about you."

"Are you sure?" she asked in a voice that sounded lost. She wrapped her hands in his T-shirt, needing him to anchor her.

"Positive." He brushed her hair back off her face. "I want you to choose a safeword. Something you wouldn't normally say. It can be used at any time. Doesn't have to be during punishment. You're to use it if you're in pain or scared or uncomfortable and you need me to stop what we're doing to talk. Okay?"

"All right. How about . . . Romeo."

"Romeo?" He grinned. "All right, Romeo it is."

"I find it hard to . . . to let other people see me without being covered up. It makes me feel vulnerable."

"I get that. Won't push you into anything that you're not ready for. If you need to stay fully clothed, then that's what you'll do. This is at your pace, Duchess. Not mine."

"You're a good man, Brick."

"Wish I was better."

"I have anxiety. I take medication for it. And I have ways of managing it. I know Reuben might have mentioned it to you, but I wanted to tell you too."

"Are you allowed to drink alcohol while taking your medication?"

She shook her head.

"Damn it, baby girl. Wish you'd told me."

"Not something that's easy to admit. But I wanted to tell you, so you know why I have the issues that I do. I think I'll always have them. Are you sure you can put up with me being like this?"

"Put up with? There is no putting up with you. I care about you just the way you are. I don't want you to change. I just want you to be happy and healthy."

"I am. I mean, I know I still have issues and have to take medication. And I wasn't really happy with my job. But with you, I feel more settled. Less like a freak and more normal."

"Hey, I don't ever want you to call yourself a freak, understand me?" His face was stern. "Or you'll get yourself one hell of a spanking."

"Yes, Daddy."

"Does Little space help? With your anxiety?"

"Yeah. It's like a stress relief. I don't feel nearly as worried about everything. Which is amazing, since I worry a lot."

"And you're sure about this sort of relationship? Me being your Dom? Having rules and punishments?"

"Truthfully?"

"Yeah."

"It's all I've dreamed of. Rules and boundaries make me feel safer. And well, it seems I have a bit of a bratty streak."

"You don't say," he drawled, making her smile.

"This sort of relationship, I think it's exactly what I need."

"You'll tell me if anything I do makes you feel like you're less or that you're being taken advantage of or need to get out—"

She put her hand over his mouth. "You need to trust me, too. I know that there's a difference between harm and hurt. And knowing that you'll punish me if needed will give me closure so I don't have to keep worrying. Anything I can do to stop worrying is a blessing."

"I get it, although I'll still check in with you."

"That's what makes you a good Dom, and a great Daddy."

"That's another rule. No drinking while on your medication."

"Yes, Daddy. I didn't really enjoy the experience."

"I'm sure you didn't. It happens again, and you won't sit for a long while."

Her bottom tingled at the idea. She still had yet to experience a spanking and she really wanted to know what it would feel like.

"What else helps with your anxiety?"

"Having you hold me."

"Good, because that makes me less anxious too."

The idea of big, strong Brick being anxious made her smile.

"Strangely, sucking on something. Like my pacifier."

"Or my fingers?"

"Yeah," she whispered.

"I have another idea for when you're ready to be more intimate. I knew a Little who had anxiety once and it helped her."

"What was it?"

He stared down at her for a long moment. "I don't know whether to tell you yet. You might think I'm trying to push you into something you're not ready for. Now, you're still owed a punishment."

She poked her lip out. "Maybe we can forget it just this once?"

He raised an eyebrow. "From what you've told me, it makes you feel more secure knowing that I will follow through. And there are several other punishments I have yet to follow through with. Although that will change tonight."

Oh, barnacles!

"Drat my honesty."

His chest moved as he laughed. "First, though, you need to decide on your limits. They might change over time, so I'll check in with you every so often. Is having me bare your bottom all right?"

She sucked in a breath. She could put it as a limit, but she wanted to test herself. "I want to try."

"My brave girl."

Satisfaction filled her.

"We'll start with just my hand, then later on, we can discuss whether you're okay with other things."

His hand was pretty big. Hm, she wondered if that whole big hands, big cock thing was true. Or wait, was that big feet, big cock?

She looked down at his feet. She'd need to ask Kiesha. She knew everything. Even when she didn't, she'd make it up.

"I won't know what to do, though."

"You don't have to take the lead. Just use your safeword if things become too overwhelming or frightening."

"All right, I can do that."

He kissed her gently. "But right now, it's time for you to get back in the corner."

She pouted as he put her on her feet then stood. "The corner's boring though, Daddy."

"That's the point. You're supposed to reflect on your naughty behavior and how you can avoid such behavior in the future."

"I wasn't that naughty though, Daddy."

"You didn't drink all your water and tried to hide that you hadn't by giving it to your dolly."

"Silly Angelique, if she'd just drunk the water like she was supposed to, then this wouldn't be happening," she complained.

"Uh, no, if Juliet had drunk her water like she was supposed to, then this wouldn't be happening," he countered as he positioned her in the corner. Then he moved behind her to lower the drop seat on her onesie.

She stiffened slightly.

He ran a hand down her back. "Easy, baby girl. You can do this."

She could do this. He believed in her. She just had to believe that she was strong enough. His fingers pulled down her panties. There was a small moment of panic, of wondering what he thought, if he hated what he saw. But then his fingers brushed down one butt cheek.

A small noise escaped her and he leaned into her, brushing his lips against her neck. "So gorgeous. Who knew you were hiding such a sexy ass under your loose dresses? Plump and pretty."

Plump and pretty? Seriously?

And yet, with each word of praise, her tension eased.

"Given how naughty you are, I'm certain to get a lot of close-ups of this ass in the future."

She sucked in a gasp at those words. "Daddy! I'm not naughty."

Before she thought better of it, she stomped her foot. Whoops.

Silly foot. It seemed to have a mind of its own. Somehow, she thought that wasn't going to go down well. Brick could be extremely gentle, but also rather stern.

Mr. Grumpy Butt.

Brick placed his hands on the wall, his front burning against her back. She gave a slight moan as she pushed her ass back into him. Arousal flooded her. Yikes. She pressed her thighs together, hoping he couldn't smell how turned on she was.

What was it about this position that did it for her?

"Are you having a tantrum, Duchess?" he drawled. "Do you need some help settling into corner time?"

Did she?

"No, Daddy," she squeaked out. Although she wasn't entirely sure about that.

"Now, I think that's a lie. I think you need Daddy's help." He moved to her side. "Push that bottom out. That's it." He drew the sides of the onesie apart, baring her bottom even more.

She let out a slight noise of surprise and he calmly placed a hand over her bottom, warming the skin. "What's your safeword?"

"Romeo."

"You'll use it if you need to. Just remember, Daddy is your protector, your guide, your confidant. I would never do anything to make you feel small or less than me. You're first. Daddy is always second. And that's the way he likes it. Because when his baby girl is happy and healthy, then Daddy is doing his job right."

The words settled around her, like a weighted blanket. Holding her together, making her feel protected, loved.

She sucked in a breath. Did she love him? Could she?

"Understand?"

"Yes, Daddy."

"Good girl. Now, Daddy is going to help you settle into position, and remember, corner time is for reflecting about how naughty you were and what you might do next time to avoid ending up in the corner."

How would he help her settle? Would . . . ouch!

"Daddy!" She moved her hands back to her bare butt. Which he'd just whacked. "No, that hurt. Bad Daddy."

"No, naughty Juliet," he countered. "Move your hands to the wall. You mustn't ever put your hands on your bottom. They could get hurt."

"My butt is hurt!"

"Your butt is meant to hurt. Now, I'm going to count, and each number is how many extra spanks you're going to get once those hands are moved. One—"

She moved her hands back to the wall, ignoring his chuckle. She was no idiot.

"That's better. One extra, so that means you have three more."

Three. She could do this. It wasn't as bad as she thought to be honest. And a small sliver of disappointment filled her.

Wait. What?

How often had she wondered what it would be like to be held accountable for her actions, to be punished? That wasn't Xavier's thing. He tended to treat her like she was fragile.

And he's not your Daddy. He never was. Never will be. So, stop thinking about him like that.

Another smack drew her from her thoughts. Oh, that was good. She might not like the way her butt stung, but she did like how it cleared her mind.

Smack! Smack!

Whew! It was over. Her first spanking. Wow. She couldn't believe she was concerned about it. She'd handled it like a pro.

If she did say so herself.

"Good girl," Brick praised, rubbing her bottom. She preened under his praise. She was a good girl. "Ten minutes of corner time. You're to stay still and think about why you're here, then I will tell you when to move."

"Okay, Daddy."

Dude. She totally rocked this punishment thing. If this was as bad as it was going to be, then she'd be free to do anything she liked with little consequence.

Ten minutes later, she was supremely bored and rethinking that stance.

Corner time sucked.

There was only so much thinking she wanted to do. And she had toys to play with. Her fort was calling her.

"All right, corner time is finished. Come here, Duchess."

Turning, she skipped over to where he sat on a high-backed chair. Where had he found that chair, and why was it in her playroom? It didn't go with any of the furniture.

She skidded to a stop with a frown. "What's that chair doing in here? Where did you find it?"

He raised an eyebrow at her questions. "Hm, I'm not sure I like that tone in your voice. Do you want to try that again?"

She swallowed heavily. Whoops. She probably did sound a bit demanding and rude. But she was never keen on change. Found it hard to adjust. And this was *her* playroom.

"Sorry, Daddy. But it doesn't suit the playroom. Why is it in here?"

"It's here because it's just become your spanking chair."

Her mouth dropped open. "What?"

"I agree, it doesn't fit the décor. But that's the point, really. Because it's not a chair that you want Daddy to sit in as that means you're going to get your butt spanked."

Her hands went reflectively behind her ass. "But, Daddy! I've already had my spankin'."

Brick looked confused, then surprised. "What? You mean those smacks you got in the corner? That wasn't your spanking, that was to settle you down. And one was because you moved your hands."

"But . . . but . . ." She couldn't even find words.

"Oh, poor Duchess. You really thought that was your spanking?" He gave her a sympathetic look and she stuck out her lower lip, feeling very sorry for herself. He held out his hand to her. "Come here."

She took it, letting him settle her onto his lap. He held her tight, and she cuddled in, her face burying against his chest. This was undoubtedly her favorite place to be. His touch settled her. She felt so safe. Wanted. Cherished.

"You're the best man I've ever met, Brick Sampson," she whispered.

He froze for a moment. "I'm not a good man."

"You are."

He kissed the top of her head. "I live in a studio apartment in a neighborhood I wouldn't allow you to step a foot into. My bank account is empty. My business is on the brink of bankruptcy. I'm grouchy and bossy. You should run a mile from me."

"Brenton Sampson," she said indignantly. Drawing back, she glared up at him. "Do you really think I'm so shallow that the only reason I'd want to be with you is because of what you could give me?"

"Well, obviously not since I can't give you any of this." He waved his hand around the room.

She cupped his face between her hands. "All of this is just stuff, you silly man. It can't love me, or hug me, or keep me safe."

"The alarm system you have will do a pretty good job of keeping you safe."

She narrowed her gaze at him. "Are you being deliberately obtuse?"

He shifted around, looking uncomfortable and her heart softened. "I don't want stuff, I want you. The man who takes care of me fiercely and without apology. Who pumps up my bike tires even though I can't ride it. Who worries that I'm not drinking enough water. Who is willing to do whatever it takes to ensure I'm happy."

"That's all I want, baby girl." He kissed her gently. "Now, enough buttering me up. Time for your spanking."

"But Daddy, surely we can forget about that now."

"Surely we cannot." He lifted her off his lap, then helped guide her so she was lying across his thighs. "I know there are things I can't give you. That will take a long time for me to give you, but there are things you need that I can give you. Like the spanking you need."

"Daddy, nobody needs a spanking," she argued.

"I have to disagree." He rubbed his hand over her bottom. "You most certainly need a spanking."

21

Damn, his luck was looking up. He couldn't believe this gorgeous, beautiful, darling girl was his. That she didn't care that he didn't have two pennies to rub together.

He knew it was shallow to worry about money, but he wanted to give her everything she deserved.

And you will. Just don't let your insecurities get to you. Do not push her away.

Yeah. No way he was letting that happen.

His cock grew hard and he knew she could feel it from the way she sucked in her breath.

"Ignore it, Duchess. It just thinks you're so damn beautiful, it can't help itself."

"Could I see it?" she asked.

Shock made him still. She wanted to see him?

"Forget it, I shouldn't have asked," she said hastily.

"You can ask me anything. And you can see my cock any time you like."

"Any time?" she asked slyly.

"When we're alone," he hastily added. "Brat. You don't ever

have to be shy or embarrassed about asking me for what you need, Juliet."

"It's not weird?"

"Uh, that you want to admire my dick? Nah, that's not weird at all. Be weird if you didn't want to."

She giggled, the way he'd intended.

"But that has to wait until after your spanking. What's your safeword?"

"Did you forget already, Daddy? I suppose you are pretty old."

He tickled the inside of her thighs until she squealed with laughter. "No, brat, I didn't forget. I want you to say it so you remember it."

"It's Romeo, Daddy. Stop!"

"Say it if you need to. Ten is the count."

He started smacking her bottom, turning her pale skin pink. She started kicking her feet, wriggling on his lap, which was doing little to help his raging hard-on.

Pausing, he ran his finger down the crack of her ass as she sobbed for breath. "Is it o-over, Daddy?"

Aww. His poor girl.

"No, baby girl. You're halfway through."

She let out a cry of despair that he was pretty sure was exaggerated.

"Five more, unless you're saying your safeword?"

"No, Daddy."

He started in again, moving his hand lower and peltering spank after spank onto her full cheeks. It wasn't a really hard spanking. Not for her first punishment, especially when she had more owing tonight.

While she cried, he turned her over and then lifted her into his arms to carry her into her bedroom. He tried to lay her down on her bed, but she held onto him, refusing to let go.

"Shh, Duchess. I'm going to come in with you. Just let me get you some tissues and a washcloth. Good girl, here's your pacifier."

He managed to get her onto the bed and she grasped hold of her blankie. Quickly, he wet a cloth and grabbed some tissues, and then he somehow managed to get into the cot-bed with her. It wasn't an easy fit.

She grasped hold of him, clinging with her hand in his shirt and her face pressed to his neck. His skin was soon wet from her tears, but he held her until she calmed. Then drawing her back, he wiped her cheeks and nose with the tissue, directing her to blow before wiping her red face down with the cloth.

"There you are, Duchess. Good as new."

She gave him a skeptical look and he bit his lip to hide his smile.

"My bottom is not as good as new," she told him haughtily.

"Hm, better look at it. Roll over."

Her mouth dropped open. "No!"

"Duchess, roll over. Aftercare is my job and I need to make sure you're all right."

"I don't think I need aftercare."

"Aftercare also includes cuddles and kisses."

"Okay, okay." She rolled and he ran a finger over her bottom, which was still bared. It was red, but that wouldn't take long to fade.

"It doesn't look so bad. I think someone is protesting too much."

"Am not, Daddy!"

She gave him an indignant look over her shoulder.

"You wouldn't be trying to fool Daddy, would you?" he drawled.

"Never, Daddy."

Yeah, right.

Reluctantly, he drew her panties and drop seat up. "I'll check on your bottom again. When Daddy tells you to get over his knee for an inspection, you'll be expected to obey straight away."

"You can't!"

"I can," he replied sternly, rolling her onto her side and facing her. He grasped hold of her chin. "I take your care very seriously."

"Maybe too seriously," she muttered.

"No such thing." He leaned in and kissed her. "Now, are you really upset with Daddy? Because if you are, I might keep my dick in my pants a bit longer. Don't want to tempt you into an act of violence."

JULIET KNEW she went bright red. She couldn't believe she'd asked to see his cock.

Hussy.

"Please, Daddy? I promise not to hurt your pee-pee."

"Let's not call it a pee-pee, yeah?" he grumbled.

"Okay, Daddy. Can I see your disco stick?" she asked sweetly.

"Nope, not using that one either."

"Cream stick? I like cream."

He narrowed his gaze. "It's not a cream stick. Cock or dick are acceptable terms."

"That's no fun, Daddy. Everyone calls them that. I think your dick needs a proper name. It's an individual. It doesn't want to be like everyone else."

"You haven't even seen it yet."

"But I can tell. Maybe we should call it sweetie-pie."

"You asking for another spanking, brat?" he growled.

"No, Daddy. That's just mean. I'm just trying to come up with a good name for your pee-wee. How about pounder? Is that more manly?"

"How about we don't name my dick anything."

"Please, can I see it?" she begged.

"You're really sure?"

She nodded. "I'm sure. And maybe, could I see all of you?"

He eyed her then nodded slowly. Sitting, he took off his shirt. She gasped as she took him in. Tanned. Firm. Strong.

Leaning in, she licked his chest, right above his nipple. He sucked in a sharp breath.

"If I lick it, then it's mine," she told him, totally laying claim on him.

"Yeah? Feel free to lick anything you like then."

Oh, she would.

He lay back. She touched his hands as he went to undo his belt. "Could I explore first?"

"Yeah, Duchess." He put his hands behind his head, indicating that she was in charge.

And she fell in love with him a little bit more.

She felt like she'd been given an all-day pass to Disneyland. Even better, because she didn't have to fight crowds. Leaning in, she sucked a nipple into her mouth. He let out a low noise and she jumped back. "Did I hurt you?"

"Fuck, no," he muttered. "Felt so good."

Oh. Wow. Okay, she liked that she could make him feel good. She sucked on the nipple again while her hands roamed over his chest.

"Duchess, you have no idea how good your hands feel on me."

She smiled as she licked her way down his perfect abs. Seriously. How did he get abs like that? She felt like there was no way she could measure up to the perfection of his body.

"You're gorgeous," she told him as she ran her thumbs lightly over his nipples.

"And you're a tease," he muttered. "Kiss me."

Moving up, she pressed her lips to his. But frustration filled her when he didn't take control. She sat back with a distressed sigh. "I'm not very good at kissing. Can you take over?"

"Come here." He moved one hand and beckoned her forward, then he wrapped his hand around the back of her neck. Then he kissed her. She sighed with pleasure.

So good.

When he pulled her away, she was swaying, pleasure making the room spin.

"You okay, Duchess?"

"Your kisses make my head spin," she told him.

He grinned. "Good."

It was very, very good.

Then her gaze lowered to his belt. "Can I?"

"Yeah, you can. Just remember that nothing happens that you don't want, okay? I'll keep my hands behind my back, and you can explore as much as you like."

"What if you . . . I mean, if you react?"

"Oh, I can guarantee I'll react. You mean what if I need to come?"

She nodded, knowing she was bright red. Dear Lord. Was she really having this conversation?

"Then I'll ask you to stop so I can calm down a bit. But I have excellent control. Or I used to, before I met you," he added quietly.

She didn't think she was meant to hear that last part.

"And if I want to, um, I mean . . . if I don't want you to calm down?"

His eyebrows shot up. "You want to jack me off, Duchess?"

She wasn't sure she'd quite put it like that, but . . .

"Maybe," she whispered. "I've never seen a man's penis, or touched one in real life. I might not do it right, but I think I'd like to try."

"Not much you can do wrong, other than hit me in the balls or use too much teeth on my cock."

Okay, she lied. She could go even brighter red.

"Not that you have to use your mouth," he added. "Maybe one

day, but not today. Although I did have an idea for your anxiety if you like the idea of using your mouth."

She blinked. "You think giving a blow job would ease my anxiety?"

It sounded odd. And as though it would be more of an ease to his anxiety than hers.

"No, not that. You ever hear of cock warming?"

She shook her head.

"Basically, it's where a sub will warm their Dom's cock."

With what? A blanket? That didn't make . . . oh wait.

"Like in their mouth?" she managed to ask.

"Or their pussy or ass, which you're obviously not ready for."

"But isn't that just sex or a blow job?"

"No, because literally, all they are doing is warming their Dom's cock. It might harden then go soft, but it's not about sex. I once knew a Little who liked to take her Daddy's cock into her mouth when she was anxious. Like a cock pacifier."

Cock pacifier? So, basically, a giant pacifier. Well, not that she knew how big he was, but yeah, those feet looked big.

Was he kidding her? He was just saying this to show her how naïve she was, right?

"I promise it's a thing. But if you're not into the idea, you don't have to do it."

"So, when this Little you knew was anxious, she would just suck his cock?"

"Not suck it. Although there might be light sucking, that's not the point. If she was feeling out of sorts or worrying, she'd ask his permission to take his cock into her mouth. He'd continue with whatever he was doing. She said it helped her focus and relax. It doesn't need to be a thing between us."

She got that. She couldn't help but feel intrigued.

"I don't know if it will help, but I . . . I kind of like the idea."

"If you want to try, that's something we can do."

"Can I look now?" she asked, gesturing to his cock.

He nodded and she started undoing the belt, then he had to help her pull down his jeans and boxers. His dick sprang free and she sucked in a breath.

Lord, have mercy on her soul.

That thing was enormous.

"Duchess, Duchess, look at me," he urged her. Reaching up, he grabbed her chin, turning her face towards him. "It's not going to hurt you."

"It's huge!" How could it not hurt her?

He grinned. Actually grinned. She smacked her hand against his pecs.

Um, ouch.

She rubbed the palm of her hand. "Are you made of concrete?"

He was frowning now. Reaching out, he grabbed hold of her hand. "Don't hit me."

"You can't tell me that hurt you."

"It hurt you. And that isn't allowed. Now, as for my dick being too large, it's not. All it means is that I have to make sure you're nice and wet before I fuck you. Which I'll do, with pleasure." He gave her a wolfish grin.

Be still her heart.

"Still want to touch?" he asked.

Yeah. She did. He drew his pants and boxers down his legs, so he was lying there, completely naked.

Wow. He was gorgeous.

"I promise, he won't bite."

Reaching out, she ran her finger along the shaft. Okay, his skin was softer than she'd thought. It twitched and she let out a startled giggle.

"You won't hurt it."

"Can you tell me what to do?"

"Nothing you do will be wrong," he reassured her. "Put your hand around it."

She moved with more confidence, wrapping her hand around it gently.

"Squeeze it tighter, that's it. Fuck, yes. Now run your hand up and down the shaft. Good girl. Yes."

His breath came in faster pants as she moved her hand up and down.

"It's so hard, yet soft. Weird."

"Duchess, when you have your hand on my dick, I'd appreciate it if you didn't call it weird."

She giggled. "Sorry, Daddy."

Some wetness appeared at the slit and she ran her thumb over it, then drew her thumb to her mouth to suck on it.

A hum of pleasure escaped her as his taste burst onto her tongue. She'd thought that it was meant to taste bad.

"Fuck, Duchess. You don't know how hot you look right now," he told her.

A flush of pleasure filled her and she moved lower until her face was right up close to his dick. She decided she wanted it in her mouth. She reached out with her tongue and licked her way along the shaft.

Oh. She liked that. So, she did it again. And again. Then she became aware that he was muttering something.

"Are you saying the times tables?"

"Whatever I need to do not to come," he told her.

"You don't want to come?"

"Not so quickly. Don't want you to think I have no staying power. But fuck, your mouth is magic."

"Yeah?" Well, now she needed to use more of her magic on him. She took the head into her mouth and sucked.

"Fucking hell!" he groaned.

Wrapping her hand around the base, she took more of him in. But instead of moving, she just suckled on him lightly.

Oh. Okay. Maybe she was getting some idea of where he was going with this cock pacifier thing. Because she really liked having his dick in her mouth.

But she really wanted to see him come as well. Moving her mouth from his dick, she sat up and knelt between his thighs, facing him.

"Daddy?"

"Yes?" He opened his eyes to stare up at her. She ran a finger up and down his dick. Ooh, it twitched again. She giggled.

Her attention landed on his balls. She forgot what she'd been going to ask him as she ran a finger over his ball sac.

He groaned.

"Can I touch your balls?" she asked.

"Yes. Be gentle," he warned.

She'd figured that. She cupped them, surprised by their warmth. With her other hand, she started jacking him.

"Fuck, Duchess. Fuck!" He groaned. "You need to stop."

She froze. "Did I hurt you?"

He was panting and a light sweat had broken out over his tanned skin, making it glisten.

"No," he reassured her. "But I'm close to coming."

"Would that be bad?"

His gaze met hers. "Not for me. Are you sure you want that?"

"I'd like to. If that's okay," she added.

"Yeah. It's more than okay. That would feel amazing."

Ooh. She liked the idea of making him feel amazing. So, she went back to drawing her hand up and down his cock, while she lightly played with his balls. He moaned, tensing, and his balls seemed to draw up into his body.

"I'm going to come!"

Good. She watched as ropes of his come landed on his stomach. Then she gentled her touch as he panted, shuddering.

"Can I touch it?"

He muttered something under his breath. "Yeah, Duchess."

"Is it wrong?"

"Nothing is wrong as long as both of us agree," he told her. "And we're not harming someone else."

Oh good. She ran her finger through his come. "There's less than I thought."

He let out a chuckle. "Don't ever lose that honesty."

"Sorry. Should I not have said that?"

He shook his head. "I love that you say what you're thinking."

She gave him a shy smile.

"Pass me the cloth. I'll clean up."

His cock was at half-mast as she grabbed the cloth, but she didn't hand it over. "Can I do it?"

"Of course."

She cleaned him up, loving that she got to take care of him for once. By now, his cock had softened. She wanted him back in her mouth. She leaned down, intent on doing just that when he tapped her nose. "You have to ask first."

She glanced up in surprise.

"I'm a man who likes to be in control. I gave up a lot of it just now because I didn't want to scare you. But unless I give you free rein, I want you to ask permission before you take me into your mouth."

"Okay," she whispered. "Can I have your cock in my mouth, Daddy?"

"You may."

She put the side of her face on his lower stomach then took half of him into her mouth. Even soft, he was huge. She adjusted, taking as much as she could. She suckled lightly, like she might with a pacifier. This was different, of course. He was much bigger and warmer. She sighed happily as he ran his fingers through her hair.

"You like that, Duchess?"

"Hm," she replied.

"That's good. I do too. If you need me, you can ask at any time. If it's possible, I'll give this to you."

Damn, that sounded perfect.

22

"Daddy, will you bathe me?"

He looked up from his phone in surprise. He'd just sent another message to Reuben. Why wasn't he answering? Maybe he needed to send Elias or Sterling to Boston to check on him.

"Bathe you, Duchess? You mean run you a bath?"

"No, I, umm, mean, will you bathe me?"

Now he really looked at her. His eyebrows rose. "While you're naked?"

"Of course while I'm naked, Daddy." She gave him a 'duh' look that he didn't appreciate.

His gaze turned stern and she bit her lip.

"Please, Daddy. I don't want to keep worrying about it, and I figure if we do it in Little space, then maybe I won't be so worried about you seeing me. Without clothes. Naked."

Okay, now the brat was rubbing it in. He thought about it. Last night, before he'd put her to bed, they'd done some kissing and heavy petting, but he hadn't gotten his hand under her pajamas.

This seemed like quite a leap.

"Are you sure?" he asked.

Her face closed off. Shit. Wrong thing to ask. He stood, but she stepped back.

"You're right. Silly me. Gotta go potty." She turned, but obviously didn't recall that she'd been building a castle with blocks and plowed right into them, landing on her knees.

"My castle!"

"Baby girl." He hurried to her and picked her up, placing her on a bean bag. "Are you all right?"

"My castle is destroyed. I spent hours on it!"

She'd spent about fifteen minutes on it. She had a short attention span and a bit of a flair for the dramatic.

She was adorable.

"I'll help you rebuild."

"It's no good! It was perfect. It will never be that perfect again." She let out a small sob.

"Hey." He cupped her chin, turning her face to his. "It can be perfect again. Just a different sort of perfect."

She shook her head. "Ruined. Never to be fixed."

"Juliet," he warned, knowing they weren't talking about the castle. "That's not true. Let me see your knees."

"They're fine."

"You landed hard, they could be bruised."

She brushed his hands away. "No, Daddy. They're fine."

Calmly, he stared up at her. "Duchess, don't push Daddy's hands away like that when he's trying to take care of you."

She pouted. "You don't want to bathe me."

"I never said that. I was worried it would be too much for you. Now, move your hands away."

He raised her skirt, taking in the red marks on her knees. Gently, he pressed his fingers against them. She hissed.

"Fine, huh?" he asked dryly. "These might bruise."

"I've had worse."

He cupped her face between his hands. "I want to bathe you. But I don't want you to offer because you think you have to."

"I'm not," she whispered. "I want to try. Please."

"Then that's what we'll do," he told her decisively.

Standing, he picked her up in his arms and carried her through the bedroom and into the bathroom. Then he set her gently down on the counter.

"What disgusting color do you want to make your bath tonight?" He looked through her bath bombs.

"Daddy, they're not disgusting." She gave him a stern look, waggling her finger. "They're pretty. I want the blue one with the silver stars. I want to sparkle like nighttime."

Right.

He ran the bath and then put the bomb in it. It started to disintegrate as he turned back to her.

"Sure?"

She nodded. "Yes, Daddy."

Gently, he lifted her down then started taking off her T-shirt. She was trembling as he took it off. She didn't have a bra on, and her small breasts were soon revealed.

"Remember, you can say your safeword at any time," he told her.

She nodded shakily then cupped her breasts once he had the T-shirt off.

"Don't hide, Duchess," he told her in a low voice. "You're beautiful."

"Small."

"Small can be beautiful. Flowers are small, but usually perfectly formed." He tugged off her skirt, nearly laughing at the sight of her panties. On the front were the words: *Lick me until* followed by an image of an ice cream.

"Lick me until ice cream?" He grinned.

She went bright red. "I thought they were cute ice cream

panties. It didn't click until I received them in the mail what it meant."

"I will happily lick you until you scream," he murmured, staring up at her with heat in his gaze.

Her blush filled her face, and he took the opportunity as she was occupied with her thoughts to whip off the last of her clothing. Then she was trembling, naked, goosebumps covered her skin.

"You're cold."

She shook her head. She had a habit of not talking when she was upset or worried.

"Words, Duchess," he reminded her.

"Nervous."

"Why?"

"That you'll think I'm ugly."

Yeah, he was feeling very bloodthirsty. Standing, he cupped her face, glaring down at her ferociously. "You listen to me. You are not ugly. Naked or not, you are beautiful."

He kissed her gently, then that kiss turned to something harder. He moved his mouth around to her ear. "I'm so fucking hard for you."

She sucked in a breath. "I . . . I . . ."

"I want you so bad. The most beautiful girl in the world." He needed to control his lust for her, though, because she needed him to help her through this. She needed reassurance. Not to be pressed up against the bathroom counter and fucked.

Thoroughly fucked.

"Come on, baby girl. Let's get you all nice and clean."

She stared up at him, her lips trembling before her gaze moved to his cock.

"Eyes on mine," he warned. "I'm starting to worry that you only want me for my cock."

"Daddy!" she protested. Although her shoulders eased and a glint of humor entered her gaze. "It is a pretty cock."

"Brat." He turned her towards the bath and swatted her ass, making her yelp. "Come on."

Turning off the bath, he tested the temperature then helped her into the water. She sighed with bliss as he knelt and reached into the bag of toys she had. "What have we here? Mermaids?"

"Those are my special bath mermaids, Daddy." Picking them up, she started to play with them, swimming them through the water. It surprised him how easily she relaxed when in the bath. Maybe she felt more covered up. Although her breasts were still easily visible, her pretty, perky nipples, calling to him.

Easy, man.

Grabbing a cloth, he started washing her, marveling at her smooth, creamy skin. He worried for a moment that she didn't get enough Vitamin D with how much time she spent inside. Maybe they'd have to make time for outside play.

When he started to clean her legs, she tensed slightly, but she didn't move away as he went higher up her thighs.

"You're perfect," he murmured to her, prepared to heap on as much praise as she needed to hear. "Most beautiful, darling, smart, and kind girl."

She froze and he glanced up at her to see tears dripping down her face. Shit. That wasn't meant to make her sad.

"You mean that, Daddy?"

"Every word, Duchess." She threw herself into his arms. He caught her, holding her tight and murmuring to her quietly. He rocked her back and forth.

"Thank you, Daddy."

"No, little one. Thank you for trusting me with you. I promise to never let you down."

∾

AFTER HER BATH, Brick helped dress her in a pair of pajamas that had pictures of mermaids over them. Then he brushed out her hair. She'd loved having him bathe her. Although, she couldn't stop herself from thinking about Xavier briefly. He'd actually given her the bath mermaids for Christmas last year. He could be so sweet.

Her phone buzzed as he clumsily finished braiding it. Brick was sitting on the rocking chair and she was between his feet. She raced over and grabbed it off the bedside table, relief filling her as she saw it was a text from Reuben. Although, usually, he hated texting.

REUBEN: *Mini, sorry I haven't called. I need to go silent for a while, if you don't hear from me for a few days, don't worry. Stay safe. Love you.*

WELL, shit. That wasn't cryptic or anything. Plus, thought she was going to worry more than ever.

"What is it?" Brick asked, walking over to her.

She turned the message around to show him. He swore quietly under his breath.

"Something's wrong, isn't it? I mean, when someone says not to worry, that usually means you should start worrying more. Oh God." She started to hyperventilate. "What am I going to do?"

"First of all, you need to calm down," he told her in a low, firm voice. "Look at me."

She raised her gaze to his and he cupped her face between his hands.

Steady. Firm. Strong.

"Everything will be fine."

"How do you know?"

"I just do."

She nodded. Everything would be all right. This was Reuben, for goodness sake. He was basically indestructible.

"Tell me you're not going to worry."

She gave him an incredulous look. Really?

"Right, what am I saying? Now you'll worry more than ever." He huffed out a breath. "Then we'll just have to keep you busy, so you don't have time to worry. You trust your brother, yeah?"

"Yes."

"You know he can take care of himself?"

"Yep. He's ruthless and smart and savage."

"And he wouldn't like it if you were worrying after he said not to, right?"

"No, he'd hate it."

"Then you need to have faith in him."

"Right. Right, of course."

Fingers shaking, she sent him a text back.

JULIET: *Go kick some bad guy ass. I'm good. I love you. Be safe xoxo.*

SHE LET OUT A SHUDDERING BREATH. He'd be fine. This was Reuben. He was always fine. It was everyone else who had to worry when he was on the warpath.

Only, she had no idea how she was supposed to sleep at night wondering what was going on. And then Brick said something she totally wasn't expecting.

"Come on, it's time we started getting your punishment out of the way."

She gaped at him as he took her hand and led her into the playroom to where the punishment chair was. He sat and patted his lap. "Over you go."

"W-what?" she squeaked out.

"Your spanking, remember? We're splitting it over two nights. Twenty-five tonight."

"But . . . but . . ."

"But what?"

"I thought we weren't doing that! You didn't spank me last night!" So she thought that meant he wouldn't.

"Because I thought you'd had enough with everything that went on. Come on, let's knock these out."

Knock these out? Was he for real right now?

"Baby girl, do you need to spend some time in the corner first?"

"No, Daddy!" She really did not. She moved as slowly as she dared, then lay herself over his lap.

"Good girl."

"Let's do them all."

He'd been in the middle of pulling down her pants and panties when he paused.

"All?"

"Yep. All forty." She crossed her fingers as she said that, hoping he couldn't see.

"Good try," he said dryly. "It's fifty."

"Drat. Thought you might have forgotten."

"Because I'm so old?"

"Daddy, I'd never say that." Think it maybe . . .

"You know, I could add on extras for you trying to deceive me," he said casually.

"What?" She turned to look over her shoulder at him. "No, Daddy! That's just mean."

"And trying to deceive Daddy isn't naughty?"

She huffed out a breath. "Sorry, Daddy."

Truth was, she could probably use this spanking to help clear her head. She'd spent so much time worrying about Reuben and Xavier, who she hadn't heard from since he'd stormed out of the house yesterday, that she was exhausted.

"I don't want to give you fifty at once when it's only your second spanking. We'll stick with the plan. But if you break a safety rule again, your punishment will be harsher." They'd spent some time today going through rules, expectations, and her limits. She knew he meant every word. He was steadfast about her following rules for her health or safety.

"You disobeyed me. Several times. You put yourself in danger. That isn't acceptable, and you earned yourself a harsh punishment. I don't like having to deliver it, but it's what is needed so you know that sort of behavior won't be tolerated, and you do not do it again."

"Yes, Daddy. I'm sorry."

"You're precious to me. I couldn't live if something happened to you."

Did he really mean that? It seemed crazy to her.

"You're precious to me too, Daddy."

He pushed her panties and pants right down and she kicked them off. Her butt was fully bare and she tensed for a moment, but he didn't give her a chance to feel self-conscious.

He started spanking her immediately. It wasn't long until she was kicking her feet, trying to wriggle away. He held her steady as he gave her the first ten spanks. She was sniffling by the time he stopped to rub her lower back soothingly.

"How you doing, Duchess?" he asked in a low voice.

"Oh, just fine," she replied. "How's your day going? Funny weather we're having at the moment."

"Smart-ass," he replied. But she heard the smile in his voice.

"Gonna give you the last fifteen without stopping. Ready for the rest?"

"Does anyone ever say yes to that?" she squeaked out.

He let out a huff. But before she could say anything else in the hopes of delaying the inevitable, he started spanking her again.

She couldn't help but kick her legs as he turned her ass into a throbbing mass of agony.

Okay, it wasn't that bad. But it was still damn sore. And by the time he finished, she was crying, lying limply over his lap.

And her brain was blessedly empty of all thoughts and worries.

Instead of turning her over immediately to give her the cuddles that she had totally earned, he ran his fingers lightly over her ass.

"Damn beautiful ass you have, Duchess."

She rolled her eyes. Was he admiring his handiwork? "Thanks. It serves me well."

A short bark of laughter.

Then she sucked in a breath as he moved his finger down the crack of her ass.

"Can't wait until you're ready for me to explore back here."

Holy heck.

He pressed against her dark hole and she let out a small noise of pleasure. How was that pleasurable?

They'd talked about anal sex and she said she was interested. Maybe not before she had actual sex, though.

"It's okay. I'm not going to do anything more," he soothed. "Not tonight. But at some stage, I'm going to play more back here."

A shiver of pleasure ran through her.

Oh, dear Lord. What was wrong with her?

"You'll like it."

All right for him to say. He wasn't getting things up his ass.

How had this become her life?

23

He was a complete idiot.

Fuck.

With a groan, Xavier rolled over to check the time. Ten a.m.

Double fuck.

He'd called in sick to work. First time he'd ever pulled a sicky in his life. But it would have been worse than negligent to take his drunken ass into work.

Still. He felt terrible about that.

It wasn't like he'd gotten any answers from the bottom of a whiskey bottle. All he had now was the headache from hell and regrets.

So many fucking regrets.

He'd messed up so bad. Taken her for granted.

What he needed was to get his shit together. The other morning, he'd acted like a child who didn't get his way. Who had their Christmas present taken away when it had never been his in the first place.

He owed Juliet a huge apology.

He owed her bodyguards a big apology. Including the guy who'd claimed her.

And wasn't that going to suck ass? But Xavier was an adult. He could own up to his mistakes.

Living in the same town as them, well, that was going to be challenging. But maybe it was better this way. This bodyguard seemed rougher than he'd have chosen for her. But he might have a gentler side. Neither of them had made a good impression on the other one.

Sure, he didn't like that they barely knew each other and he was claiming her in a bar. Then again, maybe that's what he should have done.

And now, he had to go apologize, beg her forgiveness, and find some way to spend time with her and her new man so he could ensure that this Brick guy was worthy of his angel.

"But I don't want any more to eat, Daddy."

Brick gave her a firm look. She didn't eat nearly enough on a good day, and since they'd had that visit from Xavier, her eating habits had gotten worse. She was barely eating enough to keep a mouse alive, and he knew he had to get firmer with her.

"If you want to go swimming, I want to see half the food on that plate gone."

She gave him a sulky look. Most of the time, she was very sweet-natured, with a slightly bratty side that he quite liked. But when it came to eating, she could get very stubborn.

He was also worried that she wasn't sleeping enough. She looked tired with bags under her eyes. Tonight, he might insist on sleeping in her bedroom with her. Or maybe out on the sofa in her playroom with the door open if she wasn't keen on him sleeping in the same room with her.

A long sigh left her. He raised an eyebrow. "Would you prefer something else?"

"No," she muttered, poking at the sandwiches he'd made them.

"Would you like to eat your lunch on a hot bottom?"

"Daddy! What kind of question is that?"

He leaned forward. "A serious one."

She picked up a sandwich and ate a bite. She'd just finished a triangle, which made him breathe a bit easier when his phone rang.

"What's up?" he asked Elias.

He hadn't seen either of them much since he'd been spending more of his time with Juliet.

"The Doc's at the gate," Elias told him.

He stiffened then forced himself to relax. She was his.

He had to learn to trust.

"Yeah? He didn't just come in?"

"Nope."

Interesting.

"Wants to know if he can. Said he sent a message to Juliet, but hasn't heard back."

Because he made her put her phone aside while in Little space. Otherwise, she obsessed over it, checking every few moments for a message from her brother.

"So, do I let him in?"

"Wait a sec." He put the phone on mute. "Duchess?"

"I'm eating, I'm eating," she replied hastily, stuffing another triangle into her mouth. Both of her cheeks puffed out, making her look like a chipmunk.

"Xavier is here. Wants to come in. Said he sent you a message."

He walked into her room and grabbed her phone from one of those holders she had everywhere.

She grabbed it, reading the text. "He wants to apologize and see us both." She glanced up at him and he saw the hope in her face.

"You want to see him, Duchess?" he asked in a gruff voice.

She'd chosen him.

Xavier's loss was his gain.

But that didn't mean he could cut the guy from her life. He'd taken care of her for a long time and Brick had to be grateful to him for that.

And he wanted to do what was best for Juliet. The doctor was important to her.

But he best not make a wrong move . . .

"What do you think I should do?"

He cupped her chin. "That wasn't what I asked. Do you want to see him?"

She winced.

"Duchess, that's fine. He's your friend. You should see him as much as you want."

"He was kind of acting odd last time he was here. He tried to fire you."

"Because I wouldn't let him see you. Fact is, I'd have done worse if I'd been in his shoes. So, you want to see him?"

She nodded.

"Good. Tell you what, put your bathing suit on. We'll talk to him then go swimming after."

"Where are you going?"

"Just to let him in." He kissed the top of her head. "I promise to be nice."

He ignored the incredulous look she sent him. He knew how to be nice.

Sometimes.

~

THE DOOR to the house opened as Xavier got out of his car. His shoulders tightened, but he'd known that he would be the first obstacle to go through. Reaching back, he drew out the bunch of flowers he'd brought with him.

White tulips.

Juliet's favorite.

Walking up the stairs to the front door, he felt ridiculously nervous. He eyed the big man waiting for him warily.

"I come in peace," he joked. Xavier got along with everyone. He was good at his job, a law-abiding citizen, he never even jay-walked.

But damned if he didn't fantasize, just a little, about running this bruiser over with his car. Okay, it was wrong. On so many levels. And it wasn't his fault that Xavier hadn't realized he had feelings for his girl until it was too late.

But yeah, his life would be happier without this guy in it. But would Juliet's?

Suck it up, buttercup.

He stopped as the guy didn't move from the doorway. He waited for him to tell him to piss off. Although why he'd let him through the gate to do that he had no idea.

"Hey," the bruiser said.

"Hey," Xavier replied. "I didn't make the best impression last time I was here, but, uh, I'm Xavier." He held out his hand and waited to see if the other man would reject him.

Instead, he took his hand and shook it firmly. "Brenton Sampson, but everyone calls me Brick."

Xavier could see why.

Brick nodded at the flowers. "Those for me?"

"Actually, this is for you." He held out the whiskey in his other hand.

Brick glanced down at it, his eyes widening. "Don't drink much whiskey, but this looks like good stuff."

"It is." Cost a bomb. But it was nothing he wouldn't pay a hundred times over to make things right between him and Juliet.

Brick took the whiskey.

"Listen, I was an ass the other day," Xavier said with a grimace. "I didn't know there was a threat. I was an ass. I was worried about Juliet. She's important to me. And you two haven't known each other long."

He'd expected Brick to fire up. But he just nodded. "I get it. You're protecting your friend."

He nearly winced over that word. But that's what they were.

"And from what I've seen, she inspires a lot of loyalty and protectiveness."

"She does," Xavier agreed. "She's special."

"I know."

To his credit, the big guy didn't make him grovel any further. Instead he stepped aside to let him in, shutting the door behind him.

They faced each other for a long moment.

"If you hurt her, I'll kill you," Xavier warned.

Fuck. He hadn't meant to blurt that out like that. He waited for him to retaliate. To his shock, Brick just nodded.

"Feel the same way."

"Do you . . . do you know about all of her?"

Brick eyed him for a moment. "You asking about whether I know about her Little side?"

Xavier sucked in a breath.

"I know. I'm a Daddy Dom."

All right then. That was good. He supposed. Fuck, it was hard being a good friend. A good person.

"Xavier?"

He glanced up to find her standing on the staircase. He hadn't heard her, but she'd always moved around quietly. It kind of bothered him. Not that she could sneak up on him. But that she felt the need to be quiet. To move like a ghost.

He wanted her to stomp around, loud and joyful. Happy.

She wore her hair in two braids down in front of her shoulders. She was wearing her bathing suit, which looked more like a wetsuit, covering her from her ankles to her wrists to her collarbones.

And he hated that too.

Hated that she hid her body. That she wore black to fade into the background. Why had he never helped her with her hang-ups? He knew that she'd seen a therapist when she first arrived in Wishingbone. She always said she didn't want to talk to another one again, but maybe he should have pushed her more.

Fuck, you don't deserve her and that's why you lost her.

He just needed to make sure this guy did deserve her.

"Hey, Twink," he greeted her with a soft smile. "Brought you these."

Her face softened as she took in the flowers he held up. "My favorite."

"I know."

Brick cleared his throat. Shoot, he'd kind of forgotten the other man was there. "That's what you're wearing swimming, Duchess?"

Duchess? Interesting nickname. And then he realized that Juliet had spoken. In front of Brick. She only talked to a handful of people.

And now him.

Fuck. This guy had known her for what, ten days? And she was speaking to him. Xavier eyed him assessingly. Yeah, he'd fucked up.

"Um, yeah. Something wrong?"

Brick shook his head. "No, baby girl. I'm gonna go get changed, then track down dumb and dumber. Don't go in the pool without me. I'll leave you two to chat."

Christ, he was definitely a better person than him. That sucked. He wasn't sure he could have left his girl alone with Brick if things were reversed.

But then he was starting to see that he was a messed-up asshole. The nice-guy act was just that. An act. Could he do this? Could he stay in Wishingbone and see her with someone else day after day? Knowing that she'd never be his.

You fucking fool.

"Xavier? Are you all right?"

He shook himself out of his introspection and smiled down at the best thing that had ever happened to him.

"Shall we put these in water?" he asked her, reaching out his hand to her. Then he snatched it back. "Sorry."

She looked confused. "Why?"

"Well, I, we, uh . . ."

Spit it out, man.

"Don't know if Brick would like you holding hands with another man."

"Oh. Is that a relationship rule, do you think?"

"Would be for me, Twink."

"Good to know. But accepting flowers is okay?"

"I think when they're brought in friendship, it is," he told her.

Was it his imagination or did she pull a face at that?

"At least, he didn't try to break my fingers when I told him they weren't for him, and he definitely looks like he's capable of doing that."

"He's a big teddy bear. All scary on the outside and marshmallow on the inside."

"Maybe for you." But for anyone else, Xavier was pretty certain Brick was a bruiser.

He followed her through to the kitchen, and took out a vase without asking, knowing where they were.

She pulled herself out an iced coffee and him a coke. They sat at the kitchen island in awkward silence.

"Xavy, are you okay?"

"Twink, I'm so sorry," he said at the same time. He huffed out a breath and sent her a small smile. "I'm all right."

She raised an eyebrow and he barked out a laugh. "Okay, I'm regretting some life choices I made. And really taking a look at my life. I've realized that maybe, I've been blaming other people for my shortcomings. And that I've been taking you for granted."

"Me?"

"Yeah. You."

"But how? I'm the one who leeches off you."

He narrowed his gaze, not liking that. "Excuse me? Leech off me?"

Did she really just say that? She better not mean it like it sounded because if she did . . .

Calm down.

Even if she was yours, you couldn't punish her. Juliet is sweet and gentle. She can't handle that part of you.

Her gaze lowered. "I feel like I've used you and I'm so sorry, Xavier. You deserve better. I feel terrible, and I hope I never stopped you from living your life."

Oh fuck.

She thought he'd been talking about her.

"Baby, no. I wasn't talking about you." Without thinking, he reached over to grab her hand, squeezing it. "Twink, you could never be a leech or a burden on me, understand? And I don't want to hear you say that again."

"But you've always taken care of me, and I feel like I did nothing for you in return."

"Nothing? Ever since I moved back here, you've been my best friend."

"I have?"

"Yeah, baby. And it makes me sad as fuck that you don't know it. Because I haven't said it." He closed his eyes with a sigh. "I have to apologize about the other day. I was upset because . . . well, for a lot of reasons. I shouldn't have acted how I did. Forgive me?"

She gave him a big smile. But there was something in her eyes he didn't quite understand. "You were worried about me. There's no reason to apologize for that."

"You're the very best person I know."

She blushed and he wished he had the right to take her into his arms.

"Are these tulips my present?" She gave him a sly look.

"Present?" he asked, even though she knew what he was asking.

"Don't tease. You said you would bring me home a present if I was a good girl while you were away." She gave him a pouting look.

If she were his, he'd kiss that pout off her lips.

"Ah, but were you a good girl?"

"Yes, of course!"

"I don't think you were. How often did we call or text and I asked what was going on or if you were all right?"

"Oh." She bit her lip.

"Oh," he repeated. "You never once mentioned that you might be in danger because of Reuben or that he'd hired security guards."

"I didn't want to worry you! You had enough going on with your mother's health scare."

He grimaced. Right. The health scare that he was starting to think was a fabrication to manipulate him.

"It doesn't matter how much I have going on, you are still important to me, understand?"

"I'm sorry, Xavy. So I don't get my present?" She looked so forlorn that he almost caved. But she deserved some punishment.

"We'll see," he said. "If you're a good girl from now on, you might get it."

She nodded. "I really am sorry."

"Don't ever keep stuff from me, Twink. Please."

"I won't," she whispered.

He cleared his throat, feeling awkward around her. And he hated that.

"Stay the afternoon," she asked him suddenly. "We're going swimming then grilling, then we're watching a movie."

"I think I best go." He didn't think he could stay and watch her be lovey-dovey with Brick.

God, she was so tiny in comparison to the big bruiser, he better not hurt her. Not even accidentally.

"Please." She gave him those wide eyes. The ones he could never say no to.

"All right, Twink. I'll stay. So long as it's okay with your man."

"It will be. I'm sure he'd like to get to know you."

Yeah. Xavier wasn't so sure about that. He knew how he would feel if the tables were turned. Then again, they'd already established that he wasn't that good of a person.

24

Brick strode through into the pool house, just in time to catch Elias kissing the back of Sterling's neck as he sat in front of the monitoring system.

He cleared his throat and Elias jumped back. They both turned to stare at him guiltily.

"Um," Elias said, his eyes widening. "Hey."

He needed some advice. Part of him wasn't sure if he was doing the right thing in leaving Juliet with Xavier.

You're trying to be trusting.

Fuck, it was hard though. It wasn't that he didn't trust Juliet.

No, it was the rich, smart doc that he had problems trusting. He was pretty sure that Xavier had feelings for Juliet. But he'd come here to apologize. And Juliet cared for him.

And Brick was trying to be trusting.

So here he was. But he really needed his best friends to tell him he was doing the right thing. Because what he really wanted to do was storm into the house, grab Juliet, chuck her over his shoulder, take her up to his bedroom and fuck her until she forgot everything but his name.

"Sorry," Sterling said quickly.

"Why?" he asked, raising his eyebrows. Both men looked sheepish. "I don't give a shit who you kiss or fuck, so long as you do your job."

"You really don't care?" Elias asked.

"Of course not, you idiots." He gave them an exasperated look, then glanced over the monitors and saw the one with Juliet and Xavier in it. They weren't doing anything but talking. The knot in his stomach eased. "Besides, anyone with eyes can see the two of you like each other. You need to stop hiding it."

Sterling and Elias shared a look.

"Guess that tells us," Sterling muttered.

"I'm surprised you left them alone," Elias said, seeing where he was looking.

"If I want a real relationship, I need to have trust," he muttered.

"Where'd you read that?" Sterling asked with a smirk. "Been reading one of those ladies' magazines?"

Brick shot him the bird. "You think I've given them long enough?"

"You know that Juliet cares about you, right?" Elias said to him.

"I know. It's just they have a history. And the way he reacted the other day . . . it feels like more than friendship."

"That girl is scarred," Sterling said. "She doesn't trust easily, but from the start, all she's seen is you. She watches you like you're her world."

That knot eased inside him.

"Reverse harem," Elias said on a cough.

Both men stared at him.

"Just saying. Although technically, it would be a ménage. Unless you added another guy."

Sterling stared at Elias as though he didn't know him.

The dark-skinned man blushed. "What? I like reading reverse

harem books, it's an escape from real life. It's not like you haven't done it before, Brick."

That was true.

"Even if Brick was okay with it, who says Xavier would go for it?" Sterling asked.

"You know what they say, keep your friends close and your enemies even closer," Elias told him.

He glared at Elias, but as he stormed back out of the pool house, those words played over in his mind.

Enemies closer.

Ménage.

Fuck.

JULIET WAITED NERVOUSLY by the pool.

Xavier had decided to go for a swim as well. He was borrowing some of Reuben's swim shorts. Was this a good idea? Maybe she should have let him leave? Would Brick be upset?

The heat beat down on her. She needed to get in the water. The swimsuit she wore was more like a wetsuit and it was way too hot to be wearing it.

Brick had seen her naked when he was bathing her last night. And Xavier had seen her in her Little clothes.

But still, she couldn't bring herself to put on a swimsuit. To wear anything that might reveal some skin when she wasn't in the safety of her playroom.

She stepped closer to the side of the pool.

"Hope you weren't planning to get in without me," Brick said from behind her.

She turned so fast that the world wobbled around her. Firm hands grabbed her upper arms, steadying her.

"Fuck. Got to stop doing that," Brick muttered.

Uh. Yeah. Or one day, he was going to sneak up on her while she was on the roof of some high-rise then plop! She was squished on the sidewalk.

Of course, there were no high-rise buildings in Wishingbone, and if there was, she had no reason to be on the roof of one. But who cared about logic?

"Sorry, Duchess. You okay?" He peered down at her in concern.

She straightened her shoulders and nodded. Nothing to see here. Nope. Just another ordinary day.

But oh, there was something to see when she peeked at him. Would she ever grow tired of looking at him? She didn't think so. He wore a pair of black board shorts and nothing else. His abs were damn near edible, and don't get her started on his nipples.

Shoot. She needed to cool herself down.

He tilted his head toward the pool. "Want to tell me why you were headed towards the pool when I said you weren't to go in by yourself."

He was being ridiculous. With a sigh, she crossed her arms over her chest.

"Oh, like that, is it?"

Yes. Yes, it was like that.

"You think that because we're not in the playroom that you don't have to obey me?"

"Yes," she told him quietly.

"Unfortunately, for you, baby girl, Daddy's rules have to be obeyed at all times."

That sucked.

"You'd think with the other half of your spanking coming tonight that you would behave yourself."

"I'm always well behaved, Daddy."

He gave her a knowing look. "How did your talk with Xavier go?"

"Good, Daddy. He apologized. He wasn't feeling himself. He was worried about me." She watched him with concern. "I asked if he wanted to stay for dinner and a movie."

"That's fine, Duchess. I'm not upset with you for wanting to spend time with your friend."

"Really?"

He leaned in and kissed her lightly. "Really. So long as he remembers who you belong to." He lightly tapped her ass.

Before she could say anything, a whoop interrupted them and Elias rushed past to cannonball into the pool, splashing them both.

"Hey!" Brick said, picking her up and carrying her a few feet away, as though the water might harm her. It was charming and seriously overprotective.

"Sorry!" Elias didn't sound sorry, though. In fact, he looked kind of smug as he turned and started swimming.

"You okay?" Brick looked her over, and when he wasn't watching, she rolled her eyes. When he set her down, she grinned and started running towards the pool.

But a wide arm landed around her waist, pulling her up short.

"No running around the pool," he barked.

Slap! His hand landed on her ass in warning. Her eyes widened. Not because it had really hurt, but the fact that he'd done it outside when Elias was right there.

He was insane. It wasn't like she was going to slip and crack her head open.

Actually, there was a possibility that would happen. She couldn't seem to remain steady around him. Going up on tiptoes, she whispered in his ear.

"Last one in is a rotten egg?"

A finger wiggled at her. "I don't think so, brat. We're going to walk over to the stairs and go in calmly and quietly."

"Jesus, man, what are you, a hundred? Let the girl cannonball in," Sterling said as he walked towards the pool. Brick shot him a quelling look that had him raising his hands in surrender. "Or not."

He kept a tight hold of her hand, as though she was a toddler that might take off if given the slightest bit of freedom.

Huh. Seemed apt.

The cool water was soothing on her feet as they stepped in. When they were waist deep, he drew her close, pulling her with him out to the deep. Elias and Sterling were both swimming laps.

"Do you want to swim laps?" she whispered, not that they were paying her the slightest attention. In fact, they seemed to keep sharing these odd looks.

She wondered . . .

"Will you promise to stay in the shallow end if I do?"

A huff of breath escaped her. Then she pushed back away from him, catching him by surprise as she dove back then twisted under. She swam away in long, firm strokes that took her to the end of the pool. When she turned around, she found him standing right where she'd left him.

And he didn't look happy.

Whoops.

He crooked a finger at her and she swam back slowly. When she got close, he grabbed her around the waist and drew her into him to whisper in her ear. "You're lucky we're not alone, Duchess. Or you'd pay for that stunt."

A shiver ran through her.

"Point taken. You can swim just fine. I still don't like the idea of you swimming without me."

He was completely insane. But he took off to swim his own laps, moving through the water with ease even if he wasn't a natural-looking swimmer like Sterling was. Brick kind of pounded through the water rather than gliding.

He still looked sexy as hell doing it.

Lord, she had it bad.

And then out walked Xavier.

He was wearing a pair of dark-green board shorts. His pale blue eyes caught hers as the sun glinted off his dark-blond hair. He wasn't as tall or wide as Brick, but he was definitely all muscle. With his angelic looks and tanned, muscular body, he could have been on the cover of any romance novel, and it would have sold millions just for that reason.

Friend. Friend. Friend.

Immediately, she felt ill. She was disloyal. She was a terrible girlfriend. Forcing her gaze up to his face, she smiled and waved. Then she quickly turned to look at Brick. He was staring at her with a funny expression on his face.

She smiled at him.

Please don't realize that I was staring at my best friend with lust.

She couldn't stand to have him think she was like Linda.

Then Brick winked at her and the tension in her eased.

"Twink? Want your floaties and your ring?" Xavier asked her quietly, looking over at Elias and Sterling, who were swimming laps, then Brick who raised an eyebrow at the question.

"Just my mermaid," she whispered when he leaned down.

He moved to the pool shed and came out with the huge mermaid floatie, throwing it into the pool.

"I should have known," Brick said with a grin. "A mermaid would swim well."

"Juliet's an excellent swimmer," Xavier said, slipping into the pool. "She could have been on the swim team at school."

But she'd been too terrified to try out. To even get in the pool with other people.

Always a coward.

And yet, look at her now. Sure, she was covered up. But she was swimming with men she didn't know that well.

And her best friend, who always made her feel safe. But who was also stirring her in ways that only Brick should.

She was so messed up.

"Want a hand up, Duchess?" Brick asked. Then he grabbed her by the waist, easily heaving her up into the air. Xavier grabbed the giant floating mermaid and held it steady as she climbed on. They were on either side of her. For a moment, her breath caught, wondering what it would be like if they could always be like this.

With her in the middle.

Stop being an idiot, Juliet. You've read too many ménage romances. That doesn't happen in real life.

Then Xavier suddenly pushed the floatie hard, making her spin and squeal. She hung on for dear life as he boomed out a laugh. Jerk.

She tensed, wondering if Brick would snap at him. Overprotective didn't cover that guy. But instead, she looked over to find him grinning at her.

Good Lord.

What if they decided that instead of being enemies, they could be partners in crime?

She wasn't sure she would survive.

"Duchess, out of the pool now," Brick said firmly.

He'd gotten out about an hour ago and dried off while watching her swim around and play. Xavier had stayed in a bit longer to play with her. It was easy to see they'd done this before. That they were good friends.

Xavier had gotten out about twenty minutes ago and gone to take a shower before dinner. Elias and Sterling were in the pool house getting dinner ready. He'd watched her and Xavier together with surprising ease.

Okay, he'd had to fight his jealousy a few times. He was only fucking human. But he hadn't felt the urge to murder him, which he was pretty sure he'd do with any other fucker who made his girl smile like that.

All right, so maybe he'd had some murderous thoughts, but he hadn't done it. That was what counted, right?

Now he just had to get his little mermaid out of the water.

She had the audacity to shake her head at him.

Brat.

He moved to the side of the pool, hands on hips, and glared at her.

"It's nearly dinner time, and you've been in there too long."

She scrunched her nose and didn't move.

Oh, for someone who was owed the rest of her spanking tonight, she was being quite bratty.

"Do you want to add to the spanking you have owing?"

She narrowed her eyes and shook her head again.

Stubborn. Brat.

"I'm going to count to three and you best be out by the time I finish. One."

Her eyes went over his shoulder and widened. He could guess who was moving up behind him. Didn't change anything. Xavier knew what she was. He didn't know if the other guy was a Dom or not. That didn't matter, it was obvious to Brick that he'd never taken a firm stance with her. Probably spoiled the little brat.

"Two."

"There a problem?" the man behind him asked carefully.

"No problem. Just a naughty girl who is going to find herself over my knee if I get to three and she's still in the pool."

Juliet's mouth dropped open and Xavier stepped up next to him. "You can't spank her."

Brick turned and gave him an incredulous look. "Sure, I can."

"No, you can't." Xavier gave him an angry look. "You'll hurt her."

"Yeah, a spanking hurts, but I'd never harm her." Brick eyed the other man for a moment. "This is what she agreed to."

Xavier's face blanched. He looked like he'd been slapped. "There's no way she agreed to you hurting her."

Brick sucked in a breath. "Listen, asshole—"

Then she was out of the pool and between them, staring from one to the other, her face pleading with them. She looked about as scared as he'd ever seen her. That made him suck in a breath to calm himself.

This guy was just trying to protect his best friend.

He closed his eyes. "Look, if you're not in the lifestyle, then I wouldn't expect you to understand, but Juliet told me that you know she's a Little. So, I thought you'd be more open-minded."

When he opened his eyes, both of them were gaping up at him. What?

"I'm in the lifestyle," Xavier gritted out. "I've been a Dominant for years. I know her. I know the lifestyle. And I know that she is too delicate and fragile for the harsher side of BDSM."

"Listen, I'm not doing anything we didn't sit down and talk about first," Brick told him. "A spanking given as punishment to correct a behavior isn't something I'd consider harsh. I'm not whipping her until she bleeds. She knows the rules. She agreed to them. And to be punished if she broke them. Besides, this is something she needs."

Xavier sucked in a breath and stared down at Juliet. "Did he make you agree to this?"

"Of course not," she said in that husky voice. "I wanted this. Brick is right. I need it. I like having boundaries and rules."

Xavier went so pale that Brick thought he might faint. He shook his head. "Juliet, I always thought . . . I mean . . ."

He scrubbed his hand over his face, and Brick almost felt sorry for him.

"Why did you never tell me?"

"I don't understand," she whispered.

But he didn't seem to hear her. "I just didn't think you'd want that. I thought it would scare you. That you couldn't handle it."

"Juliet isn't as fragile as you all seem to think," Brick told him, not unkindly. "I've seen the way people treat her. Like she might break with a hard word. But she's stronger than people give her credit for. She's resilient. She's a fighter. She's also a brat who doesn't listen well." He gave her a stern look. He pointed at the house. "Upstairs. Shower. Then it's dinner time."

She hesitated, looking up at Xavier.

"One," he said in a low voice.

With a huff, she stomped her foot and glared at him. "Daddy!"

"Two."

"Such a darn bossy-boots."

"Th—"

Spinning, she took off.

"No running," he barked.

She slowed then turned as they both watched her. At the door, she turned and stuck her tongue out at him. Xavier sucked in a sharp breath.

"Damn brat," Brick said with affection as she walked inside.

"I've never seen her act like that." Xavier stared over at him with something that looked like shock. "I don't think I've ever seen her that sassy."

"Like I said, she needs the boundaries and rules. They make her feel safe. Secure."

"How did I never see any of this? How was I so blind?"

Brick wasn't good at this sort of shit. Advice, emotional crap, he left that all to Elias.

"Maybe you didn't want to see it," he murmured. "Maybe you

wanted to keep her in that box you assigned her. Because it was safe. It was what you both knew."

Xavier shook his head, but Brick didn't think it was in disagreement. "So, what you're saying is I was a fucking coward."

Yeah. Kind of.

XAVIER SAT at the table feeling kind of numb.

He'd been a complete idiot. A coward. A fool.

Even though Brick didn't say any of those things to his face, they were all true.

How had he never known?

Because maybe Brick was right. He'd made assumptions about her.

Fuck. Fuck.

He'd known she was strong. But for some reason, he'd just decided she couldn't take his darker side. That he wasn't good enough for her.

So yeah, he was a fucking coward.

Suddenly, he noticed food filling the plate in front of him. Juliet was piling it high with grilled fish, fried potatoes, and coleslaw. Not unexpectedly, her plate held very little food.

Nothing much changed there.

"Enough, Twink," he told her when she tried to fit more on. "I didn't swim enough to burn through this many calories."

She'd quickly showered and wore another long, black dress.

Which he fucking hated.

Why had he never encouraged her more? Helped her to stop hiding so much?

Fuck. He'd really been an idiot.

"You need to eat more, Duchess," Brick said, putting more food on her plate as she wrinkled her nose, giving him a stubborn look.

Xavier nearly grinned. He hadn't been the recipient of that look very often, mostly because he generally let her get her own way. In everything.

Christ. Yep. Idiot.

Because he wanted a brat who wore her hair in braids and held tea parties and held onto him so tight when she was scared or afraid. Who'd never give him instant obedience. Who'd never step foot in a club.

But his happiest memories over the last two years all involved the brat currently refusing to eat any of the fish. Her eyes were narrowed, and he knew that a tantrum was brewing.

He'd spoiled her to death. And he'd loved every minute.

He should have opened himself up. Should have been brave enough to recognize his feelings for her and tell her about his needs.

Now, it was too late.

"Duchess," Brick said warningly. "You need to eat."

And now, he found himself in the unenviable position of helping someone else learn how to take care of his girl. The job that had been his for so long that he hadn't realized its worth.

He'd taken her for granted.

Ignored his feelings for her.

He probably deserved to lose her. Brick wasn't exactly who he had imagined she would end up with. He was gruff, blunt, firm.

But maybe that was what she needed.

Except he couldn't help but think she might need something from him as well. But that was wishful thinking. What could she need from him that she didn't get from Brick?

"Duchess, damn it," Brick said quietly. There was a note of frustration in his voice. And worry.

Because she wasn't eating.

Well, even if she wasn't his, this was something he could help with. The other two people at the table were engaged in a quiet conversation and not paying them any attention.

"She's a nibbler," he told Brick.

"What?"

He winced then, realizing the other man might not welcome his advice. He wasn't sure he would be gracious about it if the tables were turned.

"Juliet is a nibbler. She can't eat large meals three times a day. She has to eat small things through the day. She doesn't like red meat much, but she'll eat chicken and fish. She'll eat most fruit, but she loves strawberries. And she prefers her veggies raw with ranch dressing."

Brick stared at him, then frowned. He braced himself for the other man's ire. But Brick turned to Juliet and raised an eyebrow. "You didn't tell me."

Hm, a day ago, hell a few hours ago, he would have taken umbrage at the other man's tone with her. But now, he saw it more clearly. Her more clearly.

"That was naughty," he murmured, before he thought about it.

Brick shot him a look, then to his surprise, the other man nodded. "It was. Duchess, if you don't tell me things I need to know to take care of you, then you could get sick or hurt. You need to talk to me."

"Communication isn't her strong point." He grimaced as Brick glared at him. "Sorry. I really am trying to help. Getting her to talk about some things is like pulling teeth. Her stomach gets sore with large meals. She's usually pretty good at eating regularly, though, because she knows otherwise, Reuben will throw a fit and hire her a cook."

He gave her a firm look and she squirmed.

"Also, her stomach is tied to her emotions, so if anything is upsetting her then she loses her appetite."

Brick nodded. "Makes sense. So how often a day should she eat?"

"Six or seven smaller meals. However, she can eat more than she has right now without hurting her tummy." Xavier gave her a firm look. "I'd say at least ten more bites."

She scowled back at both of them.

"Brat, you heard what Xavier said. Ten more bites."

Both men nodded together. And Xavier found that he was enjoying himself. Brick wasn't the type of guy he'd normally be friends with. However, if he wanted to stay in her life, then he had to be friends with him as well.

Maybe it would be easier to walk away. To put distance between them.

The idea of doing that tied his stomach in knots, though.

Christ.

She leaned in towards them, shooting a glance at Elias and Sterling, but he swore those guys only had eyes for each other.

"Are you two ganging up on me?" she whispered.

He stiffened, worried about how Brick would take that. Then the other man surprised him by grinning.

"Maybe it takes two of us to rein you in, brat."

Hell. Why did that feel so right?

BRICK HELD Juliet in his arms after he finished spanking her. She was straddling his lap, her face pressed to his chest. She was wearing a nightgown tonight with a large mermaid on the front of it. The mermaid had a sequin tail.

It was sweet. He wished she felt comfortable enough to wear cute and colorful things all the time. Maybe one day he'd get her to that point.

Xavier had left soon after dinner. He'd given Juliet a brief hug which Brick had tolerated. Xavier had been quiet and thoughtful for most of the night, especially after he'd said that thing about it taking the two of them to look after her.

Why the fuck had he said that? It wasn't true. He could take care of her on his own. Sure, he might not know her as well as Xavier.

The other guy was an idiot if he'd stopped himself from making a move because he thought she wasn't ready or couldn't handle him. Still, just because Brick didn't need him to take care of his girl didn't mean she didn't need Xavier.

He waited for the anger. The jealousy. The need to rip the guy apart.

Weirdly, it didn't come.

He rubbed her back. She was calming down. She'd begun crying almost as soon as he'd started smacking that glorious bottom, which had alarmed him so much that he'd paused to check she was all right. She'd told him she was fine.

Obviously, she'd just had some strong emotions that needed a release. He got that it was that way for some subs who held things deep inside them. They needed a way to let them free, a reason to let go of that control.

"They clear my head."

"What does, Duchess?"

"The spankings. I get overwhelmed sometimes. My thoughts. The anxiety. The worries. The spankings help. They clear it all away. It's so peaceful."

Okay, he hadn't realized that. His hand paused as he thought that through. But he couldn't see how it was a bad thing.

"I'm glad it helps, baby girl. You know, if you ever need a spanking just to help clear your head, I can do that. You don't have to be naughty and earn one."

"What? Just ask for one?" She leaned back to look up at him skeptically.

He nodded.

"Isn't that weird?"

He grinned at her. "No weirder than anything else."

She smiled back at him. "Guess that's true."

Cupping the side of her face, he ran his thumb over her cheek. "You're so beautiful."

She made a scoffing noise. "With my red eyes and my messy hair and my too-thin body."

"Yes, you are. And that sounded like you were putting yourself down. Is that allowed?"

"No, Daddy."

He grunted with satisfaction. She peeked up at him. "Thanks for letting Xavier stay for dinner."

"Baby, you don't have to thank me for that. He's your friend. We might have had a rocky start, but I'd never demand you stay away from him."

She let out a small sigh of relief. Then she chewed her lip, looking off in the distance.

"What's worrying you?"

"What isn't?" she countered. "Reuben going silent. Xavier acting kind of strange. Zombies attacking and eating my brains."

Okay.

"Well, zombie attacks are frightening."

She nodded.

"But I think we can push that worry aside for now."

She sighed. "Okay, Daddy."

He wasn't sure where that fear came from. "I don't know Xavier, but it seems he's a bit . . . lost?" Fuck, he wished he was better at this.

"It feels like he's kind of been sad for ages. He doesn't have the best relationship with his parents. They always want him to be better than what he is."

Brick frowned. He had great parents who had always

supported him. They were currently doing a world trip, but they talked every month.

"Better than a respected doctor?"

"Yeah, crazy, huh? They pushed him to be good at sports, at his studies, a B was never an acceptable grade. They forced him to apply to Ivy League colleges because they were the best. He and Reuben went to Harvard together. I think his parents were pretty horrified when he chose to move back here. But if he hadn't . . . I think they would have pushed him over the edge. I wish he could see that he's perfect the way he is." She started to go red. "I mean that as his friend."

He hushed her. He wasn't going to take offense over that.

"They don't live here?"

"No, they moved when he graduated high school. His dad was the head of the hospital here for years before he got a better offer. They now live in New York. I just wish he was happy," she said. "He hides it well, but I see his sadness."

He nodded, but didn't know what to say. Because he had this inkling suspicion he knew what would make Xavier happy. And it wasn't his parents' acceptance that he wasn't perfect. The thing was, he didn't much care about Xavier's happiness.

But he did care about hers. What if she would be happier with both of them?

Shit. Damn Elias.

"I get it, baby girl."

She rubbed at her eyes with closed fists, looking so adorable that it nearly killed him.

"You're exhausted," he told her quietly. "Time for bed."

"I am. But I don't know if I'll sleep. I don't sleep well."

"I was thinking I might sleep on the sofa tonight. In case you need me."

Her hands dropped and she gave him a surprised look. "You don't have to do that."

"Feel better if I did."

She chewed at her lip. "I'd feel bad about you sleeping on the couch, though." Then she snapped her fingers. "Oh, I know. You could sleep in my bed. I'll take the couch."

"First off, you aren't sleeping on a couch. Not happening," he said firmly as she opened her mouth. "Secondly, your bed might be Juliet-sized, but it's not Daddy-sized. I'll get a crink in my neck."

"Neither is the couch."

Well, she had him there.

"It's not really a Daddy bed," he told her gently.

Her mouth opened. Closed. She nodded. Then her hand wrapped around his shirt. "We could sleep in your bed. Together."

Surprise filled him. He didn't think she would make an offer like that. "You'd be able to sleep?"

"Maybe. I don't sleep well anyway. I could try. Only if you wanted. I understand if you don't. I mean, I might snore, or kick in my sleep or punch you."

"Why would you punch me?"

"I dunno. I might be dreaming that I was a ninja fighting off a dragon."

"Would a ninja punch a dragon? I mean, I assume a dragon wouldn't even feel a ninja punch."

"All right, so maybe I'd be dreaming I was a bounty hunter, bringing in a bail skipper."

"Don't know if you'd be allowed to just punch someone who skipped bail."

"Maybe I would be dreaming I was a kangaroo."

"Really?"

She huffed out a breath. "It's just a dream, Mr. Logical."

"Okay, baby. How about we just start off with me sleeping on the couch then, huh? Ease into sleeping together in a bed."

"Probably best, since I might have been going to dream about punching someone in the balls."

Yeah, he didn't really want to be sleeping with her when she had that dream.

CRIES WOKE him up in the middle of the night.

Brick was instantly awake. Racing into her bedroom, he found her tangled up in her bedding, crying out.

"Duchess. It's okay. You're okay." He leaned over the railing but she cried out, shying back. Shit. Was she still dreaming? More asleep than awake?

"Duchess, it's me. It's Daddy."

More cries.

"Baby girl, you're all right. I'm here." The noises were heartbreaking. He wanted to wrap her up in safety, hold her tight, but he was scared of terrifying her more. Her tears kept coming, shudders wracking her body. She was gasping for breath. She sounded like she was going to hyperventilate.

Shit. Fuck.

Okay, calm. Think.

Would she be better off if he left? If this happened to her every night and she coped . . .

But fuck, she shouldn't have to cope on her own. Not when he was here to take care of her. This was his job. He was damn good at whatever job he took on. He wouldn't fail his girl.

Not when she was the most important thing in his life.

"Baby girl, it's Daddy."

"Go away. Leave me alone. Leave me alone."

Those words were a kick to the stomach.

She's upset. She doesn't know what she's saying. She's still stuck in a nightmare.

"Baby—" He reached out to touch her, but she smacked his

hand away with a pained cry as though she'd physically hurt herself.

"Juliet, listen to my voice. It's Daddy. I'm not going to hurt you." He tried again. This time she shied back so hard that she thunked her head against the rungs of the cot.

Fuck. Fuck.

"Okay, baby girl. I'm backing off. I'm just going to sit here. I'm not leaving, but I won't touch you." He sat in the beanbag chair he'd sat in earlier when reading her book before bed. She'd sucked on his fingers while he'd read. Maybe she wanted his fingers? Would that help?

"Do you want to suck my fingers?"

Another whimper.

Fuck. Fuck.

Small cries filled the room. He couldn't take it. He wasn't a man who sat around and waited for something to happen. He was a fixer.

Doing nothing when someone he loved was hurting was killing him.

And he did love her. He didn't know when it happened. He didn't care how quickly it had happened.

All that mattered was that the girl he loved was sobbing and afraid and he couldn't do anything.

He had to let out a deep breath.

Think.

What could he do other than sit here, twiddling his fucking thumbs?

The thought came to him suddenly. Could he do it, though?

Then she cried out again.

"Baby girl?"

"Please don't hurt me," she whispered.

Like he ever fucking would. Even knowing she wasn't in her right mind; the pain was real. Very real.

"It's all right. I'd never hurt you. I'm going to try and get some help."

He climbed off the beanbag, hating that she cried out again. He grabbed her phone from the holder, those things were actually fucking handy, then he moved into the playroom, thinking this call might upset her further.

He hit his name. It only rang three times.

"Twink? What's wrong?" The alarm in Xavier's voice was unmistakable.

"It's me. Brick," he said lamely.

"What's the matter?" The worry in his voice grew. "Is Juliet ill? Injured?"

"No, man. No. Let me speak, huh?" His irritation stemmed more from worry than anything else. "I need your help. I don't think she's been sleeping, so I decided to stay on the sofa in the playroom. Woke up just now to her screams."

"She's having a nightmare?"

"Yeah, only thing is, she's not waking up. I mean, I tried to talk to her, but she keeps telling me not to hurt her and when I reach for her, she shies away. Maybe I should leave her alone, but I just can't. And I'm scared she's going to hurt herself."

"Night terrors. She gets them sometimes. When she's really anxious about something."

"Reuben," he muttered.

"Has she heard from him lately? Has something changed?"

"He's gone silent. We're not sure what's going on."

"Okay. Did you turn on the light?"

Turn on the light. He was a fucking idiot.

"No. Christ. I'll do that now."

"No, wait," Xavier said quickly. "That can actually make things worse. She's got her nightlight, but turn the light on in the bathroom. You want to do it gradually, or she could get a real fright and hurt herself by accident."

"Fuck. Fuck. She doesn't know I'm here. She keeps telling me not to hurt her."

"She's out of it right now. Doesn't know where she is. Nothing she says is at you," Xavier reassured him.

He sucked in a breath. He knew that . . . but it was also reassuring to hear it as well.

"You've seen her like this before?" he asked.

"Sometimes, if she's not doing too well, I'll stay over. Hasn't happened for a long time."

"What would you normally do for her?" Brick asked.

"Like I said. Turn the bathroom light on. Don't try to talk to her straight away or touch her."

"Fucked that up."

"You didn't know," Xavier reassured him.

Fuck. He really was a nice guy, huh? Their first meeting might have been a shitty one, but Xavier hadn't been entirely to blame for that. Brick didn't like to lie, even to himself, and he was definitely not a perfect person. He wasn't as nice as Xavier. That was for sure.

"There's a scented candle on the bedside table. The scent can help cut through the nightmare. Also, there's a song she likes by this singer called Arianna. It's on her phone."

He rattled off the name of the song.

"Right. Fuck. I'll put it on my phone." He grabbed his phone and downloaded the song. There still small whimpers coming from her that broke his fucking heart.

"Is there anything else?" he asked desperately as he played the song.

"You can only wait until she comes back to you. When she does . . ." Xavier hesitated.

"What?"

"I . . . this might sound weird."

"Tell me."

"Touch helps. Skin-to-skin touch. I know it sounds strange since she doesn't always like to touch people. It has to be someone she trusts, but it's clear she trusts you."

"That's what you do for her?" he asked.

Don't get jealous. He's trying to help.

"Yeah."

"She likes to suck on my fingers."

"She's got a pacifier too."

"I know. She likes my fingers better." He didn't say it to be a prick. Well, he didn't think he did.

"All right, then it might be best to do that."

"Sorry to wake you," Brick said awkwardly, considering this guy was basically a stranger.

"You don't have to apologize. I'd do anything for her. She's my best friend."

He noticed that the whimpering had stopped. "Baby girl?"

There was a sob.

"Duchess?" he queried softly, stepping closer but not too close. The last thing he wanted was to frighten her again and have her hurt herself. "It's Daddy."

"Daddy?" she asked in a lost voice.

"Um, Xavier," he said awkwardly.

"I heard," Xavier replied swiftly, and he was sure he heard a sad note in the other man's voice. "I'll let you go take care of her."

"Thanks, man. Appreciate it."

"Anytime."

After hanging up, he put her phone back in the holder then moved carefully over to the side of her cot-bed.

He couldn't see her clearly as his phone crooned something soft and low.

"Can I switch on the lamp?" he asked in a low voice.

"Y-yes," she replied.

When the light went on, his heart nearly stopped beating. His poor girl was a mess. Her hair had gone wild. She was taking shuddering breaths; her eyes were almost swollen shut.

"Oh baby," he said, close to broken by the sight of her.

"I'm okay," she told him.

"No lying," he scolded lightly. She was far from okay. He wasn't either, truth be told. He was nearly shaking. Big bad Marine brought down by some night terrors.

"Night terrors," she told him. "I get them sometimes when I'm anxious."

He nodded. "Xavier told me."

"Xavier? He's here?"

"No, baby girl. I called him on your phone when I didn't know what to do for you."

"I'm sorry I scared you," she told him in a small voice.

"I'm sorry I terrified you so much you hit your head. Is it okay?" he asked, noticing her rubbing it. She froze.

"Just stings a bit," she admitted. She rubbed at her eyes, her hands trembling.

"Can I hug you?" he asked.

She stared up at him then nodded shakily.

"Thank fuck." He bent over towards her slowly. "I'm going to lift you up."

After waiting for her nod, he lifted her up into his arms. She wrapped her arms and legs around him.

"Baby girl, you should have told me you were feeling so anxious."

"S-sorry." He sat in the rocking chair and rubbed her back until the trembles eased.

"What do you need?" He thought about asking her if she wanted him to pull off his T-shirt, give her his skin like Xavier said.

But that felt like their thing. Was that weird? He didn't know. It wasn't a typical best friend thing, that was for sure. But then who gave a fuck about normal?

"To pee."

"Okay, I can manage that." He carried her into the bathroom, set her down by the toilet and then went to turn away.

"Don't leave," she begged.

He turned back to her. "I'll be in the other room."

"Please. I know it's weird. Just don't leave my eyesight. Please?"

"I'll do anything you ask."

"That could be dangerous." She gave him a wobbly grin. "Cause I'm in the mood for a coffee ice cream sundae."

He snorted. "Nice try."

"I thought so," she muttered as he turned away to give her privacy. She peed then flushed, and he spun back as she washed her hands. She squealed as she looked in the mirror, trying to finger comb her hair.

"Hush, you're perfect." He wet a washcloth then lifted her onto the counter to wipe her face. Grabbing her toothbrush, he put toothpaste on it.

"Open."

"My breath stinks?" she wailed, huffing out a breath into her cupped hand then trying to sniff. "Oh no. I probably smell." She sniffed at her armpit.

"Juliet." He had to fight hard to hold in a grin, not wanting her to think that he was laughing at her. When he kind of was. But not in a mean way.

"I don't care if your breath stinks or you do—"

"So, I do stink then," she cried.

"Hush, no, you don't. But I thought brushing your teeth might reset your brain. It's probably silly—"

"No, it's not." She opened her mouth. "Ahh."

God, she was adorable. "I'm brushing your teeth. I don't need to see your tonsils."

She grinned sheepishly. "Sorry. Too used to Xavier telling me to open my mouth. I mean, when he checks me over. Happens rarely. I hate the doctor. Not Xavier. Just visiting the doctor. Oh, just brush my teeth, please."

He complied, brushing her teeth for her before picking her up.

Once more, she wrapped herself around him.

"What do you need now?" He hated that he didn't just know. But there was only one way to find out.

"I don't wanna be on my own."

"Then you won't be. I can sleep on the beanbag in your room."

She shook her head, a shudder worked its way through her, and she gulped in a breath.

"All right, shh. I can climb into bed with you."

It would be a tight fit, but he'd make it work.

"The sheets are wet," she whispered, then she stiffened. "I didn't pee them, though. I just . . . the sweating."

"It's okay, baby girl. We'll get them sorted tomorrow morning. You can sleep in my bed, I'll sleep on the floor. Anything you want?"

"Blankie," she told him.

Walking to the bed, he grabbed the blankie with her pacifier attached. Not easy when he was holding her, but he managed.

Then he shifted her weight onto his hip so he had one hand free. She sucked on her pacifier, rubbing her blankie under her nose as he carried her down to this bedroom. He set her down on the bed, but she let out a tiny distressed noise. Then she reached for him.

He crouched down, placing his hands on her thighs. "Hey, what's wrong?"

"Don't go."

"I'm not going anywhere. I was going to get you a T-shirt of mine to wear."

"Oh. Thanks." But she clutched at his shirt, not letting him move.

"Baby girl, you have to let me go."

"I love you, Daddy."

He froze. Then stared at her for a long moment. "You do?"

She stared back at him, her face solemn, then she nodded. "I really, really do."

A small smile crept onto his face then it widened. "Good, because I love you more than anything."

She sighed. "That's a relief."

He let out a surprised chuckle. Sometimes she shocked the hell out of him. Well, a lot of the time. And every day, he was amazed by her strength.

Grabbing a T-shirt, he helped her take off her nightie, throwing it into a pile he had ready to wash. He'd get to them tomorrow. After she had on a new T-shirt, he pulled back the covers. "In you get."

"Um, Daddy?"

"Yeah?"

"Will you sleep with me? Please?"

"Sure. Have you had these night terrors much lately?" he asked.

"A few times since Reuben called to tell me what was going on."

"Fuck." He hated that. "Move over."

She slid over and he climbed in with her. There were several inches of space between them so he raised his arm. "Come here."

"Actually, um . . ."

When she didn't say more, he grunted and rolled to his side. "What is it?"

"I, um . . ."

"Juliet, you can ask me anything."

"Can I please, um, you know that thing about . . . about cock warming . . . can I . . ."

"You want my dick in your mouth?" he asked in a low murmur.

"Yes, please," she said in such a sweetly polite voice that it filled him from the inside out, chasing out the cold.

"You can."

She scooted down under the covers without another word. Then he felt her tugging at the boxers he was wearing. Usually, he didn't wear anything to bed, but he'd been wearing boxers and a T-shirt while he was here in case he needed to get up in a hurry.

He helped her pull them off, throwing them away, and then her mouth was around his cock. He was at half-mast, but it didn't take him long to get fully hard.

"Just ignore it. It's got no manners," he said sleepily.

JULIET LISTENED to his low murmur, letting his tone rather than his words soothe her.

She hated the night terrors. Generally, she wouldn't get back to sleep afterward. She'd stay awake until dawn broke, then spend her day moving around like one of those zombies she was terrified would eat her brains one day.

She'd gone ages without having night terrors until Reuben called to tell her he was in danger. She'd had several since and she was feeling completely exhausted. Drained.

Sometimes when she finally came out of them, she found herself in another room of the house or she'd discover that she'd hurt herself. She'd have cuts or bruises. That was more terrifying than anything else.

She'd never told anyone that. Not even Reuben. Or Xavier. Both of them would have shit fits.

In completely different ways. Reuben would yell. Then he'd go scary quiet. Xavier would never yell, but he'd give her that look like he wasn't going to put up with this. For a man who spoiled her horribly, he had some lines that wouldn't be crossed.

This time, though, she hadn't woken up alone. And now, here

she was, lying next to one of the sexiest men she knew with her mouth on his cock. He was lying on his side and reached up and dragged down a pillow to support her head as she suckled lightly.

It might sound insane or fanciful, but she swore she could feel her stress levels dropping. What would it be like to be able to do this anytime she felt anxious or unsure?

Well, maybe not every time. The poor guy would probably get a chafed dick. His erection was impressive, and she couldn't get anywhere near all of his dick into her mouth. Just slightly more than the head.

Moving on instinct more than anything else, she cupped his balls in her hand. He let out a small sound, and she slid his cock from her mouth and drew the covers down so she could see him.

"You don't want me touching you there?"

"You can touch my balls, Duchess. They're sensitive, though, and like to be handled gently."

She snorted. "No shit, Sherlock."

"Excuse me?" he asked in a deep voice.

"Nothing, Daddy. It must be those zombies, they've eaten part of my brains."

She took his cock back into her mouth, figuring that was her safest bet to keep her out of trouble.

Maybe.

Darn zombies.

25

Xavier pulled up outside the house. Someone must have told Juliet he was here, because as soon as he stepped out of his car, she was barreling down the steps toward him.

"Slow down, Twink," he commanded, surprised when she listened. She came to a stop right in front of him.

Then, to his shock, she threw herself against him, hugging him tight. It wasn't often she initiated hugs, unless she was in Little space.

"Hug?" she whispered.

He realized he was standing there, like a dummy. He wrapped his arms around her. "Will Brick be okay with this?"

Much as he wished he was her man, he didn't want to create problems between her and Brick. She was happy, and for that much, he was grateful to the other guy.

Grudgingly.

"Of course," she whispered, sounding indignant. "Brick sometimes has issues with trust after the way his ex-wife cheated on him. But if he doesn't trust me, then this isn't going to work."

"That's really insightful of you."

"Well, I've been told I'm pretty smart," she said modestly. "I baked some brownies."

"Without walnuts?"

"You're as bad as Reuben. No walnuts. Promise. I'm not annoyed with you." She winked up at him.

"Brat."

Turning, she tugged on his hand. He was still concerned that Brick would appear and knock him flat on his back for touching his girl.

"Should you be out here, alone?" he asked as they entered through the front door.

"She should not," Brick said, walking towards them both with a stern frown aimed at Juliet. "She was supposed to wait until you were inside."

"Twink," Xavier said warningly. "You need to listen to Brick when it comes to your safety."

"And other things," Brick added. "We'll be having a discussion about that later."

Xavier studied her closely, looking for any sign that she was scared or concerned about Brick's words, but she just gave the other man a pouting look.

Damn, that was cute.

"Don't even start. That won't get you out of trouble." Brick pointed a finger at her. Then he turned to Xavier with a nod. "Thanks for your help last night."

"Of course," Xavier replied. Even though it had hurt him not to help her in person. "I wanted to come over and check on her before my shift at the hospital."

"Would have thought less of you if you hadn't," Brick said. "She's a bit tired. She's going down for a nap later."

"Good idea. She doesn't sleep enough as it is."

"I'm setting up an eating schedule with meal ideas to keep her healthy. I'd appreciate your feedback."

"Absolutely."

"I'm still here, you know," Juliet suddenly said.

Xavier glanced down at her, biting his lip in amusement as he took in her red face and the way she glared at them both. Her confidence was growing and he was proud of her.

"You're so short, I forgot you were there, Twink." He pulled on her braid teasingly.

She sniffed. "I think I'm going to revoke both of your brownie privileges."

"Fighting words," Xavier teased.

"Or spanking words," Brick added.

She gave a theatrical gasp. "I don't think so, mister."

Brick grinned at her. "I'm going to work in the study. You're in charge of her for a while, Doc. Good luck."

"I'll need it."

Juliet huffed and stormed off towards the kitchen while Xavier found himself in the weird position of sharing a grin with the man who was with the woman he loved.

The world was a weird place.

XAVIER COULDN'T HELP but moan as he took a bite of brownie. "You make the best brownies I've ever had, Twink."

She let out a pleased giggle. He loved that sound. She didn't laugh enough. Or she hadn't laughed enough in the past. If Brick could get her to smile more, then Xavier would be forever indebted to him.

It was difficult to do. He'd rather hate the bastard. But seeing Juliet happy could never be something he resented.

Didn't mean it wasn't hard. Was he going to be able to do this?

To stay in this town while she was with someone else? To see them together?

It would be torture.

But he only had two choices. Stay here and somehow survive seeing them together. Or leave. And never see her.

Fuck.

"Delicious as always, sweetheart."

She gave him a shy look. "Thank you. You want more? Better eat it now before Elias sees it."

"I'm fine."

"I'll box some up for you to take home. Are you all right? You look tired." She studied him with worry.

"I should ask the same about you," he said. "It sounded like you gave Brick a fright last night."

"I know. Stupid night terrors. I wish they'd go away."

"Maybe you should talk to someone about them? It might help."

"I don't know," she whispered.

"Think about it, for me?" He put his hand over hers.

"All right. I'll think about it."

"Thank you, sweetheart."

BRICK WALKED into the kitchen just as Xavier placed his hand on his girl's hand. He saw the way Xavier looked at Juliet. With a mix of desperation and hunger.

But Xavier wasn't his priority. Juliet was. He waited to see what would happen, but all they did was smile at one another.

Then she turned and saw him. And her gaze lit up. Her face practically shone with happiness. And the knot in his stomach unraveled. Because there might be a part of her that loved Xavier. But she loved Brick too.

"Came in for some brownie," he said in a gruff voice. As he grew closer, she launched herself off the stool at him.

"Careful," he barked at her at the same as Xavier did.

Brick lifted her up so she rested against one hip while Xavier righted the stool she'd nearly knocked over. Xavier stared at them with such longing that it actually hurt Brick.

Damn it. Was he coming to like the guy?

There was no denying he'd been a big help last night. Brick had panicked and Xavier had known just what to do.

Could they take care of her better together?

"Are you sure you're all right, Xavier?" Juliet asked.

"Just a lot going on."

"Your mom?" she asked.

He sighed, shaking his head. "She won't tell me what the biopsy result was. Truth is, I'm starting to wonder if there was a biopsy."

"What do you mean?" Brick asked as he set Juliet down and then walked over to grab some coffee.

"I'll get you some coffee," she offered, standing.

"I've got it, Duchess. You stay there."

He poured a cup and stood on the other side of the counter. Xavier was frowning, looking pensive. "I think she might have lied about the whole lump scare just to get me to visit."

Juliet gasped, reaching out to touch Xavier before snatching her hand back. Brick was starting to realize just how special Juliet was. And her capacity for love. She had enough for both of them.

It depended on how selfish they wanted to be. On how selfish *he* wanted to be.

"You really think she'd do that, man?" Brick asked.

Xavier nodded. "Yeah. They hate that I work here. Not prestigious enough for a Marson. My father got out of here as soon as he could, and I think my mother regrets ever coming here in the first place. They're constantly pushing for me to work with my father at New York-Presbyterian. This time, they really upped the ante."

"What do you mean?" Juliet asked

"While I was there, they invited a woman who works at the hospital to come to dinner at their place. She was beautiful, single, and obviously someone they found acceptable."

"Oh," Juliet said.

Brick hated the look on her face. She appeared lost, sad. Xavier didn't notice as his head was down.

"Not that I was interested, of course. In her or the job. But the fact my mother is so cagey with the results of her biopsy makes me think the whole thing was a ruse."

"I'm sorry," Brick told him sincerely.

He shrugged as though it meant nothing, but it obviously did.

"I'm glad you're not leaving," Juliet told him.

Xavier frowned, looking off into the distance. "Maybe it's time I did. Don't get me wrong, I love it here. But perhaps it's not the place for me. I came here when I was in pain, to lick my wounds and start again."

Juliet had gone pale, wide-eyed. When she saw him studying her, she looked quickly away, but he thought he saw the tears in her eyes.

It gutted him.

"You're needed here," he said to Xavier.

The other man gave him a smile that didn't reach his eyes, then he looked at Juliet with such longing that Brick felt his stomach clench.

Fuck.

Juliet still had her face tilted down so she didn't see. But Brick did.

"Am I? I'm not so sure." Xavier glanced at his watch. "I've got to go. Thanks for the brownies and coffee, Twink. Make sure you rest this afternoon."

After he'd left, Brick walked around the counter and touched her back lightly. "You okay, Duchess?"

"Yeah. I think I might go up to the playroom, though."

Sensing she needed some time on her own, he nodded. "I'll be up soon."

Unable to stay away from her for long, he found himself in the playroom forty minutes later. He found her snuggling down in the corner with a huge, stuffed wolf in her arms.

"Hey, baby girl." He knelt in front of her. Pain stabbed his gut as he saw that her eyes were swollen. "What's wrong?"

"Nothing, Daddy. Worried about Reuben."

He should scold her for lying, but he didn't have it in him. Instead, he drew her into his lap and rocked her.

"Reuben bought me Wolfie when I first moved here. I call Reuben the Big Bad Wolf."

"Sounds apt."

"Wolfie has kept me safe," she whispered.

"He's done a good job."

"Xavier has too."

"I know."

"Sorry," she whispered. "I know I shouldn't be upset at him leaving."

"You have a right to your feelings. And your feelings for him don't make your feelings for me any less."

"Of course not, Brick. I don't ever want you to feel like that." Panic filled her face.

"Hush, I know you don't." He kissed her lightly. Then he drew back and held her tight.

"Everything will be all right, baby girl. I'll make sure of it."

～

Xavier walked into the Wishing Well, wondering what the hell he was doing.

But a few hours ago, he'd gotten a text from Brick asking him to meet him to discuss Juliet.

And Juliet was his soft spot.

He saw the other man sitting in a quiet corner across the room. It was only Tuesday night so there weren't many people around.

He already had a couple of beers in front of him. Xavier sat in the booth across from him, and Brick passed a beer over.

"Take it you drink beer?" Brick asked.

Xavier shrugged. "Yeah, sometimes. What's going on? Is Juliet all right? Is she ill?"

"She's not ill. But I wouldn't say she's all right, either."

Xavier stiffened. "What do you mean? What's wrong?"

Brick tapped his fingers on the table. "This is hard for me to say. But I only ever want what's best for her."

"I know." Xavier gave him a nod. "I can tell you do. And she's smiling so much more lately. That's down to you."

"She hasn't been these past couple of days. She's been upset. Quiet. Withdrawn."

"Why?" Had Brick done something to hurt her? He'd kill him.

"Because of you."

Xavier sat back, shock filling him. "What? How? I haven't seen her since that last day I came over."

"When you dropped that bombshell about leaving."

Xavier sucked in a breath.

"It's because of her, isn't it? That you're going to leave. You love her, don't you?"

Shit. Fuck.

What to say?

Swallowing heavily, Xavier nodded. "I do. But you don't need to worry I'm going to steal her away from you. I want her to be happy."

"Who said you could steal her away if you wanted to?" Brick looked amused rather than angry. "I'm not worried, which is surprising considering my ex cheated on me with my accountant for years."

"I'm sorry, man. But that's not who Juliet is. Or me."

"Juliet doesn't have a disloyal bone in her body," Brick agreed.

"Who's with her now?"

"Elias and Sterling. They're watching a movie."

"A zombie movie?" Xavier guessed.

Brick grimaced. "I think so."

"She has a love-hate relationship with them."

"She worries about them eating her brains, yet she keeps wanting to watch movies about them."

"Crazy, huh?"

They shared a knowing look. Then Xavier looked away, uncomfortable. "I can't stay here and see her with you. I don't think I'm strong enough to do that."

"I get it. If things were reversed, I'd feel the same. I married my ex because she was safe, you know?"

"Safe?"

"I cared about her, but I didn't love her. Loving someone is . . ."

"Like throwing yourself into the middle of a tornado and hoping you survive?" Xavier said dryly.

"Something like that. It's being vulnerable and shit. Stuff I don't do well. I lost people I cared about when I was in the marines, I didn't want to go through that again. When Linda, my ex, left, I was upset over the humiliation. She cheated on me for years and I had no idea. I was a failure who couldn't hold onto my business. I've always put myself first. I was driven to build my business. I'm set in my fucking ways. I had all these ideas about Juliet before I even met her based on how much money she had. Yeah, all my life I've put myself first. That's been my problem. Why did you never make a move on her?"

"Because I was stupid," he said honestly. "When I first moved back here, I was a mess. My mind was in a dark place. I didn't want a relationship. When I had to, I'd go to the club and scene with a sub. I like to be in complete control. That need grew after . . . after the incident that brought me back to Wishingbone. I didn't even realize I have feelings for her until recently. And I never thought I deserved her. Figured she needed someone who would give her gentleness, who would let her be in control, let her call all the shots."

Brick snorted. "She doesn't need that. She feels better when she has rules and boundaries."

"I never saw that."

"I get it, she seems delicate, but underneath she's very strong."

"I would never have dreamed of spanking her. Then to find that she lets you spank her, that she wants it . . ." He shook his head.

"You're an idiot."

The words were said without malice or glee. Just matter-of-fact. And yep, he was an idiot.

"She loves you. She's loved you for a long time, I'd say."

Xavier sucked in a breath. "She loves you now."

"Yeah," Brick said with an easy smile. "She does. Didn't know I could feel like this. Feel this love. Feel this secure."

Xavier didn't get where he was going with this.

"She means everything to me. I want to put her first. Her needs."

"What are you saying?"

Brick looked at him full-on. "I think we should share her."

avier gaped at him.

What?

Seriously?

Had that just happened?

Xavier suddenly became aware that he was staring at Brick with his mouth open. He probably looked like an idiot.

"Are you insane?"

"Likely," Brick admitted, taking a sip of beer. "But you have to admit, it has its advantages, right?"

"And its disadvantages."

Brick nodded. "Not saying it's the easy option. I could've just let you leave without saying anything. I'm sure with time, she'd get over you. And I'd have her all to myself. That's the option that would be easiest. Only thing is, it's also the option that leaves us all miserable. At least for some time. Juliet, because you've left. You, because you don't have the girl. Me, because I can't stand to see my girl hurting."

"You're doing this for her."

"It ain't for you or me."

Xavier sucked in a breath. "You really do love her."

"More than anything. I'll do whatever it takes to make her happy."

"Even if it means sharing her."

"Yeah, man. I actually shared a girl with a friend, back when I was far younger. I was in the marines, so I was away a lot, and she hated to be alone. The relationship itself was actually pretty good. He could be there for her when I couldn't. And vice versa. It has its downsides, too, of course. But if you set up ground rules and have good communication, I think it can also work really well. It only ended because we weren't really in love with each other. Not like I love Juliet. I'm willing to put the time and effort in to make this work. If you are."

Was he?

What was the alternative? Never see her again? He drank his beer. "I need something stronger."

"I'll go get it, give you a minute."

Xavier thought about it. It couldn't work, right?

Except, it did for Archer and Doc with Caley. They made it look easy, even though it couldn't be. Not with Doc involved. And they were brothers.

But what if it could work? Then he'd have Juliet. All he had to do was share her.

When Brick returned, Xavier met his gaze. "You really think it could work?"

"With communication. We'd need to be united on most stuff. And if we weren't, we'd keep arguments away from her. We'd probably have to arrange our own time with her, as well as spending time together with her. We'd have to be a real family, meaning you and I probably need to spend time together too."

"You really have given this a lot of thought."

"Yeah, man."

Xavier nodded. "I've got friends who are in a permanent ménage, we can talk to them as well. If you want."

"I think that would be a good idea."

"And Juliet? If she doesn't agree? If she doesn't want to do this?"

"I don't think we have to worry about that," Brick told him. "She loves you, loves us both. There are a few things we should talk about and go through. Some rules. She's not experienced. At all."

Xavier gave him a surprised look. "You mean you two haven't had sex?"

Brick shook his head. "Not yet. We've played around a bit, but nothing more."

That made perfect sense.

He let out a deep breath, feeling a sense of hope and rightness. Something he hadn't felt in a long, long time.

"Then yeah, I'm in. I'm completely in."

"Good, then let's go over some rules."

"ANGELIQUE, if you don't drink your water then you won't get any cake," Juliet scolded her naughty doll.

"Angelique is being naughty again, huh?" Brick asked.

She didn't look behind her as she was too busy dealing with Angelique. "When isn't she naughty, Daddy?"

"Rather like some other little girl I know."

"Missy? She's not as naughty."

"I think he meant you, Twink," an amused voice added.

With a gasp, she turned and saw Xavier standing in the play-room with Brick. She flushed red. She didn't know why, it wasn't like he hadn't seen her in Little space before. But it felt different with Brick here.

Wait. Why were they here together?

Brick had been acting a bit odd lately. But she'd put it down to her own headspace. She'd been sad since Xavier said he was leaving. But it wasn't like she had any right to try and hold him here.

She stared from one to the other. "Xavier? I didn't know you were here."

"I invited him over." Brick shocked her with that news. Did this have something to do with him having to go out last night and today? "That okay?"

"Yes, of course. I . . . are you staying for dinner?"

"I thought he could stay the night." Brick moved into the room then kissed her gently on the lips.

She glanced over at Xavier, who had moved to the sofa as though he belonged here. Well, he'd been here often enough. But this was still kind of weird.

"I like your outfit, Twink," Xavier told her, running his gaze over her with a nod. "Cute."

"Been trying to get her to wear something other than black dresses that cover her," Brick told him. "But she won't wear anything out of the playroom."

"Maybe take it in baby steps. Why don't you wear that to dinner?" Xavier asked her.

What was going on? Why were they talking like this?

"It's only going to be us," Brick told her. "Elias and Sterling are having dinner in the pool house. Which means I'm cooking, unfortunately."

"I could cook," Xavier offered.

"Perfect."

Juliet moved over to Brick, grabbing hold of his shirt. The move wasn't lost on Xavier who narrowed his gaze at her. But she tugged at Brick, who leaned down.

"What's going on?" she whispered.

"Trust me?"

"Of course."

"Then just go with it. I promise, everything will be all right."

He cupped her cheeks between his hands and kissed the tip of her nose. "Now, what say we build another fort?"

XAVIER WATCHED JULIET. Poor thing looked overwhelmed and confused. But after speaking quietly to Brick, she'd thrown herself into the fort building.

She really did look cute today. She was wearing a short blue and white striped skirt that barely covered her ass. And when she bent over, he saw blue ruffly panties underneath. Her top was white with ruffles down the sleeves.

They'd discussed whether to just come out and tell her their plans, then after speaking to Caley and the two Docs today, they'd changed their minds and decided to show her a united front first. To prove that this could work.

He watched as she and Brick built the fort. But then Brick looked at him, nodding towards her.

Xavier stood. "Twink, can I help?"

"Of course," she said, in a far more relaxed voice. "I want one with two levels, then I'm going to put a moat around it and have mermaids in the moat."

"Sounds like fun. Shall I get your bath mermaids?"

"Yes, Xavy! Get them!"

He had to grin over how loud and excited she sounded. But mostly, over how relaxed she was.

Two levels wasn't exactly easy to achieve. They ended up using the sofa as the second level and Brick grabbed some tall lamps from downstairs to drape blankets over. Cushions around it formed the moat, and mermaids swam in the depths. Finally,

Brick found some pieces of wood in the garage to make into the drawbridge.

Juliet grabbed an outfit from her costumes and got changed in the bedroom. When she returned, she was wearing a pale blue princess dress with lace sleeves, she wore a tiara and fairy wings. And she carried a wand.

"I'm a magical fairy princess," she declared. "And I'm going to defend my castle from the naughty, evil pirates trying to take it over."

Brick rubbed at his chin. "Would pirates try to invade a castle? Don't they tend to stick to sailing the seven seas looking for buried treasure?"

She pointed the wand at the other man. "We don't need your logic here, smelly pirate!"

Xavier had to grin. "Have some imagination, man. There's hardly likely to be mermaids swimming in the moat of a castle, either."

"You two naughty pirates need to hush!" she cried then she grabbed some swords for them. "Begone, stinky, ugly pirates!"

"I feel personally attacked," Xavier exclaimed, sniffing at himself.

Brick grinned at him. "Well, I didn't want to say anything . . ."

Suddenly, something hit him right in the face. He let out a surprised yelp then glanced down to find it was one of Juliet's soft toys.

She raised her wand into the air and let out a mighty roar. "Loyal soldiers! Unite! Defend the castle!"

"Oh, it is on!" Xavier yelled back. "You'll walk the plank, wench!"

Juliet gave him a maniacal grin. Just before she flung another soft toy in his face.

Brat.

For the next hour, Xavier didn't stop grinning as he played the part of a smelly pirate, come to raid the mermaid castle. While Juliet yelled at her toy soldiers and pretended to fight them both off.

"Die, you ugly, smelly, syphilis-ridden mongrels!" She pretended to kill them both, piercing their chests with the plastic swords she'd taken off them. Both men died dramatically, slumping onto the floor. She jumped on Brick's stomach, making him groan as she giggled.

"I think I need a nap," Brick sat up with her in his lap.

Juliet giggled. "Poor Daddy, he's so old."

"Hey!" Brick protested. "Brat." Placing her on her back, he tickled her until she cried for mercy and lay back on the floor, gasping for breath.

"Gotta pee." She climbed to her feet, leaving the two men alone.

Xavier sat up and looked at Brick. "Thanks, man. You don't know what this means to me."

Brick nodded. "I know. But mostly, I'm doing it for her."

"I know, I just want you to know, I'm committed to this. I'll do whatever is necessary to make it work."

"Good. Me too."

~

COMMITTED TO MAKING WHAT WORK?

She knew she shouldn't have listened, but she couldn't help herself. She crept away when they didn't say anything more.

There was definitely something going on. Why were they so friendly all of a sudden? What were they keeping from her? She didn't want secrets between them.

This was all rather odd.

But since Xavier was here, and the last thing she wanted was for him to leave, perhaps she shouldn't question it.

After peeing, she walked back into the playroom.

"Duchess, I thought we'd keep Xavier company while he cooks dinner." Brick held out his hand.

She glanced down at princess fairy outfit. "I should change."

"No," Brick replied firmly.

"Wear what you have on, Twink," Xavier told her. "Please. For us."

Well, barnacles.

"Okay. I will."

"Been meaning to ask where Twink came from," Brick said.

Xavier's lips twitched. She studied him for a moment. There was something about him . . . he seemed lighter almost. Happier? She wasn't entirely sure.

"It's short for twinkle toes," Xavier said.

"Ah. Because she's clumsy?"

"Exactly."

She huffed. "It could have been because I'm light on my feet."

They both just stared at her. She wasn't *that* clumsy. She had that thought right as she tripped up over a cushion and nearly went headfirst into the fort.

About an hour later, they were all seated at the dining table. She was sitting at the head of the table. Brick had put food on her plate. Shepherd's pie with green beans and garlic bread.

"Thanks for this, Xavier. It looks delicious," Brick told him.

It did look and smell delicious. But she didn't know how she was going to eat with her stomach tied in a knot. She glanced from one to the other as they dug in.

"Eat, Duchess," Brick urged.

"Is there something you don't like?" Xavier asked.

"No, I love it all." Something he already knew. She picked up her fork.

"Do you need me to feed you?" Brick asked.

"N-no." She glanced over at Xavier then shifted around on her seat.

"Do you need to go potty?" Brick asked.

"Brick!" She went bright red.

"Everyone has to pee, Twink." Xavier grinned at her.

Ass. She glared at him. "Do you have to go potty?"

"Nope." He popped a piece of garlic bread into his mouth. "Now, eat."

"I don't know if I like the two of you ganging up on me."

"Well, you certainly seem to need it," Brick told her, pulling her plate closer. "Think it will take two of us to look after you."

She sucked in a breath, freezing. "What's going on here? Why are the two of you acting like this?"

They shared a look with one another, but didn't say anything.

"Tell me," she urged. "I deserve to know."

"She's right," Xavier told Brick. "I thought it would work better this way, but we're confusing her."

"What is it that you're committed to making work?" she asked before thinking better of it.

Xavier raised his eyebrows. "Were you eavesdropping, Twink?"

"I, um . . ."

"That's very naughty," Brick said. "I think she should spend some time in the corner for that."

"I agree," Xavier said.

"What is going on here?" she cried, starting to feel completely overwhelmed.

They must have seen it too, because they both winced. Then Brick reached for her, drawing her onto his lap. Xavier moved into her chair and leaned across to take her hand in his.

"Everything is all right, sweetheart," Xavier soothed.

"I'm confused. You're both acting odd. Where were you today?" she asked Brick. "And was Xavier with you?"

"Yes, he was. We went to Sanctuary Ranch."

"Why?"

"To talk to Doc, Archer, and Caley," Xavier told her.

"About what?"

"Being in a permanent ménage," Brick told her.

She took in a deep breath. "Are you . . . do you mean . . . oh." She couldn't make her brain work in order to get the words out properly. She was completely flabbergasted.

"I'm going to ask you a question, Duchess, and I want you to answer me honestly. Can you do that?"

"I guess so."

"All I want is your honesty, remember? No lies."

"No lies," she repeated.

"Juliet, do you love Xavier?"

"W-what?" Had he really just asked her that.

"Juliet, do you love Xavier in the same way you love me?"

27

D*o you love Xavier in the same way you love me?*
That was the last sentence she was going to hear. She was certain of it. Because her heart was about to seize up. There was no way Brick had just asked her that.

Right?

Because there was no way he could know. She hadn't let it slip in her sleep, had she?

Oh God. She was going to lose him. She was going to lose Brick.

"Juliet. Juliet, look at me. Fuck."

"Maybe we should have waited," Xavier said, sounding stressed. "Maybe she doesn't want this. Want me."

"She does. She's just in shock. Juliet, talk to us," Brick urged.

"Perhaps I should leave," Xavier said.

"You're not going anywhere," Brick told him sharply. "You need to stay here. You're in this just as much as me. We agreed. If this relationship is going to work, we're all equal. No one is more important."

"She is."

"Well, yeah, obviously," Brick agreed. "But between you and me. One of us isn't more. Now, stick to the plan."

Their conversation started to penetrate. And she . . . she didn't understand it.

She cleared her throat and tried to move out of Brick's arms.

"Nope," he told her. "You're not going anywhere. At least not until you talk to me. To us."

She glanced over at Xavier who looked worried. She hated it when he was worried.

"I need an answer, Duchess," Brick prompted.

"Nobody will get angry at you either way," Xavier promised.

She looked at each of them. "Is this a dream?"

"No, baby." Brick pushed her hair off her face. He gave her such a tender look that she stared at him in amazement.

Tender wasn't exactly a word she would use to describe Brick. Unmoving. Stubborn. Loyal.

"If this relationship is going to work?" she repeated back his earlier words. "You mean a relationship where . . ."

"We share you," Brick told her. "A permanent ménage."

"I don't understand . . . why would the two of you come up with this?"

"Because I think you love Xavier. I've seen the way you both look at each other. I know how devastated you were at the idea of him leaving Wishingbone. Do you love him?"

"I love you."

"I know you do," Brick told her warmly. "And I'm not upset or mad. I was the one who went to Xavier to propose this. It's my idea. So don't think you're losing me. You couldn't even if you tried."

"I . . . I . . ."

"You don't have to answer now," Xavier told her gently, but she saw some sadness in his gaze. "If this isn't something you want, the two of us, then all you have to do is say. Then I'll go."

But she didn't want that. The idea of never seeing him again . . . Brick was right. It would devastate her. But so did the idea of losing Brick. She glanced up at him, studying him. He didn't look upset or worried. He was calm.

"I love you."

"Love you too, Duchess." He kissed her forehead. "Nothing changes that. The amazing thing about you is that I know you have enough love for us both."

"Really?"

"Really," he replied firmly. "Do you love Xavier?"

"Nothing happens that you don't want," Xavier said before she could answer. "Ever. You have to know that. Yeah, we talked about it. Neither of us knows if it will work. I didn't even think it was a possibility until Brick brought it up. He didn't have to. I know that you love him. But if you think it's possible to love me as well, I'll never give you a reason to regret it."

The fear and the hope on his face nearly undid her. She felt those fractured pieces inside her start to slide even tighter together. What Brick had healed was still delicate. But she knew she could become stronger.

If she was brave. If she took what these two men were offering her.

"You're sure?" she asked Brick.

He nodded. "I've had a while to think about this."

"A while?" she asked, confused by that. "How long?"

He sighed. "It's fucking Elias' fault. Him and those reverse harem stories he goes on about."

"Elias reads reverse harem books?" she asked. This was definitely feeling more than a bit surreal. "Wait, a reverse harem is three or more guys."

"You're not adding another guy," Brick barked.

"No more," Xavier said with a stern frown.

She held up her hands defensively. "I never said I wanted to. You brought up reverse harems, I'm just pointing out the rules."

"No more. Just him. That's more than enough," Brick said.

"Why?" she whispered. "Why would you do this?" He had her. He didn't have to share her. "If you're worried that I would have done something, I swear I wouldn't. I'm not Linda. I love you. I never want to lose you."

"I know you're not her," Brick told her fiercely. "I couldn't do this if I didn't trust you, one hundred percent. And you're not losing me."

Her stomach rolled, she felt worried, frightened, and hopeful. She wrapped her hand up in Brick's T-shirt.

"Baby girl, don't stress," Brick soothed. "That's the last thing we want."

"If you take off your shirt, that might help her," Xavier murmured.

"Nah, man, that's your thing with her. I have something else that helps."

"Are you going to do that now?"

"Well, figure I should wait a while before I show you my cock," Brick replied. "Don't want to give you an inferiority complex."

Xavier let out a scoffing noise. "I won't get an inferiority complex from your cock, I can reassure you of that. Wait, what do you do to calm her down that involves your dick?"

Her anxiety was starting to fade as she listened to their conversation.

She leaned back to look up at Brick, who was smirking. "Stick around, I'm sure you'll find out." Then he glanced down at her. "I know what I'm doing. I've actually been in a ménage relationship before."

"Not with Linda?" she asked.

"No. When I told Linda that my last relationship had been a ménage, she scoffed. She said she'd never be in a relationship like that. It's funny because there was a third person in our marriage for years. I just didn't know. No, this relationship was earlier, when I first joined the marines. And it worked well."

Brick tucked some hair behind her ear. "I know you're not Linda. I know you would never cheat on me. You've got more loyalty in your little toe than she did in her entire body. I don't think everyone is like her. And the fact is, while I never cheated, I did neglect her. I put other things first. I never opened myself up to being vulnerable with her. To giving her everything. Not like with you. If you left me, I'd struggle to find my way, to keep going."

"I'd never leave you," she said fiercely.

"I know, baby girl. You're my whole world. I'm putting your needs before everything else. Fact is, you need Xavier."

What the fuck did she say to that? If she said no, then she hurt Xavier. If she said yes, then Brick wasn't enough.

Xavier let out a low chuckle that wasn't exactly amused. "Way to put her in it, man."

"What?" Brick asked, sounding confused. He was so straightforward, he obviously didn't see the traps in what he'd said.

"My needs aren't more important than anyone else's," she managed to get out. That was safe enough, right?

Both men gave her incredulous looks.

"Yeah, Twink, they are. They're the most important."

She shook her head. "I'm not special." Fact was, she had no idea why either of them would want her. How Brick could love her. And Xavier . . . well, he hadn't come out and said exactly how he felt about her.

Brick made a low growling noise.

"I hate that you don't see how special you are," Xavier said. He looked to Brick. "Her feelings of self-worth need a lot of work."

"Yeah, so does self-preservation. She puts herself in dangerous situations without a thought to her safety."

Xavier nodded.

"Why the hell did you let her use a bike to get around?" Brick blurted out.

Xavier sighed. "It wasn't my place to do anything about that."

"It is now."

Xavier looked up at Brick then at her. "If Juliet agrees. It's a lot, Twink. You can take time to think about it. Having two men, it might not be easy."

"But we'll make it as easy as possible," Brick interjected. "If there's any jealousy or issues between the two of us, then that's where they'll stay. We'll talk it out with each other, but we'll try not to let it affect you."

She gave him a surprised look.

"Told you I've been thinking about it."

"Because of Elias," she stated.

"Because I saw the way you stared at Xavier when you thought I wasn't looking. Because I definitely saw the way he watched you. I know I didn't have to let him in. Because I know you'd never do anything to betray me. You mean everything to me, and I want to give you everything you desire and need. This sort of relationship means there will always be someone else to watch out for you, take care of you, when I'm not around. There might be times I have to work away, and I don't want you on your own. If I'm not here, Xavier will be. He'll watch over you nearly as well as I will. Because he loves you."

"Thanks for telling her I love her, man," Xavier said dryly.

"I'm trying to help you both out."

"You really love me, Xavier?" she whispered.

Xavier ran a finger over the back of her hand, and she noticed his hand shook. "Yeah, Twink. I do. I tried not to, but I couldn't stop."

She winced.

Brick sighed. "And people say I stick my foot in my mouth."

"You didn't want to love me?"

She found herself being lifted onto Xavier's lap, her face pressed to his chest as he rocked back and forth.

"Not like that. Not because you weren't worth loving."

"I'm messed up. I'm a mess of phobias and fears and anxieties. There's no way I'd fit into your perfect life."

"Perfect life? Are you fucking kidding me?" He pulled her face back from his chest. Which was a damn shame because that was one of her happy places. "I don't have a fucking perfect life."

BOTH BRICK and Juliet sent him looks of disbelief.

Is that really what they thought?

Juliet waved her hand at him. "Look at you. You look perfect. Sound perfect. You have an amazing job, you're smart, you're well-liked."

"You've probably never failed at anything in your life," Brick added. "Or lost everything and had to rebuild."

"Everything he does, he does well," Juliet confirmed.

Okay, now they were just making him mad.

"If I'm so perfect, then how come I fucked up so spectacularly?"

"Ooh, Xavy just swore," Juliet said with wide eyes. "Shit just got real."

He gave her a stern look. "Don't swear."

She stuck out her lower lip.

"Yeah, I don't think so, brat." Brick leaned over and tapped her lower lip. "Being cute is not a get out of jail free card."

"Should be," she muttered.

"Sadly, some people have let you use that cuteness to get your own way."

"Hey!" Xavier muttered, even if it was true. He brushed her hair back. "I just like seeing her happy."

"So, do I," Brick told him. "But she can be happy and not be allowed to get away with murder."

"Are you saying I'm spoiled?" she asked.

Brick sighed. "I'm having to undo years of being spoiled."

"Xavy, aren't you going to defend me? Tell Daddy I'm not spoiled."

"You're a hundred percent spoiled," Xavier told her.

She glared up at him with a huff. Then something came over her face. Something thoughtful. He fell silent, waiting for her to think everything through. Brick must have realized that she needed a moment too.

They'd hit her with a lot.

"If this is something you can't do, I'll understand," Xavier told her. "I'll walk away. We can go back to being friends."

He wasn't sure how, exactly. It was hard to have everything dangled in front of you then walk away. But Brick had shown him that putting her first should be their priority.

Brick just sighed, shaking his head at that.

He didn't get the other man. Not at all. But then, he also felt this tie to him. Because they both loved her with a passion that hurt.

Was it enough to unite them as a family? He didn't know. But he wanted to try. He didn't love Brick. Didn't know him that well.

But for her, he'd get to know him.

Yeah, it was bizarre. Could two near-strangers love the same girl? Could they become a family for that girl? Could they learn to share?

Last night, he'd gone online to search for those answers. He hadn't really found them. He'd always asked the two docs and Caley, as well as Brick, but the only way to find answers was to discover them himself.

He'd just have to find out firsthand himself.

"I don't want anyone to walk away," she whispered. "I don't want to lose either of you. That's why I'm so scared."

"You're not going to lose us," Brick told her. "Not unless you tell us to get lost. Even then, I'm not sure I could ever walk away from you. I'd become some weird stalker, watching your every move."

"I'd join you," Xavier told him.

They grinned at each other. Yeah, this situation was weird as fuck. But hey, it was a changing world. Maybe this would become the new norm. Who knew? All he knew was he loved Juliet and was tired of trying to hide it or deny it.

"I want this. God, I want this so much, but it doesn't feel real. It feels like I'm in some sort of dream."

"I get it, I felt the same way when the big guy brought it up."

"I don't live in a dreamland," Brick scoffed at them both.

Juliet rolled her eyes up at Xavier. He winked at her.

She started biting her lip. "I don't want to hurt anyone. I couldn't stand it if that happened."

"You're not going to hurt anyone," Xavier reassured her.

"We're grown-ass men," Brick added, reaching out to free her lip. "We can guard our own feelings."

She stared over at Brick. "I love you." She looked up at Xavier. "And I love you. Hurting either of you, losing either of you because I . . . because I'm a weirdo who loves two men at the same time, I couldn't stand that."

"Nope. Stop that right now," Brick barked.

Even Xavier jumped. Then he frowned at Brick for talking to her like that. Brick gave him a steady look back. "She's not going to break, man. She's tougher than any of you know."

Juliet sucked in a breath. "You can't blame him for thinking I might break," she said to Brick. "I'm the town looney."

"Nope," Xavier growled at her. "That's not happening."

"You should spank her for that," Brick told him.

Spank her? Fuck. Could he? She was so much smaller than him.

"Fuck, man, I've spanked her. And look at me." Brick held out his hand. Yeah, he had hands like dinner plates. "She didn't break. Remember, you're giving her what she needs."

Right.

"Brick's right. You need a spanking for calling yourself a freak and a weirdo. That's twenty."

"Twenty!" she squeaked.

"Damn, man. Like your style." Brick grinned.

"Twenty is a lot," she told him.

"Calling yourself those things is not going to be tolerated," he told her in a firm voice. His blood damn near boiled. "You are not looney or a weirdo. You know what you are?"

"What?" she whispered.

"Ours."

"Fuck, yeah," Brick agreed. "You know, I wasn't sure I was gonna like you to begin with. Seemed too prim and proper. But I think your shit really does stink."

"I don't know how to answer that."

She giggled. Actually giggled, and Xavier's heart lightened. Brick shared a look with him, letting him know he'd done that on purpose.

"She can take a spanking, man. What she can't be allowed to do is continue with self-destructive behavior. We work together, we'll build her up. Show her that she's a fucking goddess."

Xavier sucked in a breath. That felt so right. "And it's going to take two of us to do it."

Brick let out a huge sigh, shaking his head. "I'm afraid so. She's a handful, tiny as she is."

"I am not," she muttered.

"What you are," Xavier told her in a warm voice. "Is beautiful and courageous and smart. You are so filled with love, that

Brick and I are the lucky ones, because you have enough love for two people. You think either of us would be complete without you? We wouldn't. So, if you didn't have enough love for us both, then one of us would forever be lost, without that piece of our soul."

"Damn, man. That was good."

He shook his head at Brick, but didn't take his gaze from Juliet's beautiful hazel-colored eyes. Tears dripped down her face. "I love you, Juliet. I've been a fool for years, but no longer. I'm going to grasp hold of this chance with both hands and never let go. I will do whatever I have to in order to make this work. But whether we try, this all comes down to you."

She nodded then turned to look at Brick.

"I'm in, Duchess." Brick slipped onto the floor then reached over to grab her hand in his. "I want to do this. I think it can work. I'm prepared to do whatever it takes to make it work. I've done it before, I know what the pitfalls are. But I think it's worth trying. I didn't just suggest this on a whim. It might not always be easy, but nothing worth having ever is. I love you, and I want you to be the happiest you can be. If that's with both of us, then that's what will happen, understand?"

He leaned in and kissed her.

And yeah, Xavier wouldn't lie to himself. It was weird to hold his girl while another man kissed her.

But she wouldn't be his girl without this man.

When Brick drew back, Juliet looked up at him. "I want this. I want to try. I want to love you both, and have you both love me."

Thank God. Thank God.

Brick kissed her until she let out a soft murmur and drew back. "Love you, Brick."

"Love you, Duchess."

Then it was his turn. He cupped the back of her head with his hand, holding her steady. "I can be demanding, controlling."

He didn't know why he had to warn her. He was getting every-thing he wanted.

Don't ruin it, man.

"You?"

"Yes, me," he told her. "And if the two of you think that my life is perfect, then you're delusional." He let out a humorless bark of laughter. "Not everything I touch turns to gold, you know." He let out a deep breath. "There's something I've never told you, Juliet. That I don't talk about with anyone."

"Is it to do with the reason you moved back here to Wishing-bone?" she asked.

"Yeah." He cleared his throat. "This is hard to admit. I made a mistake. A big one. And it cost a woman her life."

28

"Xavier, no," she whispered. "I'm sure it wasn't your fault."

He gave her a sad smile. "It was, Twink. And if after hearing any of this you both change your minds, I'll understand."

"Nothing will make me change my mind about you," she told him fervently.

Brick just regarded him steadily. They both waited, their food growing cold. But he didn't have much of an appetite anyway.

"I was working at Massachusetts General, this woman came in. She was in her mid-twenties. Seemed healthy enough. The nurses told me that she was a repeat visitor in the ER, but that there was never much wrong with her. But this time, she had strep throat. I treated her like any other patient. I don't know if it's because the other doctors and nurses usually dismissed her a hypochondriac or what, but she seemed to fixate on me."

"Fixate?" Juliet asked.

"She'd keep coming back to the emergency department and asking for me. And there would never be anything wrong with her. Finally, I got sick of it. I had worked a long shift. Lost a young patient who'd been brought in after being in a car crash. I just didn't have the patience for her to waste my time. She said she had a headache. I asked a less-experienced colleague to check on her. They dismissed her, telling her to take some painkillers. She died a few hours later from a ruptured aneurysm."

"Oh, no, Xavier. I'm so sorry." Juliet wrapped her arms around his neck and squeezed.

"Not your fault, man," Brick told him. "You didn't even treat her."

"But I should have," Xavier said. "I pawned her off on a colleague because I couldn't be bothered. It was my fault."

"Xavy, no."

"It was." He blew out a breath. "Her family thought so, too. There was talk of a malpractice suit. I deserved it. To pay. Then it suddenly disappeared."

"How?" Brick asked.

"Reuben?" Juliet guessed.

"Yeah, that bastard paid them all off. I was so angry at him. Mostly at myself, but it was easier to be mad at him. I quit and I turned into a hermit for a while. Until Reuben came to give me a pep talk. I punched him in the face and told him to fuck off, that we were no longer friends."

"Oh no," Juliet said softly.

"Not my finest moment. I've kept up the anger ever since, but it's not fair. None of it was his fault. It was mine. However, something he said kept coming back to me. I could either wallow, and waste my life, and her death would be for nothing. Or I could actually help people. I found out about the opening at Wishing-bone hospital and, surprisingly, got the job."

"Of course you got it. What happened wasn't your fault, silly man," Juliet scolded.

He loved that she only saw the good in him. Fact was, there was more gray than he liked to admit.

"For the longest time, I didn't think I deserved happiness. Still don't in a lot of ways. But I'm not unselfish enough to not grasp hold of it. Of you, if you still want me."

"Yes, of course I still want you."

Unable to resist, he dropped his lips to hers and kissed her. A feeling of rightness swept through him. Of coming home.

He knew he would do anything for her. Whatever she needed, desired, he would give her.

Because that's what you did for your heart. You held it, you protected it, cherished it.

When he pulled back, he glanced over at Brick, worried about his reaction. But the other man just gave him a nod. His tension eased.

"Coming back here was the best thing I ever did. Even if my parents can't see that. They've never been satisfied with anything I've done, though. They're not terrible people. But I wouldn't call them good people, either. They care more about appearances than they do about happiness."

"Guessing they wouldn't approve of us, then," Brick said.

"That's putting it mildly."

Juliet sucked in a breath. "We don't have to tell them."

"What?" Xavier asked.

"You don't have to tell them about me. About us."

"Keep you a secret?"

"Yeah," she said.

He let out a noise he'd never heard himself make, and by the way her eyes went wide, neither had Juliet.

"You are not, nor will you ever be, my dirty little secret, you understand me?" When she didn't say anything, he narrowed his gaze. He gave her his best Dom look. "Do you understand me?"

"Yes, Sir."

Fuck if those words didn't go straight to his dick, making him shift around slightly. Brick sent him a knowing smirk.

"Suggest it again, and the spanking you're owed will seem like child's play in comparison to what I'll give you. Understand?"

"I understand."

"We're not hiding this, Twink. Not from anyone."

"But what about your job?" she asked. "People will talk."

"So?" Brick said. "Who cares what people say?"

A funny look came over her face. "People can be really mean. Maybe you think you don't care. Or you tell yourself not to, but it burrows its way deep. It becomes this rotten thing inside you, growing and growing until you can't breathe, you can't sleep, you can't eat. Their words become a mantra in your head. And maybe you know they're not right. But then you start to think maybe they are. Maybe you are what they say. Maybe you're stupid, a slut, maybe your parents wished you'd never been born, maybe the world would be a better place if you weren't in it."

What the fuck kind of hell was this she was talking about? Xavier met Brick's gaze. The other man was pale.

Brick cupped their girl's face between his hands as Xavier held her as tight as possible.

"Duchess, look at me," Brick crooned.

"Twink?" he asked when she didn't move.

Suddenly, she stiffened, then she turned and buried her face in his chest.

"Duchess, look at me," Brick repeated.

"Forget I said any of that."

Yeah, right, that wasn't going to happen.

He shared a look with Brick. Neither of them could ignore what she just said.

"Baby girl, look at Daddy."

She let out a deep breath.

Xavier sucked in his breath. "Talk to us, sweetheart. Come on, look at Brick before he loses it and starts crying. I don't need to see the big guy cry."

To his credit, Brick backed him up straight away. "I can feel the tears starting." He fake-sniffled.

Her shoulders moved. He shared an alarmed look with Brick.

"I'm practically sobbing," Brick added.

There was a small giggle. It was watery and tiny, but it was there. Then her hand reached out and wrapped itself in Brick's pants.

"Sorry, I'm sorry," she whispered.

"You have nothing to be sorry for," Xavier told her. He chose his next words carefully. "I know you were bullied before you came to Wishingbone."

She nodded. "I was."

"Why did no one do anything?" Brick demanded.

"Hard to do something when they didn't know."

Xavier kissed the top of her head and Brick grabbed onto her hand.

"When I was nearly eleven, my parents were killed. It was a home invasion gone wrong. I woke up to yelling. I ran out of my bedroom just as shots were fired. There was just this . . . this silence after those shots. I remember that silence so well. I don't know how long I stood there, but by the time I finally moved, whoever had shot them was gone."

She took in a shuddering breath.

"They were lying on the floor of the living room. My mom was wearing these flannel pajamas she loved. They had cows on them. I tried to wake her up. But she wouldn't wake and there was blood pooling under her body. My daddy, he was close to her, his arm was reaching out towards her."

She rubbed at her eyes.

"Apparently, I must have started screaming. I yelled until I was hoarse. We didn't have close neighbors, and I don't really remember what happened next. But our neighbors found me walking down the road, dressed in my pajamas, covered in blood."

"Oh, baby girl," Brick murmured. He knelt on the floor in front of them.

Xavier knew about how Reuben's father had died, he knew she'd found them, but she'd never spoken about it, and Reuben hadn't given him details.

"Did they find who did it?" Brick asked.

"No, they never did."

"Where was Reuben?" Brick asked.

"Reuben's actually my half-brother," she murmured. "Same dad. There're four years between us. He lived with his mom and came to visit sometimes during the holidays. His mom hated our dad. I think she thought he had an affair with my mom and that's why he left her. My mom was an only child and I didn't have anyone but Reuben. And his mom wouldn't take me because she hated me."

"Fuck," Brick muttered.

"That nearly killed Reuben," Xavier said. He looked at Brick. "Reuben's grandparents lived here. Whenever his mom found a new boyfriend, he'd get shipped here to live with them. Then when she got dumped, she'd take him back to Boston to live with her."

"Reuben wanted his grandparents to take me," she added. "But his granddad had dementia, and his grandma didn't have the time to take on a traumatized eleven-year-old who wouldn't talk. Well, the doctors said I damaged my vocal cords, but I'm not sure I would have talked anyway."

"What happened?" Brick asked.

"I went into foster care."

"Reuben played a game of football that weekend," Xavier said. "He was so vicious they benched him for the rest of the season. To say he didn't take it well was putting it mildly. He wanted to take you. He would have raised you himself. Except his mother wouldn't let him move full time to Wishingbone, and his grandma could barely cope with looking after his grandpa."

"I know," she whispered. "He called me every night. He swore he'd get me out of the system when he could. Told me not to give up. He was the only thing that kept me going." She let out a deep breath. "You know how you hear those bad stories about foster parents?"

"Yes," Brick said carefully.

"Well, I didn't have that experience. My foster parents, they were amazing. They were kind and understanding. Supportive. I couldn't have asked for better foster parents. For the first nine months I was with them, I didn't go to school. My foster mom taught me at home. They decided to start me in a new school year. I had just begun speaking again, but my voice was this weird, broken thing. It didn't sound like me. So, I didn't like to talk much. When I went back to school, well, it wasn't good. Not awful, but not great. I didn't have any friends. I was the weird kid with the broken voice who barely spoke, but I managed. Until freshman year, that's when it all went to hell.

"I was younger than the other kids, which didn't help. Still, the first couple of months were okay. I kept my head down, trying not to bring any attention to myself. But one day, I accidentally bumped into one of the star football players. I went flying backward. I thought he'd ignore me or blame me or something. But he was really nice. Helped me up. Smiled at me."

She let out a bark of humorless laughter. "Little did I know that would send me spiraling into hell. His girlfriend took exception to him helping me. But instead of taking it up with him, she started picking on me. She was part of the cool group. And her friends all backed her up. They made my life hell.

"It was brutal. The things they said and did. I withdrew even more. I stopped eating. I went back to not talking at all. I wore long clothing all the time, in black. I just wanted to disappear, to fade away. They found out what happened to my parents, and they told everyone that I killed them. They said I was a slut who was after everyone's boyfriend. They called me a freak, ugly. It just went on and on and on until I didn't want to be there anymore. I didn't want to be anywhere."

"I'll kill them all," Brick said in a low, harsh voice.

"I'll help you," Xavier swore. She clung to them both. He wished they could go back and help her. To shelter that young girl who went through hell.

"You didn't tell your foster parents?" Brick asked.

She shook her head. "My foster dad worked for the father of one of the girls who bullied me, and she said that he would lose his job if I said anything."

"So, what changed?" Brick asked.

"Reuben was still at school. His grandpa had died and left him this plot of land and some money. When he turned eighteen, he started investing it. And he did well, really well. He came to visit whenever he could, but it had been a few months since I saw him. I know he blames himself for that, but it wasn't his fault."

"No, it was theirs," Brick said darkly.

"I hid my weight loss under baggy clothes. I tried to pretend everything was fine. But it wasn't. And one day, right at the end of the year, I collapsed in class. I ended up in the hospital for a week recovering. I had to see more therapists. Reuben had his lawyer in the thick of things, and he somehow convinced his grandma to apply for custody of me. His lawyer didn't think that child services would give him custody of me at that stage."

She shook her head. "I don't know how he did it. He'd just graduated high school, but he was scarier than everyone else. I felt sorry for my foster parents. I still keep in touch with them. I told them why I hadn't said anything and my foster dad broke down in tears. It was awful. I wish I had been better to them."

"Hey, none of it was your fault," Xavier told her. Tears entered his eyes and he blinked, but one slipped free.

A look of amazement filled her face. "For me?"

"Sweetheart." His voice broke, and he buried his face in her hair.

"Brick?"

"God, Duchess. God." They hugged her tight.

Xavier could feel his insides breaking. Yeah, he'd known some of it, but not all the details. He hadn't even met her until she'd already been living here a few months. When Reuben had gone to get her, he'd been packing to move to college.

But when he'd come back to visit Reuben during the summer break, there she'd been. Tiny and scared, clinging to her brother like he was her safety.

"Reuben took a year off to take care of me. He'd been doing college classes in high school anyway, so he was well ahead. He got me into school here, made certain that everyone knew that any slight to me was a slight to him. I think he scared the whole town shitless. Told me that he was my wolf. That he would harm anyone who hurt me."

"Good," Brick said, looking wrecked.

"I'm all right, Daddy. I promise."

Xavier could tell that Brick was just as much of a mess as he was, his eyes red-rimmed and glassy.

"I really will kill them. All of them," Brick swore.

"I looked some of them up, tried to stalk them online," she told them. "Believe me, you don't have to go after them. Their lives are hell. Not one of them was successful in life. They went on into bad marriages or poor business decisions. It's like everything came back to bite them on the ass."

Or Reuben had. But Xavier didn't say it.

She let out a shuddering breath, and Brick stood, grabbing a box of tissues from the counter. He crouched, but instead of offering her a tissue, he held them out to Xavier.

Xavier took a tissue, then tilted up her face and carefully cleaned it. By the time he finished, she was bright red.

"I've often wondered if you were a Daddy," she told him. "You're always so patient and kind to me. But when I tried to ask Reuben once, he refused to say anything other than you weren't for me."

"Reuben introduced me to BDSM," Xavier told her. "He took me to my first club. It was a way to relieve the stress of medical school, of my parents' expectations. There, I could be in control. I could make the decisions. I enjoyed discipling naughty subs. I never went near the Littles area. Then one day, I saw a Dom comforting his Little. The way he held her, cared for her, you could see her blossoming under his attention. It struck me. I formed a friendship with that couple. The Little was a sweetheart. Her Dom was this huge guy. Turns out he owned a gym, and they'd been together for a while. Over time, they taught me a lot, but I never took it much further. I wasn't sure why I didn't feel like I could. Then I found out that you were a Little. And I had an outlet for my Daddy side. You. It's always been you." He brushed her hair back. "Forgive me for being an idiot."

"I forgive you. Idiot." She grinned as he mock-glared at her. "Does this mean you want to be my Daddy too?"

"How about your Papa?" he asked.

"I like that. Will you kiss me again?"

"Fuck, yes."

"So many f-bombs tonight, you best watch you don't get your mouth washed out, Papa."

Lord. That filled him with so much happiness he thought it might burst out of him. Grasping hold of the back of her head, he brushed his lips over hers. Once. Twice. "You sure? Once you're mine, there's no going back."

"Shut up and kiss me."

"Brat."

His mouth moved against hers, he slid his tongue between her lips and kissed her like he needed her to breathe, as if this kiss was their first, their last, and everything in between.

And when he kissed her, he found his home.

WHEN XAVIER DREW AWAY from their kiss, she stared up at him dreamily. That was . . . wow.

Then she remembered Brick.

Turning, she discovered she was still clutching his pants. Then she forced herself to be brave and look up into his face. But there was no anger or jealousy.

Just acceptance.

Dear Lord. What had she done to earn the love of two remarkable men like them?

"You're really okay with this?" she said croakily. She felt like she'd spoken more in this last week than she had in years.

He cupped the side of her face then leaned down to press his lips to hers. "I am, Duchess. I promise."

She looked to Xavier. "And so are you."

"Yeah, Twink." He gave her a soft grin. "You're our girl now."

"And our girl needs some food, then it's bedtime," Brick told her. "I'll go reheat our food."

She cuddled against Xavier, feeling completely spent.

"You've got a good man there, Twink."

"I've got two good men. The very best."

She ended up being fed her dinner by Brick while sitting in Xavier's lap. It was a weird feeling, but she wasn't certain she'd ever felt this loved. This cared for. After they'd all cleared up, Brick picked her up.

"Time for bed." He carried her towards the door. "You coming, Xavier?"

She glanced over to find Xavier staring at them longingly. Then his eyes widened. "Um, yeah. If that's okay."

"Wouldn't have said it if it wasn't," Brick replied. "We'll all sleep in my bed.

She reached over Brick's shoulder with her hand and Xavier took it, entwining their fingers. A joy like nothing else filled her.

Maybe this was crazy, insane. Perhaps they'd all had parts of their brains eaten by zombies, but right in that moment, she didn't much care.

They were hers.

She was theirs.

And whatever happened, she knew that she wouldn't regret taking this chance. Not if it could get her all of them.

They walked into Brick's room and he put her in the middle of the bed. "Back in a minute."

Brick disappeared as Xavier stood on the other side of the bed.

"You getting in, Xavy?" she asked, feeling shy all of a sudden. He was her best friend, her caregiver in a lot of ways. She shouldn't feel nervous with him, of all people.

Yet, he'd never been in the same bed with her.

"I promise I don't kick. But Brick snores sometimes," she whispered.

"Heard that," Brick said, returning from the bathroom. He climbed into bed with a groan. "Fuck, I'm tired. I feel like I could sleep for a week. Are you getting in, man, or what?"

She had to hide a grin as Xavier climbed into bed. Brick, in his blunt way, had done what she couldn't with her cajoling.

Just maybe this craziness would work, and wouldn't that be something?

Weird, freaky Juliet with two hot men in her bed. If only those bullies could see her now.

29

"Well, what do we have here?" Xavier asked, walking into playroom, and setting down the bag he was carrying.

Juliet, who was wearing a loose, pale dress that ended just above her knees, was frowning down at Angelique, who was standing with her head leaning into the corner.

"Papa!" she squealed, racing over to him and throwing herself into his arms. He'd gotten home in the early hours of the morning, sleeping in a different bedroom from them so he didn't wake them up. He hadn't spent any nights at his place since they'd entered this crazy relationship. There probably wasn't much point in keeping his apartment.

That would give fodder to the gossipers in town. They'd been keeping things quiet so far. He didn't know whether any of them were ready for the town to know about their relationship just yet.

"Hey, sweetheart."

"I missed you."

"I'm sorry. A few more night shifts and I'll have some time off to spend with you."

"Okay, Papa. I know you have to work hard."

"Congrats on another win last night." Brick had taken Juliet to her quiz last night while Xavier worked.

"Thanks, Papa!" Leaning back, she gave him a big smile.

He wiped at the corner of her mouth. "You been getting into the chocolate?"

"Just one piece."

He raised an eyebrow.

"Okay, maybe two."

"Don't eat any more today, all right? There's a lot of caffeine in that chocolate."

"Daddy thinks there's more caffeine in my veins than blood," she replied happily, adjusting the tiara on her head. "What's in there?"

He glanced down at the bag. "Well, remember when I said I would bring you back a present if you were a good girl?"

"Yes, but you were mean and said I hadn't been a good girl because I didn't tell you about Brick, Elias and Sterling."

"Right, but I thought that you've been pretty good since."

She jumped up and down, clapping her hands. "Yay!"

"Not entirely good. I haven't forgotten about you calling yourself names."

She pouted. "Papa, did you bring it here just to say I can't have it?"

"Of course not. I wouldn't be that mean. Here you are, Twink." He held out the bag and she opened it, gasping loudly as she drew out a mermaid toy. She immediately hugged it tight.

"I love it!"

"Yeah?"

"Yes, she's perfect. She's so squishy and soft. Like a giant marshmallow. Thank you, Papa." She gave him a huge hug.

"I'm glad. What will you name her?"

"Wavey!"

"That's perfect," he told her.

"I wonder where Daddy is? He's meant to be bringing up lunch, and I want to show him Wavey."

"I asked him if he'd mind me taking you on a picnic instead. I don't have to be back on shift until three."

"Yay! I loves picnics." She clapped her hands. "Can I take my paints and easel? I want to paint you a picture."

"I would love that, Twink," he replied, kissing her forehead. "Let's gather up your stuff and I'll carry it downstairs for you."

"I should change my clothes," she said hesitantly.

"No," he told her firmly. "You look gorgeous the way you are."

While she didn't look completely convinced, she did nod. Then she snapped her fingers. "Oh, wait. Angelique is in time-out for being naughty."

"What did she do this time?" he asked, well-versed in the adventures of her naughty doll.

"She threw her snack at Missy!" Juliet gave him a shocked look, shaking her head. "Can you believe how naughty she is?"

"Well, it's Angelique, so yes."

"Sometimes I think I ought to smack her bottom."

He could sympathize.

"Papa, what do you think of this?" Juliet asked, turning her painting around to show Xavier. He was sitting on the blanket he'd laid out on the floor of the sunroom. It had become really windy outside, so they'd decided to set up in the sunroom. There were so many windows that it sort of gave the illusion that they were outside.

While she'd painted, Xavier had prepared them a picnic lunch.

These past few days had been strange. But also amazing. Having them both living with her was like a dream come true.

Sure, there were learning curves, there probably would be for a while. They all wanted this to work, though.

Her only concern was Reuben. She hoped he was all right. Brick said that if they didn't hear from him soon that he'd get JSI to track him down.

After that first night, when she'd shared a bed with Xavier and Brick, they'd spent most of their time one-on-one with her. Partly due to Xavier's schedule. But it was probably also because this was new. They were trying to be careful not to encroach on each other and she wanted to keep things fair.

They hadn't told anyone about what they were doing, other than Elias and Sterling. But it wouldn't take long for Kiesha to find out. That girl was a bloodhound for gossip.

Xavier stood and walked over, placing his hand on her lower back. A shiver ran through her. Neither of them had fucked her yet. It was driving her a bit insane.

He stared at the painting on the easel. "That's so pretty, Twink. What is it?"

"Papa, it's obvious." Silly man. "It's a mermaid warrior fighting off a shark."

"Oh, right. It's obvious now. I just thought you were doing a landscape."

She made a scoffing noise. "Boring."

"Of course, my most sincere apologies." He made a small bow and walked over to the picnic lunch he'd made. "Now, time to come eat."

"Not hungry, Papa."

"That wasn't a question, Twink," he said warningly.

She barely paid attention. She was pretty certain he wouldn't spank her. Brick had ended up giving her those twenty spanks she's earned for calling herself a freak and weirdo.

"I'm okay, Papa." She stepped back, staring at her painting.

"I'm going to count to three and if you're not here, then you're going to be in trouble," he warned.

What sort of trouble?

"One."

Eh, she wasn't worried.

"Two."

What would he do?

"Three. Right, that's it." Walking over, he gently grasped hold of her wrist and took the paintbrush out of her hand, putting it in the jar of water.

"Hey, I wasn't finished, Papa."

"You are now," he told her. "No more painting for you."

She pouted. "Why not?"

"Because you were naughty and didn't listen to me." He gave her a stern look. "And now, you get to spend some time in the corner, thinking about your behavior."

"What? No, Papa. That's not fair."

He led her over to a corner. She caught a look at the picnic food, which all looked delicious. Drat, she wished she'd listened to him now.

"Ten minutes. Any shifting around will result in the clock starting over."

She turned to look at him over her shoulder. "Papa, that's mean."

"Clock starts again."

Well, barnacles. This was going to suck.

Turns out, she wasn't very good at staying still.

After two restarts, she finally managed a whole ten minutes without shifting around.

"Good girl. Come here, Twink."

She turned to find Xavier sitting on the blanket. She walked over to him and he drew her onto his lap so she was straddling his thighs, facing him.

"Now, what do you have to say for yourself?"

"I'm sorry for being naughty and not listening, Papa." She gave him a pouting look. "That wasn't very nice. I don't like corner time."

"You're not supposed to."

"Think I'd rather have the spanking."

A strange look crossed his face. She wondered when Xavier was going to trust that this is what she wanted. That she could handle his discipline.

She guessed it would take time.

"Now, you're to keep your hands behind your back. Papa is going to feed you."

Oh, this sounded like fun.

"If you eat something I give you, then you get a reward. If you don't, then no reward."

Hm. Okay.

The first thing was a strawberry. Easy. She loved them.

When she swallowed it, he kissed her gently.

All right. She was going to like this game.

Another strawberry. He kissed her neck. Another, and he moved his lips lower. Then he drew the tunic down to kiss the swell of her breast.

"Papa, what if someone sees?"

"Brick is manning the cameras. Sterling is asleep, and Elias has gone out. Besides, it's just a bit of play."

The next thing he tried to feed her was a sandwich. She wrinkled her nose. "A strawberry."

"No, a sandwich."

"Strawberry."

"Do you need more corner time?"

"No, Papa." She took a small bite. "Where's my reward?"

"You don't get one when you argue."

Well, that sucked. The next time he held the sandwich up, she eagerly took a bite.

Reaching behind her, he undid the zipper on her dress. Then he tugged the top of her dress down to reveal her breasts.

"Papa! You can't." She tried to cover herself with her hands and he gave them a light smack.

"Did I say you could move your hands?"

"No, Papa. But I . . . I . . ."

"Yes?" he asked, running his finger over her breast.

"I can't eat with my boobs on display," she said lamely.

"Of course you can. They're gorgeous."

"They're small. There's nothing to even see."

He suddenly twisted a nipple and she hissed. Immediately, he dropped his hand away. "Juliet, I'm sorry."

"No! Don't be sorry. It actually felt kind of good."

"It did?" he asked skeptically.

"A bit of pain clears my head, helps me think," she admitted to him.

"Interesting. But I don't want to hear any more insults about your breasts, hear me?" He gave her a stern look.

"Yes, Papa."

"Good girl. Now, keep your hands behind your back."

He took her nipple into his mouth and she gasped, feeling that sensation in her clit.

"Ohhh."

"Good girl." He fed her another bite of sandwich. Then sucked on her other nipple.

"Papa, feels so good."

"Tastes good too." He picked up a strawberry and bit it in half before rubbing the other half over her nipple. Then he sucked up the juice.

That was so incredibly arousing.

"More, Papa. More."

"You're still hungry?" he asked.

"Not for food."

"Unfortunately, my girl, all you're getting today is food."

What? What kind of mean joke was that? She glared up at him. But he ignored her scowl and fixed her dress, covering her up.

"Papa, you're mean." She pouted.

He tapped her lip. "None of that now, brat. Or you'll be back in the corner."

Really mean.

"Now isn't the time, okay? But soon."

Fine.

His phone rang and he reached over to grab it, frowning when he looked at the screen.

"Who is it?" she asked.

"My mother."

"You don't want to take it?"

"No. She refuses to talk about the lump or biopsy. I just . . . I'm nearly ready to wipe my hands clean of them both."

"Oh, Papa. Don't do that." She clasped hold of his face between her hands. "I know you're upset, but if you cut them off then you might come to regret it later. You don't get another set of parents. I know they have their issues, but just think about it first."

"I'm not making a rash decision. I promise, I'll think about it. You're a good person, Juliet."

"So are you." She kissed him. "Even if you won't let me come."

"It's good for you. Builds character."

If looks could kill, he'd be ash.

30

J uliet looked out the window of Brick's truck, feeling
uncertain. She didn't think she wanted to go to the diner
to eat. Her mind went back to the picnic yesterday. When
Xavier had put her down for a nap before leaving to go to
the hospital, she'd been tempted to ease the ache in her clit.

But he'd told her if she did that, then he'd know and she'd be
in big trouble.

She'd still be tempted, but he'd ended up reading to her until
she fell asleep. She missed him. Just like she missed Brick when he
was giving them time on their own.

"Look at me, Duchess."

She let out a deep breath and turned to stare up at him.

"We can go home if you want," he told her.

She didn't want to have lunch at the diner. She hated the diner.
She didn't really like to go anywhere in Wishingbone except to the
Wishing Well for quiz night.

But Elias had begged them to get out of the house for a while.
Sure, he and Sterling could have come on their own, but when

he'd stared at her pleadingly, she'd found herself nodding in agreement.

"I know I'm overly protective," Brick admitted. "I want you to stay in the house because I know it's safe, but that isn't necessarily what's best for you."

Wasn't it? Because she wasn't sure the diner was the best place for her.

"But say the word and we'll go."

"It's fine," she told him.

"Wait there until I come around."

Sterling and Elias were already out of their truck and waiting on the sidewalk. She was guessing that they'd all had a chat and came up with this excursion as a way to get her mind off Reuben. It was sweet of them.

Brick undid her belt and lifted her down. She wrapped her hand in his shirt.

She made it to the booth in the diner, mostly by keeping her face down and letting her hair fall forward. It felt like there were eyes watching her, and she guessed at least half the diner was following the four of them. And largely because of the men with her.

They'd be the topic discussed at a few dinner tables tonight, and probably these guys would be the object of several fantasies too. She had to smile at that.

A shiver ran through her and she raised her head to take a brief look around, wondering at the unease.

But she didn't see anything. When she sat in the booth, she didn't bother looking at the menu before leaning up to speak to Brick.

"I'll have fries," she whispered.

He frowned. "Just fries? You need something more substantial than fries."

She sighed. She supposed he wanted her to eat half a cow.

"Fine. Chicken salad sandwich."

He sighed but nodded and placed the order. When their drinks came, she concentrated on downing the iced coffee as the guys spoke quietly to each other. A few people came up to say hello. But she knew they were just fishing for information about Brick and the guys. After he'd made that declaration that she was his, it would have gone around the population of Wishingbone quicker than she could blink.

Finally, their food arrived and she had something else to concentrate on.

It tasted a bit funny and she set it down with a grimace, trying to figure out what that taste was.

"Eat your lunch, Duchess," Brick said to her.

She gave him a stubborn look. He simply gave her one back. She sighed. She supposed she could wash it down with more iced coffee.

"And drink some water."

Sheesh. When had he been made the food and water police?

But like the good, obedient girl she was, she sucked down some water. Then she started to feel warm. She rubbed at her chest. Why was it hard to breathe?

She swallowed heavily. There was a lump in her throat. An impending sense of doom hit her. Something was wrong.

She itched at her throat and chest. Anxiety filled her. Was it an anxiety attack? But why was she so itchy?

Shit. Shit. Fuck.

Opening her mouth, she clearly heard the wheeze and she felt the struggle to get the air into her lungs.

No. No. No.

She knew her blood pressure was plummeting. Her airways constricting.

Anaphylactic shock.

Her stomach cramped. *No. No.*

She needed her EpiPen. She tried to grab her handbag, but managed to knock it off the seat where it had been sitting beside her.

"Juliet? You okay?" Brick turned her. Then his face went pale, shock filled his features. "Fuck! What is it? What's wrong?"

There was more noise. But she couldn't talk. She could only concentrate on trying to breathe.

"She's turning red!"

"Her face is swelling!"

She didn't know who was talking or yelling. Didn't care. She just wanted to breathe.

Then she found herself being moved. Her legs were in the air. She couldn't make out what anyone was saying. But someone was shoving up her skirt to get to her thigh.

She didn't even have it in her to care that her legs were on show to the whole diner, and probably her underwear. There was a sharp prick of the EpiPen being administered.

Thank fuck.

XAVIER RUSHED into the emergency department, ignoring his buzzing phone. He pushed back the curtain, horror filling him as he saw her lying there.

"Juliet!"

There was an oxygen mask covering her mouth. She was also attached to a drip. Her face was swollen, her chest and throat covered in red hives.

Fuck. Anaphylactic shock.

Amanda, the nurse who stood next to her, quickly turned. "Oh good, Doc X. I had you paged because I knew you'd want to know. She was brought in about thirty minutes ago. Doctor Richardson gave her some steroids. She's still having a bit of trouble breathing."

Fuck. Fuck.

He managed to nod. "I'll have her admitted."

"Are you sure? Doctor Richardson thought she'd be fine under observation for a few hours."

"She'll be admitted." Where he could watch over her himself for the next twenty-four hours. His shift ended in about six hours.

"All right, I'll get onto that."

He nodded woodenly, then remembered his manners as she left. "Thanks for paging me."

Amanda smiled at him. "We all know how much she means to you, Doc X. Oh, apparently, there are a couple of men in the waiting room, upset that they aren't allowed back here. They claim to be her bodyguards, but Mary-Lee wouldn't let them in. You know what she's like about the rules."

Shit. He knew who had been calling him. "I'll take care of it, they are her bodyguards. Actually, could you go find the one called Brick and bring him in? It's a wonder he isn't tearing the hospital down trying to find her."

"Apparently, Mary-Lee did threaten to call security on the guy who claimed to be her boyfriend."

"Ah, yeah, that would be Brick."

"I'll go get him then."

Xavier read her file quickly then checked her vitals. Steady. They were steady. Her oxygen levels could be better, but they weren't terrible.

Probably admitting her was overkill, but he didn't care.

He moved towards the side of the bed. Gently, he grabbed her hand, squeezing it. His hand was shaking. He held her hand like it was made of the finest of crystal.

He could have lost her. Closing his eyes, he breathed in deep.

She was usually so careful. He'd drilled that into her over and over. How severe her allergy was.

"Oh, sweetheart. What the hell happened?" he asked quietly. Outside this cubicle, he could hear the noise of the ER, but in here, it was like a bubble.

Opening his eyes, he leaned in and gently kissed her forehead. "Jesus."

"X-xavier?" she asked.

Her eyes didn't open, and he wasn't sure if she knew he was actually there or not.

"I'm here, Twink. I'm here. You're safe. You're in the emergency department in the hospital. You had an allergic reaction, but you're going to be just fine. I promise."

He wouldn't allow her to be anything else. This fierce need to protect flooded him.

"Nothing will happen to you."

"Love you, Xavy. Always have."

His heart skipped. "Love you too, Juliet. I'll always love you, my sweet girl."

"Where is she?" a deep voice demanded. He turned. Fuck, Brick would get himself kicked out if he went around yelling like that.

Xavier went quickly to the curtain and drew it open. Brick's wild gaze met his. "Fuck, Xavier. Is she all right?"

"In here. She's fine." He nodded to Amanda, who was watching them curiously. "Thanks, Amanda."

"Of course, I'll give you some space."

Fuck. No doubt she was going to tell someone about this. There was no mistaking the fear on Brick's face. And likely on his own too.

Oh, well. They had bigger worries than a bit of gossip.

When he turned back, Brick was leaning over her. His face held a wealth of pain as he gently kissed her forehead and whispered to her. Xavier moved to her other side, taking her other hand.

"How is she?" Brick finally asked him. "Will she really be okay?"

He got it. They could have lost her.

"Her vitals are pretty good. Someone administered the epinephrine?"

Brick nodded. "Soon as I realized what was going on. She was trying to get it out of her bag but couldn't grab it. I got it out and shot her with it while Sterling called for an ambulance."

"You did good. She's had some steroids and she'll remain on oxygen for a bit until I'm happier with her oxygen levels."

"You're sure she'll be all right?" Brick stared at her, the look on his face one of reverence. Of complete and total love.

"I won't let her be anything else," he replied arrogantly.

"I know," Brick replied, to his surprise. "She fucking scared me. I thought . . . I thought I was going to lose her."

The man that Xavier bet rarely let anyone see any sort of weakness, or what he likely saw as weakness, cracked.

His head dropped. His shoulders moved up and down. Xavier moved around to the other side of the bed.

"I know how you feel," he said quietly, placing his hand on the other man's shoulder as they stood there, side-by-side, looking down at the woman they both loved. "I know."

They stood in silence for a long moment until Brick discreetly wiped at his eyes and turned away for a moment, taking in a deep breath. Xavier's hand dropped to his side. "Fuck. I've been a fucking marine. I've seen shit that gave me nightmares for years. I've lost people I loved. I've been married to someone who betrayed me. I've nearly lost everything. And nothing, none of that comes close to the terror of nearly losing her."

"But you didn't," Xavier told him quietly. "You saved her."

Brick just shook his head for a moment. "It could have gone

wrong. I could have been too slow. I didn't check that she had her EpiPen before we left . . ."

"She always carries it," Xavier reassured him. "I put two in each of her handbags. And you know they're scattered throughout the house, right?"

Brick cleared his throat. "Yeah, I just . . . she's so fucking precious to me."

"To both of us."

Brick nodded. "To both of us. I'm glad I have you with me in this, man."

"We'll take care of her. Together."

31

J uliet opened her eyes, gasping in a breath. There was something in her nose irritating her. Along with a beeping noise. And the smell of antiseptic.

It all annoyed her.

Juliet didn't let herself get annoyed by much. But yeah, it was grating.

She looked around. She was miserable. Exhausted. Her head ached. She felt jittery, like she wanted to climb out of her own skin. She raised her hand to rub at her chest, her heart felt like it was racing.

A small whimper escaped her.

"Juliet? Duchess? Oh, baby. Thank fuck."

Brick's face appeared in her vision. He looked terrible. Pale and exhausted. Black marks were under his eyes. Poor guy looked like he needed a good twenty-four hours of sleep.

"What's wrong?" she croaked.

"Nothing now that you're awake," he replied.

Aw. That was sweet. But what was going on? Obviously, she was in the hospital. But why . . .

Then it all came flooding back.

"I didn't eat any shellfish," she muttered.

Brick's face went blank. She watched him curiously. What was he trying to hide?

"Don't worry about that right now, Duchess."

Okay, even an idiot had to know that would make her want to know more. And Brick was no idiot. He grimaced. "Fuck. The sheriff is looking into what happened, all right?"

"You think someone tried to hurt me? That they what? Tampered with my food?" It was so hard to think. And something was niggling at her brain. What was it, though?

"Yeah. Maybe."

"The people who are after Reuben." Panic flooded her. "I need to call him."

"Calm down."

"No, no, I need to talk to him. I need to make sure he's all right." She pushed the covers back, trying to get out of bed.

"Duchess, get back in that bed," he told her in a stern voice.

But she was too far gone to pay attention. "I need to—"

"What's going on? Juliet, what are you doing? Lie back down." Xavier appeared on her other side.

"Xavy, I need to go call Reuben." She reached for his hand. He clasped hold of her hand in his then gently pressed her back into the bed.

"You don't need to do anything except lie down," Xavier added firmly.

She was so tired.

"Reuben—"

"Reuben is a big boy who can take care of himself," Xavier told her. "You're to stay in bed. Doctor's orders."

She gaped up at Xavier. He placed his fingers on her wrist to take her pulse. As though he didn't have a monitor that could do that.

Brick tucked the blankets around her.

They moved together, almost in sync. After taking her pulse, Xavier picked up a glass of water with a straw while Brick supported her head so she could drink.

"Be easier with her baby bottle," Brick muttered.

"Yeah, we can use that at home. Someone here might see it."

"Good point," Brick said as he eased her back.

Xavier brushed her hair off her face while Brick moved to her feet, massaging them lightly.

Oh, dear Lord. That was heaven.

Tears entered her eyes as they pampered her together.

"You're so tense, sweetheart," Xavier crooned. He drew her up then settled in behind her, pulling her back against his chest so he could rub the tension from her shoulders. Brick sat at the end of the bed and continued to rub her feet.

"You scared us, baby girl," Brick told her in a low voice. "Please don't do that again."

"I didn't like it much either."

"Poor baby," Xavier said, kissing the top of her head. "Just relax, we'll take care of you."

"She's still slightly swollen," Brick said, studying her.

"It should go down over the next few hours."

"Brick," she croaked.

"And the redness?" Brick asked.

"The antihistamines will help with that."

"Xavier," she pressed.

"Her pulse is good. Blood pressure is still a bit low. Oxygen levels are good."

"Guys!"

They both stopped talking, their attention moving to her.

"Yeah, Duchess?" Brick asked.

"Reuben . . ."

Brick sighed. "I've tried calling him. Still silent."

"Same," Xavier added.

"Oh God," she sobbed.

"Hey, stop. Stop," Xavier told her firmly.

She gaped up at him as he moved around to sit on the bed facing her. He placed his hands on either side of her face. "If anyone can take care of themselves, it's Reuben. And he told you he was going silent. Trust him."

She took in a shuddering breath.

"We don't know if what happened had anything to do with the people after him," Brick told her. "It doesn't make a lot of sense. They'd have to know about your allergy and then watch to get their chance to do something to your food. Then have the means to do it without being seen."

"Then you think it was an accident?" she asked.

"That you had an allergic reaction to a chicken sandwich?" Brick asked grimly. "I don't know. We'll see how competent your sheriff is."

"Ed is good," Xavier told him. "He'll find out what happened. He's protective of Juliet. Most of the town is, they won't like that someone tried to harm her."

Most of the town thought she was insane, they were just too scared to say so because of her brother.

"She doesn't believe that," Brick murmured.

"She doesn't see how much people want to coddle her, watch out for her."

"We'll teach her," Brick said. He sat on the chair across the bed from Xavier before taking her hand in his. A feeling of safety filled her, surrounded by them both.

"What happened exactly?" she asked.

Brick explained everything. And while he was matter-of-fact as he spoke, she could hear the note of fear in his voice.

"I'm all right, Brick."

"You are now."

"And you're going to stay that way," Xavier added.

Both men nodded at each other again, a look of determination coming over their faces.

A wave of exhaustion overtook her. "I wanna go home."

"Not happening, Twink," Xavier told her.

She fluttered her eyelashes at him, giving him her best puppy dog look. She wasn't above begging. He just raised an eyebrow.

"Does she think that's going to work?" Brick asked, sounding amused.

Xavier sighed. "Can't blame her. It would have in the past."

"Jesus, man, she had you wrapped around her little finger," Brick said.

She gaped at him. "Did not."

Xavier snorted. "You did."

She sniffed. "I feel like I'm being ganged up on."

Her eyelids were growing heavier and it was hard to concentrate.

"Go to sleep, sweetheart," Xavier told her.

"I'll sleep once I'm home." In her own bed, surrounded by her own stuff. And the two of them.

"You're not going home until I give all the clear," Xavier told her firmly.

"Not unless you want to find yourself over one of our laps," Brick added.

"Xavier won't spank me," she mumbled. By now, her eyes were completely closed, and she was barely clinging to consciousness. She felt the bed depress as someone leaned on it, then lips brushed her ear, sending a shiver through her.

"Wouldn't be so sure of that."

Damn.

Double damn.

SHE WOKE up feeling groggy and out of it

A groan escaped her as her bladder told her that she couldn't go back to sleep like she wanted. That she had to get up and go to the toilet unless she wanted to make a hell of a mess.

Not for the first time, she thought that wearing a diaper could make life a lot easier sometimes.

"Twink? You okay?" Xavier asked.

"Gots to go," she managed to mumble, not caring who heard her. She hadn't even made sure that she was alone with Xavier.

When a girl had to go, she had to go.

"All right, let's get you up." To her surprise, instead of hauling her onto her feet, he lifted her with one arm under her thighs and the other around her back.

Then she was set down on her feet. She swayed and two hands landed on her hips.

"Jesus, you're out of it, aren't you, sweetheart?"

"Where's Daddy?" she muttered.

"Asleep. Do you want me to wake him? Do you need him?"

There was a funny note in Papa's voice, but she couldn't figure it out. She leaned her forehead against his chest. "No, let Daddy sleep. Juliet gots to pee."

He rubbed his hand up and down her back. "Never heard you refer to yourself in the third person."

"Papa," she complained. "Pee."

"Right, sorry. I'm going to help you, okay?"

Well, yeah. Duh. That's why she was leaning on him. Wasn't like she could stand on her own. Or figure out how her clothing worked. Stupid clothing.

"Pee."

"I'm getting your panties down, Twink," he said, sounding amused.

"What's I wearing?"

"Your mermaid pajamas," he replied.

Oh, because she was home. She remembered that now. She'd had to spend twenty-four hours in the hospital. A lot of that time, she'd slept. But when she hadn't slept, she mostly complained about being in the hospital. She'd begged both of them to let her go home. And she'd even lost her temper once, throwing a bit of a tantrum. Which was embarrassing to think about now.

There was cool air on her butt then she was being directed back. She still couldn't be bothered opening her eyes.

"Pee, Twink," he commanded.

"Hold your horses," she replied. "You can pee after me. I gots to go."

"I know," he told her, with such affection in his voice it made her smile. She thought it was probably a droopy, silly sort of smile. "That's why you're on the toilet."

"I'm sitting on the toilet? Good. Cause I really gotta go."

He laughed and her smile widened as she peed. So good. "Why you laughing, Papa?"

"Because you're cute."

"I am?"

"Uh-huh."

"That's good." She held her hand up. "Paper me."

Some paper landed in her palm and she managed to wipe herself clean without opening her eyes. Then he helped her stand and rearrange her pajama bottoms.

It was while he was holding her up with an arm around her waist, his other hand washing hers, that she started to shiver. The shivers changed to trembles. Her teeth began knocking together and it felt like she was having a seizure.

"Twink? What is it?"

"I nearly died."

"Oh, sweetheart," he crooned.

Then she found herself being lowered. Somehow, she thought she was sitting in his lap. Her body continued to shake, though, and try as she might, she couldn't open her eyes.

"Papa!" she cried out, needing him. Needing him to hold her, anchor her, to make everything awful go away even though she knew that wasn't possible.

"Want me to get Daddy?" he asked in a rough voice.

"Don't leave me!" Yeah, she wanted Brick, but she wanted him too.

"Skin," she found herself begging, knowing he'd understand.

There was some shifting, he let her go and she let out a cry.

"Shh," he soothed. "I'm pulling my top up."

And then her right cheek was pressed to his bare chest. Finally, she was able to open her eyes and she grabbed hold of his top, which he'd bunched under his arms.

Her breaths came in sharp gasps. The panic was almost like a living, breathing dragon inside her, threatening to claw its way out. Xavier rocked her, letting her breathe in his scent, surround herself with him.

"It's okay, Twink. Take what you need. I'm here."

"I nearly died."

"I know, sweetheart. But you know that Brick and I wouldn't let that happen, right? You're safe with us. We'll take care of you. Pretty sure that Brick isn't going to let you out of the house for the next fifty years to achieve that, but . . ."

She let out a small bark of laughter, shocked she could manage it. "Maybe you can talk some sense into him."

"Me? I'll be right there supporting him."

"Papa!"

"What?"

"I can't stay in the house for the next fifty years. I deserve time out for good behavior at least."

"Those times will be few and far apart."

So rude.

She rubbed her face against his warm, smooth chest. His scent was one she knew as well as her own. The urge to lick him came over her and she did it without thinking.

Xavier made a choking noise. "Did you . . . did you just lick me?"

"Why would I do that?"

"Well, I suppose you might have thought I was lickable," he mused.

"You are lickable, and maybe I did lick you," she admitted.

"Feel free to lick me anytime."

"Really?"

"Really. I pretty much think everything you do is cute. It's an affliction." He gave a fake sigh and she giggled.

She leaned back to look up at him. He smiled gently down at her. There was some scruff on his cheeks, he obviously hadn't shaved in a few days. And it only made him look sexier.

"You're so gorgeous."

One of those dimples appeared in his cheek as he stared down at her, eyes dancing in amusement.

"Well, thank you, sweetheart. So are you."

She sighed, feeling like she was floating. Part of it was her body still recovering from everything. Part of it was Xavier.

Then his head started to lower, his lips coming towards her. The kiss was sweet, gentle, and she opened her mouth before remembering that she probably needed to brush her teeth.

Leaning back, she wrinkled her nose. "Do I have stinky breath? I should brush my teeth."

"Sweetheart, your breath is just fine." He leaned in and kissed her again. "And even if it was stinky, I wouldn't care."

She sighed. "I guess that's true love."

"I guess it is. Now, how would you like to go sneak into bed with Daddy?"

"Can we give him a fright, pretending we're zombies come to eat his brains?" she asked.

He winked at her. "Exactly what I was thinking."

32

"Oh God, run! Run!" she cried out at the TV screen. Then she hid her face behind her hands as the people on the screen ignored her excellent suggestions and went running towards the zombie-infested woods. "No!"

"Tell me again why we let her watch this shit?" Brick asked.

"I'm pretty sure that she gave you those big eyes of hers and you instantly caved," Xavier replied dryly.

"I'm not the one who spoils her. What the heck was that thing you brought home today?"

"It's a dancing, singing wolf. Once you meet Reuben, you'll get the joke."

"Oh no, they got them! Oh shit, they're dead."

"Language," Xavier scolded.

It had been three days since she'd nearly died. Tonight was supposed to be quiz night. She was upset because Xavier and Brick had made her stay at home. Like in most things when it came to her, they were united.

Things hadn't instantly become easy between the three of them once they'd decided to try this crazy idea. In fact, it was often more awkward than not. But nobody had gotten mad or insanely jealous. Well, if they did, she didn't know about it.

Ed had come to visit that first day she was home, telling her that they'd interviewed everyone in the diner and had concluded that it was an unfortunate accident.

The owner of the diner was a bit of a bitch. And she'd had her eyes on Xavier for a while. Juliet hated the way she looked at him. She'd called to see how Juliet was, but hadn't exactly apologized. Both Brick and Xavier were furious. Reuben would be too, once he found out.

God, she hoped he was all right.

"Sorry, Papa, but it's zombies. They're damn scary."

He gave her a stern look. "Last warning."

Hm. Or what? She eyed him speculatively. She thought she heard Brick give a small bark of laughter, but when she looked over at him, he gave her an innocent look back.

"Maybe you should have bought her zombie repellent instead of a dancing wolf," Brick said as she squealed as the zombies descended on some poor, stupid fools who were now getting their brains eaten.

She buried herself behind Brick on the sofa, wrapping her legs around his waist and peering over his broad shoulder.

"They have that?" she asked.

Xavier made a scoffing noise. He looked tired. Poor guy worked too hard.

"We should totally get that if they have it," she insisted. She bounced up and down. Brick let out a grunt. "Watch where your foot goes there, Duchess. Don't want to hit the family jewels."

She giggled. "Sorry, Daddy."

Then she slid out from behind him. She tried not to touch one of them too much in front of the other. So far, everyone was playing nice.

She wanted it to stay that way. When the movie was finished, she nodded decisively. "I wish we had that zombie repellent."

"There's no such thing as zombies," Brick told her in his practical voice.

"Daddy, you just watched them eat all those people."

"It's a show."

She shook her head. He had no imagination. Fortunately, she had enough for them both. Well, maybe that wasn't a good thing.

"I'll buy you some zombie repellent," Xavier told her. He was stretched out on the recliner, looking relaxed in a button-up shirt and some neatly-pressed jeans.

"You will, Papa? Yay! We really do need it because I'm worried about Daddy's brains. I think they'll want them."

"Nah, not much to eat there," Xavier replied as Brick scoffed.

"Papa, that's not nice to poor Daddy. Besides, he's got the biggest head. That means he's got the biggest brains, right? Poor big head." She knelt and grabbed his head between her hands. Then pressed it from side to side.

"Easy there, you'll rattle those brains right out of my big head," Brick said dryly.

"Sorry, Daddy."

"Come here, Twink." Xavier crooked a finger at her.

She watched him warily. "Why?"

He raised his eyebrows. "Do I have to have a reason?"

"Well, maybe. If you're in the mood for huggles, I'm all there. If you're in the mood for spankings, then I'll just stay here."

Brick laughed. "Can't say she's not honest."

"Don't encourage her," Xavier told him. "And huggles?"

"It's a combination of hugs and cuddles. Subject to trademark."

"I'm not spanking you, brat," Xavier told her. "Come here. Now."

Drat. That was his Dom voice. He'd never used that voice on

her before they'd entered the arrangement. That's what she was going to call it. It sounded like a movie title.

The arrangement.

Two men. One woman.

Possibility of zombies.

"Juliet, I'm going to start counting," Xavier warned.

She let out a squeak of worry and jumped up, moving over to him. He held out his hand and she took hold. He helped her onto his lap so she was straddling him. She glanced over at Brick, worried. But he just looked like his normal self.

"Look at me," Xavier commanded.

Sheesh, that voice did things for her. A shiver ran through her. Lord, he was hot.

"Did you just say I was hot?" Xavier asked.

Barnacles! Had she said that out loud?

Crap.

"I think you're hot too," she said hastily to Brick.

Both men shared a look.

"Sweetheart, are you worried that if you don't keep things fair between us that you'll hurt one of our feelings?" Xavier asked her.

Well, damn. She thought she'd hidden that better.

"I just want to make sure no one gets upset."

"You're gonna give yourself an ulcer worrying about that," Brick told her. "Or diarrhea."

Ew.

"Brick's right. You can't worry about how either of us feels if you touch the other one or tell them they're hot. Besides, we know I'm hotter than Brick."

Her mouth dropped in shock then Xavier grinned.

"In your dreams," Brick said.

She glanced back and he winked at her. Something in her eased. Maybe she had nearly given herself diarrhea worrying about making sure things were even.

"Now, that's settled, I want a kiss," Xavier said. "I haven't had one in ages and the well is running dry."

A kiss?

"Brick, I don't think our girl believes we can share nicely."

"Hm, well, I guess maybe we'll have to prove her wrong," Brick replied. "Why don't you bring her over here?"

Xavier stood with her in his arms and carried her over to the sofa, sitting with her on his lap again. Right next to Brick.

Then Brick turned her face towards him. He ran a finger along her lower lip then pressed it into her mouth. She started to suck without thinking. The tension in her body eased.

"Good girl. Such a good little girl. Now, you're going to kiss Xavier, aren't you?"

Damn. She guessed so. She nodded.

He slid his fingers free and she turned to Xavier. He wrapped her hair around his fist. "When I give an order, I expect it to be obeyed. Understand me?"

Oh hell. Oh hell.

Dead. She was dead.

Squashed like a possum on the side of the road. Wait, no, that was gross.

Then his lips pressed against hers. And that definitely wasn't gross. Nope, that was the exact opposite.

Xavier drew back with a groan. "She's thinking too much."

"Let's see what we can do about that," Brick replied. He drew her in for a kiss. She could feel Xavier's hand going up her thigh and she shivered with pleasure.

"Easy, Duchess," Brick told her. "Anytime you want things to stop or slow, say your safeword. Tell Xavier what your safeword is."

"Romeo," she said on a sigh as Xavier moved his mouth to her neck, pushing aside her pajama top.

He slid his mouth over her collarbone. How the heck was that sexy?

She had no idea.

Brick moved behind her back and she felt his hands on her hips, then he pressed a kiss to her back, between her shoulder blades.

Xavier slid his mouth away from her skin then leaned back, staring at her through heavy-lidded eyes. "You don't know how long I've thought about this, dreamed of it."

"Knew from the moment you met me that you'd be dreaming about me," Brick quipped as he drew the bottom of her pajama top up to kiss along her back. Again, how was that so hot?

Maybe it wasn't. Maybe it was just because it was these two men were touching her, holding her between them.

"I didn't realize you had such a good sense of humor, Brick," Xavier murmured.

Neither had she. It almost seemed like more of Brick was being revealed with every day.

"Neither did I," Brick muttered. "Or at least, I think somewhere along the way I forgot how to have fun. I owe you for showing me what it's like to be happy again, Duchess."

"No more than I owe you for the same," she whispered back.

"So sweet, our girl, isn't she?" Xavier said in a low voice. "I wonder if she tastes that sweet. I think it's time we found out."

What was happening here? If anyone had asked her who the most dominant was of the two men, she would have said it was Brick. Yet, right now, there was no doubting that Xavier had taken control. That he was steering the helm. Maybe with a subtler touch than Brick. Her Brick tended to be full steam ahead, take-no-prisoners.

Xavier was quieter, sneakier, but filled with confidence. She liked seeing him like this. It was kind of similar to the confidence he exuded while working. He was calm and competent. But this was more.

As though he was in his element. A king in charge of his realm.

Xavier reached up to cup the side of her face. "What do you say about that, sweetheart? Do you want to feel Brick's tongue on your pussy? Do you want him to lick you? To play with you? To flick that clit until you scream?"

"Yes," she groaned.

That glint in Xavier's eyes made her heart race. He wasn't looking at her like she was fragile or broken. She was looking at her like he wanted to devour her.

And she wanted that.

She wanted it all. She could feel her clit throbbing, the moisture gathering between her legs.

He lowered his hand to the buttons of her pajama top then slowly undid them. One by one. While her heart raced and her body trembled. While Brick laid kisses on the small of her back then massaged her butt cheeks.

"Brick?" Xavier asked.

"Uh-huh."

"If Juliet doesn't answer a question, she gets punished."

Xavier wasn't her kind and careful best friend right now. He wasn't even her indulgent, sweet Papa. He was the stern, commanding Dom.

Xavier spread the two halves of her top apart, revealing her breasts. "So beautiful."

Brick reached around her to cup her small breasts. "Most perfect breasts I've ever touched."

She smiled as Brick squeezed them lightly. Her nipples hardened against his palms and she groaned. Then Brick let go of her breasts and grabbing the top, drew it off her arms. Now she was sitting on Xavier's lap in her bottoms only, with Brick behind her, running his fingers down her back. He moved his hands back to her breasts, but this time he toyed with her nipples, teasing them lightly.

With a moan, she leaned against the huge man behind her. He was almost as tall as her, even kneeling.

Brick nipped at her shoulder and neck as Xavier placed his hands on her thighs, just watching her.

"Have you dreamed about Brick eating you out, Juliet?" Xavier demanded.

She blushed bright red. She could feel her cheeks heating. "Yes, Sir."

"Good girl for answering."

Brick continued to play with her nipples, driving her insane. She started to rub herself against Xavier's legs.

"Have you ever made yourself come?"

Oh Lord. She couldn't answer, could she? Why did he have to ask her these things?

Brick stopped touching her and she let out a small whimper. "Don't stop. Please."

"He'll start again when you answer the question," Xavier told her.

What kind of cruel torture was that? She glared down at Xavier.

"Now, that's not a very nice face to make at your Dom, sweetheart," Xavier crooned. "Brick, could you help me out?"

"Yep."

Xavier drew her forward, and several sharp smacks landed on her ass from a dinner-plate-sized hand that had to be as hard as a paddle, she was sure.

When Xavier helped her sit back up, her bottom was stinging but she made certain not to glare at the man underneath her. Nope, she was a good girl.

Always.

"That's my sweet girl," Xavier murmured. "Those really are the most beautiful breasts I've ever seen in my life. I need to taste them again. Bring them here."

She leaned forward without even thinking about it, and he circled one nipple with his tongue then moved to the other nipple, laving them both until she was whimpering. Behind her, Brick kissed his way down her spine before lowering the band of her pajama bottoms to kiss the top of her ass.

Then Xavier drew her back. "Now, have you made yourself come?"

Brick's fingers returned to her nipples, playing with them expertly. They were going to kill her, but she knew better than not to answer.

"Yes."

"With toys?"

"No, just with my fingers," she told him.

"Hm, we might have to change that. Order you some toys."

Did she need toys when she had the two of them? Adding something more just might kill her.

"We'll need a vibrator." Xavier's hands moved up her thighs. "Some handcuffs."

"An egg," Brick added. "With a remote. So we can drive her crazy."

"Wouldn't that be fun on quiz night," Xavier mused.

They wouldn't!

Oh hell, they would. Xavier's fingers were now on her pussy. Brick continued to torture her nipples as he moved a single finger down over her clit. She couldn't feel it that well through the layers of clothing and she let out a frustrated noise.

"Do you want to come, sweetheart?" Xavier asked her.

"Yes, oh, please, yes."

"Doesn't she beg so pretty, Brick?" Xavier asked.

"Sweetest thing I've ever heard," Brick told him.

"We need to make that pussy nice and wet. Ready to take us. Are you ready to take us, Juliet? To have your men fuck you?"

"Yes."

"Hm. I'm not sure. You don't sound desperate enough yet. Does she sound that desperate, Brick?"

"I'm damn well desperate," Brick muttered.

"Have you ever given someone a hand job?" Xavier asked

"Yes," she moaned as that finger moved slowly and steadily up and down her slit.

"Who with?" Xavier demanded.

"Brick," she managed to squeak out.

The anger eased. "That so? Thought there was just heavy petting?"

"Very heavy," Brick told him.

"I see."

"Fuck, I need to taste her," Brick groaned.

"You're driving Brick insane."

"You're both driving me insane," she complained. "I need to come."

"Who knew you could be so demanding," Xavier murmured.

And who knew he would enjoy torturing her? Where had he hidden this mean side? She had no idea.

"Ask us nicely, beg prettily, and Brick will eat you out."

"Please, Sirs, please. I want to come. So badly. Please."

"Good girl," Xavier crooned, then he reached up and grasped her around the back of her neck, drawing her in for a long, drugging kiss. Her head was spinning as he drew away then lifted her off his lap. She hadn't even realized that Brick had moved away from her until then.

Hands grasped hold of her pants and whipped them and her panties down her legs. Then she was standing there as bare as the day she was born. The shock of it cleared her head and she realized she was standing there.

Naked.

Where they could see every inch of her scrawny body. Not that

Brick hadn't seen her naked and Xavier had seen her breasts, but this felt different. She felt more vulnerable.

Her arms reached up to cover herself.

"No," Brick said from behind her. He turned her to face him, then he cupped her face with his hands and kissed her gently.

Oh, so gently.

Her forehead, her nose, her chin, then her lips.

"You're perfect. The most perfect creature created just for us. There is no part of you that you should be ashamed of. And I won't accept it. And neither will he." He nodded behind her to Xavier. "You're mine. You're his. And you're fucking perfect."

Tears entered her eyes.

Then she felt Xavier press against her. "So don't hide your loveliness from us, my sweetheart. It makes us sad to think you would believe we don't adore every single piece of you. And remember, we don't want to make the big guy cry. It would be messy."

She let out a watery laugh but dropped her hands to her sides.

"That's our girl," Brick murmured. He stepped back and stared down at her. When his gaze reached hers, the heat and love in his eyes blew her away. "Fucking perfect."

Two large hands cupped her breasts, holding them up, and Brick leaned in to suckle on one then the other. Her legs nearly buckled as she swore she could feel the suction of his mouth all through her body. Her clit throbbed mercilessly.

"I wonder how wet she is," Xavier murmured.

"We should definitely check that," Brick agreed. "Spread your legs, Juliet."

She pushed them apart, hardly believing that she was doing this.

She was going to be with them both. Her. She was weird and damaged.

And loved.

Reuben loved her. Her friends loved her. But this went beyond that.

It was everything.

Brick moved his hand down to her pussy, cupping it. "Fuck, that's smooth." He ran a finger along her lips then slid the tip into her pussy. "And tight."

He pushed his finger deeper inside her. Then she felt a hand on her ass, sliding lower and lower. Until another finger joined Brick's. There was a slight twinge of pain, but nothing she couldn't handle.

Oh, holy hell. What new sort of torture was this?

One finger moved in, the other moved out. She grabbed hold of Brick's shoulders to hold herself steady as they thrust into her. She could hear how wet she was. Maybe that should be embarrassing. But in that moment, she really didn't care.

Then their fingers disappeared. She let out a cry until she opened her eyes to find Brick sucking on his finger.

Wow. That was so hot that it was a wonder she didn't burst into flames right then and there.

When she turned, she found Xavier sitting back on the sofa, doing the same.

Holy. Hell.

These two would kill her. Seriously.

"Delicious," Xavier said.

"Yum," Brick added.

Dear. Lord. Save her.

Xavier patted his lap. "Scoot back."

He lifted her onto his lap, so she was sitting with her back to his front. Then he arranged her legs on either side of his and spread them wide. That left her open to Brick's gaze. And from the way he stared down at her, he liked what he saw.

A lot.

"Oh, hell yes." Brick slipped off his T-shirt so he was just wearing a pair of jeans. She'd seen his bare chest before, of course. But it never failed to take her breath away. All those muscles, his bare skin.

All hers.

Lucky girl.

Then he crouched between Xavier's feet and pressed her thighs even further apart. "I could be here for a while. Settle in."

Then his mouth dipped between her legs, his tongue sliding along her lips.

"Lean against me, sweetheart," Xavier told her. She pressed back, her heart already racing as Brick expertly ate her out.

Felt. So. Good.

Seriously. This could become addictive.

"Good girl," Xavier told her. "Now lift your hands behind my head and keep them there."

She lifted her hands up, unable to think, unable to do anything but obey.

"While Brick licks that delicious pussy, I'm going to play with your nipples." He lightly twisted her nipples as he spoke, sending sparks of arousal through her blood. "Have you ever thought about having your nipples clamped? They'd look so pretty with little jewels hanging from them. Then a chain that led down to your clit. I could clamp that as well. Then push a butt plug nice and deep in your ass and run the chain over it. You'd be dressed up like our cherished, beautiful sex slave. Would you like that?"

It wasn't something she'd really thought about. But the imagery he painted made her squirm. Then Brick thrust his tongue into her passage and she cried out.

"I think you'd like that. A collar. Your hair up high to reveal this gorgeous neck. So beautiful. In our bedroom, you'd be our cherished little sex slave. Outside of our bedroom, our beautiful baby girl. We're going to take such good care of you, sweetheart. I promise."

She knew they would.

And she was going to do the same to them.

"Are you ready to come yet? You can come whenever you like. It won't usually be that way, but today is a special occasion. Your first time with us."

Wait. She wouldn't be allowed to just come whenever she wanted other times?

Did she really know what she was getting into with these two? They seemed to like torturing her.

But then all thought left her mind as Brick started flicking at her clit in earnest. He pressed one finger inside her, moving it gently in and out before adding another. Again, a little uncomfortable but nothing major. Then she felt it. It started to build and build.

It burned deep inside her. She strained towards it. Oh Lord. She rose and then she crashed. She clenched down on his fingers as she came. Her cries filled the room as she arched. It was almost too much. Too consuming. Xavier pinched her nipples, making her scream as it added to her pleasure.

By the time she fell from the high, Brick had slid his fingers free from her pussy and was lightly lapping at her folds. She collapsed against Xavier who wrapped his arms around her, holding her tight.

"I have you. I have you. You're safe."

How did he know she felt slightly fractured in that moment? That she needed an anchor. She didn't know and it didn't matter. Because they gave her everything she needed.

"Thank you," she whispered.

Brick sat back on his haunches and actually licked his lips. Cripes. Then he grinned. "Thank you."

She smiled back shyly. "You liked it?"

"Baby girl, if I got to do that every day for the rest of my life, it still wouldn't be enough."

She sucked in a breath. Well, then, if that's what he wanted to do, who was she to stop him?

XAVIER WALKED behind Brick as he carried their girl up to their bedroom. They entered, and he laid her on the bed before stepping back to pull off his jeans. Xavier had suggested they take this upstairs. He didn't want their girl's first time to be on the couch.

Another day, for sure.

It would be even better once this risk to her was past and Elias and Sterling left. They could have sex in every room in the house. And in the pool.

Hm. The ideas.

Brick quickly stripped and grabbed hold of his cock while Juliet watched, riveted. She licked her lips and then climbed onto her hands and knees to crawl over to the side of the bed. She sat on the edge. He was pleased to see that she'd lost a lot of that inhibition over being naked in front of them. He was certain she'd still have moments, but they'd be there to reassure her.

"Can I please have your cock in my mouth?" she asked Brick.

Xavier raised his eyebrows. But Brick just nodded and stepped closer to her, letting her dip down and take his dick into her mouth. Xavier had to grin as the other man's eyes practically rolled back into his head.

Then Brick turned towards him. "So, you gonna strip or what? You shy?"

Xavier took a quick glimpse of Brick's cock. He wasn't used to studying a man's dick, but Brick seemed surprisingly comfortable with just stripping off in front of him. And it was pretty damn hot watching Juliet suck the other man's cock into her mouth.

If he was less confident in his own skin, then he might get a complex about the size of the other man's dick. But it wasn't all about size, was it?

Besides, he wasn't exactly small. He just wasn't behemoth-sized.

Stripping, he placed his shirt over the back of a chair, then took off his jeans and folded them. Then his boxers.

Brick just rolled his eyes at him. There was nothing wrong with being tidy.

Climbing onto the bed, he moved in behind her, gathering her hair in his fist to pull it to one side so he could kiss along her shoulder and neck. She let out a small murmur of satisfaction.

"Come lie back on the bed," he told her. "I want to explore."

She slid her mouth away from Brick's dick. The other man grumbled good-naturedly, but climbed onto the bed on her other side as she scooted up the bed and lay on her back. She stared at Xavier, running her gaze over him, taking all of him in.

"You're beautiful, are you sure you want to be with me?" she asked.

"Brick," he said sharply.

"Fine, but at some stage, you're going to need to spank her." Brick sent him a knowing look before rolling her onto her front and spanking her ass several times. Her white skin grew pink, and Xavier had to reach down to grasp hold of the base of his dick.

That was hot.

Then Brick rolled her over and Xavier cupped her chin. "None of that, understand? You're worth a thousand of either one of us. And we'll tell you that until it becomes ingrained in your brain, understand me?"

"Yes, Sir."

"Good girl. Now raise your hands above your head and grab hold of the headboard so that Brick and I can explore."

She raised her hands up and they went to work. He licked her nipples, took as much of her breast into his mouth as he could then let it fall out. Brick whispered quiet words of reassurance to her as Xavier worked his way down her body. Then he knelt between her legs and drew them up into the air, pushing them back and spreading them wide so he could take in her pussy.

"You need a taste, man," Brick told him.

"Yes, I do." Then he let go of her legs but kept them spread so he could ravish her. He ate her pussy until she was screaming, until he knew she was close, then he drew away, his mouth damp with her juices. He licked his lips. So sweet.

"I've never tasted anything better," he told her.

Her eyes were wild, her hair a mess, there were red marks on her skin from where they'd sucked and lightly nipped her.

She'd never looked more beautiful.

"Please, I need to come," she begged.

"I know," he told her.

"Then why did you stop?" she wailed. Well, as close to a wail as she got in that husky, broken voice. Her voice kind of cracked, but he didn't pay any attention and neither did Brick. Her voice was a part of her, of her past, it made her what she was today.

Oh, she was going to be fun to train, though. He could spend hours teasing her, bringing her to the edge without letting her fall over.

But not tonight. A small taste, but he'd let her come soon.

"Shh," he told her. "You'll get to come soon. But we need to make sure you're ready for Brick's dick."

Brick looked over at him for a moment, his gaze dropping to his dick.

"You should take her first."

"Why? Because I'm smaller?" he challenged.

Wait. Why was he asking? Didn't he want to fuck her?

Hell, yes.

"Yep." Brick grinned. "She can suck my dick. That's what she loves, don't you, Duchess?"

Her nod was eager. Xavier ran his finger up and down her slit. Then he circled it. Her legs started to come together and he frowned up at her. "Keep still."

"It's hard."

"Sometimes you have to do something difficult in order to get your reward."

"Is my reward coming soon?" she asked as he kept up that movement, up, circle, down. Repeat. His touch was far too slow and light to send her over the edge, but it was definitely enough to drive her insane.

"If you're a good girl," he told her. "Do you have condoms in here?"

"Yeah, but they're extra-large," Brick told him.

Xavier narrowed his gaze. Lord, he was full of shit. "I'm sure they'll fit."

Brick snorted then reached over into the bedside drawers to pull out several condoms. He threw one at Xavier, who ripped it open and rolled it onto his cock. Juliet watched him with wide eyes.

"You sure about this, sweetheart?"

"Yes."

"If it hurts or you need me to slow down, then just tell me, all right?" He moved between her legs, then leaned over her to kiss her while he lined the head of his dick up with her entrance. Slowly, so very slowly, he inched his way in.

"Put your legs around his hips. That's it, Duchess. You're doing great. Just breathe. Good. You're so beautiful. I bet you feel so good, surrounding his dick in your wet heat. Good girl."

Brick kept talking to her, praising her as he slid inside her. Fuck. So tight. So damn delicious.

He was panting, sweating by the time he was fully seated inside her. Then he drew up so he could look down at her. "All right, sweetheart?"

"Yes. Sort of."

He looked to Brick, who slid a finger between their bodies to rub at her clit. Okay, that was weird having another man's hand on him, so close to his dick.

But he could deal.

It wasn't long until she was panting, wriggling underneath him. "I need . . . I need . . ."

"Want my cock, Duchess?" Brick asked.

She nodded.

"Good, let go of the headboard," Brick commanded as he moved up the bed. But there wasn't quite enough room. Xavier slipped out of her pussy then moved to the end of the bed, standing. Grabbing her hips, he tugged her down. Brick threw him a couple of pillows which he put under her ass to raise her. Then he took hold of her hips and drove back inside her.

Brick lay on his side, his dick by her head. She turned her face towards him and took him into her mouth. The other man let out a deep sigh then turned and gave Xavier a thumbs up.

Xavier rolled his eyes, but took that as his signal. He drew back then gently pushed forward.

Felt so good.

SHE'D NEVER IMAGINED sex could feel this good. She sucked on Brick's dick as Xavier drove himself into her. It had hurt initially. Burned as she'd been stretched wide. And she hadn't been confident she could take him. Luckily, she was wet enough that it eased his way.

Reaching up, she wrapped her hand around the base of Brick's dick, jacking at him as she took him into her mouth.

"Open wide, Duchess. Let go so I can fuck your mouth."

Okay, that sounded like something she wanted to try. A finger flicked at her clit as Xavier drove himself in and out of her. And her arousal started to peak again.

Then Brick used her mouth, driving his dick in until she almost started to gag. But he drew back at that point. She kept her mouth wide, tonguing his shaft when she managed to, but otherwise, she was simply along for the ride.

"Fuck, fuck, I'm close to coming," Brick told Xavier.

"Same. Let me just get her there." His finger flicked her clit more firmly, and she felt herself moving towards the edge. Then she screamed around Brick's cock as she came. She felt him come in her mouth, his taste along her tongue, and she swallowed him down.

Xavier thrust deep. Once. Twice. Three times. Then his own yell filled the room. He actually swore, making her smile as she continued to suck on Brick's cock.

Xavier pulled free, then lay next to her on the bed. She could hear his heavy breathing. He moved to the side and wrapped his arm around her waist. "You going to let Brick go, sweetheart?"

She made a negative noise in the back of her throat.

"Think she needs a minute," Brick told him, running his fingers through her hair. "This calms her down."

"Yeah?" Xavier asked. "What does it do for you?"

Brick chuckled. "Drives me fucking insane. But I wouldn't change that for the world."

33

Juliet stood in the corner and fumed.

This wasn't fair.

She'd just needed a drink. She shouldn't be punished for that, right? Okay, so she was only allowed three iced mochas a day. And maybe she'd been trying to sneak in a fourth drink.

But how was a girl supposed to survive on just three? It was making her cranky.

"Come here, Twink," Xavier called out.

Last night, after they'd made love to her, they'd bathed her together. She'd thrived under their care. But sometimes, she wished they didn't pay such close attention. Like now.

Turning, she huffed out a breath. Xavier raised an eyebrow. Brick was doing some work downstairs in the office, so it was just the two of them.

"Maybe you need another ten minutes in the corner."

"No, Papa! I don't. Really."

He crooked a finger at her and she slowly walked over to

where he sat on the sofa. He settled her on his lap sideways. "You want to tell me what's wrong, Twink?"

"My tummy." She placed her hand over her stomach. "It's all tied up in knots."

"Because of Reuben?"

She nodded.

"I'm worried about him too. I know we haven't gotten on that well for the last two years, but I miss him. I still love him."

She sighed and leaned into him. He held her tight, rocking her back and forth gently. But then he pulled back and tilted her head up. "But that worry is no excuse for being naughty. Too much caffeine isn't good for you. I'm worried about what all this stress is doing. I think you need to have a check-up."

"No, Papa, I don't."

"Yes, you do," he replied sternly. "Now, you need to have some lunch."

He carried her over and sat her in a chair by Angelique.

"Angelique, you're in charge. You tell me if Juliet doesn't behave."

She gave an outraged gasp. "Papa, you can't put Angelique in charge! She's so bossy and a total tattletale."

"Ah, but she's a good person to keep you on your best behavior."

She sent Angelique a stern frown then glanced down at her sandwiches. They'd been cut into shapes so they looked like mermaid tails. She nibbled at one, studying her clothes. Papa had dressed her this morning in a pretty dress with a full skirt. It was pink and sparkly. Underneath, she had ruffly panties and a pair of long socks that went up over her knees. She looked super cute. She wished she was brave enough to wear something like this out in public.

She ate a sandwich and some fruit.

"Papa, I'm done."

"Let's see how much you've eaten." He glanced down with a nod. "Good. Now drink the water in your sippy cup."

She tilted up the sippy cup, gulping down water as quickly as she could. She had things to do. She'd just put it down when her phone started to ring.

The sound of wolves howling filled the room, and she dropped her sippy cup and stood, racing for her phone on its holder. It was a video call. Her fingers shook as she answered it.

"Reuben?"

"Hey, Mini." He looked exhausted, sounded even worse. But he was calling her. He was alive. He was safe.

She burst into tears. Immediately, he looked terrified.

"Mini, stop crying. Stop. Please. I'm all right. Hey, hey, stop now. you'll make yourself sick."

Xavier stepped over to her, wrapping an arm around her. "Twink, it's all right. He's safe. He's fine."

"Xavier? What are you doing there?" Reuben stared up at them both. Confusion filled his face.

Xavier took a deep breath. "Juliet and I are together."

"What?" Reuben barked. "The last report I got said that asshole I hired to protect her had fucking claimed her in front of everyone at the Wishing Well. Now you're with her? What the fuck? What is going on there? I couldn't do anything about that other asshole at the time, although I will. He's number one on my shit list." Reuben pointed down the phone. "And you're about to go to number two."

"Reuben, please," Juliet told him. "That doesn't matter."

"Doesn't matter?" he yelled.

"Reuben, are you safe? Is it over?" she asked.

Reuben let out a deep breath. When was the last time he'd slept? Eaten?

"Yeah, Mini. It's over. You're safe. I'm safe. I managed to get everything into place to take control of the situation. So you no longer need bodyguards. That asshole, Sampson, is the next one I'm calling. So I can damn well fire him." Reuben narrowed his gaze. "Although I'd really like to know why you think you get to date my sister, Xavier."

"Because she wants me and I want her," Xavier replied calmly.

Reuben glared at him. "Not happening."

"It already has," Xavier told him. "And if you don't have anything nice to say about it, then I'd appreciate you not saying anything at all."

Reuben's face started to go purple. Oh barnacles. Boy was about to blow.

"I love him, Big Bad Wolf," she told him quickly. "I love him, and I have for years. Please be happy for us."

Reuben seemed to take a moment to calm down. "Mini, you don't know everything about him—"

"He's been my best friend for the last two years, Reuben. I think I know him well."

"Do you know that his parents are going to throw a shit fit over this? What if they don't want you with her, Xavier? Are you going to break her heart? Not. Happening."

Xavier stiffened. "You were right about my mother. She lied about the lump."

Poor Xavier. He'd finally answered a call from his mother this morning and she'd confessed. She'd demanded that he forgive her, but he'd told her to give him time and to let him come to her.

Juliet was so proud of him, even as she worried about him losing his parents over this. It was their own fault, of course. But she didn't want Xavier to have regrets later.

Reuben's face softened. "I'm sorry. That must have hurt."

Xavier gave him a short nod. "My point is that I don't care what my parents think. I'd certainly never allow them to harm my relationship with Juliet. And I would never break her heart. She's my family now."

"You are not tying up my little sister and beating on her ass."

"Why not?" Juliet asked. "I might like that."

Xavier winked at her while Reuben spluttered. "Juliet, you have no idea what you're talking about."

"Reuben, I'm a grown woman. And I'm a sub."

"You're a Little."

She blew out a breath. "So that means what? That I can't enjoy being submissive during sex? That I'm not allowed to like being tied up and spanked? Or plugged? Or clamped?"

"What the fuck have you done to my sister?" Reuben roared.

Xavier sighed.

Double barnacles.

"What the hell is going on in here?" Brick grumbled as he walked in, looking all sexily mussed. Apparently, he was dealing with his accounts today, which seemed to put him in a grumpy mood. "I could hear yelling from outside the room." He looked over at Juliet. "Duchess, I need you to come downstairs and suck my cock while I work to put me in a better mood."

Oh hell. He didn't.

He fucking didn't!

Brick sat on the sofa in Juliet's playroom with a sigh.

Juliet was curled up in his lap like a tiny kitten while Xavier sat across from him in the punishment chair.

"The bastard fired me." He was still in a bit of shock over the call with Reuben that he'd interrupted.

"Well, you did ask your client to suck your cock," Xavier said.

"She's not my client! She's my baby girl."

Juliet smiled up at him.

"And you started dating her while you worked for him," Xavier added.

"No one likes someone who's so logical all the time," Brick grumbled.

Juliet and Xavier shared a look.

"I saw that," he told them. "He hates me."

No one said anything to that.

"If it makes you feel any better, he's not fond of me either," Xavier told him.

"But you have a tie to him. Unlike me. I'm just the guy who violated his sister."

Juliet made a noise of protest.

"I know, Duchess. But that seems to be how he sees it." Jesus, the threats he'd made. Brick could feel his balls shriveling up inside him. He was going to have nightmares over those threats.

"Good news is that he said he can't come visit for another week," Xavier pointed out. "Bad news is that he doesn't have to be here to make our lives a misery."

"I'm going to call him later when he's calmed down," Juliet whispered. "I'll make him see sense."

Xavier still looked pensive.

"On the positive side, at least the danger is gone," he told her, trying to cheer her up. "Your brother is safe. You're safe. Elias and Sterling can leave. Your life can get back to normal. I think if Elias and Sterling want to leave tonight, I'll go with them."

For some reason, she stiffened in his hold, looking completely stricken.

"Duchess? What's wrong?"

"You're going to leave," she croaked.

"What?" He looked down at her in shock.

"You're gonna leave me. You were only here for the job."

"Like hell I was," he growled. "What the hell are you talking about?"

"Think about what you just said," Xavier said dryly. "I'm going to go check my messages. I'll be back soon. Oh, and don't fuck her until I've checked her pussy. I want to do a complete check-up on her." He got up and left.

What he just said? He thought about it. Oh shit.

"Duchess, look at me," he said firmly. She raised her gaze to his, her eyes glassy.

"Jesus, my girl, why would you think for even one moment that I would leave you? My life would be fucking empty without you. It's . . . you . . . you fill me up. Fuck." This shit didn't come easy to him. He wasn't a smooth talker like Xavier. "I love you. Do you still love me?"

She nodded. "Of course."

"Then that's all that matters, isn't it? And you should know that as long as you love me, I'm here. Even then, you'd be hard-pressed to scrape me free."

"Like chewing gum on my shoe," she said with a small smile.

"Exactly. Although, gross."

"Even though my brother threatened to chop off your balls, sauté them in butter, then feed them to you?"

"Still not leaving you."

"Even though he said he would smash your dick with a mallet?"

"Still gonna be here."

"Even if he makes it impossible for you to find another job?"

"Think you or the Doc have enough money to keep me in the style to which I've become accustomed?" he joked. Although that threat had hurt more than the rest. "Point is, Duchess. I'm going nowhere. When I said I was going to leave with Sterling and Elias, it was so I could go get my stuff and move here. I mean, if that's what you want." He realized then that he hadn't actually asked her.

"Of course it is. I want you here. I'll come help you."

He shook his head. He knew she didn't like to leave Wishing-bone. "There's not much to pack up. I want to get there and back as quick as possible, and I don't want you traveling for hours in my truck just to turn around and come back. You'll get too tired."

She pouted for a moment then nodded. "Fine, Daddy. But I'm going to miss you."

"I'll miss you too. Let me text the guys and see what their plans are."

He sent off a text to Sterling, who was more likely to answer his phone.

"They're leaving in the morning. Hm, I guess that means that I get to be here for your check-up."

"Oh, goody."

34

"I don't like this," she complained.

"It doesn't matter whether you like it or not," Xavier said patiently as he pulled things out of his bag.

"But why do we have to do it in the office?" she asked, looking to Brick, who just watched with an amused twist to his lips.

"Because the table is at a good height," Xavier explained patiently.

"What if Elias and Sterling are watching?" she asked desperately.

"They've turned off the camera in here," Brick reassured her. "I have a panic button if we need help."

She grumbled.

"Brick, can you strip our girl for me?" Xavier asked in his dominant voice.

"Certainly. Come here, baby girl."

"Daddy, I don't like visiting the doctor."

"Now, that's not very nice, is it?" Brick scolded.

Luckily, Xavier didn't take offense to that, he just made an amused noise.

"But he'll poke and prod me."

"You didn't mind when he poked and prodded you last night," Brick teased as he started to undress her.

"Daddy!" she protested.

"Hush, you're going to be fine," Brick told her. "You need a check-up. You've been under too much stress."

"Exactly," Xavier agreed as she stood there, naked.

She shivered.

"Cold?" Brick asked in concern, running his hands up and down her arms.

"She gets like that when she's nervous." Xavier came over and cupped her chin. "You're fine, Twink. Brick, would you help her onto her back on the desk? Arrange her so her legs rest over the end."

Xavier had laid out a sheet on the desk so it wasn't that cold when Brick helped her on. She grabbed hold of his T-shirt. "Don't leave, Daddy."

"I won't," he soothed.

"Actually, sit up," Xavier said. "Let's do the basics first."

He checked her throat and eyes, her glands and looked in her ears. Then she had to breathe in deep while he listened to her lungs. She didn't know why, because he was acting very professionally, but she was starting to get aroused. She could feel the moisture gathering between her legs.

"Right, now lay back," Xavier told her. "Put your hands behind your head."

She moved her hands obediently, and he started to give her a breast exam.

There's nothing sexy about a breast exam. There's nothing sexy about a breast exam.

Yeah, she could say it as much as she wanted, but her body didn't believe it. Then he reached her nipple and lightly pinched it.

She was pretty sure that wasn't part of a routine breast exam.

"She's very responsive," Xavier commented to Brick. "Look at how stiff her nipples have gotten."

"Prettiest color too," Brick agreed. "Her breasts are spectacular. Same with her plump, pert ass, and that pussy. Pretty and it tastes amazing."

Xavier stared over at Brick, nodding seriously. They both seemed to ignore her as they spoke, but Xavier kept lightly pinching her nipple while Brick ran a finger over her other nipple.

They couldn't be oblivious to what they were doing to her, right?

She wriggled around on the desk, wanting more.

Xavier's gaze shot down to her. "She's having problems staying still."

"I've noticed that," Brick said.

Xavier sighed. "I might need to get you to hold her down if she wriggles too much. It's essential that she remain still."

"I understand."

"What? I can stay still!" she told them.

Xavier shook his head. "I doubt it. But let's have a test. Let's see if you can stay still while Brick sucks on your nipples."

She gasped then Brick's lips surrounded her nipple. He sucked and she moaned, arching her back without thinking.

"Nope, she can't stay still as I suspected."

Brick slid her nipple free from his mouth and lapped at it with his tongue a few times before straightening. "Just tell me when you need me to hold her."

Xavier nodded gravely before he palpated her stomach. Then he walked down to her feet, running his fingers over her arches. She giggled, trying to kick out.

He tut-tutted with fake disapproval. "We might have to get a proper examination table with restraints."

"Good idea," Brick agreed.

Killing her. They were trying to kill her.

"There's a tube of lube in the front pocket of my bag, and in my bag, you'll find a rectal thermometer. Could you get both for me?" Xavier asked.

What? Lube? Rectal thermometer?

No way. That wasn't happening.

"Xavier, no!"

He stared at her for a moment. "If there is anything you don't want me to do, then you can say your safeword. Are you saying your safeword?"

She thought that over. Was she?

No.

Yikes.

She shook her head.

"Words," he told her.

"No, Sir. I'm not saying my safeword."

"Good girl."

Brick handed them over. Xavier set them down next to her hip. Grabbing her feet, he placed them flat on the desk and far apart. He grasped hold of the chair and set it at the end of the table. Then he spread her pussy lips wide apart and ran a finger along her folds.

"Wet and a lovely color. Someone likes her examination, don't they?"

She groaned as he played with her clit. She wriggled, trying to get more friction.

"Brick, some help."

Brick laid an arm over her hips then grinned down at her with a wink as Xavier continued to play with her clit.

"She's very wet. It took very little to get her to this point. That's a good sign."

Holy hell. He was speaking in a clinical sort of voice, and for some reason, even that was turning her on.

She had problems. Seriously.

"I'm not even going to have to use lube." He then turned and reaching into his bag, pulled out a headlamp.

Holy. Heck.

"Let's just make sure that she looks good after being fucked for the first time last night."

Xavier slid a cool finger deep inside her. "It looks good. Not too red and she's sucking on me. That's it. Good girl. A second finger. Well done. Now, let's see how you go with something in your bottom hole."

She stiffened at that. "No!"

"Yes," Xavier said firmly.

She turned to Brick. "Daddy, don't let him."

Brick shook his head. "Baby girl, we need to start stretching you to take our cocks there. And Xavier just wants to make sure you're ready for that."

She wasn't. She really wasn't. How had she thought she was?

"If you could hold her legs back for me," Xavier asked as he squirted some lube onto two of his fingers. Brick pulled her legs back into her chest, exposing her ass.

Oh, Lord. Help her.

"Shh, you're all right, baby girl," Brick told her. Then Xavier pressed a finger against her asshole. "Deep breath in. That's it. Now let it out slowly."

Xavier pushed his finger into her back hole steadily. It was weird, but it didn't hurt. And as he wriggled it around, she sucked in a sharp breath. Okay, that actually felt really good. She'd read somewhere that there were a lot of nerve endings back there, and she now believed it.

A moan escaped her. Especially when his other hand moved to her pussy and he started to rub her clit.

"Like that, do you, baby girl?" Brick asked.

She couldn't reply, she was practically panting with need. Then Xavier stopped.

"Noo," she cried out.

"Answer Daddy," Xavier said sternly.

"Yes, Daddy. I like it."

"Good, then I want you to come with his finger in your ass," Brick ordered.

The finger on her clit moved faster as Brick leaned down to kiss her. Xavier drove his finger in and out of her ass and she came, her orgasm so hard and fast, that she swore she saw stars. Her head spun, and she was grateful for Brick's hold on her as she might have rolled right off the desk.

By the time she returned to her body, Xavier had removed his finger from her ass, and they were rolling her over, tucking her legs up against her chest as she lay on her side. She whimpered as Xavier parted her ass cheeks again then slid the thermometer into her bottom.

"Do you need Daddy's cock?" Brick asked quietly.

"Yes, please."

He helped her shuffle over slightly before he released his dick from his jeans and boxers. It was at half-mast, and by the time she had her lips around the head, it was hardening further. He ran his fingers through her hair as she suckled, taking comfort.

"She really does enjoy that, doesn't she?" Xavier mused.

"Yeah, it's more about comfort than pleasure. Although, there's that too," Brick replied.

She tuned them out as they talked and she lay there with the thermometer in her ass.

"Okay, I'm going to take it out now."

Thank God. She breathed out a sigh of relief as he slid the thermometer from her bottom.

"No fever. Other than being a bit underweight and stressed, she's doing well otherwise," Xavier said.

"That's a relief." Brick continued to soothe her by running his fingers through her hair.

"I think we need to start stretching her bottom, though."

She made a small, distressed sound.

"Hush," Xavier said, not unkindly. "We'll start with a small plug. Just keep warming Daddy's cock and I'll warn you when it's going in."

Her bottom cheeks were soon parted again. This was so embarrassing. Then a plug was pressed against her back hole.

"Deep breath in. Now let it out. That's it. Good girl. Here it comes."

The plug slipped inside her bottom with surprising ease.

"Now, that wasn't hard, was it?" Xavier asked, rubbing her butt.

She kept her mouth around Brick's cock, her hand cupping his balls to soothe herself as she lay there.

"Ten minutes," Xavier told her. "I'm going to go wash my hands."

Ten minutes later, the plug was slowly pulled from her ass. Then she was rolled onto her back, losing Brick's cock from her mouth.

"No. Want Daddy's cock."

"Oh, you can have it soon," Brick told her. He grabbed a condom from his back pocket before he stripped off. Did he just carry those everywhere?

Brick picked her up.

"Xavier, you sit on the couch," Brick commanded. "She can suck you off while I fuck her from behind."

She half-expected Xavier to protest being bossed around, but it was like he'd decided it was Brick's time to be in charge or something.

Stripping off, he sat on the sofa, then Brick carried her over and set her down. She knelt between Xavier's legs and leaned forward, licking her tongue around the head of his dick.

She hummed with pleasure. That was delicious. She took the head into her mouth and suckled, loving the way he groaned. He was soft yet firm. Silky and hard.

Damn, she was lucky.

FUCK, he was the luckiest bastard in the world.

Brick knelt behind his girl and grabbed hold of her hips, situating her how he wanted. She was a bit short, but if he leaned right over, he could make it work.

And his dick really wanted it to work. He pushed his way inside her, hearing her moan. A groan escaped his lips.

Perfect. So perfect.

He knew he wasn't going to last long. He needed her too much. He held her steady and pumped into her with shallow, short thrusts, then he made them longer, gliding in and out of her. Then faster. Fuck.

It wasn't long until he was panting. He had to come so badly that it hurt. He glanced up at Xavier, seeing the way the other man's breathing had shortened, and knew he wasn't far away. Reaching around their bodies, he played with her clit until she cried out, clenching around him.

"Coming! I'm coming!" Xavier told them.

That's when Brick let himself go, driving deep into her, his orgasm burning through him as he claimed their girl.

His. Theirs. Forever.

They all ended up in a pile on the floor of office. Brick rolled onto his side and leaned up on one elbow to look over their girl to Xavier.

"So if I'm moving in, then don't you think you'd better do the same?"

"I . . ." Xavier swallowed and then sat, looking from him to Juliet. "Are you sure? People will talk."

"I don't care. Do you, Juliet?" Brick asked.

"No. People already talk. Personally, I think if they have a problem with our relationship, it's because they're jealous."

Brick leaned down and kissed her. "Yep, jealous of how we managed to get the most beautiful girl in town."

Juliet went red then she looked up at Xavier. "Please, Papa. I want you here."

"Then that's where I need to be," Xavier told them. "With the two of you."

"A family," Juliet pledged.

"Family," they both repeated.

35

The race was on.

Well, not exactly a race since she was the only one on the track. But off she went! Over the ramp. Airborne! Yes!

She landed with a crash, the wheels wobbling, but she quickly recovered. She had this. She raced around the corner, it was time to take on the big beast.

This was it. She was prepared.

She had her helmet.

She had her knee pads.

She had her magic flying cape.

All she had to do was hit the ramp and she'd fly off the other side.

Something registered in the back of her brain. A noise. But she pushed it aside. She could do this.

Brick, Elias, and Sterling had left early this morning. She was going to miss Elias and Sterling, even though they had promised to visit. Brick promised he would be back soon, so it was just her and Xavier here. But Xavier had gotten called in to the hospital about an hour ago.

This was the first time she'd been left on her own in weeks.

Then she started pedaling her bike towards the ramp she'd set up, and out of nowhere, a body appeared. Oh God! She was going to hit him! A squeal left her as she darted around him, nearly falling off her bike. She came to a stop, panting, her pulse racing.

Turning, she saw him stomp towards her. He was breathing heavily, thunder filled his face. Uh-oh.

"What the hell did you think you were doing!" he roared.

She winced.

"Hi, Papa," she said cheerfully.

"Don't you 'hi, Papa' me, Twink. What were you just about to do!"

Well, she thought that was obvious. "I was going to take the jump, Papa. But you got in my way. You should be more careful. I could have hit you."

His hands clenched into fists and his jaw clenched.

"In the house. Now."

"But, Papa. I need to try."

"Now."

"Papa, I was being safe."

"How?"

"I have my helmet on."

"Nope."

"And my knee pads." She was proud of herself for remembering them.

"Nope."

"And I can fly."

"What? Why do you think you can fly?"

"Because I have my cape on." That was obvious, right?

"Because you have your cape on," he repeated.

"Uh-huh."

"You think you can fly because of a cape?" he asked.

"Well, yeah."

"Get in the house."

"What?" she asked.

"Now."

"But I have to try, Papa. Don't you know how hard it was to put together that jump? I had to get the wood and the crates and set them all up and . . ." she trailed off. Wow, had he always had that vein in his forehead?

"Inside. Now. Up to your playroom. Strip and get in the corner. I'll be in to deal with you when I've cooled down."

"But—"

"Now."

"I guess I'll just go do that now."

She wasn't sure how long it took him to come into the playroom, but she felt like she'd been standing there for hours.

"Come here, Twink."

Turning, she eyed him warily. He was sitting in the punishment chair. That wasn't a good sign. He pointed at the floor in front of him. "Here. Now."

Yikes.

"I was safe." She dragged her feet as she moved towards him.

"You could have hurt yourself."

"I had my helmet on."

"It wouldn't have stopped you breaking your fool neck."

"Hey, that's not nice."

"No, what's not nice is coming home to find that the woman you love is about to risk her safety by racing a bike off a makeshift ramp. What were you thinking?"

"That it would be fun."

"No." He slashed his hand through the air. "That is not to happen ever again, understand me? You will not risk your safety like that. Do you know how devastated I would be if something happened to you?"

Okay, now she felt pretty terrible.

"Well? What do you have to say?"

"That I'm sorry for worrying you, Papa."

"And?"

"And I won't do it again," she sighed.

"Damn straight, you won't. Especially after I spank your ass so hard that you don't sit for a week. Come here."

CALM. Calm.

Xavier let out a deep breath. He'd been avoiding punishing her. Brick had given her all the punishments she'd earned. And now, the other man wasn't even here while he gave her this first punishment between them.

He didn't know why he was so hesitant. Some part of him thought he might go too far. But that was ridiculous. This was Juliet. His heart.

He'd never harm her.

He adjusted her on his lap with her legs dangling over the side. He squeezed her plump ass. She needed this. And he needed to give it to her. She'd nearly turned him gray when he came home to find her about to ride over that ramp.

Lord help them. She was coming totally out of her shell. Reuben had once told him she'd been a daredevil as a child, but he'd never seen it.

He had a feeling that he was going to be seeing more of that side of her.

But putting herself at risk was never going to be acceptable.

He rubbed her ass then started smacking it, using quick, firm spanks. He covered the two cheeks turning them from white to pink to red. She started off squirming, protesting, then trying to push her way off his lap. But he held her firm, applying spank after spank. He stopped partway through.

"Okay, sweetheart?"

"No," she sobbed.

His heart stopped for a moment until rational thought returned. That wasn't her safeword.

"Are you saying your safeword?"

She sniffled. "No, Papa."

"You're ready for me to continue?"

"Do you really expect me to say yes to that, Papa?" she asked in a tart voice that let him know she wasn't hurting as bad as she was letting on.

"Awfully sassy for a girl getting her butt walloped, aren't you? Maybe you need some extras. Maybe I'm being too lenient on you."

"No, Papa, no! You're not. I promise. I'm sore. I won't sit down for a week. I'll never do anything naughty again."

He found himself grinning. She was something else. "I don't think you need to promise that. Especially as you won't be able to keep that promise. Right, here come the rest."

He spanked her. Sharp, hard spanks that soon had her crying again and kicking her legs. Eventually, all the tension in her body left her, and she lay limply over his lap, accepting her punishment.

He lifted her, then turned her so she straddled him, her weight off her sore ass. She leaned into his chest, sobbing her poor heart out.

Rubbing her back, he made soothing noises as she calmed down.

"Good girl. You're okay. You're Papa's good girl, aren't you?"

"I'm s-sorry, Papa," she told him.

He drew her back then kissed her lightly on the lips, ignoring the tears flowing down her cheeks. "I love you, sweetheart. I want you here for a long, long time with me. I hate when you're hurt or sick or sad. I know you just wanted to have some fun, but it was dangerous. Please don't do that again."

"I won't. I promise. I love you too."

She flung her arms around his neck and held on tight. He rocked her back and forth. After she'd calmed down, he grabbed some tissues and cleaned up her face.

"Now, how about I grab a baby bottle and you can take a nap."

"I don't wanna have a nap, though."

"Be a good girl and have a nap then afterward, I'll grab some snacks and we can have them in your fort."

She wiped her eyes then stared up at him. "Hm, I'm not sure, Papa. Usually, my forts are girls only."

"Girls only? No Daddies or Papas allowed?"

"I guess I might make an exception. But, see, Angelique isn't keen on boys. She says they smell."

"I don't smell. And when was the last time Angelique had a bath?" he asked, feeling slightly offended.

"Papa." She cupped his face in her hands, giving him a chiding look. "Angelique is a doll."

"Does she know that?"

She broke into giggles that made him smile, feeling like he'd won the lottery.

Being in a relationship meant being vulnerable. It was letting someone see all of you, not just the good parts. The safe parts. It was messy and sometimes confusing.

And fucking rewarding when you did it right.

36

J uliet always felt nervous walking into quiz night at the Wishing Well.

But tonight felt even more nerve-wracking. Because tonight, she was going there with both of her men. She grasped hold of their shirts in her hands and they both glanced down at her. Brick winked.

"It will be all right, Duchess."

Xavier looked a bit nervous as well, but then he leaned down. "If you're a good girl and win, then we'll take turns making you come when we get home."

She sucked in a breath. Well, she always won. And he knew that.

Ever since he'd spanked her, it was like Xavier had stepped things up. He'd grown more confident. And more dominant.

It was a hell of a turn-on.

And in contrast, Brick seemed to grow more relaxed. He smiled more. He laughed more. And joked.

She loved them both so much. Tomorrow, Reuben was coming to visit.

She really hoped he didn't try to kill them.

But after tonight, everyone was going to know they were together. That she was with both men. Xavier had gotten rid of his apartment and moved in with her. He'd told his boss at the hospital about their relationship and he'd taken it surprisingly well. Brick had moved what little things he owned here, and he was talking to Kent Jensen about working for JSI. He'd decided he was tired of trying to resurrect his business. He'd told her that the idea of working for someone else actually felt right.

As they walked in, she stared down at her jeans. Yep, she was wearing jeans and a long dark blue top that came to her knees.

She was going to be sick. Especially when everyone seemed to stop and stare at them. And then she heard them. From way at the back.

"Juliet! Hurry up, dude! We need you!" Kiesha yelled.

"Whoop!" Isa screamed. "We're going to kick your butt, Loki!"

"Only because Juliet is here," Loki yelled back. "Are you sure you won't marry me, Juliet?"

Both of her men growled and gave Loki the death stare as around them everyone started talking again.

Maybe, just maybe, this was going to be all right.

THEY'D WON.

Not that there had been any doubt. But it was always nice to win. As Kiesha and Isa danced around, she grinned over at her guys and waggled her eyebrows.

Brick grinned back while Xavier gave her a heated look.

Oh yeah. That was happening tonight.

Her insides twirled with happiness. Leaning over to Kiesha, she took hold of her arm. "Toilet?" she whispered.

"Yep, let's go." Kiesha turned to the table where Brick and Xavier sat with Ed. "Doc and bodyguard boy, we gotta go pee."

Brick stood. "I'll come."

Kiesha waved her hand. "You're not on duty anymore, bodyguard boy. I got this. I can help her pee."

Kiesha weaved them through the crowd to the toilet. She got that feeling of being watched but shrugged it off. Juliet peed and came out of the cubicle before Kiesha, who was muttering something about her jeans not fitting because she'd eaten too much dinner. Juliet smiled as she washed her hands. She didn't pay much attention to the door opening.

Then turning, she froze as she saw who walked in.

"Always got to win, don't you?" Gladys said in a snarky voice. "Perfect, precious Juliet. Who everyone has to take care of. Everyone has to coddle and protect. Including your brother. What kind of sick relationship do you have with him, anyway?"

What the hell? What was Gladys talking about?

"You're the reason Reuben broke up with me, you know."

Um, what? When had Reuben ever been with her? Juliet was careful not to look over at the cubicle where Kiesha was. She didn't want to clue Gladys in, just in case she didn't know they weren't alone.

"We were going places. He loved me. And then he got a phone call and had to go rushing off to save you. Poor little Juliet was all broken and needed her brother to fix her. We were supposed to go to college together. But he broke up with me because he needed time for you."

Was that true? Reuben never said anything. They must have started dating during senior year when Reuben moved to Wishingbone while his mother dated some rich party boy and was overseas a lot.

"It was always about Juliet. It was your fault that he left me. It was your fault I didn't get that promotion at work."

Now she was delusional because Juliet had nothing to do with that.

"He knew you didn't like me. He made sure I didn't get that promotion. You and I have never gotten along, but you didn't have to get Darin and I fired!"

Wait. She'd been fired? And Darin too?

Uh-oh. She could guess who had done that.

"I know it was you. Can't you take some criticism? Apparently not. Jesus, you can't even just die quickly, can you?"

Wait. What?

"That's right. I tampered with your food at the diner. I'm working there now. Washing dishes. I saw you enter, and I knew about your allergy. I'd been watching you when I could, waiting for the perfect opportunity to get revenge. So I chopped up some shrimp into tiny pieces and put it in your sandwich. But you just wouldn't die!"

"Kiesha!" she cried in her broken voice. But it was enough. The door to the toilet opened and Kiesha came out with a yell. She had a stun gun in her hand, which she pressed to Gladys' arm, then she shocked her. The other woman collapsed onto the floor with a pained cry and Kiesha stood there, staring down at her. Then she grinned wildly.

"Oh my God! I'm a total badass!"

The door suddenly opened, and a huge man stepped inside. Bigger than Brick, he had an olive complexion and short, black hair.

He turned his gaze to her. His eyes were dark. Cold. Emotionless.

Oh, shit.

"Hey, who are you?" Kiesha demanded.

Juliet moved closer to Kiesha, prepared to step in front of the other woman and defend her. Because she had a bad idea that she knew who this guy was.

"Hey, Goliath." Kiesha waved her hand in front of his face. Bad idea. "You're in the wrong bathroom, Big Foot. See? No pee boxes."

Okay, under other circumstances, she might have laughed at that. But this was not the time to laugh.

"Who are you?" she managed to ask.

Kiesha shot her a look, tensing. No doubt she could see the stark fear on Juliet's face.

"I was hired to send a message. To your brother. He thinks he's clever, but he should always remember there's someone smarter, stronger, and more deadly."

The guy started reaching under his jacket.

"Shit! Wait! I have a taser in here," Kiesha cried, reaching into her handbag. "Just wait. Don't worry, bestie, Kiesha is here!"

This guy wasn't going to wait. Fear flooded her as he drew out a gun, right as Kiesha pulled out a pink, bedazzled taser.

Too late. She was going to be too late.

Then the door slammed open, hitting the guy in the back and knocking him forward. Kiesha pressed the trigger on the taser, and the prongs latched onto his chest.

He groaned, tumbling to the floor, his big body twitching.

"Oh my God!" Kiesha cried as Brick raced into the room, gun in hand, his eyes focused, deadly. Ed came next, his gaze eating up the room, his gun drawn. Xavier followed. He looked pale, terrified.

"Do they hand out awards for being a badass?" Kiesha asked. "Because, boss man, I totally deserve one."

"Juliet, sweetheart, are you all right?" Xavier was suddenly in front of her. He ran his hands over her, as though searching for injury. She was vaguely aware of people gathering in the hallway outside the bathroom door.

Ed was securing the big guy on the floor, while Noah was talking to Gladys. Georgie was hugging Kiesha.

Where was Brick? Then suddenly, he was in front of her as well. They were both here. They sandwiched her between them.

"I think she's just in shock," Xavier said. "She doesn't appear to be injured."

"Thank fuck," Brick said, drawing her close and kissing the top of her head.

"Kiesha, what happened?" Ed asked.

"Gladys came in, she was talking about how Juliet had ruined her life," Kiesha told them. "It was all bullshit stuff about how she used to date Reuben and he'd dumped her because of Juliet. She blames Juliet for losing her job. And she tried to kill her by cutting up shrimp and sticking it into her sandwich at the diner. Actually, it kind of sounded like she'd been stalking her or something. Then this big guy comes in and says he's sending a message to Reuben. He was a real looney." She sneered down at the man.

Juliet looked from the big guy who was still twitching, to Gladys who looked to be in shock then up at her men. "Reuben is going to be so pissed."

THEY WERE CODDLING HER.

She had a feeling they weren't going to let her out of their sight after this for a long, long time.

They'd called Reuben on the way home. That hadn't gone well. He'd exploded. Then he'd told them that he would make certain nothing like that happened again. Apparently, this guy hadn't been called off like he should have been or had gone rogue. She wasn't sure exactly which. Reuben was being his usual vague self.

Now Brick was carrying her into the house. She was wrapped around his front like a monkey, unable to let go.

"I'll check the house is secure," Xavier told them. "And get her a drink so she can sleep. You want it in your baby bottle?"

She nodded. She liked the baby bottle when she was extra anxious.

Brick grabbed her some pajamas, but she shook her head. "Skin."

"All right, baby girl," he soothed. He stripped them both off, then they brushed their teeth together. As soon as they were in bed, she started scooting down.

"Please, can I have your cock, Daddy?" she asked.

"Take whatever you need."

She took his dick into her mouth. For the first time, it wasn't at least semi-erect. She guessed that everything that had happened had dampened his arousal as well.

Surprisingly, her eyelids soon started drooping. She'd been certain that it would take her forever to fall asleep.

"SHE'S UNDER THE COVERS?" Xavier asked as he walked into the bedroom.

Brick gave him a tired nod. "Pretty sure she's fallen asleep. Help me move her and we'll talk outside, yeah?"

Xavier nodded, setting the baby bottle down on the bedside table next to her pacifier. Brick managed to slide free from her mouth, with only a small murmur of complaint from her. Xavier carefully moved her, tucking her in while Brick put some pajama pants on.

Xavier picked up her pacifier, pushing it against her lips. She immediately took it into her mouth, sucking on it.

They stepped out into the hallway, leaving the door open.

"Fuck," Brick said. "Fuck, I can't believe we nearly lost her tonight." He started pacing up and down the hallway, while Xavier leaned against the wall.

"I know. I'm going to have nightmares, thinking about what could have happened."

"He had a fucking gun. How could I have let down my guard like that?"

"You couldn't have known, man. We all thought the threat was gone. Sounds like this guy went rogue."

"And that bitch from the library? How did I not know she was a threat? She nearly killed Juliet. The sheriff messed that investigation up." Truthfully, he was more angry at him himself than the sheriff.

"Ed will be beating himself up," Xavier told him.

"I want one of us close to her at all times," Brick stated. "If I can't be with her, then you have to be."

"Guess that's the beauty of a relationship like ours, huh?" Xavier mused.

Brick stilled, then turned to face him. "Yeah, it is. I'm glad you're in this with me, man. There's no one I trust more to take care of her than you."

Xavier nodded. "Same." He straightened. "Don't beat yourself up over this. We both feel guilty, but we thought she was safe."

He'd try, but his gut still felt sick. When a woman had raced up to the sheriff to tell him she'd seen a large, shady-looking man enter the woman's bathrooms, he'd just known she was in trouble. He'd nearly lost his mind.

But they'd gotten there in time. She was fine. She was safe.

"She's the very best part of me. She saved me from a life of bitterness and misery. I can't lose her."

"I get it. I feel—"

A chilling scream interrupted Xavier. They both rushed into the bedroom. Brick's heart pounded with terror.

Juliet was sitting up in bed, her eyes wide and unseeing. She appeared terrified.

"Juliet! Baby!"

She didn't reply. Instead, she climbed off the bed, her movements surprisingly forceful.

"Fuck! Night terror," Xavier said.

"Where is she going?"

"Don't know, but don't grab her. She might become aggressive."

Her body shook with trembles, her breathing was labored.

"Sweetheart, Juliet, why don't you get back into bed," Xavier said in a soothing voice as she stood there. She reached up to tug painfully at her hair.

"Xavier," Brick said in a low voice. He couldn't take this. It was killing him.

"I know, man. We'll help her. She'll probably come out of it soon, we just have to keep her safe."

She headed towards the door, but Brick blocked the way. She came to a stop in front of him.

Fuck. Fuck. He really needed to touch her.

"Juliet, come back to bed," Xavier said in a low voice.

Another pain-filled cry left her. Brick's heart broke. Then she blinked and looked up at him. "Daddy?"

"Baby girl." He reached out and touched her arms. She let out a sob, and he drew her close, holding her against his chest. Xavier moved up behind her, sandwiching her between them.

"Papa," she cried. "Daddy."

"We're here, sweetheart," Xavier soothed. "You're safe. Nothing is going to happen to you. We'll keep you safe."

Brick wasn't capable of saying anything. All he could do was hold on to her and reassure himself that she was safe.

∾

SHE SHOULD HAVE GUESSED that something like this would happen.

She'd been so terrified when that man had drawn a gun on them. Scared that he'd harm Kiesha, that he'd kill her.

Now, pressed between her two men, she let them soothe away that terror. Xavier continued to whisper to her, while Brick held her like he thought she might slip away from him.

"Come on, why don't we get you back into bed," Xavier said.

"Don't leave me," she told him as Brick picked her up and carried her to the bed, setting her down in the middle.

"I'm not going anywhere," Xavier told her. "I just need to get ready for bed. You want my skin?"

She nodded as Brick climbed into the bed.

Xavier used the bathroom. Then he stripped down to his boxers and got in on her other side. He grabbed the baby bottle from the bedside table, then raised his arm.

"Come here."

She settled into his chest and he held the nipple to her mouth so she could drink the chocolate milk it held. That was a treat.

Yum.

When the bottle was empty, she rolled over to face Brick. Xavier curved around her back. Brick held out his fingers and she sucked on them for a while until she'd calmed down.

"I don't understand how Gladys hated me that much. I mean, I was bullied by people who hated me, but at least they never tried to kill me. It's scarier than having that other guy come after me, because I knew her. I spent every working day with her and I never realized how insane she was."

"That was all on her," Xavier reassured her. "She'll get a psych evaluation."

"None of it had anything to do with you," Brick added.

She knew that. But still, she wished people would just leave her be.

"They were likely jealous of you, you know," Xavier told her.

"Those kids that bullied you. Even then, you were gorgeous. All legs and eyes. So sweet. You've always been so sweet."

"She is. Our sweet, darling girl," Brick murmured. "You realize you're not allowed to go anywhere without us."

"For how long?" she asked.

"The rest of your life ought to suffice, what do you say, Brick?" Xavier asked.

"Yeah. That will do it."

Suited her just fine. She didn't want to be without the two of them. Ever.

They were her family.

Her happy ever after.

And she'd never let them go.

EPILOGUE

Xavier felt his exhaustion fade away as he turned into the driveway that led to home.

His home. Their home.

Never in a million years had he thought he would end up in this sort of relationship. With his best friend.

And his best friend's boyfriend.

He snickered. That sounded like it belonged in one of those romance novels that Brick liked reading to Juliet before she had a nap. Of course, then he usually ended up having to eat her out because she'd get so worked up that she couldn't sleep.

Xavier was pretty sure Brick did that on purpose.

He pulled into the garage and got out to stretch. It had been a long few days. But he was off for a few days now, and he intended to spend them all with his girl. Brick was due to leave for a job tomorrow for JSI. He'd be gone for about a fortnight, and Xavier knew Juliet was feeling anxious about it.

So it shouldn't have surprised him to walk into the living room and find her on her knees in front of Brick, who was naked from the waist down.

"You spoil her," he said, while Brick ran his fingers through her hair. He had the news on the TV and was scrolling through his phone with his free hand.

"Like you can talk," Brick countered.

It had taken some getting used to, the three of them living together. They were different personalities. Xavier liked every-thing in its place. He tended to be more reserved in some ways and more open in others. Brick was blunt, but found it hard to talk about anything that had to do with his feelings.

But they were making it work. Because there was no other option. They both wanted Juliet more than they wanted to breathe.

For her, Xavier would do anything. Because there was no living without her.

Juliet turned at his voice with a smile. "Papa!"

"Hey, Twink," he said to her, sitting on his favorite recliner. It was pretty much the only thing he'd brought from his house and didn't really go with her furniture, but Juliet didn't seem to care.

He kept his gaze on her face, trying to avoid looking at Brick's cock.

Yep, there were definitely weird things about this situation. But other things that were hugely rewarding.

"Come here." He crooked a finger at her. She stood, and he took in her outfit with approval. She was wearing long blue and white striped socks and a loose, pale blue dress that ended just below her ass. In fact, he was willing to bet if she bent over that he would be able to see her panties.

Actually, why not look?

He held up his hand for her to stop. She came to a stop and stared at him in confusion.

"Turn around and bend over," he commanded.

Red filled her cheeks, and she huffed out a sigh.

"Now," he told her. "Or do you need to go over my lap for a bottom warming first?"

"Yes, I want to have a spanking first," she said sarcastically.

"All right. Over you come." He held out his hand.

"I was joking," she said in a squeaky voice.

"You were? I didn't get the joke, and I have an excellent sense of humor. Don't I, Brick?"

"You do?" Brick retorted with a grin.

Xavier glared at him. "Why haven't I smothered you in your sleep yet?" When they were all home, they usually slept together. Neither one of them wanted to sleep on their own away from their girl if they could help it.

"Like to see you try," Brick dared as he drew up his boxers.

Xavier didn't reply. He knew he didn't have a chance of smothering him. Not unless he drugged him first. But then his girl would be sad, and he couldn't have that.

"If you don't want that spanking, then I suggest you bend over," he warned Juliet.

Biting her lip, she turned and bent over. Sure enough, her dress slid up, revealing a pair of light blue, ruffly panties. Damn, that was hot. She had a gorgeous ass. It was plumping up even more now that they were making certain she was eating regularly. Well, Brick was. He was more on top of things than Xavier was with his long hours at the hospital. But over these next few days, it was his turn to take charge of her care, and he was looking forward to it.

He'd told his parents about their relationship three weeks ago. Shortly after that bitch Gladys attacked his girl. They'd told him they would disown him if he went down this path. He hadn't heard from them since. Juliet had been upset initially, but he'd told her that it felt like a weight had lifted off him when he'd told them that he was choosing his happiness over theirs.

His kind-hearted girl had spent days fussing over him afterward, which had only cemented his resolve.

Their other troublesome family member took more finessing. Reuben had stormed into town on the warpath, prepared to wrestle his sister away from him and Brick. That was when Xavier had really seen the upside of having a partner to help him look out for their girl. Brick had stood side-by-side with him when they'd told Reuben they weren't going anywhere. And when Reuben had tried to get Juliet on her own, to convince her to get rid of them, one of them had been around to circumvent him.

In the end, Juliet had convinced him that she was the happiest she'd ever been with the two of them, and Reuben had backed down. Well, he'd threatened all sorts of bodily harm to their dicks and balls if they hurt her, but that was only to be expected. If he had a sister, he'd do the same. Of course, the fact that Reuben wasn't speaking out his ass and would actually do it made things a bit more worrying.

But since neither of them intended to harm Juliet, it didn't matter.

He figured that it helped that Reuben had noticed how well Juliet was doing under their care. She'd started wearing different clothes outside of the playroom. When they left the house, she would often cover up with more clothes than were needed, but she was changing things up and not always wearing black.

Her confidence was growing. And so was her sassiness.

He loved it. Loved her.

"There's a surprise there for you," Brick told him. "Lower your panties, baby girl."

Xavier swore he could hear her grinding her teeth. A surprise, huh?

"Daddy, no," she cried.

"Duchess, now." He looked over at Xavier. "Someone is wearing her sassy pants today."

"I can tell," Xavier replied. "She's going to find herself unable to sit tomorrow at this rate."

"That might already be a problem," Brick said with a grin.

Oh, was that so?

"Juliet, panties down, now."

With a huff that he didn't appreciate, she lowered her panties down under her ass, but slid her hands over her butt.

Oh, this brat.

"Move your hands."

"But, Papa, this isn't fair. You two don't have to get plastic logs up your butt."

Plastic logs? Did she seriously just say that? He looked over at Brick, whose shoulders were shaking as he held in his laughter.

"If you're talking about a butt plug, and I hope you are, then I've been plugged before."

"Me too," Brick said cheerfully. "And I didn't complain half as much as this one did when I was plugged. She's lucky I only used my hand on her ass."

"Your hand is enough, Mr. Grumpy Butt," she muttered.

"Excuse me," Brick said in a low voice.

"Sounds to me like someone needs another spanking," Xavier told him.

"Followed by some corner time."

"Noooo," she cried out.

"Lower those hands, Juliet." Xavier made sure there was no room for argument in his voice.

Although whether she'd still try was up for debate.

With a sigh, she lowered her hand. A red crystal poked out from between her ass cheeks at him. Her pink cheeks.

His eyebrows rose. "Very nice."

"I do take pride in my work," Brick said with a satisfied sigh.

"Daddy!" she protested.

"Hush," Xavier said firmly. "You were obviously naughty while

Daddy was putting in your plug. I think you might need to be plugged more often."

"That's not fair." She stood, turning to look at him.

"Did I tell you that you could move?"

She huffed out a breath then turned again.

"I think that's an excellent idea," Brick said. They'd been plugging her nearly every day for the last two weeks in preparation for them taking her together.

Xavier thought they were all ready for the next step.

He knew her complaints were mainly for show. Whenever they played with her ass while having sex, she went off like a rocket.

Tonight was the perfect night to take that next step before Brick left tomorrow.

"Juliet, come here." He held out his hand to her as she turned.

She gave him a suspicious look. "I'm not sure I want to."

Brat.

"Believe me, you don't want me to come get you. That will result in you getting tied to the headboard and teased all night long without getting to come."

The longest they'd teased her with was around two hours and she'd acted like she was dying. She couldn't handle a whole night.

"Coming, Papa. Coming!"

BRICK GRINNED as their girl practically threw herself at Xavier. It was always a fifty-fifty shot whether being threatened with a spanking would work to curb her behavior. Corner time had a better response rate. But being threatened with some edging. Yep, that got her to co-operate really quickly. Their girl hated not being able to come.

When he woke up each morning, Brick was still shocked to find Juliet lying beside him. Just a few short months ago, he'd been feeling grouchy and depressed. He hadn't seen the light at the end of the tunnel. And he never thought he would get involved in another relationship, never mind find someone to love and trust.

Now, it felt like the sun had come out, brightening his world. All because of her.

Sure, he had to share her. But he knew she wouldn't have been as happy without the Doc. Brick would find it extremely difficult to leave her if he didn't believe she was in good hands. Sure, there was a part of him that wasn't happy that Xavier would have her to himself. But then again, Brick spent more time with her day-to-day than the busy doctor did.

Besides, Xavier wasn't a bad guy. Mostly. His obsessive tidiness made Brick want to smack him, but other than that, well, he might actually miss the guy over these next two weeks.

By now, Xavier had their girl positioned over his lap. Her panties were on the floor, her skirt up over her ass, and that crystal was peeking out. His dick grew even harder, and he reached in under his boxers to squeeze it.

Fuck. Last thing he wanted was to come before he got inside her.

"Now, you're getting ten for that sassy mouth of yours. Then you can spend ten minutes in the corner."

"But Papa, my butt already hurts."

"I can make it twenty," Xavier warned.

"No, no, ten is fine."

Xavier shared a look with Brick. They were surprisingly in-sync on how to take care of her. Sure, there would be times they probably wouldn't be. But they'd already come up with protocols on how to deal with disagreements. The last thing they ever wanted was to stress her out. So all issues would be dealt with between themselves.

Working on her anxiety and nightmares was their priority. When it came to her best interests, they were united.

She came first and always would.

By now, Xavier was smacking his hand down on her ass.

Aww, fuck it. He started slowly moving his hand up and down his dick as Xavier turned their girl's ass red. By the time he finished, she was sniffling but not crying. He turned her over and whispered something to her that made her face grow red, then she jumped up and raced over to him. She stood there with her hands holding up her skirt so he could see her pretty pussy.

He quickly glanced at Xavier, but his gaze was on their girl's ass. Not that Brick could blame him for that. It was a damn nice view.

"I'm sorry for calling you Mr. Grumpy Butt, Daddy," she blurted out.

Huh? Oh, right. He'd already forgotten. Hard to remember something like that when you were looking at your half-naked girl.

"Forgiven, Duchess." He crooked a finger at her and she leaned in. He put his hand to the back of her head and kissed her. Long and hard and hot.

When he drew back, her face was dazed and his balls ached with the need to come.

"Corner, now," Xavier said. "Stay in there until we're ready for you."

She made a face but moved into the corner. Slowly. After giving them both her version of puppy dog eyes. Brick just shook his head.

Such a brat.

CORNER TIME WAS THE WORST. Corner time was the worst.

Oh-ho-ho, corner time was the worst.

How long did she have to stay here? With her sore ass poking out and her hands holding up her skirt. It was so embarrassing.

Thank God they had alarms and an electric gate. Imagine if someone else saw her right now.

She'd never live it down.

And if that person was Reuben, well, he'd probably shoot first and ask questions second. She was kind of surprised by how well he'd taken her being in a relationship with Xavier and Brick. Oh sure, he'd tried to change her mind and he'd threatened to castrate them several times.

But he hadn't actually done it. So, that meant he wasn't totally opposed to the idea. Nothing terrible had befallen either of them. Not like it had with Gladys and Darin. Oh, he'd been enraged when he'd learned what Gladys had done. From what she'd heard, Darin had to move away to find a job that wasn't scrubbing toilets. And Gladys, well, after Reuben paid her a visit, she'd suddenly pleaded guilty to all charges.

Yep, Reuben had gone on the warpath. So really, his reaction to her new relationships had been mild for him. She didn't think he and Xavier would ever be best friends again, but she thought they could mend things so they could be friendly. She worried about her brother, he needed someone of his own to fuss over. And she already had two bossy men to deal with. That was more than enough.

She'd had a few more night terrors, but nothing as bad as the night of the quiz. She'd terrified the guys that night. They'd talked her into speaking to Archer about what happened. About her past.

"Come here, sweetheart," Xavier told her.

Turning, her eyes went wide as she saw what they'd been doing while she'd been stuck in the corner. There was a large, soft-looking blanket on the floor along with lots of cushions piled up on one side. Around the room, candles had been lit. Brick hit the lights and the candlelight created this romantic atmosphere that made her heart flutter.

Xavier held out his hand and she moved to him. Then Brick

slid up to her other side and they led her towards the comforter. Brick turned her to him and started to pull off her clothes. He was only wearing his boxers and the thick head of his cock was pushing out of the band. She reached out then looked up at him.

"May I?"

"Yes," he told her in a gruff voice.

She slid her hand under his boxers, pushing them down so he could run his hand up and down his shaft. Brick let out a small groan before throwing her dress away.

She heard Xavier sigh at the untidy gesture and had to smile. Naked, she dropped to her knees and slid his boxers down his legs and over his feet. He kicked those away as well.

"Lucky I like you, man," Xavier muttered.

Glancing up, she saw Brick grin and knew he was doing it to wind the other man up.

The ass.

Then she drew his dick to her mouth and licked the head. Brick groaned.

"Fuck me."

Oh, gladly.

She took his cock into her mouth and sucked, cupping his balls at the same time. He started muttering something she couldn't make out. Probably trying to distract himself from coming. She had to grin, loving that she had the power to make him lose control.

"Enough," Brick commanded, pulling his dick free. "I can't come yet."

"Come here, sweetheart."

Turning, she crawled over to where Xavier lay on his side, watching them. He looked like a Greek god, lying there in the soft candlelight.

Sheesh.

She laid down on her side, facing him, then turned back to look at the huge bruiser of a guy moving in behind her.

They sandwiched her between them, Xavier kissing her while playing with her breasts while Brick laid kisses down her back and reached down to play with the plug in her ass. He turned it then tugged on it lightly, making her groan.

"Put your leg up on my hip," Xavier commanded.

She raised her leg and he moved his hand down to her pussy, running a finger through her slick lips while Brick moved his finger to her entrance and drove it inside her.

She moaned in pleasure as Xavier toyed with her clit and Brick drove two fingers deep into her pussy. Xavier lowered his mouth to her nipple, sucking on it hard.

She was so close. So close.

Then Xavier moved his finger away from her clit.

"No," she cried out.

"Shh," Brick said, sliding his fingers free. Xavier handed Brick something and she heard a squirting noise.

Lube.

Then the plug was slowly slid from her ass before two fingers pressed against her bottom.

"Take a deep breath," Brick commanded.

She breathed in and Brick pushed his fingers into her. Xavier thrust two fingers into her pussy, and together, they drove them back and forth.

Oh hell. Oh God.

This was insane. Pleasure flooded her, and she would have squirmed restlessly if she could have moved. Just when she was at that peak, Xavier muttered something she didn't hear to Brick, and they slid their fingers free.

She whimpered, unable to remember how to speak, how to do anything but breathe. And even that was hard. Then she was being moved, positioned over Brick's wide body as he lay on his back. Her legs straddled his hips, and he raised her up.

"Grab my dick, Duchess. Guide me inside you. Fuck. Yes," he groaned as he lowered her onto his cock.

Lord. So good. So damn good.

When she was fully seated, he reached up with one hand, wrapping it around the back of her neck to pull her in for a kiss that made her head spin. She'd gone on the Pill so they didn't have to worry about condoms anymore.

Then she felt Xavier move in behind her. He ran a finger down her asshole before pushing it slowly inside her. He must have put some lube on his finger because it moved effortlessly in and out of her ass.

Damn. Felt so good.

She wanted to move, but Brick held her hips, keeping her from thrusting up and down on this thick cock.

Two fingers. Three.

Were they trying to kill her?

"Please. Please. Please." It was all she was capable of saying. Over and over.

"Ready for my cock, sweetheart?" Xavier asked. "Do you want to be filled with us?"

"Yes, oh God, yes. Please!"

"Good girl," Brick told her. "Now, take a deep breath in. You know what to do. He's not that much bigger than your plug."

His thick head pressed against her tight entrance as she breathed out. There was some burning, but they'd prepared her. So it didn't last long. Then Xavier was inside her. Both of them filled her.

Too much. Not enough. She didn't know. All she knew was that she had to come. Desperately.

Xavier drew back. Then thrust forward as Brick started to move beneath her. She couldn't keep up with the rhythm they created. All she could do was hold onto Brick's thick shoulders and keep herself grounded by looking into his eyes.

"She's so tight. So hot," Brick groaned.

"I can feel you moving inside her. I didn't think that would be hot, but it is," Xavier told him.

"I can't . . . I can't . . ." she cried.

"Come whenever you want, Duchess," Brick told her. He reached between them and lightly tapped her clit.

That was all she needed. There was no holding back. She came, clenching down on their dicks. Her orgasm made the world around her fade. She gasped for breath. It was like nothing she'd felt before. It was overwhelming. She barely heard Brick's own yell of satisfaction or Xavier drive deep, coming in her ass.

But she felt them roll her over, whispering to her quietly of their love, their hands petting her softly as she came down from the high.

How had she ever managed to get this lucky to have not one but two men who loved and adored her?

No freaking idea. But they were hers.

Maybe she had quirks. And her quirks had quirks. But these two men loved her just the way she was.

And that was worth more than anything else in the world.

DIRTY DADDIES ANTHOLOGY

Have you pre-ordered your copy of the Dirty Daddies Anthology yet?

You don't want to miss out! My story involves a grouchy, gruff hero with an optimistic, sweet heroine. It's going to be fun!

Dirty Daddies Anthology
    Coming Sept 28th

A DADDY FOR EVERYONE...

Available for a limited time, this collection of twenty-five sexy-as-sin romances star Daddy Doms who demand obedience and require your total surrender.

Whether you like Cowboy Daddies, Dark Daddies, Doctor Daddies, Stern Daddies, Shifter Daddies, Alien Daddies, or LGTBQ Daddies, there is a Daddy waiting for you. This deliciously naughty collection of all-new stories, penned by some of the best authors in the genre, is bursting with HOT, raw Daddy Dom action that's sure to leave you breathless.

Don't Keep Your Daddy Waiting...

Printed in Great Britain
by Amazon